CW01496480

Also by Barbara Kastelin

THE PARROT TREE

WHEN SNOW FELL

Book cover painted by the author
Web: www.barbarakastelin.co.uk
Facebook: @BarbaraKastelin
Goodreads:barbara_kastelin

A
BAD
LOT

SHORT STORIES

BARBARA KASTELIN

Matador
9 Priory Business Park,
Wistow Road, Kibworth Beauchamp,
Leicestershire. LE8 0RX
Tel: 0116 279 2299
Email: books@troubador.co.uk
Web: www.troubador.co.uk/matador
Twitter: @matadorbooks

ISBN 978 1789014 976

British Library Cataloguing in Publication Data.
A catalogue record for this book is available from the British Library.

Printed and bound by CPI Group (UK) Ltd, Croydon, CR0 4YY
Typeset in 11pt Aldine401 BT by Troubador Publishing Ltd, Leicester, UK

Matador is an imprint of Troubador Publishing Ltd

For my daughter, Samantha

CONTENTS

DON'T LOOK UP

I wish I lived somewhere else, away from all this. Perhaps the sea; I would like to live near the sea in a house with a tower. Dramatic storm waves would battle against my stronghold. Nobody I know lives near the sea; it's too far away.

We live outside Cambridge where the land is flat, in a double-fronted house with four bay windows. Over each set of windows the roof-tiles are pitched and between them lies a flat roof. In front of our property, there is a paved drive to the double garage with lawn on the side. Behind the house, facing north, is our large garden, close to one acre. It shames us into gardening most weekends.

Colin, my husband, left this morning in the dark to go and play golf. A queue for tee-off forces him to get up even earlier than during the week for work. Today is Saturday.

I idle around the garden where the first leaves have fallen from our walnut tree. The light has already turned autumnal, a glow of tarnished gold, a beautiful day, a clean sky, no clouds spoiling it. A short-breathed breeze barely nudges the swing we have hung on the begging-out branch of the apple tree.

I have a daughter. She has been married for three years now and lives twenty-five miles away.

The sound of an aeroplane makes me tilt my head up. It is a biplane and makes an impressive noise for something so far up. Private plane owners have to make the best of ideal days for flying around and around, a hobby without much purpose.

My first grandchild, a girl, will be in this garden tomorrow. Colin and I look after her to give my daughter and her husband a break. My daughter's husband limps from childhood polio. The toddler would point her pink spittle-slimed finger at such an airplane. She is alert for her fifteen months, but overall she is a pensive child, depressed almost at times. My daughter says that she laughs a lot at home, but when with me, there is a little pulled-up muscle right over her eyebrow, giving her face a heart-grabbingly adult expression. When I seek complicity with the baby and she avoids it, my daughter notices my disappointment. A new tooth must be coming, she says generously, because she too has muscles in her forehead, often raised. The toy plane has made a wide loop over the vast harvested wheat-field next to our garden, its soil now ploughed to show only scars in the brown earth.

It is like an unearned miracle that my daughter, whom I have reared, now has a daughter of her own. A perfect little girl, a new human being vulnerable to future hurts, already knowledgeable about sadness.

'Did you think I was perfect when I was born?' my daughter has asked me.

That annoying aeroplane is going round in tighter circles over me and with increased noise, revving up or something from time to time. I am not familiar with how aircraft stay in the air.

As a young mother I was not myself at times. Of course, things were different then. I did not have my daughter's advantages.

That droning engine should not be allowed over housing.

I remember hitting my daughter when she was a toddler, hitting her hard, with all my pent-up anger. She fell from the impact, flew almost, and hit the corner of the glass-topped coffee table. The impact cut a gash into her peach baby cheek by the force of my hand. Blood seeped out. I picked her up, shocked, and told her that it was nothing, putting a cold flannel against her feverish face, staunching and wiping away my shame.

At the next toddler check-up in the baby clinic, they asked what had happened to her face, and I said she had hit the tap while I bathed her. 'It should have been strip-bandaged,' is what they said, but they left it at that. The round clear eyes of my silent daughter made me add, 'She wriggles around a lot. You know what they're like.' Often, I wish my daughter would blame me for the scar I carved into her innocent face by my selfish loss of temper. Heaven knows, guilt creeps up on me at any moment, and I have to take two sleeping pills to find peace at night. But she is stoically loving towards me. Deep down, love knows.

Tomorrow, my granddaughter will stay the day with us and I am frightened of myself.

The aeroplane has corkscrewed itself further down closer over our house, glinting silver now and then. As it reappears right over the crown of the walnut tree, its noise changes; it is more like a dry cackle. Out of the blue, the noise stops altogether and I gasp. The plane is over our garden and the engine has cut out. As it is not a glider, it will surely just fall out of the sky. It is still able to fly somehow, though, and I see that something about the shape of the plane's hull is changing. From where the door must be, a dark shape is starting to bulge out like an ungainly growth. A person has come out of the aeroplane in mid-air – perhaps doing something desperate to restart the propeller? I stand and stare, my neck muscles starting to hurt.

All of a sudden, when the plane is practically above me, the bulky shape outside the aircraft detaches itself and starts to fall away, fall down, a person falling through the air, growing in size, growing in horror. The fluttering, dark coat-like garment is that of a woman, a woman in free fall. Aghast, both my hands smack against my face. I hear the landing thump of the body. The airplane, from which I had diverted my attention, is puttering away again over the field, and its shape has returned to compact metal, doors closed.

Once the overwhelming surge of panic abates, I dare look around me. The woman has not fallen on the grass near me, nor on the pergola roof or the patio. She must have landed in the front garden. With trepidation, I walk alongside the house to the front. Only after a while do I dare open my eyes fully. No body is lying there. Maybe I was mistaken about the fall-line of the woman; perhaps she is on the road. I go and check. The road is empty – no pedestrians, one slow cyclist and two cars driving past. No body.

No body. I laugh hysterically, my nerves as taut as hawsers. That's where nobody comes from. I turn my head back to look at our house and up at the roof. Something strong compels me to do this, something ominous. Of course – the woman is telling me that she has landed in the middle of our flat roof. It is wide enough to conceal her.

I feel singled out, targeted. I have just witnessed a murder, and the victim is sprawled on our roof. I approach, pause and listen, but no noise comes from above and now even the wind is holding its breath. A fall of that distance had to be fatal. I should get the extendable ladder out of the garage and tilt it against the house to see, but I know I can't. I should climb into our loft and perhaps something of her would show from the Velux window. I cannot. In fact, my muscles are still stiff from terror.

Now the red car turns into our drive. Colin is home, and I will have to make a salad lunch and boil water for instant soup and play-spar over who will get the last mushroom sachet – the preferred choice.

I watch him take out the golf bag and carry it into the open garage. I watch him roll his golf trolley inside too. All is so normal that I say nothing. Normality has a controlling effect on something outrageous. I lack the courage to unleash the force of such a repugnant incident.

Colin's habit is to drink a can of beer after golf. He is looking for it, but I had not noticed the last can had been drunk. I offer to dash to the SPAR in the village, and he asks me 'while I am there' to post a letter for him.

While Colin changes his clothes, I get into the red car and drive out, first away from the village to get a look at our house from the brow of a slight slope. Stopping and looking back, I can see nothing of the body because the peaked roof over the nearest bay obstructs the view.

In the local shop I pick up a pack of four lagers from the Indian couple. They recently took over from Richard who had been good to gossip with. I wait as they serve an elderly man from the sheltered housing complex, who babbles on about the zebra crossing which should be repainted. The Indians smile gently, politely. Richard would have involved himself. He is now retired.

At the red letterbox outside, I check the envelope to see whether it has the right stamp and notice that the addressee lives on Airfield Road. I push the envelope into the dark oblong mouth. Local ads and notices are nailed to the gnarled trunk of the old village chestnut tree. One is a photograph of a middle-aged woman. *Have you seen this woman?* The hairs all over the surface of my skin bristle. I bend closer to the picture. She was photographed smiling, a pronounced canine tooth giving character to her otherwise unremarkable face: layer-cut hair, maintained; silver ball stud earrings. She went missing five days ago.

Clever. The murderer put this up as a decoy. There is a number to call but I do not take it down. I drive back home.

Colin and I spoon the soup from bowls at the table. He tells me that he now needs his winter golfing clothes.

That makes sense to me. Then he says that last spring we put them up into the loft.

Surely not.

He's gone through everything in his wardrobe while I was out, he assures me.

I am adamant that all clothes not in the wardrobes were given away to charity and that no clothes are left in the loft and that it was he who had said last year that we should not clutter it up. He contradicts me and says he will go up there after lunch. Our Velux window is just where the flat roof ends and the tiled slope starts, facing north.

My 'No' is harsh. He looks at me with surprise. 'I'll go. If there is still a box with clothes, I know where to find it.'

My hand shakes as I pull down the loft ladder. Tread by tread, I ascend in my slippers; soon my head will be above floor level. The mushroom soup is rising in my oesophagus. I force it down and pause until the nausea is under control, before I climb one tread more. The glass of the window is dirty, thank God. I pull at the plastic storage box with winter sports clothes, open the flaps from which dirt drizzles and pull out a dark blue, cable-knit sweater, Colin's winter golf pullover.

With more confidence I take another look at the grime-caked window and my heart hops into my mouth. Over the top corner is not just grime, but a dark belt made of raincoat material. It has a metal buckle. Now it is proven. With the last of my strength I throw the box down the hatch, which reminds me of the death plunge and the thump. I turn round and scramble down the

7

ladder in haste. Misjudging the last three rungs, I slip and my right knee hits the metal. The skin is broken, a long gash. Blood appears through the cut, starts to gush and flows freely down my shin.

The scar on my daughter's cheek is still prominent. Especially in cold weather it shines up red, a red hook which has grown with her face because the wound was not stitched or taped at the time. I once heard Colin tell her that it was a birthmark and only special children were given those. Colin never mentions it to me. My daughter never mentions it. When she was a teenager, she always held her hand against that side of her face.

The cut on my shin starts to sting, and the blood is dripping onto my slippers. I hobble into the bathroom to press a soaked towel against it and sit on the rim of the bathtub in a state I have never been in before.

From below comes the noise of Colin watching a rugby game on television, and on the roof is splayed a murdered woman and I fight for breath so I don't asphyxiate.

Saturday ends with the sky clouding over. They predict rain and strong winds. Colin tells me this while we eat supper. I have prepared winter vegetables for my granddaughter's lunch tomorrow and put them into the fridge. I desperately need to go to bed and recover from my ordeal but it is only eight o'clock and Colin has chosen a DVD for us to watch. *Skyfall*.

In bed finally, almost out of my mind, I cannot find sleep. Right above our double bed is the cadaver of a woman and, as predicted, the wind is getting up. The neighbour's trees shake and swish. A strong enough gust could push the body to the edge of the flat roof where it would topple down the tiles. Legs or arms might appear in front of the bay window, dangling. I strain my whole worn being to discern a scraping noise different from the racket the wind is making outside. Colin snores in deep sleep, the repeated rasping and gurgling of his vegetative state. I shiver between the sheets, which frost my skin. At what moment is one actually overcome by sleep? What are the last telltale signs to indicate that, in a second, soft dark forgetfulness will deliver us from the stress of being awake? I have fallen asleep all these years and still have no idea. Thankfully it just happens, always, eventually, and will now, even despite my trauma today.

Sunday morning, the body has not moved enough to show. I have to get through this day and not ruin it for the others.

Just as my daughter arrives with my granddaughter, in a pretty new dress to visit Grandma, it starts to rain and we rush the child to the house. I am relieved that we have an excuse not to spend time in the garden. I could not bear it.

My daughter leaves us, and we urge her to enjoy the free hours we're giving her. She says she will, definitely, but I know she is now going home to clean and wash and pre-cook. She has had to go back to work after ten months' maternity leave.

The weather is worsening and my granddaughter, who has just learned to walk, toddles to the bay-window to look outside at the driving rain. 'Come away from the window,' I shout and frighten her.

It occurs to me that rain will probably speed up decomposition. Up to now, I have seen the body as an immutable fact, but of course slowly – or less slowly – it will spoil and fall apart. Heavy rain would speed this process up. I ask Colin to be with his grandchild while I go into our office where the computer is dozing. With a click I bring it to life. I have to know.

How long does it take for a body to decompose outside in the elements? I type into Google.

After the rigor mortis phase of about three hours, enzymes start to cause the organs to digest themselves, and putrefaction results in the emission of a green substance as well as gases and strong smells, and fluid drains out through orifices.

'Are you all right?' asks Colin when I reappear with a peek-a-boo at the door. 'You look very pale.'

My granddaughter does not like winter vegetables. She picks out bits with her fingers and tosses them over the high chair's table with regal disdain. I caress her cheeks, which are unharmed. They feel cold to the touch. The body on the roof has by now turned totally cold, deprived of warm blood circulating. Perhaps the raincoat she is wearing preserves her body heat.

'What are you thinking about?' asks Colin.

'I am wondering what to give the baby to eat. She is rejecting the vegetables.'

'Give her chips and ketchup.'

'Her mum won't appreciate what will come out of her after that.'

I grab my forehead, feverish from suppressed despair. The dead woman will have eaten food and her body processed it. With slack guts, it will come out of her anus and seep through her clothes, run to the rim of the flat roof and then drip down the tiles.

As we wave energetically goodbye to the child strapped into the baby car seat, my daughter drives away. Colin reminds me that tomorrow is black bin day.

I roll the wheelie bin out of our drive at the same time as our neighbour is putting out hers. She bothers to walk down the road to meet up with me.

'More bad weather is on its way. Not surprising, we're close to November. It'll bring down the leaves and fill the gutters.'

I had not thought about gutters, and the Irishman who will soon come, about this time of year, to offer to clear them out, just when the decomposition has started to run into them. Perhaps I should find a way to claw the body down from the roof, and then others can get involved. I will simply say, 'I have no idea how it got to be on our land in that state.'

The neighbour is now chatting about the rabbits still out and about. I am barely listening. Was it a large woman who fell through the air or a small one? It is hard to recall, as the memory is shrouded in horror. If she was small, perhaps there would be a way to put her into a sizable bag. We still have one with strong handles, which the builders, who had brought sand, never came to pick up.

The neighbour's husband has now apparently put out a rabbit trap and caught one. 'One cannot just put the poor dead thing into the black bin, can one?'

In bits it would be possible, gruesome bits. Such a project is out of the question. What am I thinking? I did not kill the woman. Some hobby pilot did, or one of his chums pushed her out of the small aircraft. I saw her fighting for survival, clinging onto small metal protrusions with her fingernails, while the wind tore at her whole being. Beneath her was the unforgiving precipice into which she was to plunge. Pulled by her own weight, one finger after the other had to let go. No kindness or forgiveness saved her and, having failed, she plummeted through the air at increased speed to splat on my roof.

I put the toys away into their red box. Today, my grandchild hugged Minnie Mouse to her face saying 'Ah' lovingly and walking around with it. Colin or I followed, making sure she did not fall over.

'I had forgotten how exhausting it was doing this with our daughter,' Colin said, sighing, 'to make sure she came to no harm.'

We go to bed early because we are worn out after babysitting.

Monday morning, after Colin drives off to work, our gutter-cleaner Mr O'Grady comes round. It's too early for the leaves yet, but he is in the neighbourhood and wants to warn me that he has had to put his price up just a little because of all the costs he has. 'I have pencilled you in for the last week in November, if that's all right with you.'

'That's in four weeks.' He has no idea that I am calculating at what stage the corpse will be by then. 'Out of the question this year.'

'But…' He steps a little further from the house and looks up at the gutters. 'They're already mucked up.'

I don't want him to step further out and see. He is a lean and very tall man.

Baffled and displeased, he leaves.

On Mondays I pay bills and answer letters and e-mails and should delete unwanted messages in the inbox, something I am apparently not good at doing, according to Colin.

One of my friends calls. She is a volunteer at the hospital, like me. In fact, she is the only one I ever befriended more than just 'Hello, keep up the good work'. There is little contact between us volunteers. Some visit patients, some distribute newspapers on trolleys, some guide outpatients to their appointments in the growing warren of a major teaching hospital. I am a guide and still don't know where everything is.

My friend tells me that she will not be able to do guiding with me in the main entrance tomorrow as she has to go to a funeral. A woman friend of hers has unexpectedly died. This means I will have to do more, walking further along the corridors.

The morgue is on the lower level. I wear a badge saying Volunteer and this allows me through most doors. When I used to help out in the wards, I learned that patients who die are wrapped into a white sheet like a cocoon, a flower close to where the head is. They are loaded onto a special trolley with a canvas coffin box and pushed into a special elevator, from the elderly and critical wards down to the morgue.

If I can somehow get the body down with a rake, load it into my car in the builder's bag and drive it into the hospital, I would be let into the compound with the car. There is a ramp leading down to the lower level near the morgue at the back of the building. It is not busy, I know that.

Open boot, pull at bag with strong handles. Leave bag pretty much where I manage to get it. Close boot and drive up the ramp to park the car, and guide confused outpatients with a smile. It almost enters the realm of the possible, something I could handle, in my head at least. Not many have access to such facilities.

Mid-morning, the rumbling of the refuse truck makes me look out of the window. Our bin lifts, tilts, the contents are chomped up and the bin is returned onto its feet, lid closed. It is eleven in the morning and I walk outside, checking back and up at our house. Nothing. I retrieve our bin from the pavement. Just then a green-and-yellow-striped car slows down on the road. *Police* is written in thick black letters on its door and the car comes to a halt five metres from our gate. I stand with the tilted bin and need the loo.

The car door on the kerb-side opens, and an officer steps out and looks at me. They have training sessions where they are taught to detect people trying to hide things from them. He eyes me through narrow lids. His mobile is against his ear. I should just turn away but my body is without force.

He holds the mobile away from a pink ear nestled in dark hair. 'Is this a dead spot?'

My incomprehensible grunt is linked to my involuntary floppy hand movement.

'Cell-hell?' the officer asks.

Once the trolley is next to the garage, I hear the police car drive off. I fetch hot water and bleach in a plastic bucket and swirl it around in the wheelie bin, rocking it roughly, then tilting it to disgorge the brew into the hedge. There is no way that bits of a body in black bags would go unnoticed.

I skip lunch. The mere thought of food is difficult, any food.

By four o'clock and a cup of tea, I curl myself into my house and, in some bizarrely familiar way, accept the presence of the dead woman over my head. It is a relief. I have been exposed to far too many frights to stay sane. If I continue to fret as I have been doing about this crime, I might perish faster than the corpse.

At five o'clock the neighbour knocks on our back door. She always takes the neighbourly route which goes through our linking back gardens. Surely she can't have seen something now? It has been drizzling for hours and the temperature has fallen below two digits.

'Hello!' The annoying 'Is anybody home?' follows. Having to drop what one was doing or thinking in order to go and respond.

'There is a man over at our house who says that he flew over us two days ago.'

The murderer. 'Sorry,' I say and start to shut the door in the face of the neighbour.

'I've sent him round the front to your house.'

I can't display civilities towards the neighbour I shut out; I need to think and think fast. He might not be the pilot. Perhaps he is the man whose wife was pushed out of the aircraft. Perhaps the pilot had an affair with the woman with the crooked canine tooth, and the husband found out. Maybe the pilot invited the couple for a flight in a perfect autumn sky and then an argument broke out. There was tussling at the door of the aeroplane in full flight. The husband might have thrown her out because of her infidelity, or the pilot had because the husband took over the controls of the plane, threatening to kill them all, and the pilot had to prove that he did not love the woman.

I have walked through the house and am standing behind our entrance door. My cheeks are burning hot. I see a dark shape obscuring the coloured-glass inlays. This has to be faced. My right hand turns the brass knob because I think I am balanced enough to do so.

A young man with shorn hair and a Tintin quiff says, 'Sorry to bother you but I flew over your house on Saturday and something dropped out.'

Yes, she is decomposing on the flat roof of our house.

'We had some engine trouble,' he goes on. 'Quite some panic ensued. I had a couple with me as passengers.'

I know.

'You might have seen us from below. Your house and garden are about the place I am looking for.'

He had doubtless imagined that he could get away with the whole thing.

'Did you see anything fall out of my plane?'

With shame, I look at the ground on which I am standing and then, with an effort, raise my head to look at him. 'She's on the roof,' I manage to say.

'Hey, thanks. How are we getting it down?'

'Easier now that rigor mortis is over.'

'Funny lady. Do you have a ladder?'

'In the garage.'

'Can I borrow it?'

His casualness was unbearable. I am rigor-mortised myself.

'Sorry about this. It should not have ended up on your roof, but parachute packs are expensive items, and I would be glad to have it back please.'

LUXURY CRUISES

He told her a little querulously that his belly had made a mound when he wore the silver lamé. 'It degrades a man to be made to wear women's clothes,' he grumbled. 'Even worse if they don't fit.' His role, he reminded her, was to be suave, even when cross-dressing.

'Montgomery,' she said, keeping her cool. 'The corset we bought yesterday in Marks & Spencer will put this right. Try it on and you'll see.'

With a little hesitation, he went into the small bathroom where he forced his soft body into the corset, knocking his elbow against the sink tap. He held his bruised arm under the cold water. When he bent for loo paper to wipe his elbow, he realised his mother was using newspaper cut into squares. Holding his breath, he forced the garment upwards into place and felt squeezed by a rubber clamp.

Mumsie held out the slinky silver dress and helped him wriggle into it. 'See, you look lovely.' She stepped away to admire. 'Slim like a reed.'

A fifty-five-year-old tranny more like.

A salvo of young laughter came from outside the window. 'Faggot! Faggot doing his mother.

Motherfucker!' A stone hit the glass but did not break it. Montgomery stumbled back into the bathroom to squeeze himself out of the garment.

'Sorry, they saw me. They will give you trouble.'

A few months ago, the council had moved his mother down to a one-bedroom ground floor flat, since her son did not count as living there.

'I'll be fine. I have you.'

'But I'm away most of the time.'

'I have my love for you. We are a team. You give me money to live and I work for you.'

But he gave her so little that she used newspaper in the loo. He could not afford more because he lived on perks and a token salary from which he had to fork out for his image. Grooming was increasingly costly. He now needed moulding gel to structure hair, volumising mousse to conceal its thinning, liquid crystal pomade for it to gleam under artificial light, manicure and pedicure. And that was as well as the dry-cleaning and quality underwear. The women he entertained had the habit of pulling his trousers free of his body at the belt when they were tipsy, and sometimes worse.

Montgomery sagged down on the bed. At his feet stood Mumsie's beige slippers, so familiar, and correctly settled as a pair like obedient little pets.

'Doing your best will always be doing your best.'

He got up to add the high-heeled shoes, the new foam-padded bra and the make-up bag to his two laundered dress-shirts. He picked up the closed case and released the catch to allow the wall-bed to go back up. Closed, it resembled a narrow useless cupboard.

'Now I have all that space to myself. Montgomery, dance with me before you go,' she begged.

There was no time left for that, not today. He pulled twenty-five pounds from his blazer pocket and put them onto the small table pushed against the wall. She thanked him in silence. Her dry skin was stuck to her bony cleavage; the garnet ring on her sparrow hand had dulled. And yet, there was a bounce still in his small positive mother, of unbreakable nerves remembering when there had been time to dance, waltzing to hummed Strauss.

When he was at the door ready to leave, she scuttled to the kitchenette corner, opened the refrigerator and came back with a silver-paper-wrapped packet. 'Like a first-class aeroplane sandwich.' Light was in her eyes as she handed it to him. 'It's fancy: soft bread to spare your teeth, napkin and all.'

'It's only a short flight. I won't starve.'

'Silly boy. Give us a kiss.'

Looking fixedly straight ahead of him, he walked through the council estate over worn grass. The loitering kids shouted insults. One threw an empty can at him. He kept on walking towards Lambeth tube station, which would bring him eventually to Luton Airport. Not having been able to do anything to improve Mumsie's existence left him with an overwhelming feeling of impotence, caused by his filial need to protect her.

Fighting his way down the stairs of the underground, he took refuge in bumping against all those active humans, hiding the shame of his uselessness.

The EasyJet flight took off on time. When the *ping* allowed him to get up, he threaded his way towards the front lavatory. There, slumped on the metal loo, he sat, Montgomery, named after the WW2 general whom Mumsie's father had served with. Suffocating in the confined space, he reached into the pocket of his twenty-year-old Harrods blazer, unfolded the foil of the sandwich with care and then barely managed to chew the liverwurst as sobs filled his mouth. Tears ran out of his eyes and trickled down his cheeks. The drops made mush dells in the white bread. His mother had made this for him. She had nothing in life, a lonely existence since his father had walked out thirty-two years ago, leaving bills but no pension. Her happiness over nothing grabbed his heart every time anew.

She believed them to be a team. She kept up with the latest from newspapers and magazines she pulled from bins. *Research for Monty* was what she called waiting for glimpses of MPs and visiting heads of state in the Palace of Westminster's central lobby, where the public was allowed. She endeavoured to take pictures with the miniature Canon he had given her. The guard at the entrance seemed to know her name.

More challenging was celebrity-spotting. Mumsie waited hours close to fashionable eating places, bars and nightclubs, sitting on her seat-stick, using restaurant loos without ordering. Prince Harry coming out of the Cuckoo Club and Victoria Beckham from The Ivy were her triumphs.

Little did she know how fast he had to paddle underwater to still glide as a credible rich charmer, connected, a snob about money and style. His wit during cocktail hour and at dinner tables was threadbare, his status to make introductions to stars, art dealers, politicians, a sham. With vintage good looks, seductive smiles, the hint of a bow, right hand over his silk pocket square before complimenting and kissing the hands of rich cruise-widows on the Mediterranean, he could still just about get away with it, if they were tipsy.

The pilot announced turbulence, and Montgomery could not remain in the lavatory any longer without drawing attention to himself. He looked a mess in the facilities mirror, puffy-eyed, far from the Cary Grant features of his youth. There was no way out. The kindest, most useful thing he could do was to put an end to his existence once and for all.

★

Monte Carlo spread before Monty on this June morning as he stood on the two-foot-wide Juliet balcony of a modern apartment block. The harbour was hatched with masts from yachts and daubed with the bodies of motor-cruisers. A sleek cruising ship glinting in white gloss enamel was berthed against one pier arm: his ship. All this against an azure ocean backdrop.

He turned away and went into the studio he was sharing with Giuliano, the other undercover luxury cruise *enhancer* hired by the shipping company: 'illusionists', Coco, the manageress of the boutique on board, called them. Somehow it was appropriate, as Montgomery and Giuliano pretended to be part of the guests' circles, their wealth and connections. Sometimes the role extended into escort territory; it was a grey area and not taken into account by the basic salary. The shipping company rented this studio for the two to occupy alternately. One was at sea, while the other spent the night and got organised. There were two liners, sister ships: *The Prince Regent* and *The Silver Princess*, each with two hundred and forty guests and around one hundred staff. Montgomery used to do both regularly, but now Giuliano did more of the longer cruises on *The Silver Princess* as booking management pushed it for the younger generation.

Waiting for the elevator in his white blazer and the Christy's Panama hat on his way to the harbour, Monty asked himself again how Giuliano, at thirty-seven, functioned in his job. The style of clothes on his side in the cupboard spelled *jet set*. Judging by the jumbo box in the bedside table, he ordered condoms in bulk. Clearly he offered young flesh. Did he pretend romance, or was it just raw sex? Did he do older widows as well? And if so, how did he go about it?

Crossing the staff gangplank onto *The Prince Regent*, Monty ran into Bruno, the chief engineer, who said disparagingly, 'Here we have *him* again!' – about as unwelcoming as a shipmate could get. They had sailed together nearly two dozen times, not that this brute would consider them equals. Black epaulettes and embossed gold buttons had the power to lift his nose to show two holes, as Mumsie would say.

In the foyer, the rich and pampered guests started to cover the oval marble floor with their important being; the majority were English, many of them widows who had lost the bloom of middle age. There was just the right leavening of foreigners of the right kind to reassure the English that they were abroad, not enough to restrict their eccentric behaviour and *laissez-aller*. For them, he, Montgomery, had to be a playful tool, an amusing holiday romance or provider of quaint moments. He was the charming sophisticated bachelor, a regular passenger on bespoke cruises, where the vulgar deck-pool had been replaced by a *wellbeing suite*, and in the kitchen was a French chef with two Michelin stars under his belt.

The corona chandelier above them was still on land electricity. The two curved gold-trimmed staircases glittered like fool's gold. The glass cubicles of elevators brought people up to the promenade and upper decks, and down to the royal suites and further down to the deluxe veranda state-rooms. Where the staircases converged in front of the gigantic oil portrait of the Prince Regent stood the tanned-faced second-in-command, in precision-pressed naval whites complete with rigid black epaulettes, and peaked cap with nifty gold insignia. The captain always boarded the vessel at the last minute; he was most probably bored of going round and round the Med.

Montgomery was lodged, as usual, in deluxe veranda aft. It started with an elegant sitting room with a door to a coffin-sized bunkroom with just a small porthole. The deception was that Monty could afford an owner's suite.

'Monty!' A voice rose above the hubbub. Walking hurriedly with tiny steps in expensive shoes in front of a luggage handler pulling two large cases behind him, Lucinda looked less ostentatious than usual. She wore white trousers, a tailored navy-blue sailor-top and a white cotton hat with a soft brim perched on curls the colour of freshly polished copper. For her fifty-six years, she could still be called foxy.

He planted a mimicked kiss on the back of her hand. His job had started and he was feeling wretched.

'A new Italian stylist, some smooching and tada, a new me.'

'It works,' he said. 'Especially for the Italian.'

'Oh, Monty.' Lucinda bent close to him, her hat rim lifting his carefully gelled hair. 'Still debonair I see, and not yet snapped up. We're going to have us a ball, you and I.'

'Hello!' Over by the mirrored wall Henrietta, another regular, gave him a little wave with her spangled arm. Lucinda and Henrietta tossed each other chin butts. They would fight for his favours. *How could he possibly keep this up?* The artifice – twenty hours a day exposure to guests determined to leave technically advanced society behind and sway unburdened in the romantic cradle of a dream boat, the *Titanic* before the iceberg, feather boas and the anticipation of never-ending elaborate appetisers.

At sunset, after sonorous tooting, *The Prince Regent* glided from the harbour and picked up speed on its overnight sail to Livorno. In the cabins the passengers, helped by maids and stewards, installed themselves for the four-day cruise.

Monty consulted with the *maitre d'* about the placement on his table before striding to the bar for cocktails. In his elegant yet casual Italian pewter-grey jacket – with a safety-pin holding back the lining at the cuff – he said, 'Showtime,' which was more effective than 'Cheese' for a good photo face. He felt moisturising cream pull at the corner of his eyes. Nausea was close to his diaphragm as he reminded himself not to slouch, to appear aloof and interesting. Taking them all in, he could have sworn they were the same group as two weeks ago, a month ago, eleven years ago. The pianist was *house*. The jazz singer sang her Sarah Vaughan and Ella pieces; she was hired until Livorno only.

Dinner was announced by a waiter blowing a bugle. They filed into the Regent's room and searched for their names on the board.

Monty let them cope with their disappointments or hopes, their demands for changes, while having another fake gin and tonic at the bar. When the cold entrées appeared on high-handed plates, he deigned to take his seat.

'Who is everyone?' He flicked open the damask serviette lotus flower.

Lucinda, sitting to his left, smelling so heavily of perfume musk that he felt like falling off his chair, introduced herself around. On the other side of him sat Henrietta. That way they cancelled each other out.

A single woman in her mid-fifties called Nancy Frankl had tinted jet-black hair pulled back, giving her face the appearance of a mask. She was thin and her tight head snapped left and right during conversations. Monty had been briefed: an American, newly divorced, who was left with a large house in Connecticut while her financier husband had moved to the city. She herself revealed that a friend had urged her to take this cruise as if it were against her will.

'Uptight. Jewish,' hissed Henrietta.

'Psychiatrist,' Monty corrected her as he picked her hand off his thigh and placed it back on the table.

The tall gaunt Frenchman with a Rolex on one pale wrist and anti-seasickness band on the other was Claude Grès, in banking, Paris, in his early fifties.

'Wow,' Lucinda said admiringly when he divulged that he lived on the Champs-Elysées.

'How sad for him,' Henrietta sympathised. 'The traffic in Paris these days. My chauffeur nearly lost his nerves. Lucinda, when were you last there?'

Daniel and Arabella, the couple who made up the table, were on board for a fortieth anniversary, that of their company: Chelsea Interior Design.

Monty turned to the sommelier. 'What can you offer us?'

'Sir, with the boar-en-croute a vintage claret and—'

'Don't bore me. Bring me a Baron de Rothschild; we need sparkle. And drag a few champagne stands over this way.'

Apart from Nancy, the others all ordered the same champagne at eighty-five quid a bottle.

The entrée on frosted-glass plates was placed before the guests and Monty poked at the food with his silver fork bearing the Prince Regent's crest. 'You must all know that Sir Evelyn Rothschild's daughter is to marry Sacha Gervasi in December.'

'We were contenders for the interior decoration contract for Evelyn's thirteen-thousand-square-foot Belgravia property.'

'Fourteen million pounds and he never lives in it.' Claude was plugged in.

Monty chipped in with, 'I bumped into an incognito Evelyn at Sotheby's pre-auction not long ago; I was after a little something in oil for my wall.'

Once the waiters had installed the coolers and served the champagne, Monty ostentatiously slipped the sommelier a bundle of folded notes.

'No point tipping at the end of the trip when they are glad to see the back of you.' Monty grinned around the table.

They toasted the Queen, *The Prince Regent* and several heads of state, and told jokes about them and ordered second bottles.

'Politicians and bankers are all borderline sociopaths, with their delusions of grandeur, visceral isolation and anxiety disorders.' Nancy chilled the convivial air.

'I know I'm a sociopath,' Claude said, surprising them.

'Really?' Lucinda threw her bread roll at him but missed.

They were clearly warming to each other; he was doing his job.

On the move to the ballroom, Lucinda hung from the crook of one of Monty's arms, Henrietta from the other. He stifled a burp from the heavy food and excused himself in order to discreetly recover his tip from the sommelier. This bundle of money would go round several times more.

The first evening entertainment was low-key, a juggler from Sicily and two Serbian boy acrobats using just a metal ladder and a garden chair but making the audience gasp. And the Contessa in a ballgown trying unsuccessfully to sing an aria while her poodle jumped onto her shoulders and ran under her dress. It pleased the audience.

Monty slipped away when the poodle ran away with the music sheets. Tired, he stretched out on his bunk, the vitamin cream on his face, and eyes closed. Often at moments like this he saw his mother, against lamplight, head bent, brushing out her long hair.

The propeller's faint throbbing churned, *I can do this job no more, no more, no more,* and put him to sleep.

On the morning of Full Day One, they rocked gently in the harbour of Livorno. Monty had to participate in the excursion to Pisa. His head hurt. His guts were filled with gas from soda water and watered-down champagne. He told the same jokes about the phallic tilting tower. Organised lunch in the authentic family-run trattoria would be a strain. The brilliantined village youth spontaneously broke into *O Sole Mio*. How deliciously, innocently Italian it all was! Monty knew that the family owned a Ferrari hidden in the barn.

Nancy looked as if she were part of it but he could almost see the little cogwheels turning behind her high brow. She unnerved him because she did not fit into any mould.

Back on *The Prince Regent*, they rested in deckchairs, a harpist blurbling strings, the glass doors open to the aft deck from which a soft breeze wafted in.

At cocktail hour on the foredeck, a fashion runway slanted up to the bow into the sunset as they motored to Ajaccio. Cloth-covered chairs were in place either side and elaborate cocktails offered.

Coco promised them exclusives from France and Italy. Beethoven's Seventh played while a bride in a white column dress with a headgear resembling a Nike swoosh on her head walked up the plank, turned and pouted.

'The bride has to come at the end!'

Coco singled out Monty. 'She's got to marry first before she can afford labels.' Guests invariably liked that and even more the male model in a wedding suit, rocking up the plank to kiss her pouty mouth.

The show went on with leisure and formal wear of top quality and design, but actually wearable. It was perfectly rehearsed and came to an end when the sun sank beneath the horizon.

The after-dinner entertainment was a mini Vaudeville theatre performance in multi-language jokes of misunderstandings.

Monty gave it a miss and walked slowly along the deck, feeling caressed by cooler air. Wave chased wave, silvery sheen giving into black.

'May I ask, what's your role on this boat?'

Nancy's bluntness startled him.

'You seem to like Lucinda but avoid any intimacy. Why is that?'

He had no answer and walked on. She kept up with him, hands clasped behind her back. Cocking her tight head a little, she persisted, 'I suspect depression in you, deep-seated.'

'I…' he started. 'I see no merit in knowing too much about people. Finding out who Lucinda really is would serve no purpose.'

Nancy waited for him to go on.

'She wouldn't want me anyway.'

'Do you perceive *that* as your problem?' Nancy asked and walked away.

'I hate shrinks,' he muttered into his double chin and went to his cabin to lie there and reprimand himself for not having asked Nancy about the failure of her marriage.

Much later he was woken by repeated knocking on his cabin door. His first thought was *Lucinda wanting sex? Has the shrink had a go at her?*

Monty clambered out of the bunk and, owning no dressing gown, held the lapels of his striped pyjama top together with one hand while opening the door with the other.

Claude, in a dinner jacket, stood in the corridor's emergency light, pale-blue as a ghost. He held a dangling champagne bottle and licked his glossy lips suggestively.

'Bugger.' The word escaped from Monty.

'Bugger? Brilliant! I've got you right.' The bottle neck slipped from his butter-fingers and the bottle bumped onto the carpet runner. 'Can I come in?'

'I am engaged to Lucinda,' Monty heard himself say in falsetto.

'Come on, don't be a spoilsport.'

'You… You walk down that corridor and never, ever knock on my door again. Get it?'

Just then Bruno turned the corner of the corridor.

'This man has just propositioned me!' the drunk banker complained to the chief engineer.

Monty shut the door. He would get reprimanded.

All the while, *The Prince Regent* sailed at twenty knots through the straits of Bonifacio and the Tyrrhenian Sea toward Civitavecchia.

★

Monty appeared for breakfast in his linen suit for Day Two. The heat was already intense. He was determined to tie Lucinda to him to avoid further incidents and realised that he knew absolutely nothing about her.

She appeared when they were already clearing the tables, an antique diamond rivière around her neck. 'Don't stare. They're just stones from a South African mine.'

Once, thugs had broken his mother's window. She had brushed the pieces off the carpet and held out the pan. 'How precious! They look just like diamonds.'

'Lucinda dearest, we ought to be better acquainted by now.'

'Can you get me a latte, please?'

'Are you married? Do you have children?'

'Monty, don't get heavy. Can I have sweetener in my latte?'

Lucinda turned the spoon round and round in the cup. 'Monty, you seem stressed somehow, almost worn out, and not at all the same as you were on previous cruises.'

Day Three was spent visiting Civitavecchia. They swooped into the Roman harbour with the Michelangelo

Fortress on the right. On deck, passengers watched the thrown hawser being caught by an Italian boy who looped it round an antique metal capstan. The sun shone; spirits were high. Monty trudged through St Francis of Assisi Cathedral for the umpteenth time and afterwards made an effort to tell jokes in the fish restaurant overlooking the sea.

Back on board, he was asked to appear in the captain's quarters.

There were complaints. Monty had been depressing to be with. He walked out of his duties every evening. He had been overheard being rude about Nancy Frankl. During the cathedral visit, he had called the saint *Francis of All Asses*. He swore a lot under his breath.

And, unforgivably, a French banker reported that Monty had made indecent approaches to him. When the Frenchman rebuffed them, he had been verbally abused by Monty, threatened even. The chief engineer had overheard part of it.

Such behaviour was a contract breaker. The captain informed Monty that this would be his last voyage and that back in Monte Carlo he should contact the shipping company manager.

★

Roulette tables were installed for pre-dinner entertainment. Lucinda, without batting her glued-on eyelashes, put down one thousand euros and got her chips. Monty would not have to pretend to bet to get things going. The croupier spun the wheel. Lucinda's chips were raked away. Monty put his hand on her shoulder, warm under his touch. She bet again.

Just before the bugle, the captain graced them in person to tell them that during the night they would sail to Naples for their last day, and the last gala evening, as was traditional on board, would be a cross-dressing party. The guests clapped with enthusiasm.

Monty's table companions could, of course, talk about nothing else but cross-dressing. As an experienced cruiser, he explained that the way it was done was for the couple to go to the boutique, she to choose a gown for him and vice versa. The most effective cross-dressing couple would win a free cruise.

Arabella decided Daniel should come as Elizabeth Taylor, and she would be Richard Burton, which made Nancy laugh out loud. It was unpleasant.

Lucinda assumed that she would pair up with Monty, and Henrietta, instead of manoeuvring herself into that role, convinced Claude to be her partner.

Fatigue for champagne drinking had set in. It always did. Monty was prepared and pushed neat brandy, which rich Chinese drink with their meals.

After dinner there was dancing under the stars. Monty hated this because it was personal; he had to share himself around and feared for his private sphere. He escaped after two dances with Lucinda, who moved with little rushing steps forward and backward, her body jerking with small elbow wriggles. Not one of them could dance like his mother, with elegance and in time with the music.

He was standing, looking down at the bow ploughing soporifically through the water, when he heard a pattering behind him. Lucinda had caught up with him. 'I've been looking all over for you.'

'Lucinda, why do you take such small steps when you are as tall as I am?'

She looked down at her feet protruding from the hem of her Mischka tulle gown as if they could speak for her. 'Probably because as a child I was raised in an antique shop.'

'Your father was an antiquarian?'

'Yes, in Bond Street. He specialised in curios. My house is full of them.'

'Like what?'

'A rosewood desk with two secret drawers, unlocked by a little lever concealed in the leg. But the best is the library wall which rotates when you pull out Homer.'

'What is behind it?'

'A square room, every wall filled with rare books right up to the ceiling. I now own his collection of first editions.'

'Tell me more.'

'My parents live in a luxury sheltered village. Mother's dementia is advancing and Dad can't do anything but look after her. As their only daughter, I live in the Mayfair flat.'

'All alone?'

'My first and last husband and I divorced amicably ten years ago. I don't know where he is – not in England, I guess. Rosie, my teckel and best friend, poor thing, is in a kennel right now.'

'Any drinking companions?'

'Apart from you twice a year, I meet up with father's old friends in the Ritz for tea once in a while just to air my clothes, and I am a member of the antiquarian society but they're mostly old fossils.'

'How do you spend your days?'

'Walking Rosie, reading, this and that.'

'Cleaning the house.'

'TipTop Housecleaning do that. Next you'll ask me about my dentist.'

'I was just going to but am more interested in your hairdresser.'

'Why all these personal questions? It started this morning over my latte.'

'I have been advised it would be good for me to be more interested in people around me. So how about your hairdresser?'

'I'd rather not say.'

'That exclusive?'

'If you must know, it's a wig. I have short grey hair underneath which stopped growing years ago for some reason. There, you know all about me.'

'Thank you for your trust.'

She grabbed his arm. 'You're not building up to propose, are you?'

A strong gust of wind lifted the stole from her shoulders. It tumbled and twirled along the mahogany planks. He ran, retrieved it and draped it back across her.

★

Henrietta, in a silvery tuxedo, was practising nonchalant stances, one hand in her trouser pocket. 'Am I doing this right, Lucinda?' she asked her approaching friend.

And then with urgency, 'You're not dressed as a man yet, and the bar is open. Wait till you see Claude in the lace dress I chose for him. He keeps falling over in the high heels. And Nancy made the effort to come as a male psychiatrist – Freud, I'd say. I have a mind to buy her a grey beard from the boutique.'

'Henrietta, stop chattering as if I were Lucinda.' It was Monty's voice.

'Monty? I'll be damned. You look exactly like her.'

'Isn't that the plan for tonight?'

'It's well done,' she said, flustered. 'Really well done. You fooled me completely.'

★

In the dining room, candles flickered in the cut-glass candelabras. The rowdy guests, shouting and laughing hysterically, did not suit the décor. Cross-dressing releases inhibitions.

Lucinda, also in a dinner jacket and with a Coco-purchased short-haired wig, turned to Monty. 'Now I look like you, but what do I know about you? Come on. Out with something personal.'

'I'm a romantic.'

'Prove it.'

'Not likely in this brouhaha.'

Just then, Henrietta noticed the slipped bra cup under Claude's armpit and the table erupted in mirth.

'Let's go out on deck,' said Lucinda.

'That suits me. The dress you chose for me is so tight I can't swallow food.'

Up on the promenade deck, salty fine spray hit their faces. A storm was building up. South-westerly waves crashed against the hull in the whistling wind, and *The Prince Regent* laboured through the aroused oil-black Mediterranean. It grumbled in the clouds above them.

Despite it, Monty made them take off their shoes. 'It's not cold; it's just moist.'

'Moist? There is thunder, and waves throwing themselves over the deck. It will hail any minute.'

'Romantic, admit it,' he shouted back into the squall and pulled her towards the ship's bow. Taking hold of both her hands, he started to turn, leaning out, turning and leaning, faster and faster, and she had to take wider and wider steps to prevent herself from falling over. 'Don't let go of me. Don't!'

He slowed and she regained her balance, her chest heaving.

'Now, the ultimate trust game,' he yelled, voice shredded in the wind. 'We will take turns perching in the bow, arms out, eyes closed, swaying in the wind. The feel of flying away from oneself, from the hell that is life.'

★

The captain and Bruno on the bridge scanned the screens with concentration to steer the forty-eight tonnes through the churned and sluggish waves. The visibility was getting worse.

'Fucking hell!' The captain leapt across to the windscreen. 'Some drunken guests are playing silly buggers on the bow deck.' Just then, a squall slashed against the glass, obscuring his sight. When it cleared he could make out a man in a tuxedo standing crucified on the bow. 'Bloody DiCaprio!'

*

The storm raged for most of the night but the guests were unaware as they appeared bleary-eyed for their last breakfast on board. Their journey would come to an end in a few hours.

'Where is Monty?' Lucinda asked the table.

Just then, Bruno, accompanied by the cabin steward, came to the breakfast table and enquired whether Monty had left dinner last night and not returned. The guests affirmed this, and Lucinda said that she had gone with him.

'I would be grateful if you would accompany me to see the captain.'

'Just a minute.' Nancy put her napkin on the table. 'Perhaps I should come too. I am a psychiatrist and have a hunch that something unpleasant has happened to a man who was depressive.'

In silence, heads bent, Lucinda, Nancy and Bruno stepped onto the navigation bridge. On a leather-covered bench stood a pair of gentleman's patent dress shoes and a pair of high heels. Lucinda recognised them as the ones she and Monty had bought in the boutique together and explained that they had gone out on deck and taken their shoes off to enjoy the elements. When it had started to rain hard, she had gone back to her cabin to dry and avoid catching a cold, which, as they could hear from her hoarseness, she had got anyway.

Did she see Monty later that night?

No, she had remained in her cabin until breakfast.

'Did Monty show any signs of depression during the meal or afterwards?'

'He jumped overboard, is that what you are thinking?'

Nancy nodded meaningfully.

Lucinda looked down for a while to compose herself. 'At dinner he asked me to find out more about him. I have sailed with him several times before. This time he seemed tired, worn out. Out on deck, he did say he wanted to fly away from the hell of life.'

'You were the one person in whom he confided when he came to realise that he was untrue to himself, playing the role of someone he could not identify with any longer. The hell was the void of despair calling him to destroy himself. Weariness is the forerunner and if ignored—'

The captain interrupted Nancy. 'It probably did not help that we had sacked him the day before.'

Lucinda was bewildered. 'You fire guests?'

'I'll analyse it for you,' said Nancy. 'Monty was an employee, an activity promoter, a children's party clown. You, and you,' – Nancy pointed at the captain and Bruno – 'are responsible for his plunge into the raging ocean.'

'Oh, poor Monty!' Lucinda started to cry.

A subsequent search of Monty's cabin produced a grey Italian jacket held together by safety pins, several metal strips with Valium pills, a pile of cuttings relating to the Rothschild family and an old and bent foil-wrapped liverwurst sandwich.

The captain informed the police in Monte Carlo about their man overboard at approximately 23:30, latitude 7°30 and longitude 42°.

★

Less than a year later, Lucinda boarded *The Prince Regent*. In a tulip-shaped mint jacket and bell-bottoms, a canvas beret atop her copper curls, she walked across the marble oval with tiny steps. The elderly woman next to her, in a suit with a brooch pinned to the high collar of her blouse, advanced slowly, gaping around her. 'To think you can indulge in this three times a year!'

'Actually, I'd like better staying in my large flat enjoying the antiques. Of course, if they allowed the teckel on board that might make a difference.'

'Look, here comes a ship commander, smart as a whip.'

Bruno, the chief engineer, had spotted Lucinda. 'Nice to have you with us on board again, despite last year's tragedy.'

'Never found, I gather?'

'Not any more now.' Bruno personally escorted the two women to their adjoining royal suites.

'We must look forward, not backwards.' Lucinda lifted her chin in a gesture of courage. 'Or, indeed, downwards.'

The old lady had gone to look into the en-suite. 'It's all real marble and sandstone.'

Lucinda introduced her to Bruno as Mary, a travelling companion.

Bruno left them to unpack.

'This is a dreamboat, isn't it?' Now sitting on the soft bed, bouncing a little, Mary held the soft towelling dressing gown against her parchment-skinned cheek. 'If I picked out *The Prince Regent* I could smuggle this home.'

'You promised not to embarrass me.'

'I hope I can stand all the quality and pampering.'

'You deserve it and you can.'

'Are you sure there will be waltzing under the stars, Montgomery?'

MINERAL WATER

Astrid strode along the white gleaming corridor with a determined arm swing, short cropped hair and that feel about her: a rock of a nurse one can depend on in tough moments. For weeks she had ignored letters addressed to her from her home town, Rémy in the Rhône-Alpes, and now found to her utter annoyance that an envoy of the municipality was here in person to speak to her. She was a staff nurse at the busiest hospital in Paris.

'What can I do for you?' she asked rather sharply of the man in a suit in the waiting room.

'Your father, Benoit Blanc of Rémy, convicted of murder, was released three months ago after serving twenty years in prison, and you are his only daughter.'

'I know, but I turned my back on my father when he went to prison.'

'Well, he is out now and has become a liability in Rémy. He spits on and curses the passers-by from a little balcony overlooking the road.'

'Prison couldn't have killed him, could it? Tell me that he is dead and then I will come back to Rémy.'

'Look, he seems to be performing black magic rituals. It frightens people, children and tourists, and will soon cause an accident.'

'I don't care. I don't have money to spend on my father. If you believe that hocus pocus, send him back to prison or put him into an old people's home. He is seventy-two years old now.'

'Both cost the state money. His flat is already subsidised by the commune. He has some savings and contributes – that's why he has the balcony.'

Astrid laughed with a sneer. 'Nothing will ever change in parochial France!'

'We, the municipality, have determined that you and your spouse or partner are responsible for Benoit. Here, read for yourself.'

'I don't have a husband. Who would marry the daughter of a murderer?'

'When a ground study of Rémy was made, it was discovered that a new mineral water source had sprung up under your father's land, and he had to move because all Rémy waters belong to the commune. He was offered compensation and alternative accommodation. Shooting the geophysicist was not a solution.'

'It was Dr Finley and his bloody fancy clinic next door who instigated the study! He bribed the geologist to pretend there was a new source. My father argued all this in the mairie to no avail. You don't think Mayor Maxime paid for her own boob-job, do you? We all know it was a fix for Finley to enlarge his property on my father's land.'

'Your father achieved nothing by resorting to murder.'

'Hah! I was still at nursing college then. Once I got back, with Father safely removed to prison, our garden had been tarmacked to provide a better access road to the Clinic Céleste.'

'Look, Miss Blanc, whatever happened in the past, the decision to make you responsible for your father has been taken.'

Astrid had no choice. She sacrificed her annual leave entitlement and went back to Rémy, where she had spent a childhood in a pleasant house, playing in a green garden, until her mother died of leukaemia slowly and painfully, which is probably what made Astrid become a determinedly good nurse.

*

In a cheap concrete apartment block on the road near where her home had been, she rode up in a narrow lift to the fourth floor. The human being who opened the door to her was an emaciated wretch of a man. Only the porcelain-blue eyes reminded her of happy days in early childhood.

'You turned your back on me,' he said in a low, bitter voice when he recognised her and let her in.

'I took a job in Paris, one which occupies my time and mind.'

She stepped into the one-bedroom apartment and noticed that the walls were covered in pinned-on notes and pictures, like fish-scales. Papers were even stuck to the cupboards in the small kitchen. 'What's all this?'

'I didn't shoot that geologist. I'm innocent and am going to prove it.'

'After twenty years?'

'Finley is already eighty-two, and I wanted you back so that we can confront the most famous French plastic surgeon of our time. That's why I wrote to you. His wife, Eloise, died of lung disease five years ago. Mayor Maxime retired looking like a young Vivien Leigh with all the facelifts she got as pay-offs. I spat at her when I met her in town.'

'Pay-offs for what?'

'In prison, I heard that drilling had revealed that the so-called aquifer pool under our house had dried up as miraculously as it had appeared. Finley bought the land from the commune for a song and got permission for a wide drive, parking and whatever else. He, Maxime the bitch and the inspector-general were as thick as thieves.'

'That happened way back. I see no reason why I had to come home.'

'I met up with my defence lawyer, who's old too and not practising any longer. When I threatened the bastard, he admitted that he had thought at the time there were things which did not add up. He allowed me access to the files, if I left him in peace.'

Astrid followed her father onto the small balcony, on which was a chair and a plastic storage box containing binoculars, a camera and a clipboard with notes.

'They say you act like a lunatic on this balcony.'

'If I hop up and down covered in a sheet with a mask, someone has to do something about me and reopen the case.'

'But instead they dragged me back here.' She picked up the binoculars and scanned the park belonging to the clinic. Although the trees had grown majestically, she still recognised the one against which the man had been shot.

'Look at this picture.' Benoit brought an enlarged grainy photograph onto the balcony. 'The position of the victim is wrong. He has been dragged and propped against the tree. His cap is sideways on his head. One side of his jacket is off his shoulder and one foot has almost slipped out of his laced-up shoe. There are yellow blobs on his beard, gunge from his lungs.'

'You can't erase the fact that they arrested you in our garden fifteen metres from the body, holding the pistol the geologist was shot in the heart with.'

Benoit produced the front page of *Paris Match*. It showed the picture which had appeared in papers all over France: the inspector-general with a white handkerchief picking the gun out of Benoit's hand.

'I heard a shot and went outside to where the bang had come from. I picked the gun up by its barrel from the grass and inspected it, as anyone would. Not one person in all of France sussed that I was holding the gun by its barrel.'

'Did you get access to the autopsy report?'

'Clean shot through the heart.'

Father and daughter went back inside where he riffled frenetically through papers in messy piles on the dining table. 'Here, these are the pictures the press took at the clinic on that inauguration day, and I can't figure it out.'

Astrid looked at the photographs of the opening of the orangery in the clinic. There was one of her listening to the speeches, looking so young. And there was one of a young and blond nurse standing behind a patient in a wheelchair. It was Yvette, her best friend from nursing college, who had landed that fancy job in Clinic Céleste and who had invited her.

'If you look closer... In this picture, Maxime is making her speech and Yvette is in the background at the rose arch with the patient in the wheelchair under a green blanket. In this one, the sculptor is unveiling his plaque and, notice, no one is behind the wheelchair! But what drives me crazy is the geologist, clearly visible in that upper window looking down at the sculptor. He was shot very soon after.'

Benoit continued, 'Yvette is still working there. I can see her from my balcony. Surely you stayed in touch? I need you to go and talk to her about what happened at that inauguration party, before we both confront Finley.'

'Is that why you acted like a lunatic on the balcony? To get me back here to help prove your innocence?'

★

Twenty years ago, Clinic Céleste had inaugurated its new wing, the largest orangery in France. It contained a twenty-five-metre pool, soft-cushioned recovery areas and a stone fountain dispensing fresh Eau de Rémy at the push of a button. Finley paid the commune thousands of euros a month for the supply. It had been in late June, Astrid remembered, because the roses were at their best.

Yvette, a nurse in the clinic, had been one year ahead of Astrid in nursing college. She had blond locks which danced on her shoulders off-duty, and she and Astrid had built up quite a bond during that time. Everyone in the college admired Yvette for having landed such a prestigious job, and it was indeed Yvette who had invited Astrid to the inauguration.

After being shown around the clinic, and before the cold buffet at the end of the formal rose garden, there were speeches; Maxime welcomed the guests and singled out other eminent doctors, local politicians and representatives of the Rémy police. To Astrid's annoyance, it was clear that she and Yvette would not be able to chat because the latter was on duty with her green-blanket-covered patient in the wheelchair, his face wrapped in bandages. A wink had been all they could share plus a gesture of Yvette's finger turning on an imaginary wristwatch meaning *later*. She had noticed the bearded geologist in his checked trilby at the window above, looking down at Finley who was by then describing the new procedures which defied the signs of aging.

After the unveiling of the plaque for the orangery, Finley declared the buffet open. Just then, a loud dry shot came from way down the garden. Everyone started to run towards where the noise had come from, and they had to push through the rose arch where the helpless patient had been parked awkwardly to one side. Dashing over the lawn, Astrid bumped into Yvette.

The inspector-general shouted for people to stop running. 'Go back to your lunch. Turn and go back.

Except for medical staff.' He tried to bar their way with outstretched arms.

Yvette and Astrid ran on beside Finley, followed by the press. They were all brought to a stop by the sight of the geologist slumped against a tree near the park boundary facing Astrid's garden. His mouth was slack and open, and on his white shirt was an almost neat red spot where a bullet had entered his chest.

Finley confirmed that the man was dead, and the inspector-general insisted they all leave the crime scene, while he pursued his investigation.

Astrid remembered that Yvette and she had walked back to the guests but the party had been spoiled and the wheelchair-bound patient taken into the clinic.

It was only the following day that Astrid became aware of the accusation against her father.

★

Three days after arriving in Rémy and sleeping on her father's couch, Astrid, a rolled-up newspaper sticking out of her handbag, announced herself at the Clinic Céleste. The receptionist tapped with pink oval fingertips on the keyboard and then pointed down a carpeted corridor to the door of the orangery. 'Dr Finley's wife is in there.'

Indeed, a young-looking blond woman was sitting on the rim of the Rémy mineral water fountain, idly scooping the water with her hand. 'There you are!' she said to Astrid and pulled her hand out of the expensive water.

'Read!' Astrid proffered the newspaper. 'Father started to piece together the truth.'

'I see,' Yvette said slowly, after having read. 'Prison life did not kill your father, but yesterday he fell to his death off his balcony, wrapped in a black cloth and holding a cross. Why am I not surprised?'

'I had to answer some questions from the police, not many, and then was let go. Death by misadventure is the verdict. So that's it for me then. I did have to wait for twenty years. How are you doing?'

'Well…' Yvette invited Astrid to sit close to her on the marble fountain rim. 'I got Finley to marry me in the end, three years after his wife's death.'

'Ah, the beautiful Eloise – lung damage, wasn't it?'

'You know my old-fashioned nursing specialities. I kept them up.'

'I remember you rubbing a home-made vapour mixture of petroleum, turps and nettles on my breasts when I had a cold.'

'Your chest, not your breasts. Eloise took daily primrose oil capsules on my recommendation.'

'Only some days they contained something else, right?'

'When Finley was away at medical symposiums, I harassed her with problems and then administered my homeopathic calming solution. That and the stingy rub made it possible to use the longest 001-size liposuction cannula needle several times without her feeling a thing. Push into the lung, pull out. Flesh and skin close up at once. No suspicion of foul play, nor an autopsy. Finley put his signature on the death certificate without concentrating; his eyes were on my cleavage.'

'That brings me back to the geologist. It was you. But why him? He wasn't in our way.'

'He was having a fit of conscience, and I didn't trust him to stick to his lies about the fake spring on your father's land. He was endangering my plans for this clinic.'

'He was up at the window and then not. That's one thing my father pointed out; that and you not being with your patient in the wheelchair all the time.'

'In a nutshell, when Finley was making his speech, the beardie-weirdie geologist came out of the house. I left my patient, trusting that the green blanket would stick in everyone's mind and they would all assume a wheelchair had a nurse behind it. I lured the bloke down the garden with a story about a hollow noise and gurgling. Once there, I made a pass at him and pulled him to the ground. Pinning him down, it had to be one stab into the heart and a twist with a 012 cannula. Everyone else was busy in the rose garden. I had a hell of a job propping the limp body up against the tree. I think he was dead by then, and it was easy enough to shoot him in the heart with my back against your garden fence and throw the weapon into your garden. The damage of the bullet erased the earlier wound from my stab. After that there was chaos with everyone running around. I simply joined them.'

Astrid clapped her hands. 'Brilliant, but never offer me a chest rub again, promise? Now tell me what's going to happen next?'

'My husband, now sufficiently conditioned by my old-fashioned treatments, will have a heart attack tomorrow afternoon, if that fits in with your plans.'

'Perfectly. After that we can be seen together mourning a deranged father and the passing of a brilliant surgeon-husband. Naturally we will be drawn to each other, nurse to nurse, old friends.'

'Remember at college when you pushed your hand into my knickers under the desk? I was so gooey.'

'Now we'll have a sumptuous bedroom and millions, not to forget the officially non-existent mineral water under the park.'

'No more stinking Paris drunks with cuts on Saturday night; no more curled blue toenails of wheezing down-and-outs for me.'

'No, darling, just love and luxury.'

THE DUTCH
ARCHITECT

From the wings of the Pocket Theatre in Amsterdam, Anais watched the rehearsal of *Parabolic*, which she was directing under guidance of the author of the play. Guidance was a polite word for hectoring, pouting and calling her incompetent.

Beyond sackcloth curtains, on a lit stage which was tilted forward at a slight angle, was a simple setting of empty white cubicles, each leading to the others by black doors. One cubicle had no door; inside was installed a high-legged throne in red velour, and to get to it there was a white ladder in one of the other cubicles. Actors in track suits meandered, without apparent purpose, through the set.

'White and bare' – 'Denied delusion' – 'Angst,' the performers enunciated with exaggerated diction.

'No, no, no!' interrupted the author. 'You've got to be *spiritually* in the play, not interpret it *physically*. You act like prospective house-buyers!'

The playwright liked to portray himself as the bohemian artist in black mohair, but in fact was fastidiously groomed, eyes with a cold glint, always narrowed. He was sitting in the stalls sideways, one long leg over the next seat, one arm draped over the back of another.

Like an upside-down black spider, Anais thought, *negative vibes oozing from his furry body.*

Anais's partner of three and a half years, Jan, was a salesforce developer in a company in Leiden. He took the train back to Amsterdam for the weekends, where the couple had recently bought the leasehold on the top-floor apartment in what had been a wealthy merchant's house. It was on Kulpengracht, right on the canal, the last house before Raadhuisstraat – a house with an ornate façade and a stepped brick gable and a wall plaque, *Tulphuis*. Anais felt uplifted every time it came into view when she cycled over the canal bridge.

She and Jan were proud to have made a positive move towards cohabitation – and a good investment – but found it difficult to stay within their budget furnishing the Renaissance-style apartment. They had set themselves high standards. The quality premises deserved it.

The spacious high-ceilinged living room faced the canal. In its square oriel window, their favourite spot with an all-round upholstered bench, they sat, their knees up, watching people cycle or walk past. When it rained and boats glided on the pitted green water, they imagined who had sat there before them in the seventeenth century when this patrician house had been built – the Dutch Golden Age.

So far, they had invested in a designer table, but not yet the right chairs, and a bookshelf. Pouffes and large cushions scattered on the floor mats, but not yet the carpet they aspired to, made up the rest of the furnishings.

As a statement, they had bought an Italian king-size bed for their large bedroom. Apart from matching bedside tables, they had to content themselves with rolling clothes racks and stacked crates for pullovers and such. This room looked out onto the internal courtyard with its bicycles and undesirable clutter.

Next to it was a narrow room with a tall slim window. Its shape had a charm they could not put a name on. It was a bonus space that had not been mentioned in the estate agent's brochure, and they believed they had got it as a bargain. Their use of the space changed regularly: a cosy office, a treadmill room, a reading and reflecting space. It was just too small to be called the spare room.

The modernised kitchen and bathroom also gave onto the inner court.

The straight corridor through the middle of the apartment started at the front door and ended with a blank wall, one which must have had history for it was bumpily plastered. Many before them had fixed or hung things on it. They baptised it the *art wall* and spent hours debating how to conceal its flaws. She wanted an old Venetian mirror, which would take them six months to save up for, and he preferred a ceiling-to-floor tapestry. It was not a priority and so they bought a modern, reasonably priced machine-made tapestry to cover most of the wall. If it looked disappointing, they did not say that to themselves. Perhaps with the right chest of drawers? They were both only in their late twenties and had ample time before them to change things.

Jan, of course, was now looking for a job in Amsterdam, but it is harder to undo the familiar, the established, than an agile young mind would wish.

On Friday, Anais left the theatre, pushing her bicycle. Her mind ticked off: *Sunday meal in freezer; Saturday will go out; croissants for late Sunday morning; white wine in fridge; need a new bra. Can wait, won't wear one.* As she passed the shopping arcade, her mind stopped burbling. The lamp for the living room was way down the priority list, but she could just pop in to have a look at the styles they were selling. She steered towards the cycle racks, pushed the front wheel into a clamp and hooked her bag over her shoulder.

Inside Van der Beek Lamp and Mirror Shop, the spotlights and their bounce almost hurt the retina. She felt exposed, reflected in all the mirrors: a pale-faced young woman with long strands of naturally tumble-waved strawberry-blond hair, held back and out of her green eyes by a twirled scarf. They were large and peaceful, an actor had once said to her. *Such an overdose of cold light could be effective on stage for the right play.* She binned the thought as soon as it had risen. The Pocket Theatre had to save money, and electricity was expensive.

In the next showroom, she noticed the type of lamp Jan and she were after, a modern dome-like milk-glass head on a bent chrome stem with a noise-activated switch. The price tag had one zero too many.

At the exit of the arcade, she hopped into the glass revolving door but, once she was retained between the glass separations and the curved wall, it stopped. Another person was caught in the triangle opposite her. Anais was fascinated by the potential of this situation in stage choreography but, when the door stayed put, she became aware of an intense personality close to her. Looking up, she saw a man like a dark-blond late-thirtyish George Clooney in the other compartment. A large leather satchel was strapped across his chest. He gave the glass in front of him a push but it did not budge. And then he smiled at her, inclining his head slightly, an almost personal gesture, while encompassing her with a frank blue look. Just then there was a squeak, and the revolving door was released. She ended up in the road and the fair-haired Clooney in the shopping gallery.

The weekend that followed was uneventful, mostly because Jan had returned worn from long hours of work, all the socialising and the rush hour train back from Leiden. 'If I were not coming home to you, I would have already downed three beers.'

He did not have the energy to go and see the lamp and suggested just an IKEA piece in the meantime. Even the mention of IKEA seemed an insult to the room in which they were relaxing on piled-together cushions, her svelte body awkwardly contorted with one of her legs under the other and he sitting cross-legged. They ate microwaved lasagne with small round tomatoes, a concession to the five *musts* to stay healthy. The film she had let him choose glimmered on the plasma screen. When she brought in the bowls of fruit salad, he noticed that she was not wearing a bra and put the dessert beside him. Even though it is good for them, men do not like fruit salads. She had to give up on hers as well, because he came crawling over to her to investigate this lack of underwear. Not long after, they went to bed and made love in the domesticated style.

Sunday morning was reading the papers, coffee by the bed and croissant crumbs in the bedsheets. The sun was out and they walked along the canals. She pulled him into an art gallery she had read about. The painter was present, and Anais praised one of her works, giving the impression that Jan and she would be interested in buying it for their new apartment.

Outside again, Jan asked her why she had felt the urge to encourage the painter who had produced such an awful picture. Anais did not admit that she had liked it.

Jan left her at six in the evening for the train back to Leiden, a word which in German means *Suffering*.

*

On Rosenstraat she could freewheel downhill but had to heed others doing the same. She felt her hair playing behind her. A hint of spring was in the air. In the plane trees, brown buds showed glimpses of tender green. Once she reached the flat by the *gracht*, her legs, clad in distressed jeans, had to work again. Close to the theatre, she pedalled backwards to diminish her speed and hopped off.

The rehearsal of Scene Two encountered problems because the writer wanted a minute of silence starting in mid-sentence and kept changing the choice of sentence.

'Contrast, emotional contrast – is that so hard to act? Again, from the beginning.'

Patience ran out, and the black spider let out his bad mood on her. First, the ladder had to be somewhere else, then he wanted it on the floor to visually deny its use. When an actor tripped over it, Anais was blamed. 'My piece is written for the cubes to actually rotate. Imagine how you would all fuck that up!'

Moving cubicles? Now he was getting treacherously close to Ibsen, having skirted round Sartre and *Huis Clos*. Whatever.

On the way home to her empty flat, she hesitated again in front of the shopping arcade. This was not for a second peek at the lamp, was it? She observed the revolving door and the people turning in it, asking herself what she was hoping for.

On Tuesday, she was sent out to buy a crown to hang from the back of the throne. For that, she needed to cycle all the way through the centre of town. Luckily, the weather was fine. The party goods shop, which stocked gold crowns according to their ad online, only had ones with fake rubies stuck to the rim. Hopefully the glue was weak, she thought, as she approached her cycle, wondering how to transport the crown, when someone said to her, 'On the way to your coronation?'

'Oh, Clooney. Sorry. The man in the glass triangle.'

This time he had not just the satchel but a brown leather art-tube slung over his shoulder. 'I believe, in a circle cut into four, the triangles are called quadrants, not that I want to put myself above someone who walks around with a crown.'

'It is annoying being corrected, but perhaps you know all about geometry as I guess you are an…' She hummed the *an*.

'… architect,' he finished for her, 'one who has just finished work for the day.'

Her heart was pounding in her chest. *Let's have a coffee* hovered in the air.

'Lucky you,' she said. 'I have to work every day until six, though on Wednesday the theatre is booked by schools.'

'You are not an actress but the stage manager. Do they need you in the evenings too?' An invisible *Let's have a drink this evening* was in the air now.

'The play I am *directing* at the moment opens next Saturday. The theatre is in the Central Canal District, near where I live.'

'So do I. On Raadhuisstraat.'

'Kulpengracht, one of the streets off Raadhuisstraat. We have just bought a lovely top-floor flat.' *Don't brag, Anaïs. It's not a big deal for others.* 'Funny to meet here.'

'Yes, it is.'

Puff, the coffee possibility was gone. It would have been inappropriate anyway, with a man seen through glass and for a couple of minutes by chance encounter.

She threaded the crown onto the handlebar, where it would rub against the lamp and perhaps scratch. Then she considered the metal clamp at the back. He had not moved away, nor said goodbye. He was watching her movements before he intervened and gently took the crown from her. With care, he set it on her head. 'Do not hesitate. Your reign will be long and prosperous.'

She felt the heat of her blushing, climbed a little clumsily onto the cycle and pedalled off regally, giving him a backward wave.

That evening, in the king-size bed, she talked to Jan on her mobile about the author and the crown prop she had had to buy, leaving out Clooney and her coronation. Then, she snuggled deeper into the duvet and fantasised about him. How could she not? He was good-looking, intelligent, imaginative, and dangerous as hell for her, should she ever see him again. Of course, she now knew that he lived on Raadhuisstraat but that was one kilometre long. Her side street gave him a better chance of finding out which house she lived in. Why would he want to try? He was at least thirty-five, almost certainly married, possibly with small children, and she was a Boho-waved woman with a steady partner. End of impossible story. *Anais, I said stop thinking about it.*

★

One week later, on Wednesday, she could go out without the Nike fleece. Walking away from the house, she realised with a heat-rush of intense pleasure that he had been looking for her, because he was standing, his back against the canal railing, checking up and down the road.

When his eyes met hers, he bounced off the metal and straightened up. She approached him in a controlled gait until they were within touching distance. In the plane tree above them, the leaves were unfolding in pleats. Beside them, the water of the canal was still clear and not yet murky with algae bloom.

It was important what they would say now, and so she said nothing and nor did he. In a gesture of togetherness and tenderness, he cupped her elbow and led her around the corner into Raadhuissstraat. In unison, they entered the first café, and he chose a table in the furthest corner. When they were sitting, which seemed to be a leap further into intimacy, he smiled at her as if she were finally all to himself, and she did not care whether he had ten children.

Hansen de Groot was his name. He still lived in the house where he was born and brought up, a house his grandfather had built. She told him her name was Anais Bakker, and he thought Anais was a cute name. She told him she did not like the word cute, and he agreed with her.

'Kulpengracht has seen me walk up and down a few times.'

She revealed that she lived in No 22, Tulphuis, with Jan, a friend – the end one with the oriel window and the very tall gable.

'It's called a crow-stepped gable.' He shook his head, and she watched his barley hair ruffle, and noticed for the first time the hint of a cleft in his chin. 'You won't believe the coincidence.'

She moved forward on her chair.

'I inherited the freehold on Tulphuis and the adjoining one at the angle on Raadhuisstraat, making the corner. I believe that my grandfather wanted the right address but also the view onto the canal.'

Coffee was brought and gave her a chance to let this sink in. While he turned his spoon in his cup, he went on to tell her that, on the death of the grandfather, his parents and he had occupied the Raadhuisstraat house, while his Aunt Rose lived in 'hers', Tulphuis. By the time his parents tragically died in a plane crash, they were already living in the top floor of the straat house, and Aunt Rose had moved into the lower floors. He was twenty-two at the time and inherited both properties. 'Far too much.' He sighed. 'I divided your house and sold off the leasehold to the apartments, one of which you and your friend have bought.'

He rearranged his weight on the chair. He had just made her part of much of himself; hopefully, he was comfortable with that.

Suddenly he looked up, his face shining like a boy's. 'Now I do remember the name *Bakker*. I always insist on checking the credentials my agent submits.'

'So, in fact I am now living in your property and practically next to you? What were the chances of that?'

'Friendly fate.'

More than that, she thought. *Magic*. But then, why should this be so amazing? After all, they were just two people who met by chance and happened to be neighbours.

'Your turn to talk,' he invited her and reached out for one of her hands. His touch was warm and tight on the captured hand on the cool table. She told him about working for the black spider playwright and *Parabolic*, which had opened the previous Saturday and provoked positive comment in *The Cybernetics*, a magazine only geeks read. Carefully, she told him about Jan, who was away during the week, still calling him 'her friend'.

Then she pulled her hand from under his and blurted out, 'Are you married?'

'Not yet. I have failed to find the right woman so far. My Aunt Rose is giving me a hard time about it.'

This was the most dangerous answer he could have given her. Now she almost wished he had ten children.

'Whenever I bring home a young lady friend, Rose bounces up the stairs to check her out and never leaves us alone. If the truth be known, she is an incredibly possessive woman, as was my mother.'

When it seemed time to leave, Anais rose, moved her hands up to tighten the knot on the foulard around her head, and then picked her Titian-red jacket from the back of the chair.

'It's a good colour for you,' he commented and paid by drizzling cash from his palm into the saucer with the paper-slip bill.

Hansen and Anais agreed to meet again at the bridge of the canal. It already seemed to be a natural thing to do.

★

Wednesday next, they were strolling through the tulip garden where colourful flowers glistened new and upright under clear sky, the pride of the Netherlands. She chatted about existentialism playing such a part again in current experimental plays, being and nothingness, Sartre's *virtue and character in claustrophobia*.

'Aristotle had a different take on it. He thought character doesn't determine our actions and destiny – freely chosen projects do. My grandfather worked with the famous architect Gerrit Rietveld in the Bauhaus era: the Unesco-protected Rietveld Schroder House with movable walls.'

'Art and architecture clearly go hand in hand. Add to that surrealism…'

He searched for her hand and held it tight. 'In reality, the Rietveld House was commissioned by a mother of three who wanted the rooms to suit the kids as they grew older.'

'Thank you for that.' She smiled openly up at him. 'I can use that with my playwright.'

How much they had in common. How close they seemed to grow. How lightly they bobbed against each other as if they weren't so much walking as floating. No alarm bells had rung, not even a little tingle. She feared that she could fall in love with Hansen if she did not force herself to battle against it.

They left the flower beds behind and entered a yew-shaded arbour with a nude statue on a plinth. The mood changed with the light – it turned serious, consequential, inescapable, impatient, tense, needy, fated. Suddenly, as if a frustrated divinity had forced them into each other's arms, he began to kiss her hard and urgently, trying to suck her life into his. His face pressed against hers; she felt the pulse in his temple. Her legs trembled; her whole body was consumed with fire for him. *Maul him, eat him, suck him into her.*

When they let go of each other, she knew that this was not a play she could direct or control. She was panting and had lost her scarf. He too was breathing heavily and said sorry, he couldn't help himself, and then they leapt at each other again.

Eventually the fire of passion abated. Somehow, she managed to get back to the park gate. When he said goodbye to her, he had lost his voice, and she felt as if she had battled through a tornado.

★

The next day, they met in Sloter Park. It was overcast, with rain predicted. They did not pay attention to their surroundings – trees, pond and benches – and hardly acknowledged the developing drizzle which was falling on them, nor the few people left in the park. They headed at a decisive pace through the grey. At the fake Greek temple, they looked at the concrete floor and both knew what the other was thinking, unashamedly and in desperation. Surrounded by the whispering of the rain, they stood pale from wantonness under the painted dome, like two dancers waiting for the tango to start, their glistening wet faces almost touching. *Animals* – it flashed through Anais's mind that they were like animals, appearing to be locked in a fight but in fact preparing to mate.

On the raw hard floor, they explored their bodies with keen hands, irritated by their clothes, which conspired to frustrate their lust. They entwined and pawed at each other in a frenzied desire to be locked together.

Afterwards, he drew her from the floor by her arm. He looked like Peter Pan with his tousled spiked hair and gloss-blue eyes. He picked up his crumpled raincoat. 'Did you get hurt?' he asked with concern.

'Wasn't it a feather bed?'

'In future I hope to offer you better.'

That was the moment when they knew they could no longer meet in public, not without getting arrested.

Later, in her apartment, she had calmed down enough to know where this would lead in the immediate future, and a case like this probably did not have a further future. She surrendered herself backwards onto the king-size bed. 'I want you. I need you, Hansen. I am crazy about you. I will do something stupid and come round and bang on your door, which is only metres away from mine. Can you feel me, Hansen? For I can feel you, all over my body.'

★

At the weekend, Anais made an effort to be pliant and cuddly with Jan. They did buy the lamp and decided to make up for it by drinking less wine and by not going out on Saturday night. It seemed to them a satisfactory deal.

When they had stepped through the revolving glass door of the arcade, Jan carrying the large box in front of him, she had an involuntary physical spasm which he noticed.

The lamp was perfect for the living room. They moved it a bit to the right and then the left. They clapped to switch it on and off. In the evening, they took in a Chinese, which did not count as eating out, and sipped wine they still had.

'What is the matter with you today?' Jan asked. 'You seem so distant, preoccupied. Has something happened with the black spider? He doesn't fancy you, does he?'

71

'What makes you think that?'

'I am not sure. The last three weekends you've been different. For starters, you don't listen to a word I am saying. You shiver and touch your belly a lot. Are you pregnant?'

He seemed only half-convinced after she put her head on his shoulder and reassured him that he was making it all up.

During the night, Jan woke them both with his thrashing. He said his stomach did not feel clever and blamed it on the prawn noodles. With sudden rapid movements he left the bed. She heard him retch in the bathroom. Sitting upright in bed, she forced herself to look at their individual clothes racks, reminding her of the theatre dressing area, rather than imagining Hansen's warm welcoming body right behind the wall.

'I mentioned to my boss that I am looking for another job in Amsterdam,' Jan said, returning.

'Was that wise? I think you should say nothing until you have signed a contract with someone else.'

'That wouldn't be fair to them.'

'Your boss has crossed you out. He is busy looking for someone to replace you. It might take months for you to find something here.'

'He is not like that. Most people are decent. You have a warped perception because you work with actors who are vain, and actresses who are nuts. Not to mention those who cook up modern plays. And I rather hope to find another job soon.'

She thought for a moment. *Was she wishing he would not?* 'You are right,' she said with the sigh of realisation that she had massively complicated her emotional life by accepting that first coffee on Raadhuisstraat. 'I do work in a warped theatre world where make-believe is the only reality. Of course you will find another job any day now.' *How could she be so fickle and unfaithful?*

However, when she met up with Hansen on Wednesday at the bridge over the canal, his embrace, despite her resolve to become detached, took her over the edge again and rekindled her passion for him. Tasting his lips, smell, existence, eventually she stepped back. 'I am worried. Jan wants now definitely to come back to work in Amsterdam. What will we do then?'

'Do you want to say goodbye to me?'

'No!' Her protestation made pigeons flutter up into the air. 'I am besotted with you. I love you so, I'm half out of my mind.' And after a pause and a frown, she asked him, 'Do you love me. If you do, say it. Say it.'

'I love you,' he whispered into her ear, 'but I don't want pigeons to distribute this message all over the city.'

Then, they leaned over the bridge railing, watching the water flow past and feeling the pleasing pressure of the metal bar against their abdomens. Behind them, people, mostly tourists for it had become May, passed hither and thither.

'You could come to my flat when Jan is not home, but I already know that I could not de-stress, and we have only one bed, and it would be unacceptable. Perhaps we could disappear for an hour or so from time to time.' After a pause she added, 'A hotel room,' and felt uncomfortably cheap.

'There is something you don't know about me. I abhor hotel rooms – the décor, room service, the smell of the shampooed carpet, the little wrapped soap.' He turned his head to look at her sideways. 'Anais, do you trust me?'

'Hansen de Groot, I trust you with heart and soul,' she confirmed and stopped looking into the water.

He pulled her close up against him. 'Good. Then let's go to your apartment – don't make those eyes – to investigate something.'

In the apartment, without looking left or right, he walked straight to the 'art wall' and lifted the tapestry. Then he knocked with his knuckles against different parts of the plastered wall.

'Are those bumpy lines the framework of a door? These two houses, are they linked?'

He turned to her. 'We can open this door again, if you agree. I will put a man on the job I know and trust.'

'But your aunt?'

'The door on the other side is also concealed. There is dead space between our houses, on purpose as it seems. Grandfather designed it that way.'

'But outside? It must show.'

'Not with a good architect.'

This was madness, but she needed Hansen. Surely she could come up with an innocent explanation should Jan notice the door – Jan, who might find a new job. She agreed to it. 'Let's do this.'

Indeed, the next evening someone unlocked the door of the apartment, which made her jump out of her seat. Hansen? Jan? A short stout man had let himself in.

He was carrying a box with tools. She helped him take off the tapestry and then watched as he chiselled out the metal frame of a door. Set into it was a thick wooden panel, which he prised out in one. After that, he mixed plaster in his bucket and made good the damage his chisel had made. 'Needs to dry. I'll be back tomorrow.'

He left with the panel, the bucket and the tools in two trips.

The metal door had no handle but a keyhole, which was blocked because a key was in it on the other side.

The handyman returned as promised and painted the plaster. She helped him hang the tapestry back on its hooks. 'Pretty soundproof,' he muttered.

Anais had to investigate. From the pavement on Kulpengracht, the false corner was not noticeable. Leaning out of the kitchen window at the back, a wall at a diagonal joined the corner of the house, with narrow windows running across the top under the roof. No one but an alert architect could put two and two together.

Jan called to tell her in triumphant joy that one of the jobs he had applied for had accepted him. It paid better too. 'Aren't you pleased? Amsterdam, here I come!'

It had been arranged that he stay for three consecutive weeks in Leiden for the handover and introductions and then pack up.

'Wonderful!' she exclaimed with fake enthusiasm. She shuddered with guilt mingled with joy and fear at the three weeks' chance of an irrevocable destiny between lovers. 'I promise not to buy expensive furniture while you're gone,' she joked on the phone with Jan, and they finished the conversation with their usual exchange of endearments.

After these blessed weeks, she would have to wean herself off her infatuation with Hansen. Or perhaps they could still meet in that secret room? It was an unnerving, yet exciting thought. But what if Jan lifted the tapestry for some reason? She would simply say that the owner of the building had sent someone to uncover the door in preparation for improving the wall. Clever, wasn't she?

On the agreed day, Hansen was to cross from his apartment. She heard him struggle with the lock on her metal door and, when he let her through, she saw that it was like an airlock with a second door about a foot inside. Both the doors and the walls and ceiling were thickly padded. 'Your builder said that it was completely soundproof.'

'He is right. All round, including floor and ceiling.'

'Alice in Wonderland must have felt like this'. She found herself in a magic triangular room, dominated by a large antique sofa. 'Ours. The world outside does not exist, only our feelings and the sounds we make. I wonder who was in here last. And how long ago?'

'Well, I spent quite some time dusting this magic room.'

Not only that, but he had made it cosy for them: on a small table was a three-armed candlestick with burning candles, the only source of light. On the floor stood a bottle of red wine and two glasses, and a little heater, its cable coming from the door of his house. She would have loved to have a peek inside, but he said that too many doors were in the way. Besides, they had to heed Aunt Rose.

'So, in fact this room has been used to escape the jealous rants of spouses since your grandfather's time. Probably your father, and now you.'

'Maybe that is why I haven't married. I would hate to cheat on my wife.'

She lowered her eyes. A bucket of iced water had just been thrown over her.

'You are not married. Come, come,' he said, trying to put it right.

She contemplated the worn red sofa against the long wall of the triangle, with its high back and low sausage armrests. It was the length of a bed and covered in a patterned velour. All in all, a decadent set for a major play about infidelity.

'I know you're thinking of changing the two props around. Forget about it; the sofa only fits against that wall.'

'I am glad that you don't *always* guess what I am thinking.'

'I pretty much do.'

He made her sit with him on the plush upholstery and apologised for not having brought anything to eat.

'Chewing food is…'

'… vulgar,' they said at the same time, and then she came to life and peppered his mouth with kisses for fun.

The frenzy of the park pavilion was absent. Almost as if they were different people in a different play.

'Anais, let's have some wine.' He poured them two glasses. He smiled, but the blue of his eyes was porcelain hard.

She tried to read him. Was he nervous? Perhaps opening up this hidden room brought memories of his father. His parents had died in the Pacific; she had checked it out. Tentatively, she suggested, 'There must be memories in here to do with your father, aren't there?'

'Not at all,' he said sharply. With his teeth, he pulled open the condom packet and put it next to him. He pushed back her thick hair with both hands and grabbed her neck either side in an awkward move to kiss her hard and with urgency. It hurt.

Then, he ordered her to take her clothes off. She had clearly unleashed something guarded in him. Playing the same game, she grabbed his shirt, undid a few buttons and then tore it open, which made a further button fly off. When they were naked, he threw himself over her, trapping her under him, and with a violently pounding heart against her, forced himself into her dryness.

Repeated pain shot through her, and she tried to ward him off with her spread hands, but he had to have it his way until he was satisfied. She had not needed to be there at all. Perhaps she was even bleeding. What had just happened?

They withdrew into their own space at either end of the sofa.

'You scratched my chest with your long fingernails,' he complained with resentment, bent and picked up the button of his shirt from the floor. 'Could you please cut them?'

'You attacked me like a wild animal.'

They had their first serious argument, each sounding hurt to the core. And their shadows, thrown by the candles onto the wall, projected their agitated gestures.

'Why do you turn into a beast? Do you know? It hurt. I can't allow you to do this to me, or to any other woman.'

'Look, I am only half-aware of it. OK?'

Once Anais had put her clothes back on, she approached the episode calmly. He could not really say why he had acted that way, except that he had been so worked up for their first naked sex. Never before had he roughed up a woman, but never before had he felt such a craze for anyone as he did for her. He got dressed like a scolded boy and came back to sit next to her, saying sorry so many times and promising to control himself better in the future that she, in the end, reassured him that it had not been that bad.

They ended friends and agreed to meet there again in two days' time.

Back in her living room, she rationalised that Hansen was a romantic/aggressive. According to a Dr Hayley, some men suffer the Madonna-whore complex. They feel the need to elevate women into a realm of purity and chastity, but their natural urge of penetration and therefore violation of the perfect creates frustrated aggression in them. Dr Hayley thought that it was a compliment to women generally and suggested bringing the man back to reality by acting as his pal, his equal.

*

At the Pocket Theatre, her new job was a play written by two gay men, set in the seventies. The problem for the director, apart from a gender collision, was that the two writers kept shooting down each other's ideas, and she had to play referee.

On Friday evening Jan would not come home. They had talked lengthily on the phone to make up for it.

Shortly afterwards, at precisely eight thirty, she heard the key in the metal lock and pulled in a deep breath. She had bought pralines and was now dressed in a full-length calico tunic with nothing underneath.

He had not brought wine, and she was almost glad for she had not eaten all day. There was only one candlestick with a candle stump, and no heater as the weather had warmed up. He loved the tunic and nuzzled close to its softness. And then he noticed her short-cut nails and lifted up her hand to kiss each finger one by one.

Once she had dropped her robe and he had taken off his clothes, he slowly approached her and kissed her gently on her mouth, a fairy-tale kiss. *We're OK with that so far.* She knew that he was trying his best and the sex would be good.

They started gingerly, exploring again as if for the first time, and in that instant all the chemistry came flooding back through her. He touched her breasts, leaned to them and aroused her nipples with his warm lips, which sent shudders through her. When he stopped to seek approval in her eyes, she noticed how aroused he was. He tipped her back onto the upholstery with care and, with mutual caresses, they joined. They were moved by the same forces, giving and taking in tension in the same space. When it was over, she felt vulnerable and like crying from relief and the knowledge that he was a gentle man.

Surprisingly, he begged her to walk around the room for him and to toss her hair back over her shoulder. She obeyed and felt the heat of his adoration of her in a goddess role. Slowly, however, the post-coital blush on her cheeks turned chill from the prolonged exposure, and the conflicting sensations of heat and cold coiled around her nudity as she paced in the sparse light of the candle.

'You are divinely beautiful. Painfully so. Being in love with you is like slavery, a little mad. I have no other choice but to make you my possession. I want to put this sight into my mind forever.'

'These are romantic compliments, but I feel a little lonely in all this.'

'Come here, my queen.' He laid her out on the sofa and stroked the mass of her hair over the low sofa arm. With a brush he had brought, he started to go through her hair in downward strokes, the bristles massaging her scalp. At the end of each stroke, he gave her head a little tug and the metal brush handle knocked against the side of the sofa. The repetition was soporific, and she closed her eyes.

Then came a subtle change in the clicking noise and the tugging. She raised a searching hand to make contact with him, but he did not respond, breathing hard in his concentration. She had a presentiment that something was amiss and abruptly sat up. 'That's not the brush. Scissors! You're cutting off my hair.' Her hand jerked up to her head. 'You bloody cut off all my hair. Are you insane?' She jumped off the sofa and saw a shoebox next to the sofa with her hair in it. With cruel calm, he was gathering blond meshes which had missed the box.

Screaming invective, she flew at him ineffectively, as she had no talons left. She punched him and kicked him, equally ineffectively as she was barefooted.

He picked up the box while she drummed her fists on his back. Then, he blew out the candle and stored the candlestick in his box, turned and walked towards the door of his house.

She pounced on his back and locked her arms around his neck. Dragging her with him, he reached the door. She bit his face and screamed until he roughly shook her off him, and she tumbled to the floor.

'Nobody will ever hear you.' Hansen closed the padded door behind him. A faint noise was the final crunch of the key.

★

Thirty-six hours later, the sun rose for the second time in the world of the living, visible to her only by the light growing slowly in the high windows. Her mouth was filled by her tongue, swollen and dried with thirst, and her teeth throbbed. Her chest hurt from yelling in vain for help as the horror of her situation had crystallised. She felt faint from the two nights of blackness, which had tortured her mind with visions of falling into a deep shaft.

She had intended to lean the sofa up against the padded wall to reach the window, but its feet were fixed into the concrete.

Lying on the floor like a worthless discarded creature, she noticed something stuck under the sofa. It was a piece of paper, rolled into the shape of a cigar. Sitting up, she unrolled it with care to find it to be a page from a small prayer book, parched and faded. Against the light she could make out: *Almighty and most merciful God, of thy bountiful goodness keep us, we beseech Thee, from all things that may hurt us…* Another ill-fated woman who had been here before her had at least been left with some comfort.

This discovery drove Anais to hunt for other clues. The drawer of the little table might have been a source but it had been taken out long ago – for that very reason, no doubt. Perhaps by the father, or even grandfather. Psychopaths! Murderers, if the door of this prison was not opened soon.

Pinched between the upholstery and the wood frame of the sofa was a minute piece of pale blue fabric, silk, an old-fashioned material. Dizzy from lack of everything except fear and dread, she nevertheless managed to rip away the velour. The white cotton which emerged was stained dark brown – blood. Had they been virgins?

She fell on her knees exhausted, joined her hands and recited a prayer she had to make up, because she was not a believer in organised religion. Prostrating herself in utter despair, she reached out for the leg of the sofa and felt striations in the otherwise smooth surface – tiny notches, perhaps made by long fingernails trying to leave a message.

I am sorry, Jan. You will be looking for me everywhere, but I will be lying dead, jagged-haired, stump-fingered, a few feet from you. And you will not know, because the heinous little man will have hidden the door behind the tapestry, the little man who will know where to put my body.

She had not shed one tear since being closed in. Tears were for the still human, not for those in damnation. There would be a brown stain on the concrete floor where she was going to knock her head until she could mercifully die from a stroke.

TEUFENSEE

In shadow, the two sisters walked down the path of a narrow valley tucked between steep mountains. Ursina, already nineteen and a Post Office trainee, led and ten-year-old Beata followed behind her. They ignored the triangular *DANGER* panel driven into the cliff-face and progressed, stepping over fallen stones, to the flat ledge rocks, the lower of which allowed two people to sit at the water's edge of Teufensee.

Seven hundred metres away, at the other extremity of the lake, where the mountains eased off to give room for a river running out of the lake into a green valley, more access to the lakeshore was possible, giving the lake the shape of a Williams pear. That side was Italy. Where the girls now stood, looking over the oil-dark waters, was Romansch Switzerland. The border between the countries ran across the lake. It was said to be the deepest lake in Europe and, for its size, the most treacherous.

'Why are you following me?' Ursina turned round. 'Don't you have homework?'

'I want to find out why you come here all the time.'

They stepped onto the lower ledge, and Ursina sat on the rim of the upper rock and folded her hands in her lap while Beata contemplated the curling waves of lugubrious water close to her feet.

'When the sun shines, I always think the other side is like an Italian painting. There's the wide dark frame of the mountainsides, and then the umbrella trees, a few scattered farmhouses, and the convent with its shiny green copper roof and pillared cloister on the upper floor,' Ursina said dreamily.

'What good is having a lake when we can't swim because it's freezing and can't boat because it's haunted, or even have room to spread a rug for a picnic? Can we go home?'

'Not yet.'

'Mum says you're hyptonised by the lake and trying to see the witch's hair floating under the water.'

'The word is hypnotised.'

'I know things. You will be pulled in and drown like the others if you want to get some gold from the bottom. She is guarding it, pretending one can see it, but it's only her floating golden hair.'

'Next term the teacher will tell you about the Romans who crossed from north Italy into Switzerland two thousand years ago. They misjudged the lake, and the boat they had probably cobbled together broke, and they went down with their caskets of gold and silver coins.'

'How do we know this happened?'

'Your class will go to the museum, and you can see the leather pouch which was washed up after a storm with the coins in it. And the other artefacts found in our valley.'

'A diver's bubble.'

'That was used when our grandmother was young and came up with two divers dead in it, looking as if they had seen a ghost.'

'Eek! What else is in the museum?'

'Shreds of clothing, lots of boot nails, bits of tiling and sandstone with paint on them, because those Romans set up dwellings. The archaeologists think it is because too many of them drowned and they stopped in Teufen because their army was depleted. They also found a horse's bridle. Imagine! Horses across Teufensee! They really didn't know anything about high valleys.'

'Is that all?'

'We are jolly lucky to have a museum which interests archaeologists from far away, seeing as we're only nine hundred and forty inhabitants in a Romansch valley at the back end of Switzerland.'

'I guess so.' Beata stared out at the lake, from which nebulous mist was rising in patches, as the sun must have set behind the mountain. Even in summer, the valley only had four hours of sunlight. A north-easterly wind shivered down the valley behind them. It twined the mist white against the rock walls, and the waves, born from the underwater springs which fed the lake, lapped in self-destructive repetition against the rocks.

'Look!' She suddenly pointed excitedly. 'Out there! There she is – the witch. I can see her big head bobbing. Let's run!'

'I saw,' said Ursina calmly. 'It is the border guard in his boat on the Italian side.'

'What about our Swiss guard?'

'Where could his boat be moored? The strongest undercurrent is right below us. Besides, one able young man is enough to guard this bit of border.'

'Maybe he is old, craggy and mean, and that's why the gold witch has not pulled him down yet.'

'You have too much imagination.'

'I am still a child. I'm allowed to.'

Now, the small moving figure in the distance, pulling at his oars, disappeared into the invading darkness, which amalgamated the rock colours with the lake in which they were mirrored. Chilled, the two sisters walked back to their village, Teufen, just as on the Italian side one light came on.

★

It was the end of September and Beata, sitting at the kitchen table, was writing with a pencil in her exercise book under the pulled-down ceiling lamp. Pondering on a problem, she noticed her sister's silhouette outside the window and got up to go outside.

Ursina, wrapped in the red shawl she had been crocheting during the summer, was contemplating clouds sailing fast across the gap between the mountain tops.

'This light is eerie,' said Beata with a shiver. 'Everything looks blue and pale.'

'Wait till the harvest moon appears over the peak; then you can feel like a ghost in a shrine.'

'I know exactly where you're off to,' Beata said and went back into the chalet. She ran along the corridor and pulled open the *Stube* door. 'Ursina and I are going to look at the moon.' Before her parents could react, she went into the kitchen, closed her exercise book and switched out the light, not caring about the pencil rolling over the tabletop and falling to the floor. She unhooked her jacket at the back door while kicking her slippers into a corner to step into rubber boots and run after the receding figure of her sister.

'Can't you leave me be?' Ursina said with frustration, without turning back to the heavy breathing right behind her.

When the waters turned to blue ink at their feet, the harvest full moon hung over the Italian side, exactly in the centre between the mountain tops, pink in colour and casting its enigmatic light into the moonscape.

'It is brighter than daylight. Total magic to be given an extra day of light after July and August are over for this year.'

Teufensee glinted in viridian patches and seemed to hover in conscious silence, as the sheer mountain walls swayed in the noiseless breathing of the electric moonlight.

'Spooky. You should see your face, pale like cheese with your dark eyes like holes in a rock.'

'It is said to be a beckoning light.'

'Will the moon suck up gold in pouches? Is that why you came? Is that light stain on the water over there where the witch will come up?'

'Stop asking so many questions. The water has light patches because it is a prismatic phenomenon.'

'You're trying to be clever. But then you can read all the magazines which come to people through the post.'

'Can we please just be quiet for a while?'

Beata pushed her lips together, and Ursina rose on tiptoe to scan the surface of the moonlit lake. Only three electric lights were visible on the Italian shore, plus the red of the mountain-top beacon close to the eagle's nest – the privileged predator which could circle in sunshine while they had to dwell in the dark valley.

Beata checked over her shoulder and then turned behind her. 'I have such a long shadow. It goes on and on over the boulders, and so does yours. As if we disappeared behind ourselves slowly.'

'Maybe that is what we are doing in Teufen.'

'Will you get married soon?' Beata changed the subject to something comfortable.

'I am not looking for a suitor.'

'But you like the new teacher at the school. When you came to pick me up, he sort of made a gooey honey face when he saw you.'

'That does not mean I like him.'

'Mum said he is your best chance.'

'You discuss suitable husbands for me with Mum?'

'So you don't want to get married. You want to stay home?'

'I am wishing for something special, more valuable.'

'You *do* want the gold.'

'Something meaningful with lasting value.'

'Diamonds then.'

90

'Oh Beata, more even than diamonds. Let's go back. I was hoping for the full moon to be on my side. But not tonight.'

Beata repeatedly kicked her foot against a moss-covered rock, clearly not at ease with the conversation any longer.

★

Back in the chalet their mother, who had heard the planks creak, picked the needle off the gramophone, and came out of the *Stube* to give Ursina one of her quick suspicious frowning stares, totally ignoring the presence of Beata.

'The lovesick pander to the full moon. But that is not your case. It is also the possessed who yowl to the moon. And some say you can scoop moonlight off water like gold. What hold has Teufensee over you? It's just a deep mountain lake with coins at the bottom, where they will stay. Perhaps it is your long blond hair making you identify with the heroine of myth?'

Ursina looked at her mother without really hearing what she was saying.

'According to the postmistress, the new teacher's parents are moving to Teufen. So you see, Hans is not just on a short scholarly assignment. They'll become Teufen people. You'll be twenty soon and have to look out for yourself and not moon around that lake at night or stay in your room depressed, listening to Sibelius. And what about filling your sister's head with stories of ghosts and waterlogged witches? I won't tell Dad about this if you promise to leave that lake alone. Those who were besotted with it perished, dozens of them.'

'I'm going to bed,' announced Beata.

Mum spun round to her. 'Off with you. You shouldn't have stuck around and listened.'

Beata shrugged her shoulders and tromped up the stairs, making as much noise as she could.

★

Mid-May was Ursina's twentieth birthday, for which Beata had made her a painting of a gold-haired woman standing on water in which were flowers and fish. Mother had sewn her an apron and made her a *Gugelhupf*. She had even invited some people from the village, including Hans, the teacher, and his family, who had moved into the dead butcher's chalet.

Ursina did not come home from the post office when it closed. They waited. Beata was sent out to look for her. She even went to the lake but returned alone. Eventually, they had tea and ate most of the cake. It was incomprehensible. Night came, but Ursina did not.

Nor did she the day after. The postmistress said she had done her job in the post office, sorting and recording as normal, and left as she did every day. She had not told the postmistress that it was her birthday.

The policeman from the town at the entrance to Teufen valley was called. He thought it urgent enough to get into his Wolseley and motor up to Teufen. Sitting in the *Stube* of the chalet, he noted down what was reported to him. The concern of the family of the missing person did not ruffle him. Crabby, with his fat neck in a starched collar, he pointed out that Ursina was an adult and could have decided to make her life somewhere else without telling anyone.

According to Ursina's parents, that was not how things were done in Teufen. 'Perhaps in your town, where foreigners come and go, neither known nor trusted.'

Beata watched her mother trying to spin the policeman's visit out with cake, tea and cream. Asked whether there had been anything unusual in Ursina's behaviour, Mother confessed to her daughter's obsession with the legend of the gold at the bottom of Teufensee.

The policeman got up to leave, saying they should telephone him if she did not turn up after a month.

'A month!'

*

Midsummer arrived, and they stood in the fields waiting for the midday sun to creep over the mountain peak, clapping when everything around them turned from black and white into colour. The grass was green and roses were red. Ursina was still missing, and nothing had washed up on the shore ledge.

The next day, the postmistress brought Ursina's felt hat to her mother. It had been found in the bottom drawer of the girl's desk.

This caused great distress. Ursina, wherever she had gone, had not taken her hat. What could that mean? Most likely, she had been secretly depressive. Realising her hope of gold and riches was just an illusion, she must have drowned herself in the lake the day of her coming of age. A mental health study of people living in the permanently shadowed valleys of Norway was quoted.

They telephoned the Italian guard hut, but nothing had been reported there and the nearest Italian town, thirty kilometres south of Teufensee, showed no interest in the case.

Hans, who had taken Beata under his wing for comfort, convinced the municipality to pay divers but not one volunteered. However, the Teufen men did take turns, standing on the rock ledge in twos and casting their long fishing rods with strong hooks. The undercurrent brought line and hooks swiftly back to their feet. One day, after a rainstorm, the anglers retrieved a nest of red wool and a piece of white linen with lace. Mother identified both as being parts of Ursina's shawl and petticoat. She sat at the kitchen table, her head buried in her locked arms, softening the wood with her tears.

Teufen people whispered to each other rather than talking in their normal voices. Ursina had drowned, beckoned by the gold witch. One more human being had perished in the cursed lake they had to put up with. A boy in Beata's class showed off by clambering like a monkey along the rock wall over the waters, because he thought he had seen a black object moving. He returned with one of Ursina's booties between his teeth.

In Ursina's room, her mother laid out the boot, the bit of petticoat, the wool tangle and the hat on the bedcover, as if she were piecing together the puzzle of her missing daughter.

Nothing more was found, even after the end-of-August tempest, which threw the black water about, whipped to frenzy by the devil wind from the south. Trembling on the upper ledge and wet from spray, Beata implored the witch to give them back her sister, be it just to say goodbye.

Mother locked Ursina's bedroom and hid the key. Dark winter came, and shutters remained closed behind piles of snow. Only smoke curling from the chimneys showed that people in the snowed-in chalets were still alive and warm. Before Christmas, school was closed until the middle of January, and Hans, who had started to make gooey honey eyes at another young woman in the village, had left Beata with a pile of books and extra homework.

Another year passed, during which Beata became the only daughter of sad parents. She applied herself at school and was on the way to becoming the best in upper class.

On the first of August, Swiss national day, the mayor of the valley-dwellers included Ursina in their loving remembrance, calling her a troubled soul.

Just when it had been decided that Beata should go to the upper school, in the town down below, war was declared and Switzerland mobilised. She had to stay and help the womenfolk with the farming. When she turned eighteen, she became assistant teacher in the school, as Hans had been drafted, leaving his new wife and a toddler behind.

At first, the war brought some welcome excitement into their uneventful lives, and ears were glued to radios.

The border across the lake was closed. No troops would ever be as foolhardy as the Romans had been.

In 1943, when Mussolini was ousted, the Germans occupied northern Italy. News came that officers had been billeted in the houses they saw across the lake and indeed Beata, from the rock ledge, noticed groups of men marching through the landscape Ursina had called a painting. Uninvolved, up in the rays of sun, the eagle sailed on thermal currents. There was an agreement with Italian partisans to signal if the Germans did plan to cross Teufensee or rope themselves up the mountains. Parachuting into Teufen Valley was impossible.

When Beata turned twenty, the war was over. All was to be as it had been, but people felt they had missed out, had been cheated of six years of good life. Beata became the teacher and took the classes to the archaeological museum, remembering her sister, showing the children the nails which had been in the shoes of Roman soldiers, the gold and silver coins found in the pouch. The children liked the story of the floating witch with golden hair, who had become, in Beata's mind, her sister's ghost, her tresses undone by the currents. Probably there was only her skull remaining in the cruel murky depths, resting on top of Roman coins. That image of her sister with her gold now, if that is what she had wanted, had lulled Beata into a peaceful acceptance over time.

An archaeologist from Bern visited the museum and suggested some updating and spotlighting. He was young and flirted with Beata, who showed him around. His name was Ueli, and she married him and moved into the town at the entrance to the valley, where the school had classes for every age group.

And then she became pregnant and had a little girl with gold fuzz surrounding a face which resembled Ursina's. Beata hugged the infant against her and missed her big sister. She brought the baby, wrapped in a pink shawl, to Teufen to introduce it to her parents. Before returning to town, she took her daughter to the lake, where a roll of barbed wire from the war still lay on the rock ledge. She lifted the baby bundle up in the air to introduce her to her Aunt Ursina.

Two weeks later, an envelope addressed to Beata arrived in the chalet. On her next visit home, she found the envelope contained a simple beige card on which were the words: *May you and your baby girl be blessed.* No signature. Beata smiled, believing it was from her sister, now a spirit.

From then on and without telling anyone, Beata took the post-bus from time to time and returned to the lake, in order to 'talk to her sister'.

When her baby daughter started to walk, she conceived again. With the pregnancy came visions and fever dreams: Ursina, rising from the black waves of the lake, was calling out to her. Beata claimed that she had seen Ursina under the surface of the water, floating and smiling.

Ueli tried to calm her and talk her out of this nonsense. The doctor prescribed bedrest and milk with honey. With the foetus growing inside her, she became more disturbed and agitated. Ursina was out in the lake, pleading to her.

Beata was forbidden to go to the lake, but she sneaked off with her daughter. She was discovered trying to hitchhike and brought back, half-demented with frustration; it was full moon. The same happened when the moon was full the next month. Beata's high fever was starting to be dangerous for her growing baby. Her husband was at the end of his patience. The night of harvest moon, Ueli was at a conference in Zurich. He had asked the nurse at the doctor's surgery to stay with Beata. Beata, however, tricked her and sneaked away in the late evening. The post-bus brought her to Teufen and from there, unseen, she walked to the lake to sit on the slab bathed in eerie moonlight.

The frantic nurse called Beata's mother in Teufen, and the pregnant woman was found, passed out on the rock ledge. She swore that she had seen her sister in a grey coat and with floating blond hair, standing on the water way over on the other side, her small oval face white as cheese. Over the magically lit lake they had connected as in a dream, and slowly the figure of Ursina had lifted an arm and waved once in a gesture of greeting.

'I can't bear witnessing this,' Mother bewailed. 'She too will perish in the lake.'

A baby boy was born, but Beata had slipped into a postnatal depression, incessantly talking about the ghost of her drowned sister and of full moonlight. The doctor made the decision to tackle the problem head on and expose it to Beata as the nonsense it was. He pretended to believe her and asked her to show them what she saw at the lake.

First, her reason not to go was that the moon was not entirely full, and then there was not enough fog. Ueli, the parents and the doctor gave each other knowing looks.

Finally, Beata considered the conditions appropriate. Her babies stayed in the care of the nurse while the doctor drove them to Teufensee. The moon was full and electric. The other shore showed in precise clarity. Vapour lazily swirled above the mesmerising surface of the water.

The wind got up slightly, and Beata said that was necessary. The wind blew stronger and took the vapour with it. The doctor shuffled with impatience, his lips shut so as not to say something to spoil the exercise. Mother pulled her jacket tightly over her chest.

And there the small figure was, standing on the other shore in a ballooning grey cloak and white hair, as if singled out by a moonbeam.

'I love you, Ursina. I love you,' Beata shouted.

The figure raised an arm and waved once, as Beata had told them, but then she waved one more time.

'That's for you, Mum. She doesn't know the doctor.'

The doctor did not hear this because he was running back to his parked car. Beata supported her mother by the elbow as she stumbled through the rough undergrowth to get away from the horror.

★

Fifty years later, on the first of January 2000, the start of a new millennium, the Teufen Valley people wanted to mark the event. After multiple municipal meetings, it was decided to commission a monument, to be placed at the head of the lake.

All the local people were invited, including some from the Italian side, as they shared Teufensee. No expense was spared. A wooden platform had been built over the snow-toasted rocks, large enough for a flag-scalloped canvas canopy with three sidewalls and a dozen gas heaters, spotlights, chairs in rows and a podium. Refreshments were offered back in the schoolhouse.

The festivities started with an alpine choir in national costume, followed by speeches, and then the mayor unveiled the monument in full view of everyone. It was a gold-bronze figure of a reclining woman whose bronze hair flowed down over the rough plinth-rock, seemingly entwined with it. The plaque against the stone remembered all those who had drowned.

The artist-sculptor explained that the bronze woman was nude, that nudity symbolising the innocence of the victims and, indeed, of the witch herself.

'Artists' piffle,' the mayor was heard to say because his microphone was still switched on.

After that, the mayor and the Italian *sindaco* told the tales of the lake and spoke of the lure of the dark, and the memory of all those who had drowned in Teufensee, including the unknown Romans, but the two men cut into each other's sentences repeatedly and animosity broke out, and everyone warmed to the event.

A Swiss accordionist and flautist played a piece, followed by an Italian couple in costume dancing a tarantella, the woman's layered skirt wheeling.

The *sindaco* helped an old man onto the podium. He was eighty-three and used to farm sheep close to the lake on the Italian side. 'My younger brother, Florian, drowned in the lake in 1935 when he was a twenty-one-year-old lad,' he said. 'He was working as the border guard in a small boat. He believed in the gold witch and had seen her floating hair. It cost him his life. Early one morning we found his clothing in the drifting boat.

'And then came the war. I was a handyman up at the convent with the silent nuns. When German soldiers were billeted in the convent, the nuns, who could not protest, were pushed into an upstairs corner of their own house. I happen to know that one or two of the soldiers tried to get at the gold – and we all know the outcome of that. They're not included in the monument, I hope.'

There was laughter, and he almost toppled sideways and was helped back to his seat.

Now it was for an old Swiss inhabitant called Beata to come forward to tell her story. She was seventy-five years old and her sister had drowned at about the same time as the border guard. She had been only nineteen and mesmerised by the witch whose golden hair she had seen floating. 'We found bits of her clothing and that was all.'

'The witch keeps them down there with her,' someone said out loud.

'Their bodies are never found,' contributed another.

In the back row of seats, a hand was raised. The woman was invited to talk.

She got up slowly, leaning on her stick. Everyone turned to her. Against her gun-grey dress, the gold cross on her chest reflected the rays from a spotlight. She was clearly in her eighties, with short snow-white hair. She said nothing. The noise of waves dashing against the rocks filled the silence. Invited twice to speak up, she finally cleared her throat.

'Forgive me. I have seldom spoken since the dissolution of my order. I believe that sightings of the golden witch represent a yearning for light and love in a dark existence. I have had time to meditate. The gold coin seekers, weak and undistinguished, were in love with themselves, but the nineteen-year-old woman was in love with Florian, a beacon of hope so remote that she could only guess at it in the darkness of the lake. He must have been in love with her too, the figure with blond hair waving a red shawl to beckon him across the border, offering him a dream which he could not attain. One day she took the risk of love and plunged in to reach him. Teufensee made it impossible. He drowned while trying to save her, but she managed to catch the rope of the boat, and the current brought her onto the Italian shore. The brave romantic lover died in the dark waters, having been able to love her, while remorse and guilt gave her reason to repent for ever more with divine purpose.'

The old nun stopped talking, to smile an entranced private smile.

'Good heavens!' Beata exclaimed. 'Ursina, it is you!'

THE TOP SHELF

Andy and I have been married for thirty years. Looking back, time seems like a continuum. During the process, though, it was a step-by-step progress: the nurturing of two babies, their first days away in nursery, and then proper school, the stress of children's illnesses and endless tests. Memories float up, rising with the tastes and voices of the past. Photographs make sure nothing is erased. Our children have both flown the nest and I remain, typing LOL at the end of e-mails. I say 'big hug' on my mobile, aware of the sound of my own voice.

Does my life have significance? My children's successful evolution was theirs alone, and in spite of my mistakes. My guilt is that of a woman; I know that Andy's man-shell protects him from such nagging discomforts. Who has he become over the years? We will both soon be fifty. Who is he?

I drink my tea sitting at the table, caressing the mug between my hands. Tea is comforting.

When Andy was still affectionate, he used to cut my wet hair, combing it clumsily but with concentration.

One day it did not happen any longer. Things have a way of rearranging themselves. Andy now has time for football, and I have enrolled in a beginners' drawing course. Saturday morning, I indulge in a hairdresser's appointment. It is my treat. It is also where I meet Linda and where we compare notes on articles in women's magazines about diets, miracle face creams, Botox – *should we dare?* – and even imagine getting tattoos.

The hairdressers know that we have to sit next to each other and share Emile, even though it prolongs the procedure. I have found out that habit is something you can impose on others.

Emile is a French coiffeur, a short energetic dark-haired man with impeccably trimmed sideburns, who performs grand exaggerated gestures to give the illusion that he is creative. When he is tired, his lispy accent wanes to reveal plain English, like a battery-operated doll. These pretentions are endearing to us. We have come to love him. We indulge in jealousy about his inequality of treatment of us, his hand massaging our scalps, slow rotating movements with his palm on our temples and upward under the cranium.

We have some fun, goading him to tell us about *Maman*, his mother who lived in Dieppe, grooming the dogs of rich Parisians for whom holiday-homes there were fashionable. We remind him of the Afghan dogs which made her good money as it took three hours to groom the poor things.

It was just *Maman* and Emile living cosily in a flat with many uncles visiting.

As a mere toddler, Emile told us dramatically, he had to stand on a stool and hold the dogs – and then sweep up the cut fur in the dog parlour.

'Did *Maman* make you groom the dogs as well?'

'No, I was only eight when we left Dieppe.'

'Why?'

'Everyone is eight once.'

Linda can hardly talk from withheld laughter at times. 'Did another uncle make you come to the UK?'

'No. *Maman* married Norman, a car salesman from Dagenham.'

'English sheepdog grooming from then on?'

'Norman hated dogs. He was allergic to them.'

Fascinating story. *Maman* apparently turned to hairdressing because 'it is a little the same'. We sincerely hope Emile did not believe this.

'And then I went to hairdresser school and helped her.'

'What happened to Norman?' we ask eagerly.

'He left us.'

'Died?'

'Prison. Lots of crooked dealing with cars. *Maman* was in debt over her ears. We worked every day to pay it back.'

'She should have stuck to uncles.'

It is lost on him because he is naive. Perhaps we are a little cruel to him.

'Not once did we take a day off. *Maman*'s motto was: *Only for a monumental accident do we not work*.'

It sounds exhausting.

He concludes that whatever was in the way, *Maman* and he would never give up on hairdressing.

'So, *Maman* is still around.' Linda leans over to me. 'That's good – there will be more stories.'

I know Linda so well because Duncan, her husband, and Andy work as a team for a company which erects conservatories in pretty much most parts of England. Perhaps Andy chose this because of the greenhouses he spent time in with his father, a market gardener in Norfolk.

Duncan and Andy are men's men. I have seen their naughty calendars on the wall in their office in Bury St Edmunds. In their drawers, Linda told me, were dog-eared magazines for men with almost-naked women, blush-brushed, foundationed and photographed with a soft filter. With that help even we, she and I, could look like that.

They treasure football. We have decided that men don't know that the ball is their air-filled head. They kick it around the field, missing the obvious: the net.

★

It is Saturday. Clouds play with the weak autumn sun and I set out on the bus to the hairdresser's. Linda is already there, waiting for me outside instead of being installed in the chair.

'I'm so upset, I could spit,' she starts and continues to tell me that she has found out that Duncan is doing personal things on his computer. He has chosen a new password, saying it was because he had to do business at home with people with emergency needs. 'How plausible is an emergency for a conservatory salesman, huh?'

To placate her, I say that Andy almost certainly has his own password for e-mails and that it is normal.

'Normal? There is nothing normal about Duncan any more. He's trying to fool me. Underneath he's a dirty fink.'

'Tell me what really happened.'

In a hissed voice, she tells me that twice she woke during the night to find Duncan missing from their bed. Getting up herself to pad around the house, she found him sitting at his desk in the small study, typing. In the morning, he pretended to have slept like a log. 'When a lie is born…'

We leave the conversation at that because Emile appears at the open door, urging us to come inside. I sit through washing and styling to cheer Linda up with pathetic jokes. After all, things said in the hairdresser's are meant to stay light and inconsequential.

★

I can't get Linda's words out of my head. Why does her discovery have such a strong effect on me? Andy is not Duncan. And yet…

As I can't concentrate, my sketching is neglected. A last weeding of the garden is more urgent, but Andy has neither the time, nor the patience. He says nettles have a right to prosper. *Like poisonous Duncan, lying to his wife?*

I go online, looking for something I would not know how to find. We have a joint e-mail address. Nothing in or out is abnormal. I rifle through our hanging files in the cabinet where Andy keeps our paperwork, but all is as it should be, so I feel guilty for not trusting him. I manage to keep my worries in check. However, in the supermarket I do glance up at the top shelf magazines: the soft porn lads' section under plastic.

Soon enough it is Saturday again, and for the first time I dread going to the hairdresser's for fear of hearing disturbing things. *Why do I sense something unsavoury lurking under the surface of my conventional everyday life?*

Our heads wrapped in warm towels, I fear what is coming as Linda leans close to me. Apparently, three nights ago she felt Duncan check she was sleeping before creeping out of the room.

She took her make-up mirror and followed him. He was at the computer again, completely involved from the way his shoulders were hunched. Cleverly, she positioned herself at the door, tilting the mirror so that she could see the screen. First, the line he had typed remained sitting there. A response came back, and he typed again and again. She could not read the words.

Then, he pulled out a magazine which had lain in his lap and put it next to him on the table, and then a long line appeared and another underneath, and she heard his breathing accelerate, and then the age-old noise of slapping and breathing, and she knew that he was… Linda's painted mouth is close to my ear. '… you-know-what, while he was still typing with one hand.'

Boom. There it was, said out loud.

★

A crevasse is widening on gender lines, my loyalty naturally being on Linda's side. The casual weekly salon pampering is undermined by mistrust all round. In need of support, we are now calling each other when the coasts are clear.

Cybersex. It is not disgusting in a physical way like exchanging bodily fluids. Just one little mess. However, it is strangely disturbing from a mental point of view.

Who was on the other end of this satellite beam? What woman sat in the middle of the night exciting herself with Linda's husband?

Unless she lived in China, where it was Sunday morning.

Linda believes that Duncan is cyber-bonking an Asian woman, a type he fancies.

Then the worrying thought crops up that it might be someone he knows, or even Linda knows. Our husbands meet a lot of people, not just the clients, who are often women, and they also stay overnight in cheap hotels if the job is more than a hundred miles away. We seem to both know what these Midland lasses are like.

Perturbed, we decide to watch out for more.

★

Linda has found more. We meet for coffee in town, something we never did before. First, she puts a card in my hand, which she found in Duncan's blazer pocket.

I read *Nougat*.

'How sticky is that?' Linda, who has looked it up, believes it to be a shady nightclub, almost a brothel.

Really, how could she tell from an ad?

And then she found a magazine, rolled and zipped into the outside pocket of his sports bag.

Linda is thorough. I dare ask about the magazine, and she tells me that it is a disgrace and against the law. Apparently, there are pages and pages of photographs of women exposing their genitals or assholes. They have code numbers and offer shaven pussies and treats, like peeing over men. Linda is now talking through tears. The favourite ones are underage and look like angels.

'What?'

'Fourteen-year-olds. Children with downy pubic hair and immature breasts.' Linda is vehement. 'He disgusts me. I'll never be able to let him touch me again.'

If she does not tell anyone, she will be an accomplice in a punishable crime. If all this really *is* happening, Duncan belongs in prison.

★

The first frost has come overnight and it is only the start of November. Not long ago I was still pulling weeds from the soft earth. Tomorrow should be another Saturday morning with Emile, but what state of mind is Linda in? I run upstairs, *to fetch my cardigan* as far as Andy is concerned. So far, I am the one who is lying in this household.

The bedroom is dark. I dial Linda without switching the light on.

She has a plan. She is going to pretend to go to the hairdresser's, leave the house, and then ambush Duncan.

By now, Emile is something we do together or not at all. In the dim light from the outside street lamp, I make out Andy's worn dressing gown on the hook at the door. His online sexually aroused paramour would never smell its mustiness.

'What shall we say about why we did not go to have our hair done, just in case we find them not at it?' I ask.

'We just say that Emile wasn't working today.'

'Because…' I start to say, and she joins in, 'because of a *monumental accident*.'

★

With my decision to spy on Andy, I try to hide my nervousness.

'You're going to be late for your hairdresser, if you don't leave now,' he says before I have finished my coffee. There is an undertone of urgency in his remark, like a dog who needs to be walked and can't put it in words.

He surely has to be innocent. He is only playing along with Duncan: alpha males, an A-team at work. In bed, Andy is rather reticent and unwilling to ever change the same old just-get-it-over-with exercise, while Duncan has a hairy chest, maybe even a furry back. Dark pelt is visible in the triangle of his shirts. That and his hairy eyebrows almost certainly indicate oversexed glands.

I make ready to leave, fussing over a pashmina wrap around my neck, pulse thumping. Andy, watching me from the living room, shows just the tip of impatience.

I stand alone inside the plexiglass bus shelter, from where I can see our semi-detached house through the cold November fog.

I suck in my breath at the sight of him coming out of the door in his burgundy Norwegian jacket and the snowflake motif woolly hat with fleece-laced earflaps. He gets into his Vauxhall, reverses out of our drive, makes a backward half-turn and speeds up the road away from me. Watching the back of the car, I feel the vehicle is hostile toward me. The brake lights come on at the top of the road, like the eyes of a mean creature in the gloom.

A bus slows and stops. The folding door opens, and passengers wait for me to get on, but I don't. Waving them off, I see myself expressing my apologies with drawn-up shoulders and a pressed-together flat-lipped mouth, and I hope that is good enough.

Swiftly, I walk back to our house. I need to know all sorts of things. I discard my coat, the scarf, my handbag, messily in the entrance. I run up the stairs, open his side of the wardrobe and go through all the pockets in his clothes. His sports bag is empty. I pull open the drawer of his bedside table. There are his father's cufflinks, real handkerchiefs not used any longer, an open packet of extra strong mints and, rolled in a box, the special tie he wore on our daughter's graduation.

In his office upstairs, I find no brochure renting out children for porn. In his presentation bag are only pictures of conservatories, a piece of roof plastic, price lists and an order pad. I am almost appeased, but then I see his old presentation bag tucked under the desk, kept for no reason, its clasp locked. No small key is in the narrow desk drawer. I burn hot and cold, as I shake the case and hear things in it thumping around.

Andy might be back any time from wherever he has gone. In my haste, I trip over my own foot but catch the railing in time to avoid falling down the narrow stairs. My head, however, hits the wall. This will leave a bump or a bruise.

I spin round at the foot of the stairs and run back up, taking two at a time. My intention is to snoop around Google, the way Linda has told me to do. There is no ground for fingers dripping with sweat – e-mailing the children is what every mother does. I come up here to do this normally.

OK, I am sitting at the screen. We chose the password together; that's how our marriage works, not like Linda's. It's *Ricky2L*, which was our old dog to love. I open his business e-mail, the password for which he has also given me. There are rows of text about technical things and material. I search around a bit and become aware that I know so little about his work. What I find strange is that not one e-mail is from Duncan, nor is there one sent to Duncan. They work as a close team after all.

Linda must be right. It is so easy to set up new e-mail addresses. I look at the shadow-outline of a stylised head needing a password. I type in my name: *Jenny*. Denied. *Jenny1*. Denied. *Jen1*. Denied. We once had a cat called Sheba. I try *Sheba2L*. Denied.

I concentrate, trying to slip into his brain. The telephone extension rings right next to me, and I jerk in the swivel chair.

It's Linda, her breathless voice hardly recognisable. 'I've caught him red-handed and confronted him,' she puffs. 'There is something going on. I am calling from the garage. We had a huge fight, and he deleted his history when I asked to see it for the last week and shoved me away. Now he is watching sport, shouting into the living room that I am a bitch because I forced the password out of him. *Babe4babe*. Foul, isn't it?'

'Linda, I'll call you back.' I hang up. Andy might drive up any minute. Quickly I type in *Babe4babe* and hope that there is not a hidden camera somewhere in the machine, checking who gets in.

A ladder of e-mails appears. *3:15 am.* I click that one open. It's from Duncan. Amongst the jargon and half-finished words and references to things I don't know about, Andy is urged to go to a seedy-sounding website called *The Trinians*. At three in the morning!

I open Google and type in the address. A black screen appears, with an ad for a sex shop in Soho on the right. The video promises 'Puberty funk. She has to go.' I am horrified: astride a motorcycle, a blonde in knee-high black boots and panties, with a frozen expression of urgent wantonness. I double-click on the right hand side of the mouse for the picture to go away, but it starts moving. She moans, gyrating her pelvis. I switch off the speaker. Chin over her smooth shoulder, she blows Andy a baby puff-kiss. Heart in my mouth, I see the proof that she is no older than fourteen because of the little swollen red meningococcal vaccine shot in the shoulder. It is given to children at that age. My father was a GP. Heaving, I clutch my jacket against my throat, and the computer sends a yellow message over the screen that the site is not safe. I shut down the computer and wait with impatience for the light of the monitor to disappear.

Anger makes me pull out the black case. With a distorted paperclip, I fiddle around in the clasp lock. It springs open. Inside, I find two rolled periodicals with beige rubber bands around them, twice each. I undo one, and the magazine unravels to show me hundreds of small pictures of naked women showing off their vaginas or their bottoms. They are numbered, many in partial school uniform, many ready to be spanked, and their abilities to degrade themselves are described. I roll it up and put it back.

How could I not have known what is going on in Andy's head? I can't call Linda. I don't know what stage she is at with Duncan.

Still, how could I not have noticed my husband's real thoughts? Suddenly, I think of how he was with our daughter when she was growing into a young woman. I hear the Vauxhall turn into the drive and will have to think about that later. I descend the stairs, trying to walk normally, head high and looking ordinary as he comes in.

'You're home,' he says, not pleased. He is carrying a plastic supermarket bag.

'The hairdresser had a serious accident and didn't turn up. Linda and I didn't want to go with someone else.'

In the bag, I can see a magazine that is not yet rolled up with a rubber band and hidden. A new edition to rush home with, so he can have time alone to get his blood thick about it? *Please, mind, do not produce imagination; just bring down the swelling on my forehead, which is throbbing.*

'I want you to drive back to the shop for me right now and get me a packet of disposable shavers. What an idiot – I forgot them. Here…' He holds out the Norwegian jacket he has just taken off, lifts the earflap hat over my head and taps it down. 'It's nasty out there,' he says and opens the door for me.

In my stunned condition I obey in silence.

'Any brand,' he shouts after me, and I drive off to the shop, fog-lights on in the murk. Even the street lights are obfuscated.

In the supermarket, I grab the packet – disposable, pivoting, *for shaving pussies?* – and walk with it to the express till, passing the rack with magazines wrapped in cellophane – *to protect the innocent pubescent children from seeing themselves naked?*

I feel weak and weepy. Andy was a normal husband and surely a correct father. There would have been signs if something were wrong. What signs?

When I get back home, Andy reminds me that he will be off to Peterborough with Duncan early the next day.

I notice that the magazine is nowhere in sight and that he has put the shopping away; the bag is folded in the kitchen drawer with the mats and the candles in case of a blackout – he, who never puts anything away.

'I'm picking up Duncan around five. It's my turn.'

'How long?'

'Three days. You know what…' He seeks my eyes, but I avert them. 'You are such an angel. Could I ask you to wash the car?'

'Now? It's foggy, dark and freezing out there.'

'I wouldn't ask if I didn't have to redraw the conservatory plans before I leave. Look, we haven't put the hose away for the winter yet.'

'So now I am the hubcap scrubber.'

'I can claim for it and will pay you. It doesn't look good if the reps arrive in a muddy car, and you do such a beautiful job.' He gives me that smile which makes his face handsome and deepens his eyes.

Outside, in Andy's Norwegian jacket and having taken new yellow rubber gloves out of a packet, I stand on tiptoe and douse the Vauxhall with water from the hose. Up in his bay window Mr Russell, our neighbour, is looking down at what I am doing, his arms crossed before him. He lives alone and has nothing else to do. Perhaps he spends hours watching online sex.

I apply myself with the shampooing of the metal, starting at the front and working to the back. I need to do it fast to make my car-washing believable, because I intend to make a thorough investigation of the inside. The soap bubbles slide slowly downward over the doors. My loafers do not prevent my socks from getting soaked. I should have taken the trouble to put on Andy's wellies.

'Aren't you worried that all that water will freeze and ruin your car paint?' Mr Russell is now standing at our separation fence.

I ignore him.

'The way you're scouring, one would think you're trying for a prize.'

Mr Russell can't help it; he has to give advice. Otherwise, he is an all-right neighbour, tidy around the house which, after all, is the most important.

Luckily, he is getting too cold to interfere any longer and leaves me alone to wipe down the dashboard, under the dashboard, and go through the glove compartment, where I find lots of packages of extra strong mints. Who will he be kissing that much? Under the seat is nothing special, nor under the rubber mats on the floor. I check the inside of the boot, but do not find what I am not sure I am looking for. I shut the boot with a bang. Up at his window, Mr Russell looks down at me. If it were not Mr Russell, I might think this neighbour was lusting after me. *Get a life.*

Just as I start sponging the hubcaps as a last touch, Sunita walks past our house, a letter in her hand. She is our friend and neighbour on the other side.

'My, my! You're washing the car in weather like this?'

I straighten up and wipe the moist hair tendrils out of my eyes with the back of my yellow hand.

'Shouldn't you be at your cute hairdresser's?'

'Emile had an accident,' I say and move to the next hubcap. I want to get this chore over with. There is so much gossiping in this road. One can easily lose an hour a day just being polite.

As I hose down the foamy hubcaps, Sunita, who has posted the letter in the pillar box further up, passes again. She has a stunningly beautiful teenage daughter. Perhaps this girl is making some extra money. Kama Sutra and all. Unbeknown to me, there might exist a whole web of abomination and perversion spread underneath everyday life.

The temperature is dropping with the wind getting up, ice-needling me. *Why did I agree to do this?* Most probably because I feel guilty for thinking that Andy is capable of damaging children.

After energetically rolling the hose onto its wheel until the nozzle reaches me, I peel the gloves off and hesitate before lifting up the lid of the bin and stuffing them in. *Rubber goes into blue, doesn't it?*

With the pail, I return to the warmth of the house.

Eventually, Andy comes down from his office. He hands me a white card on which he has drawn a red heart and written: *To thank you for your help, I'll take you out for dinner to your favourite on my return Tuesday evening.*

My favourite has a name one can mention in broad daylight; it is La Taverna, not Sticky Willy or Gooey Nougat. I prop the invitation on the mantelpiece.

Guilty men bring women flowers; even more guilty men invite them for supper. No, that is rubbish made up in *Marie Claire*. A really guilty man would not willingly expose himself to a lengthy dinner with the very one he is trying to hide himself from.

'Tell me about your job in Peterborough.'

'What do you want to know?'

I have never asked him before. 'What do you and Duncan do in the evenings?'

Panic: he cannot tell me. He will start lying. I will start to tremble, and then he will notice and know that I have found out things.

'We'll have a lot to discuss with this job.' Oh, *that* he can talk about. 'It's a smashing order, a large attachment to a garden centre, the biggest order any conservatory company in south-east England has ever landed.'

He and Duncan have to present a first-class act for the prospective client. It sounds overdetailed to me.

★

It seems to be the middle of the night when I wake to see Andy dressed and putting on his shoes.

'I'm sorry I woke you.'

With gungy eyes, I watch the elaborate way in which he winds the laces into each other and then secures the double knot with a tuck.

'Thanks again for the car. I reserved a table for us at La Taverna for half past seven on Tuesday. Is that OK?'

He approaches the bed, bends over me and kisses my furrowed brow. 'You've got a bump on your forehead.'

The door closes with a clonk. He is gone. I can luxuriate in bed but must not concoct images of Andy and Sunita's daughter online, nor waste time on ineffective excuses for men who are turned on by corruptible purity or by pictures of women with balloon breasts. It is all just an industry for men who never grew up. In particular, I have to refrain from clicking open *Babes4babes* and imagining a scenario where I expose Andy and he writhes in self-loathing.

I will spend time writing to my son and daughter, Ellie, who has just moved into a flat share; she might need crockery or even furniture. These three Andy-free days have to be used to make progress with my drawings. Our art teacher has his own new method. Instead of making us sketch objects we see, he hands out paper sheets on which part of an object is already outlined. By guessing and drawing the rest, we will apparently make headway.

By mid-morning the sun has come out, and the leaves are dripping guiltily. I listen to music of the eighties, the time my children were babies and in my care, my clever beautiful kids. I hope to be able to draw them pictures good enough to hang on their walls one day. So far, we have done sheets with plants, fruits and kitchen utensils. Our homework this week is to finish vehicles. I choose the motorcycle and start shading and hatching.

That evening, my mobile rings on the kitchen counter. It's Linda; she has received a call from Duncan in Peterborough. He was very upset and hardly able to talk, but it seems the police have been to see them and are bringing them back home.

My throat knots together. I must not get hysterical. Talking slowly, I try to get more details but Linda has none. She is almost one hundred per cent sure, though, that it was not the police from Peterborough; it was our local police.

Ungenerously, I do not suggest going to give her support right now, mainly because I am far too worked up myself. Besides, the art teacher told us that we had to be selfish with our time – that is how artists become artists. I tell her to make herself a cup of tea; we'll just have to wait to see.

I try to draw but can't. I try to read a book but can't. Finally, I unscrew the metal top from the brandy bottle and pour myself a generous amount into a kitchen glass.

The police will get two dirty-minded birds with one stone. I'll have to make up defences for Andy, temper things down. Would I lie to protect him? I am his wife; I am probably allowed to lie.

Time is glued to the clock. I feel floaty but pour myself another brandy. It is a mistake, I know.

It is nearly midnight when a car-transporter pulls up outside with the Vauxhall loaded on it. A police car arrives, and Andy gets out. His face is pale and strained. He and a man in a dark blue suit, obviously a detective, come in.

Andy says, 'He wants to talk to you.'

Ominously, the policeman still has not said anything. He lifts my drawing off the table and studies it. Glancing at the brandy bottle, he says, 'I will have to ask you to take a breathalyser test.'

An irrational flash of hilarity takes hold of me; he can't object to me drunk-sketching. But I comply.

The policeman goes into the kitchen, then upstairs. *Andy's office.* He returns rather quickly with a bag into which he has put things. Andy watches all this with concern. I give him imploring looks, skidding sideways a bit when trying to reach for his hand to squeeze it in support.

With the breathalyser tube and the bag in his hand, the policeman looks at Andy's invitation to La Taverna on the mantelpiece and wants to know whether Andy wrote it. I nod. The invitation goes into the bag.

Outside, the car is still visible on the truck, with Mr Russell watching and talking to a uniformed policeman.

My legs feel like buckling. I sit on the sofa a juddering heap, and Andy joins me and puts his arms around my shoulders.

'Andy,' I whisper, 'I'll protect you whatever you have done.'

The policeman gets a message on his radio. He asks me to put on shoes and a coat. My head is in the clamp of inebriation. Dad once explained that feeling of pressure on the brain.

At the police station, I follow the man into a small ugly room, place my bag on a chair and stand with my hands on the chair back. The policeman leaves me that way and closes the door behind him. I have sobered up considerably from the shock of it all.

The door is wrenched open. A man comes in. He is tall and thin.

'Sit down.'

I lift up my bag and take a seat.

'You are here to make a statement. It will be videoed.'

I see the black contraption with a camera eye pointing at me. I look back into the grey cold eyes behind metal spectacles of the man sitting across from me.

'I ask you questions and you answer them.'

It started easy: whether we owned the Vauxhall, its registration number, did I drive it to Sainsbury's at about a quarter to ten on Saturday morning?

More like ten thirty.

Was there fog and bad visibility?

I put my fog light on.

Did you wear a red Norwegian jacket and hat with flaps?

Did you, almost immediately after your return, wash the car?

Was the temperature around zero?

Did you scrub the hubcaps of the car?

Were you wearing new rubber gloves and did you discard them in the blue bin?

Did Mr Russell watch you?

Did Mrs Sunita Patel ask you why you had not gone to the hairdresser?

Was your excuse that your hairdresser, Emile, had had a serious accident?

'That was just a joke.'

'Was it? You have a bruise on your forehead. How did you get it?'

'I bumped my head against the wall.'

'You had 2.3% alcohol in your blood an hour ago. Would you say you are a regular drinker?'

'That's because I found pornography on the internet.'

'Does that turn you on? Would you say your marriage is sound? Did your husband write the dinner invitation card for you?'

'Sorry, you are confusing me with your questions.'

The man leaned over the table, and his eyes behind the steel spectacles were those of a reptile.

'At about ten on Saturday morning, in bad visibility, a man on a Vespa was knocked down by a speeding Vauxhall on Tamson Road. He was crushed against a car on the grass verge and lay undetected for some time because a delivery vehicle parked in the road and concealed him. The casualty was blue-lighted to hospital but died shortly afterwards from a wound inflicted to his head. The name of the man was Emile Dufour from Dagenham, originally from Dieppe, a hairdresser.'

'Can I have some water please?' I manage to ask.

'You'd better get yourself a lawyer. We have to keep you in custody. It's not looking good for you.'

LA GIRAFFE

In Challon-le-Prélot, the café-restaurant was situated on the main road just before the bend. White-painted tractor tyres planted with geraniums defined the terrace. Denise liked flowers. The terrace could have extended much further were it not for the dirt road leading up to the Bourins' farm. This cut the café off from a triangle of tarmac which belonged to nobody in particular and was therefore common property. Logically, it should have been the café's car park, but not everyone respects logic – in this case, particularly not the Bourin family.

'You got something to say?'

'You can't just leave your trailer full of rubbish in our car park for days on end.'

'Watch us.'

More words were exchanged, but finally Denise gave up. *Foutez-moi la paix* was language she abhorred.

Later, a large pile of old roof tiles was dumped next to the trailer. The short and stocky Bourins with their wiry black hair and bristly moustaches had been farming there before the village existed.

Before the house had become a café, Denise had raised a family with her husband, whom everyone called Képi. They had a son, Alain, while Képi worked as a foreman in the packaging factory near Challon-le-Grand. Denise had assisted the caterers during receptions and weddings in the Château de Champlitte thirty kilometres up the road, but had stopped working when she found herself pregnant again, secretly wishing for a girl. But another son was born, pale of skin with a quivering, salivating mouth who did not dare open his tightly closed eyes until his second month. Denise had called him Jules, and Képi disliked everything about him.

This unfortunately coincided with the factory being bought out and modernised. Képi was kept on part-time because he had once shaken the hand of de Gaulle, but also because of his fearsome temperament. Denise, almost guilty for having given birth to a boy who dribbled, had suggested she put her domestic skills to good use and, after a year of bureaucracy, they were granted a commercial licence for a café-restaurant. The family had moved upstairs, and the downstairs and kitchen were expanded. They set up garden furniture with parasols.

Képi ordered a canvas baldachin from the nearby town of Gray to display the name of the establishment. Képi had been set on something which would stand out. The restaurant in Challon-le-Grand was called Café du Mur Blanc and the one in Framont, Café du Rond Point: banal names. Denise feared what was coming, and indeed three weeks later their café was named La Giraffe.

With all this, Denise had forgotten about baptising Jules, who by then was two years old. She asked the young curate, Matthieu, to call round. Képi, who swaggered proudly about La Giraffe like a proud patron on the rare occasions he was there, did not throw the priest out, although he was allergic to anything to do with the church. He must have been drunk because he even agreed to have Jules baptised.

The ceremony had been performed in the church in Challon-le-Grand which also served smaller Le Prélot. Denise had adapted a little girl's white dress to fit the toddler for the occasion. Only the family was present, Képi smoking in the vestibule of God's temple to avoid the curate's solemn preamble. When the blessing came at the font, Matthieu lifted Jules up, which revealed that the child was not wearing a nappy. His pink bottom was cupped in Matthieu's hand and warm urine ran down into the sleeve of the chasuble. His elder brother, Alain, sniggered; Képi turned away. The curate, with the invocation of the Father, the Son and the Holy Ghost, kissed the baby boy on his forehead, whispering, 'God will love you, and so will I.'

★

Jules followed his brother through local school but their experiences had little in common. Alain was popular and good at football, went on to college in Gray, and on graduation joined the immigration service. Jules shied away from people and was not sporty. He sat with the girls and loved religious study, at which he excelled. The teachers thought him peculiar; Matthieu, now the village priest, took pride in him. Képi, rumoured to be having an affair in Challon-le-Grand, called him a 'waste of space'.

The road through Challon-le-Prélot was a scenic off-motorway route to the Midi, and Denise was run off her feet during the summer season. Jules served as waiter and washer-up. Képi, when he was in the mood, entertained the locals at his *table du patron* in front of the Dubonnet mirror, which had safari postcards of giraffes tucked into the frame, and a large stuffed toy giraffe stood in one corner. In Le Prélot, the gossip was that he now had an established mistress in Challon-le-Grand.

★

Right at the start of one high season, the Bourins dumped tons of rubble onto the tarmac triangle. The number of customers dropped because passing traffic could not park. Képi blamed it on Jules for mincing between the terrace tables and hanging out with 'that pederast priest' – it just provoked the Bourins. His *real* son would have taken them on, Alain having inherited his father's protruding lower lip, challenging anyone at any time, but he had been posted to Calais.

In July, when the English and Dutch started to drive through, the Bourins demanded their tractor tyres back, cleaned of paint, flowers removed. On the fourteenth of the month, Bastille Day, with every table on the terrace occupied, the Bourin sons walked in, closed the parasols above the customers and threw them onto the gravel; their father would not be able to see the procession pass on the road.

Képi spent nights away and it was said he had now moved in with his mistress. Denise served *croque-monsieur* and *steak-frites-salade* with a dour face. Few locals looked her in the eye for fear she saw their knowledge of her husband's betrayal.

Every Sunday Jules cycled to church in Challon-le-Grand but finally an exasperated Képi smashed up the bicycle. From then on, it was the priest, Matthieu, who cycled to the café. Jules would perch on the back and, in smooth balance and harmony, the priest and the young man would set off down the road, to Mass on Sunday and for Bible study twice a week. In the panelled church library under the vaulted ceiling, the two of them sat at an oblong table strewn with ancient texts about the life of Jesus. They shared an ambition to look back past the metaphysical interpretation of a divinity, to find the original Jesus – a young 'guy' in first-century Palestine.

'Bloody Church,' grumbled Képi, 'getting its claws into that boy. How much longer will it go on?'

'You're not interested in him. Be glad someone is. Besides, he helps and I need him. Alain is away all the time and has a salary and prospects. I was thinking we should leave La Giraffe to Jules after we're gone.'

'La Giraffe is not for you to give. You came into the marriage with nothing. Now that you mention it, I will be wanting a divorce and will keep the café.'

'I would have nowhere to go.'

He got up and whisked his army beret off the table. 'I've got a meeting with the town council.'

'One called Jolande, with a leather miniskirt and fake tits?'

Denise's sixtieth birthday was approaching and she saw nothing to celebrate. As his mother's tears dripped into the cheese of the *croque-monsieur*, Jules, with Père Matthieu, decided to mark the milestone with a family meal.

On the day, the sun shone and sparrows twittered in the maple tree. La Giraffe was closed to customers. Denise and Jules had worked hard to prepare everything. Képi had left Denise and sought a lawyer, but he agreed to attend, just to see Alain.

In the oven a rabbit stew slow-cooked and a gratin was bronzing. The large wheel of brie was ripe. White tufts of beaten egg sailed on caramel: *îles flottantes*. Denise wore eyeshadow and lipstick. Matthieu had cycled from Challon-le-Grand, bringing fresh baguettes and a potted orchid, while Jules had walked up to the Bourin farm and suggested they remove the planks and sandbags and let Jesus into their hearts. On his return, Denise put make-up on his bruise. Luckily the jaw was not dislocated.

Alain arrived from Calais without his 'partner' and her son. He talked derisively about hordes of eager English tourists passing through border control, their tongues out for decent French cheese.

As they were taking an aperitif on the terrace, Képi was driven up in a powerful car. He got out and the female driver roared off, nearly clipping one of the rusty agricultural machines parked opposite. The family went into the shade of the café and took seats at the table laid with white cloth. Képi slapped his tall sturdy boy on the back.

Over the meal, he could not resist telling Alain that Denise was going to have to pay him rent for the café and a percentage of the profits. 'If she falls behind, I can throw her out and you can have the café.'

'According to civil marriage law, Denise already owns half,' said Matthieu, 'and the business is in both your names.'

Képi's anger at the priest swept over the table. 'I've lost my appetite. Let's go somewhere where there are men.'

He and his son left. The door banged shut behind them. From the brie, a smooth delta had oozed out onto the cheeseboard.

Without a flicker of an eyelid, as if Képi had not existed, Matthieu said to Jules, 'You might be interested to know that, at the Last Supper, the apostles almost certainly ate lamb, bean stew and bitter herbs, apart from the bread and wine mentioned in scripture.'

They moved the dirty dishes into the kitchen, and the priest asked for an apron.

'My goodness!' Denise laughed for the first time that day. 'Why on earth should you?'

'Your birthday is important.'

Tears rose in her eyes. 'Thank you both. It really has become a special day.'

The grace with which Denise contented herself with so little made both men stand either side of her at the sink, their hands on her forearms. It felt to her as if they flooded her with strength and radiance from a joyful bond between them, a weightless elevation caused by their spiritual unity.

Long into the night in her cold bed, Denise thought about that boy of hers, who had no place in the world, and the priest. Their minds were somewhere inaccessible to 'ordinary' people, and yet perhaps they might be able to bring to light the 'ordinary' person that Jesus of Nazareth had been.

★

After a thunderstorm which marked the dramatic end of summer, cars and caravans filed back through the village, heading north.

Jules sat at a metal garden table in the gravel, which was coated with fallen leaves. He was exposed to the road because the flower-filled tyres had indeed been removed by the Bourins. Inside, La Giraffe was a darker scene, drab from wear and tear and stained by cigarette smoke, and his mother looked older. Her hair had lost its lustre and her face was sallow with sadness. In order to keep the café, her income had been savagely reduced, and Képi's unscrupulous lawyer kept demanding more.

Twirling an autumnal leaf by its stem, Jules thought that Paradise was not lost because of the tempting flesh of an apple; it had been the question of who owned the apple tree.

He watched as, across the road, a young Iraqi refugee who had recently arrived worked on the garage he was building. Three walls already stood. Now, he seemed to be contemplating the next task while rubbing his beard. Long wooden beams lay on the ground. Jules's fascination grew as Ahmed parked a pick-up truck close to the building, moving it several times to find the perfect position. He hoisted up the first beam, pushing one end onto the roof of the driver's cabin. Climbing onto the truck, he lifted the other end, trying to position it on the supporting wall. As he moved the beam from the cabin roof, it rolled off and fell to the ground with a thud. Then, Ahmed built up a brick pillar on the back of his truck to bring the beam into a more horizontal position before trying to move it. It rolled off again with another thud.

Jules crossed the road. 'Can I help?'

An odd conversation ensued.

'You could if we were compatible.'

'Isn't it rather a question of strength to lift the heavy beam?'

'The beam is, in fact, too heavy for us. I must rely on the Mesopotamian theory of weightlessness. If one manoeuvres the heavy object into the correct angle of equilibrium, and two people in harmony and balance exert their influence, the mechanical forces of gravity and matter are negated, and the object is moved without effort. I was a physicist in Mosul University before coming here.'

'Can't I be in balance with you?'

'No. You'll have the wrong touch. It can only work within one culture – Islam in this case. My Algerian friend was going to help me but he miscalculated gravitational forces and came off his motorbike. Now he is in hospital.'

Ahmed resumed his labour alone, and Jules returned to the café, chewing over his words.

With a ground-shaking thud, the beam hit the ground again.

'Bon Dieu!' Jules exclaimed, ran into La Giraffe and picked up the telephone.

Twenty minutes later, the figure of a fast-cycling man appeared. Jules climbed onto the back rack, holding onto Matthieu's shoulders. Off they cycled as if twinned.

Jules had experienced a revelation and, during the following months, he stayed with the priest while they researched it. In the panelled church library under a vaulted ceiling, the two of them sat at their oblong table strewn with manuscripts and parchments. In the forbidden gospels, they sought evidence, and made copious notes with cross-references.

Finally, after many sleepless nights, they completed their thesis. Matthieu booked a session with his bishop who, a busy man, sat at his desk steepling his fingertips and controlling his impatience while listening to the priest and his friend present their findings.

'Why should it be so unusual that the neighbour cannot put heavy beams on his building without a crane or lifting device?'

'He could have done with the perfect partner. In the olden days carpenters had no mechanical help of any kind.'

'What has any of this to do with your study of the life of Jesus?'

'The Thirteenth Apostle.'

The bishop sat stunned for a moment. 'Look,' he said, 'we've had Jesus being a woman, Jesus as a hirsute superstar, Jesus born in Africa and black. I cannot bother the cardinal with your theory. I've got to be somewhere.'

Jules and Matthieu left their thesis with him. They were standing in the corridor, wondering where they might be taken seriously, when Marie-Louise, the secretary, was buzzed into the bishop's office. The two waited in the hope of reprieve, but she emerged with their scrunched-up thesis and tossed it into the waste paper basket next to her desk. Heads hanging, they left the building.

Marie-Louise, bored, took the paper ball out again and flattened the pages. The words revealed an extraordinary discovery: that of a further apostle, an intimate secret friend of Jesus. She looked up at the picture of the Last Supper on the wall. Twelve muscular men, net-pulling fishermen mostly and probably hammering carpenters. She contemplated Jesus in the picture: tall, slender, elegant hands, the hue of delicacy on his soft face. He would have sat with the mild and the weak and studied philosophy and poetry – the one to be bullied for sure. To protect himself from mockery and earn respect and attention, he had to use his more refined intelligence and find ways to amaze them with miracles. They bullied him to death anyway when he was only thirty.

She read that the secret and most endearing aspect of his humanity was that he had a boyhood friend who was also misunderstood: a mathematician and scientist. The desperation of the two, alienated from society, would have created a strong bond which, according to the paper in her hand, had enabled them to lift beams onto stone walls.

There *was* a Thirteenth Apostle; Marie-Louise was convinced. In fact, that one had more importance than the other twelve. The bishop had obviously not had time to study the papers but she, Marie-Louise, did not give up easily. She found out that the cardinal was due in Reims for an ecclesiastic conference and would process across the square to the cathedral for prayers. She got a soft-wave perm and bought high-heeled shoes. She also called *Le Nouvel Observateur* and met with a journalist before driving to Reims.

The weather was just right. The cardinal processed at the head of a gaggle of clerics across the granite slabs. People gathered and knelt, except for the tourists. Marie-Louise, in a low-cut blouse and with a cross between her breasts, steered herself towards the procession. She had borrowed a dog from her neighbour and she bent down to pinch the mutt with her sharp fingernails. The animal, in howling protest, pulled her into a collision course with the cardinal.

'*Oh-là-là*, my child. You shouldn't step into my way – security.'

She melted into a genuflexion and the press cameras flashed. 'I am secretary to Bishop Claude. I sent you an e-mail about the Thirteenth Apostle?'

'Ah, the theory dreamed up by some man from a village?'

'He lives in La Giraffe in Challon-le-Prélot and his name is Jules.'

'A giraffe in Le Prélot? A hoax, my dear, and get that mad dog away from my ankles.'

She raised her joined hands in a beseeching plea as the cameras flashed.

★

'What were those photographs in Reims all about?' asked the Pope. 'The press was full of it.'

'Your Holiness,' the cardinal said, squirming. 'It's some nonsense about a thirteenth apostle. The young woman on the ground was pleading for a hearing.'

'There are twelve hours in the day, and twelve in the night, twelve months in a year and a dozen eggs in a carton. Everyone is comfortable with that.'

'I have read the thesis put together by a priest and his friend from the local café, La Giraffe. It is largely based on their neighbour's garage extension, and was presented to Bishop Claude. The priest at least graduated top in his seminary and is an expert on the gnomic gospels. It has a certain sort of logic, somehow.'

'Smother it. No more press.'

The Pope and cardinal underestimated Marie-Louise. An article appeared in *Paris Match* showing Jules with Ahmed having a beer in La Giraffe, Priest Matthieu on the bicycle, and Marie-Louise gardening in shorts.

Are these people forcing the world to rewrite Christianity?

A conclave of the cardinals was summoned. Could there be some truth in the claim of a Thirteenth Apostle? There is no smoke without fire. The Pope was consulted but handed the problem right back to the cardinals.

They all read Jules's and Matthieu's paper. Did any of them give this credence? A few raised their hands. One asked for permission to speak. 'I had a professor of Cairo University demonstrate to me the theory of weightlessness. It works miraculously. Did Jesus not promise the faithful to raise up a temple, practically overnight? We have always feared science as being in competition with us. Would Jesus not more likely have brought it onto our side?'

The Pope replied, 'Should you be right, every Bible will have to be re-edited, every religious book rewritten, every what you can think of and more changed to include this extra apostle – a secret soulmate of Jesus. The majority of you clearly believe this claim to be upheaval without foundation. The Church will nevertheless offer this Jules Giraffe the merit of having had a saintly vision.'

'Your Holiness, La Giraffe is the name of the café where Jules serves at table.'

'Well then, let us have it that Jules What's-his-name heard the voice of some divinity.'

'What should it have said to him?'

'It spoke to him of the true humanity of Jesus.'

'Should it be a classified miracle, or canonisation and sainthood?'

'Let's not overdo it. A vision is sufficient.'

★

La Giraffe became famous worldwide. Denise accepted the divorce and was awarded the family home. Ahmed built an extension to the café-restaurant with the help of machinery. A cook, a waiter and a cleaner were hired. Marie-Louise showed customers the place on the terrace where Jules had the epiphany. A chiselled marble plaque was laid in the gravel.

Inside the café, a gold-framed picture of the Pope hung behind the stuffed giraffe.

The local commune had the access road up to the Bourins barred, which enlarged the parking space for all the curious and worshippers. Le Prélot was given three Michelin stars for tourist interest.

Képi moved with Jolande to her childhood home in Corsica.

Jules ensconced himself in the seminary to substantiate their theory about the Scientist Apostle.

For Canal+ television, Ahmed was approached by the producer of Religion Around The World: Does a giraffe have mystical powers?

THE FERRIS WHEEL

On a cloudless June day, a young woman in a cream dress covered with small blue flowers pushed a toddler in the newest 1992 Italian-designed buggy across Parker's Piece, a diamond-shaped green space in the centre of Cambridge.

The mother, though proud that her baby had the latest, felt deprived by the baby-face-ahead design. Twenty-three-months-old Clarinda already looked into her future, and her spontaneous reactions to things new were hidden from her mother. All Heather saw was the Armani–Baby label against the pale immature neck and the calf-leather Start-Rites tapping against the metal footrest.

Heather Courtney stopped again, this time to put a straw hat on Clarinda's head, pushing the elastic under the little round chin. It was not easy for Heather to control her questing fingers, or to take her eyes off the baby girl with curly honey-blond hair and cornflower-blue eyes. The little angel's endearing expression was born from a dainty nose and a pink oh dear mouth. The prettiest baby ever, thought the people who passed, every one of them. Chin up, Heather resumed pushing the buggy.

From the words 'Mrs Courtney, you have a daughter', the overwhelmed new mother with the torn vagina had a single focus in life. Clarinda, she named her – a lovely name she thought, as she herself had never taken to her own. *Heather* was a short plant, dry and prickly, which smelled unpleasant and only thrived in rough climates.

A fair was set up in the middle of the common, a colourful group of stalls and rides with the Ferris wheel as its most prominent feature.

As they approached, the din of taped modern tunes mingled with a mechanical pipe-organ; the smell of chargrilled sausage mixed with the whiff of diesel from the generator.

She parked the buggy close to the Ferris wheel, positioned so that Clarinda could not see the ghouls and skeletons of the ghost train.

'Look, darling, at this turning fairy circle; it's called a Ferris wheel. These people go all the way up into the sky and down again and up.' Heather's arm made a loop, but Clarinda could not see it behind her. Her brain probably recorded the vertical wheel going round and the people on the attached shiny red sofas having to go with it. Neurologists claim that even birth is retained in human brains in every detail.

Just then, a grating mechanical noise came from the Crazy Hopper, which gradually, menacingly, escalated. To Heather's alarm the screeching contraption hit its extreme, as spinning humans, thrown into a centrifugal loop, howled as if in purgatory.

Clarinda pulled her hat off and threw it into the grass. As Heather bent to pick it up, her skirt was lifted by a single gust of wind while the thrill-ride went into another loop. A second squall turned the highest Ferris wheel-riders into flailing, writhing creatures. The wind whistling in from nowhere shivered along her skin. Heather looked around with unease; there was something deliberate about it, personal even. Up in the turbulent air, a tethered balloon of the grinning ectoplasmic blob from *Ghostbusters* tore at its rope, rocking and mocking, taunting, and dipping into the smoke which wafted from the cooking stands of the fair.

Heather crouched down to her baby to see how she was coping with all this and was reassured by Clarinda's unruffled calm interest in the fair. Meanwhile, the Ferris wheel operator had left her post at the boarding platform and was walking towards them. She was one of those fairground people, perhaps a traveller. The baseball cap backwards on her head left some long strands of brown hair dangling free, framing her angular face. She could have been considered attractive, beautiful in some way even, but for the look of disenchantment, so sour, and frankly a little disturbed. Her blue eyes darted erratically around her. She wore a silver sheen zip-up top and tracksuit trousers over which was belted a leather money-pouch. Chafed and much-worn Mule Skinner boots were on her feet. Behind her, her customers rode around the wheel, the bursts of wind a bonus thrill.

With the next gust, the fairground woman's cap flew off and sent her long hair flying across her face. She did not go and retrieve the hat; her haunted blue eyes were now fixed in shock on Clarinda. The child sat rigid, obviously holding the stare.

'What do you want?'

The woman, confused in her intentions, turned unwillingly away, picked her cap from the ground and walked back to her post.

Heather saw with some relief that the ghost blob had become caught in the spindling out branches of one of the poplars on the north side of the common.

'Let's get away from here.'

'No!' shrieked Clarinda, and followed it with a yelling tantrum.

The Ferris wheel slowed down and came to a stop, as did the music, all music, and even the thrumming of the generator, to leave a funfair in freeze-frame. Only the howling of Clarinda persisted. Then, isolated shouts began to break the silence, voices conveying the fact that the power was out.

The Ferris wheel operator was looking at them from her distance, and Heather did not know what to do, feeling as if she were the victim of some vile conjuring trick. Slowly, shoulders hunched, the traveller advanced on them again to stand even closer to the buggy. Suddenly, she crouched so that her head came level with Clarinda's. 'Don't you cry, me darling.'

Clarinda hushed and sat back into the canvas seat. Heather tried to turn the buggy away as the woman reached out a hand towards the baby.

'Don't you dare touch Clarinda.'

'What sort of name is that, when she is Irish?'

'She is no such thing. Get away from us. My husband is meeting us for lunch and he's an important lawyer. You'll be in so much trouble if you don't leave us alone.' Heather managed to turn the child away from the traveller. Instantly, Clarinda started to scream again. She writhed in her seat, twisting her head back, trying to keep contact with the fairground woman.

'Stop this at once. You can see the Ferris wheel another time.' Heather careered over the grass while Clarinda had a meltdown. Over her shoulder, Heather still felt the stare of the woman, an odd sensation, a prickle of tension in her back.

Behind them the fairground came back to life, refilling the eerie void with natural agitation and sound. Heather stopped and leaned forwards, pressing her lips gently upon the child's hot cheek, begging her to calm down.

But then the fairground woman was alongside them again and stumbling to her knees to block their way. Clarinda became instantly silent and docile, while the vulgar woman smiled at her as if acknowledging a long wait over, the reanimation of lost intimacy. It was unbearably intrusive.

Clarinda tilted her head to one side, and Heather knew the expression without seeing it; the child was flirting.

'What on earth are you doing?' Heather asked Clarinda as if she were an adult.

'Mummy,' said Clarinda and stretched out her arms.

The traveller threw back her head, crying out, 'She *is* me baby. Look, she knows it too.'

Never before had Clarinda said 'mummy' so clearly; jealousy and dread disabled Heather. Up to now it had been 'mum mum'.

'My little Daisy, I have been sick, but now Mummy is better and can take care of you.' The traveller's fingers, snake-like, curled around one of the tiny hands held out to her.

'I'm calling the police,' Heather gasped. Holding the mobile in her shaking hand she tapped in 999 and reported that a woman was trying to steal her daughter in bright daylight a few yards from Cambridge police station.

'Daisy, me darling.'

Heather then called her husband while two police officers, a male and female, strode towards them with a rolling gait, the strict tough types, thumbs in belts. From the Ferris wheel came the shouts of customers left rocking on the stationary wheel.

'Now then, Lorry, what's all this about? You've got people stuck up there. Why aren't you at your post?'

'I have just seen my daughter.'

'There you go, officer. See, she is trying to abduct my child, as these people do.'

'You'd better get your customers off that wheel safely or we'll close you down.'

Lorry reluctantly let the policewoman lead her back to the fair and watch her operate the wheel, permitting the riders to get off. And when all the seats were empty, she pushed down the lever and locked the gate, with the policewoman still breathing down her neck.

Heather had been held in place by the policeman and to her great relief she saw her husband walking briskly across Parker's Piece towards the University Arms Hotel where they were to have lunch.

'Theodor,' she shouted ineffectually, the name being long and the distance longer. 'Theo!' she yelled with all her pectoral force, waving both arms, aware that this was unladylike.

'Can you go and get my husband? I can't run with the buggy. He's the one in the grey suit with the John Lewis bag.'

The policeman strode off, legs trained to run, just as the policewoman returned, holding Lorry solidly by her arm.

'Now then, what makes you think this is your child?' Policewomen had special ways of handling female criminals, Heather knew. 'You'd better have a good story for this one, Lorry.'

As the traveller dithered, the policeman and Theo ran in step across the grass, detouring a rounders game played by schoolchildren in purple T-shirts.

'OK,' said Theo panting. 'There seems to be some sort of misunderstanding here. What is certain is that Clarinda is our child, has always been and always will be. Can you do something about this traveller, officers?'

'I'm not a traveller. I am an amusement park attendant.'

'Her name is Lorraine Manning,' the policeman said. 'And let's be careful with the racism, sir. Lorry came to the fairs some years ago with her boyfriend who ran a shooting gallery.' Heather looked at her husband, her eyes filled with suspicion. 'It's a stand where you shoot with a rifle at targets moving on a mechanical belt. The boyfriend decided to shoot at more than just cardboard ducks and is in prison. Lorry took it badly for a bit but has now taken over the wheel. Isn't that right, Lorry?'

'I'm completely well now. You can go and ask my doctor.'

'Is she well?' asked Theo.

'She's had her licence renewed for the last three years. These fairground people have to be vetted by the SPD.'

'She is a baby-snatcher. She went straight for Clarinda the minute she saw her and put a spell on her or something. My baby said *Mummy* for the first time, and to *her*.'

Theo did this thing he did in court to distract; actually, Heather knew it was to give himself time to think. Head down, he rubbed his nape and then snapped the head up. 'To sum up, we have a well-to-do mother strolling with her baby on the common on the way to lunch with her husband. We also have the ex-girlfriend of an incarcerated gypsy, a woman with a history of psychiatric illness, claiming that the baby is hers. Good sense, if you are here, make yourself known to us.'

In the following silence, a dog ran past, skidded to a halt and picked up a ball in his mouth. Clarinda laughed, delighted. Heather remembered to breathe and sucked in air in quick short gasps. And then she noticed that it was entirely calm, the wind having disappeared.

'For God's sake,' Theo continued. 'Heather gave birth to Clarinda in the Rosie twenty-three months ago. End of story.'

'On the second of July 1990,' stated Lorry.

'That's correct. Theodor, how does she know that?'

'Many ways,' said the policeman. 'Did you make an announcement in the papers?'

'*The Telegraph.*'

'There you have one possibility.'

'You – sorry, what's your name again?' Theo asked belligerently. 'Lorry, right, like in truck; you should apologise to my wife for putting her through this, and we will all go our separate ways.'

'What about the similar looks?'

'This is a beautiful baby and you are, well, what you are.'

'We have the same hair colour.'

'You are a brunette.'

Heather nudged her husband. 'Dyed.'

'Clarinda has my blue eyes.'

'So you go around attacking every mother with a blue-eyed baby.'

Lorry became agitated and screamed, 'Stop that! Stop saying things like that about me!'

The police officers exchanged looks. 'We'd better pop into the police station over there.' They made it sound light.

'This is torture for us. Can't we just leave you to deal with this?'

'We are going to have to insist.'

In the police station, Lorry was escorted away and the Courtney family were asked to remain in a waiting room.

'This is the most awful day. Why did I have to show Clarinda the Ferris wheel?'

A female detective sergeant in plain clothes introduced herself. 'Lorry Manning is known to us even though she does not have a criminal file. She became unstable after her partner was put into prison and was hospitalised for quite a while.' The sergeant left the Courtneys to go and question Lorry. Clarinda had fallen asleep in her buggy.

Theo started to pace up and down. 'Such crazed, ugly people should not be allowed to run funfairs. They are a menace to society and should be locked up in institutions.'

'Hush, Theo. They can hear you.'

But Theodor was in full flow now. 'This lowlife trash could easily have attacked you and run away with our daughter.'

'I believe that Lorry is depressive, not aggressive. I bet she had a miscarriage or an abortion at one stage.'

'Good Lord, so now you are defending her?'

'No, but actually I feel a tad sorry for her. She must have been quite pretty when she was younger. Just think how badly life must have treated her.'

The detective sergeant returned with Lorry. 'We have to do this by the book so we are all going to the Rosie Maternity Hospital for a data-check.'

Heather remonstrated strongly on the grounds of putting a small child through all this. Theo just spat out, 'Ridiculous.' Despite this, they were bundled into separate police cars and driven to the maternity hospital. During the drive, Theodor threatened the sergeant and the entire Cambridgeshire Police Force with unpleasant legal consequences.

At the Rosie, the receptionist floundered a bit, faced by the task of checking the records of birth from nearly two years ago. She excused herself and got someone else to fill in while she walked away with the request.

'Clarinda is getting hungry and needs a nappy change,' Heather said accusingly, looking at Lorry.

'What happened to my baby's hand?' asked Lorry. 'Three of her fingers are all twisted.'

'A birth defect,' said Heather. 'It can be put right once she is five.'

'Don't talk to each other,' ordered the sergeant.

The receptionist returned with a man from records. He brought a printout from which he read that, indeed, on the second of July 1990, a female baby had been born to a Heather Courtney weighing 3.65 kilos, and that delivery had taken twenty-five hours as the baby lay back-to-back. He concluded that on that day all babies were matched to their mothers, no still births, no premature births.

'There,' said Heather. 'Can we now go?'

'How about my birth? Early that morning I gave birth to a baby girl too.'

Theo puffed derisively.

'Her name is Lorry Manning,' filled in the sergeant. The employee checked on his list and then shook his head: no birthing mother of that name that day.

Lorry began blinking rapidly while repetitively tucking her hair behind her ear with a trembling hand.

'Did you register under a different name?' asked the sergeant.

'I don't remember, don't remember.'

'OK then, what was your address at the time?'

'Lived in a caravan of course.'

'Did you come for antenatal check-ups, scans?'

'No.'

'Did you leave a contact number, next of kin on the registration form?'

Lorry shook her head.

'Mummy.' The sudden piping voice of a child just woken up and still in the twilight of dream world.

'Oh, darling Daisy.' Lorry's whole body seemed to quiver.

'Do you mind?' interjected Heather.

The sergeant asked to check the list herself. 'Jen Smith,' she read out. 'Could that have been you?'

'Maybe? I said I don't remember.'

'Will this help? Jen Smith gave birth to a female early that day. It shows that she checked herself and her baby out sometime around noon.'

Lorry said nothing.

'So if you chose to be Jen Smith, where is the baby?'

Lorry let out a frustrated moan.

The registrar said, 'It seems a bit unusual that we would discharge a mother only a few hours after giving birth.'

'Well, you fucking well did then.'

Theo could not restrain himself. 'This Jen Smith and her baby are living a normal life somewhere. Can't you see that your cock-and-bull story stinks?'

'Was it not after this alleged birth you were admitted to Fulbourn Psychiatric Hospital?' The sergeant gave the list back to the hospital employee.

'Yes, all right, I walked out. But I didn't take Daisy, and when I came back here the next day, she was gone. And all of you in this shithole hospital treated me like I was a lunatic.' Lorry tapped her chest with her flat hand, and Heather thought of Clarinda doing exactly that when she was denied something. All babies did that; Lorry had just never grown out of it.

Heather got up from her seat. 'Now we're going home.'

'With this outcome,' resumed the detective sergeant, 'Social Services will look into the psychiatric side of things. You can go, by all means. If something more comes up, I have your details.'

'Thank God.' Outside on the pavement Heather lifted Clarinda into her arms. 'What a nightmare! I can't believe the police had the right to take us to the station and then drive us to the hospital.'

'This has saved us all a lot of time and money,' Theodor said, and she knew that he was right, as he was most of the time.

★

Back home, Heather baked a carrot cake in haste as she was desperate to recover Clarinda's affection. When she crawled happily into her play-tent, Heather and Theodor relived their shocking experience.

'That creepy way Lorry claimed my baby. I will never be able to forget it.'

'My dear.' Theodor squeezed her arm gently. 'It's all over now. She picked you and Clarinda by chance.

155

She has probably done this to other mothers before, from a collection of birth announcements. I agree that she probably went through a miscarriage or abortion. The police and social services will sort this out between them. Don't walk across Parker's Piece again!'

Clarinda crawled out of her tent and stood up, clumsily holding the handle of a toy wheel which, as she flicked it, produced a ratchet noise while coloured plastic peas tumbled around inside it. Shrilly she shouted, 'Mummy, Mummy.'

Theo laughed out loud. 'It's the Ferris wheel she has christened Mummy.'

My daughter is not that stupid, thought Heather. *Nor am I*. Lorry had recognised someone in Clarinda and poured emotions over the child. Clarinda was responding by mimicking the emotions. In the psychologist's baby book, it was described under *Validation*.

'But how did she recognise me? All she had was a *Telegraph* announcement.'

'Easy,' said Theodor. 'She hangs around the Rosie Clinic and watches mothers leave with their newborn, knowing they gave birth the day before, or two days before. Perhaps she poses as a relative to get more information.'

'How appalling!'

*

Three days later, Theodor drove out of his firm's private car park. He noticed Lorry sitting on the metal railing. As he had to wait for his turn to drive off, she was given plenty of time to note down his car registration. He did not tell Heather. She had just started to come over her hysterical fear of having her daughter snatched from her, had relented and sent her back to nursery school, although she remained outside on a bench most of the time, guarding. Clarinda had learned a few new words but did not say *mummy*.

★

One week later, when Heather left the house with Clarinda in a full-size pram, hood up, Lorry suddenly stepped from behind a parked delivery van. Heather was paralysed with fear.

'Me baby can't see anything in that pram. She can't stretch her legs. You are a bad mother. Give me back my Daisy.'

Hunched forwards, head bowed, Heather managed to get them home, where she closed all the curtains, shut the shutters and hid Clarinda in her play-tent. Theodor, who rushed home, called the police and made a formal complaint against Lorry, requesting a restraining order. It was settled out of court and an injunction was slapped on Lorry, prison if she broke it.

Lorry was a broken woman. She was diagnosed with a serious personality disorder and lost her fairground licence.

Heather wanted more, but Theodor said that enough was enough. 'Let's get on with our lives.'

Again, he was right, as he almost always was.

Heather insisted they move, because Lorry knew where they lived. It was a bad time to sell property, but there you go: a mother is a mother, and will always protect her child even to her detriment.

★

Clarinda's hand was much improved by two operations. At school she was lively and popular but, when the time came, she only scraped through her GCSEs. Theodor, with a hint of desperation, enrolled her in a private day school for A levels. Heather knew that he harboured the dream that one day his daughter would become a partner in his firm, and she seemed willing to give it her best, but the studies were contrary to her nature.

Thanks to extra private lessons to boost mathematics, she did pass the three A levels, but Heather had watched in dismay as Clarinda became rebellious and recalcitrant, a teenager who had discovered boys, went out too much, and argued incessantly with her parents.

To celebrate the passing of A levels, Theodor invited his family out for dinner, with the purpose of discussing university.

At dessert, he spoke. 'I know that your teachers made you all write applications to universities and that they helped with your CVs and interview tactics. Have you decided which university you want to go to?'

Clarinda stopped fingering the charm on her wrist and looked her father in the eye. 'I'm sorry, Mum and Dad, but I don't want to go to university. I never wanted to go to any university. I'd be bad at it anyway.'

158

Almost exactly on Clarinda's nineteenth birthday, she packed a few things and left home to become a croupier at the roulette table in a Luton casino.

★

Without her daughter, Heather felt as if the world had darkened. She sat around brooding and waiting for phone calls that seldom came. Theo took on far too many legal cases and drank irresponsibly. Some years later, he had a heart attack. His secretary called an ambulance and, as he was being blue-lighted along Parker's Piece, she informed Heather.

Arriving at the hospital, Heather was directed to the emergency cardiac department and learned that the patient had been moved into an intensive-care ward. She walked along busy corridors, stepping aside for medics in green jogging along with computer-trolleys.

She was asked to take a seat in a waiting room. A young woman sat plunged forward, weeping into her hands. It was then that reality shocked Heather. The thought that Theo might die had not occurred to her, ever. Now, her husband was fighting for his life. If Theo did not make it, she would become a widow.

Despite the urge to retch from fear, she went up to the desk and begged them to let her see her husband. Eventually she was called and rose unsteadily from the bench like an aged woman.

At the ward entrance, the doctor held up his hand, spreading the fingers. 'Five minutes only.'

On his bed, Theo, in a shapeless hospital gown, was linked up to tubes and ticking devices, a clip in his nose. His face was ashen, the paper-thin folds of his skin coating the cheekbones, his eyes hollow.

'Heather,' he breathed weakly.

'You'll pull through, dearest. It's one of the best hospitals. They know what they are doing. Remember the happy day Clarinda was born in here?'

Theo emitted a sonorous growl.

'Don't upset yourself. The heart of an honest hardworking respectable man will be saved. Trust in God.'

'I am not a respectable man. I am a despicable criminal.'

She shook her head in dismay and tried to reach for his hand, which he pulled away.

'You don't know the real me, yet you loved me. This is hard to bear. I need to tell you about me before it is too late.'

'Hush, Theo. Save your strength to get better. I need you.'

In a dull voice, he started to speak. 'After you gave birth, I was given the newborn girl to hold while they repaired you. I left the birthing room because they were stitching around inside you. Outside, I tripped over my attaché case, and the baby slipped out of the blanket and fell onto the concrete floor. She was dead instantly from the impact; her skull broke open.

'I panicked. I ripped off our baby's identity bracelet and stuffed the tiny body into my case. In the baby-station, I went for a pink-covered crib, wrenched the bracelet off and replaced it with Clarinda's. I had to hurt the little hand to get it on.

'When a nurse appeared, I duped her by explaining that I needed to take my daughter back to her fretting mother.'

'Sweet Jesus,' came from Heather, who tilted her head back, closing her eyes. The gesture led into a silence. When it was broken by the wailing of an ambulance siren outside, anger boiled up in her like lava in a volcano.

'You are admitting killing our daughter.

Not just that. You stole a child from its mother.

You destroyed that mother.

You made a fool of me.

You crippled an innocent baby's hand.

You destroyed Clarinda's future by pushing her too hard against her nature.

And now,' she yelled, 'you have wiped out my trust and love for you.

You sure are not going to die in peace!'

One of the monitoring machines started to beep, and the doctor rushed in. From the lack of presence in the gaunt figure and the sunken eye sockets, Heather knew that Theodor had just died. She stood over him, glaring down with hatred.

IT GETS COLD

Charlotte had just reached the porch on her way out when a thud followed by a scraping noise came from the upper floor. She felt the palms of her hands getting moist. What on earth was he up to now?

Hottie, her little dog, was pressed against the door, equally eager to escape from the haunted house. One of her outdoor shoes was wedged into the umbrella stand. Surely he had not pushed it in there, dead as he was.

Outside, the sun shone and the dog trotted alongside Charlotte, who went through the courtyard past the stable building, now used to store outdoor equipment. Daddy had turned the servant rooms above it into one big art space for her when she had graduated thirty years ago as an illustrator for children's books. Dear Daddy, now dead for quite some years. They went through the metal gates and up the little mound, where Charlotte stood under a vast expanse of sky. Clouds sailed as far as one could see over the flat fields of the Fens – over a tall and thin woman in wool trousers and a beige cashmere sweater, her brown hair gathered up in a toothy clip.

She was an only child and had inherited Tudor Manor and the nine acres of land. It had been a tranquil spot, in which she had raised her two children, but now, vexingly, a new A-road had been built, an ugly grey strip cutting close to them. Objection had been pointless.

Modern times. Henry VIII clearly could not just grin and bear it. Or was it her he was objecting to? At first it had just been muffled sounds coming from upstairs, but then the night air was ripped with deep bellowing, and she knew that Henry's soul was not at rest, turning her slowly into a heap of shattered nerves.

Tudor Manor was famous for Henry VIII's visit in 1546 when he had founded Trinity Hall College. The west wing was glorious Tudor with bricks filling in the wood structure, a long row of uninterrupted stained-glass windows and chequered and twisted chimneys above. The interior had remained untouched: the sumptuous oak-clad banqueting hall on the first floor, with a pair of encased mirrors and, on the coving, a row of painted heraldic shields. In the gigantic stone fireplace the spit roast was still workable. The historic part was linked to the newer twelve-bedroom Victorian structure by a second wood-carved staircase from the vestibule and a narrow corridor on the first floor.

Hottie, finely attuned to Henry's presence, ran off. Charlotte furtively glanced back at the Manor, avoiding any kind of mental link which could provoke paranormal activity, but the house stood innocent. A sudden squeaky shriek stabbed her with fear but the dog had merely disturbed a cock pheasant.

She was *forced* to live here, she thought, crestfallen. Here she had grown up and, as if with the gradual loss of her innocence, the Manor was daring to manifest its inherent malevolence.

Hottie on a lead, they walked back. Up at Henry's windows, nothing unusual showed.

With a cup of tea in the drawing room, she felt less stressed. It was a large and pleasing room with its cherry-wood grand piano, a unique piece, the shelves filled with books and mementos, the well-sat-in soft furniture and the Bonington and Turner paintings on the silk-tapestried walls. It was in this room that Alexander had first met her parents before the dinner served by Rose – parents who had never taken her illustration job seriously but put much emphasis on attracting a substantial son-in-law.

Alexander had graduated from Fitzwilliam with a first in History and Politics. Whilst others organised booze-ups in local pubs to celebrate, he approached Charlotte to rent Tudor Manor for a feast for his student friends. Dad would not approve, she told him, but her father was intrigued by the request and asked to meet Alexander. They got on, and she was pushed into dating him as subtly as a chequer piece is manoeuvred across the board. Alexander had just got a job as a trade envoy covering the Far East.

Sitting on the sofa as she did now, Alexander had looked at the paintings and speculated whether Turner's attraction to dreamy sunsets had much to do with the newly discovered chromium yellow oil pigment at that time. Encouraged by this art talk, she had revealed that once she had been commissioned to create a flier for *A Midsummer Night's Dream*.

'And admire this too,' her father had said, laughing. 'Our Charlotte illustrated *Boggie the Froggie*.'

When Rose announced dinner, Alexander's 'Hop along, Froggie' caused hilarity. Father proposed a toast with decanted Morgon, and Alexander recognised the wine. That was it. Her soft-focus photograph was in *Tatler* magazine announcing the engagement of Charlotte Emma Ffrench-Jones to Alexander Gardiner. One year after the lavish wedding, Olivia was born and two years later, David. These had been the happy times amidst the warm, loving, baby-smelling bodies. Alexander was already career-minded.

Now she was middle-aged, the children flown and her husband rarely home. Tudor Manor, with its peculiar smell and inexplicable noises, was increasingly a burden and so frightening that she could barely function. Alexander brushed it off. It was her property, her problem. He went on lengthy trips to the Far East and during the week stayed in his London mews house, convenient for Whitehall. Olivia was married and lived in Cornwall, and David was a student at Nottingham University, having changed his course yet again – an expensive son.

Rose gone, Charlotte had domestic help, women sent from an agency who arrived in their own cars. They showed little pride or interest in their work. The old wing was not cleaned any longer. In fact, Charlotte had not checked Henry's room, the banqueting hall, for some time.

She still had the little Lhasa apso, Charlotte's sweetest and dearest companion who, lost in this large house, bravely waddled over the large expanses of inlaid parquet, determined to follow her mistress. Hottie hated the place.

★

Long after Charlotte had drunk her evening hot chocolate, Alexander came home for the weekend. Following his desire for order, he unpacked his overnight case and laid out his pyjamas on the double bed. In a casual shirt and cashmere sweater, he sat poised on the sofa, one arm resting on the upholstered back, legs crossed, one calf-leather shoe whipping, and talked about the traffic in London.

She watched his slow sipping of whisky and thought that he rarely smiled at her or shared more than a traffic jam in St James's. When he was away, she never yearned for his intimacy. His marital right was performed in cold sheets so that she never quite knew when it was over. He had shown little more application in making their two children. He was like a cactus that bloomed only twice in a desert. Eventually, he enquired how her week had been, and she told him no more than the cleaner banging the hoover into the skirting boards. He would not believe her if she described the noises from Henry's room, and it would only make her feel foolish. When he was home, nothing of the sort manifested itself – devious Henry!

By late breakfast on Sunday, they had warmed to each other. He even brought up the idea of her accompanying

167

him to Hong Kong one of these days. She proposed a walk in fresh air because she wanted to say things that Henry should not overhear.

They walked from the house in a dull late April day.

'The Manor is proving too much for me, left here by myself,' she began.

'If you can't cope, have them send more domestic help, more gardeners.'

'It's not just that. There is the smell and the unexplained noises; there is Henry watching me and taking advantage of my loneliness. I have come to loathe this house and my life in it. Nobody visits. I never go into town unless I need to buy something. And what for? The kids don't come, let alone stay. I want to sell up and move into a practical modern bungalow.'

Alexander, who had walked along without interrupting, only fingering his chin, recoiled at the word bungalow.

'Are you insane? You have the privilege of this Manor. You owe it to your family to look after it. And you don't have to be alone. Go out, invite friends. Read, improve your intellect. And for God's sake, stop talking about Henry's ghost. It's childish.'

Charlotte felt an impulse, almost a call, to turn her head over her shoulder back to the house. When she gave in, the sight of a large dark head at one of the Tudor windows slowly faded, once it had telepathically communicated with her. The experience had a taste of unwelcome familiarity.

'We ought to go on a holiday,' Alexander concluded.

'Ought?'

'OK then, have it your way.' He picked up a stick lying on the path and threw it from him out into the grass. 'Fetch.'

Hottie did not move from her side.

'Useless dog,' he grumbled and they walked on. She felt Henry at the back of her head like a heat burn, while Alexander, next to her, was brewing thoughts. He had detected mutiny in her.

'Unfortunately,' he restarted the conversation, 'I will have to go back to Hong Kong for about two months, but when I return it will not be far from a birthday.'

'Mine. Forty-seven. Say it.'

'From your forty-seventh birthday, when we shall give a lunch party for our friends. In the meantime, I'll have a word with our children. And if I were you, I'd get a bigger dog. Train it to bite your spectre.'

★

Alexander drove back to London earlier than usual. The weekend had not gone well. Charlotte came back into the house after waving goodbye to his Jaguar. Her complaints about life in the house seemed to hover like malodorous gases. The chill now blowing down Henry's staircase smelt of rotting carcases; the acridity was definitely aimed at her.

'Oh, stop it,' she said in a dull empty voice. 'You don't exist.'

To her horror, a clear liquid came dripping down from the top of Henry's dark staircase. In the sparse light from below, the silvery puddles grew larger and more tangible, approaching step by step unnaturally slowly, and not in the way that water moves.

She sprinted into the kitchen, slapped together a quick sandwich, and picked up Hottie with one scoop of her arm. Locking the door of the drawing room, she plunged onto the sofa.

It could not be real, she reasoned, strong heartbeats at her jugular. The ghost had somehow created the illusion of liquid. If she went to check, it would be gone. She had not fainted, only fled. His trick had not worked. Her heart slowly calmed only to lead her into a different state of upset – that of her conversation with Alexander. *Read, improve your intellect.* Who did he think he was? From the shelf, she pulled out a book by Macaulay. She read from a page chosen at random. All the words were English; however, their sense escaped her. Was Alexander right to think she was stupid? She put the book back and returned to the dog on the sofa, stroking its soft fur. The house was silent. She had to find the courage to go upstairs to the bedroom.

In the hallway, the telephone rang. *Alexander to apologise to her?*

'Mum, are you OK?' Olivia's strong young voice was immediately refreshing. 'Dad called me.'

'And he asked you to show more interest in me?'

'Don't be silly. I am interested in my mother. I could come and visit Wednesday.'

'That is wonderful. Just you, not… For lunch? Supper?'

'Certainly lunch. See you. Take care.'

And stay put. Don't pack your bags and move into a bungalow.

Finally it was Wednesday. Apart from a moan and some creaking, Henry had kept to himself. From upstairs, Charlotte saw the small white car turning into the drive. She hastened downstairs in the new tunic top she had bought.

She was greeted by Olivia, smiling, smooth-skinned, svelte in jeans and a top which was purposely too short at the waist. 'Hi, Mum.' Then she gave her attention to the shimmying Hottie. 'Well, hello, little you.'

They went inside, and Charlotte offered her a salad lunch and home-made lemonade.

Olivia, tossing her hair exuberantly, recounted things happening in her life.

To fill the distance between us with words, thought Charlotte.

'Henry is apparently giving you a hard time. Dad told me,' Olivia admitted, broaching the reason for her visit.

'You must have had quite a conversation.'

'Dad is worried. I said I would help. Can we go upstairs? I haven't been in Henry's room for years.'

'If you must.'

Together, they tapped along the low-ceilinged corridor leading to the studded gothic door.

'There is quite a smell up here.' Olivia twisted the large loop-headed key in the lock with a crunch and then with a carefree gait, she went straight in, which produced a jolt of concern in Charlotte.

'Wow! It's larger than I remember. Very dusty.'

'Nobody cleans in here any more.'

Olivia was peering around. 'Rose refused to do it after seeing Henry doff his cap to her!' She laughed.

The lead-framed window glass, with its air bubbles, was dulled by dust. The milky light threw patterns on the floorboards. The only pieces of furniture left were an upright oak armchair, a carved Tudor chest and a floor-standing iron candelabra, a wax candle in each of its four arms.

'It's easy to imagine a feast – the crackling skinned boar roasting in that fireplace, men and wenches eating off pewter plates, drinking out of mugs, coarse laughter, Henry in the chair at the head of the table commanding the scene. You know that they pissed in the corners; that's why it still reeks.'

Olivia seemed to get on with the room.

'Why did Granny get rid of all the other furniture?'

'Something about the draught shifting things around.'

To Charlotte's horror, Olivia sat down in the armchair. In a loud voice she proclaimed, 'Stop pestering my mum, you old lecher. Go and die. You are not welcome here any longer.'

'I wish you had not done that.'

'Let's wait and see whether he reacts.'

In anticipation, they remained motionless. 'It's getting cold,' remarked Olivia. 'Can you feel it?'

Stepping backwards, one tentative foot after the other, Charlotte retreated towards the door, while in the candelabra one of the candles tilted in slow motion and then clattered to the floor, rolling for a while before lying still.

'Fuck,' Olivia breathed and then slowly, without touching the armrests, lifted herself out of the chair and ran out of the room, where she collided with her mother.

Hottie, who had sprinted ahead of them, was waiting at the top of the stairs and whimpering.

Downstairs, Olivia rationalised. 'The candle fell down because we caused a vibration moving about. There is always a logical explanation.'

Charlotte knew that her daughter did not believe this.

They remained idling in the hallway, and Charlotte guessed that Olivia was now going to leave. She went up to her daughter and hugged her tight.

'Listen, Mum, I had a friend who was a member of the Paranormal Society in Cambridge. It was run by a guy who called himself a ghostbuster.'

'Good heavens!'

'They did experiments using telepathy and investigated mediums. My friend thought he was great. I'll give her a ring.'

Olivia's positive being gone, Charlotte's life went on. Henry had done worse than knock over a candle.

★

The month of May brought a lot of rain and strong wind. On an evening when the gusts could be heard outside and rain prattled against the windows in spurts, Charlotte sat in the drawing room, going through her art portfolio to see whether she could convince herself to take up illustrating again. The phone rang in the hallway.

A gruff voice said, 'I hear you have a ghost. I run the university Paranormal Society. I am a ghostbuster.'

'Do those really exist?'

'I'm interested in your case.'

'It is not a *case*. There are just some unexplained noises.'

'I'm on my way.'

'No!'

But he had hung up.

Charlotte, returning to her art folders, said to Hottie, 'A crazy man has just called.'

Not long later, there was an imperious knocking on the front door. The dog jerked up. The pounding was repeated, harder this time.

Charlotte switched out the lamp and cowered down below windowsill height, her breathing shallow.

A rapping at the window pane of the room was accompanied by, 'I know you're in there.'

She recognised the gruff voice. *What has Olivia done to me?* She steeled herself and went to open the front door, and he pushed himself into the hallway, so eager was this hunter of apparitions.

Now they found themselves facing each other under the globe lamp – he, looking like the devil, black hair plastered to his head, in a black roll-neck sweater and black trousers with an onyx ring on his index finger.

'Superb,' he said with glee, looking around. 'I'm Mervin.'

'Charlotte Gardiner.'

He pumped her hand up and down.

Inbred politeness compelled her to invite him into the drawing room. It was late, raining hard, and she was alone with this dark and wet-haired man who snuffled around the room rudely, lifting up a Chinese vase to check its make. 'Authentic Kang Shi.' He examined the photographs on the grand piano. There seemed no limit to his offensive behaviour. From a shelf he picked up a jade ring. 'A gift to your husband from his Chinese mistress? Did he tell you what it is?'

Charlotte was increasingly uncomfortable at his presence.

'It's a Chinese penis erection ring.'

'I am asking you to leave my house.'

'It's not your house; it's Henry's. And I did not come to see you. Where is the blackguard? Take me to him!'

'Certainly not at this time of night.'

'Ghosts are most active in the dark. You should have figured that out by now, Mrs Gardiner. It is most probably *you* who is making Henry act up.'

'Leave at once or I will call the police.' She strode into the hallway.

He shuffled after her. As they stood there, the fat lamp above them dimmed slowly. They both looked up to see the bulbs turn orange, and the last dots went out, leaving them in the pitch black.

'That's a start,' he said, but she pushed him out into the rain.

★

He returned, of course, the next day. She, in the meantime, had called Olivia who, satisfied her mother had taken her advice, added that Mervin was a Cambridge personality. He was a city councillor and author of several books. He was big in hypnosis and psychokinesis. The students were enthusiastic about him. 'He can help with Henry. You'll get to love him too.'

Charlotte almost apologised to Mervin when she took him upstairs to the banqueting hall. 'I'm not used to manners like yours.'

'You should be, living with Henry.'

From downstairs came a hollow bang. She jumped. 'What was that?'

'You didn't close the front door properly.'

'I did,' she muttered to herself.

'I heard that. Go downstairs, open the door and leave it open, and we'll see. Our first experiment.'

On her return, he said, 'Now before we visit Henry, let me make one thing clear. Charlotte, what we are going to do together in the next few weeks is serious and will become personal. You do have a ghost. I saw his head up at the window as I drove up.'

'I've seen it too.'

'Careful handling is important. Henry has to trust us as an entity. We don't want him to start rolling his severed head down the stairs, do we?'

She looked up with a quick smile and a faint blush, but a vehement shake of her head. *No.*

'Now, let's go for it. I'll define his presence first, and you stay at the door and make sure your cat doesn't walk in.'

'Hottie, *my dog*, is far too frightened to cross the threshold. Do you believe she can see things we don't?'

'A real dog could. Your type would be skinned and eaten as a meatball by the spectre floating around in here.'

'There is a spectre floating around in here?'

'Don't just repeat what I say. I know what I am talking about and you know zilch, you stupid woman.'

He had gone too far this time.

'Leave now,' she ordered him in a shaky voice. 'Before I show you more of my home, I need to know about you. Just because you run this society does not make it acceptable or legal.'

'I love the *or* between the two. Paranormal phenomena may be legal but unacceptable. Or for some, they are acceptable but illegal. The debate goes on.' Mervin slipped out of his loafers and, eyes closed, padded around the room, his hands like radar wheels in front of him. 'I can feel you, stinker,' he said in a low voice and came back to her. 'Your turn, barefoot. Feel him if you can – it's like a bouncy resistance – and tell me at once if you think it has become colder.'

'You did it in socks.'

'I don't want to get a cold on account of a ghost playing silly buggers.'

After making it into the middle of the room, she let her arms hang by her side. 'I haven't got the nerves to do this.' She capitulated. 'The mere thought of bouncing into a ghost…'

'I know, dear. I was just testing you. You have a heightened kinetic link with the ghost. He has had time to own you. To separate the two of you, you'll have to invest your psyche into another force, a living one ideally, before I can bust Henry, otherwise you'll get hurt.'

This made some sense to her.

'Let us try to find out whether we're dealing with a jealous ghost.'

She shrugged her shoulders at first but then told Mervin that Henry never manifested himself when Alexander was home.

'That's it.'

In a familiar gesture, Mervin took her hand, and like two small children they walked round the room.

'It's a splendid example of the Tudor era *you* own here,' he whispered into her ear, and his warm lips touched her lobe. Silence. Henry was not reacting. '*Your* fireplace is a marvel and the heraldic shields against the ceiling represent…' Still no reaction.

Suddenly the telephone rang downstairs. Marvin let go of her, ran to the door, sprinted along the corridor and rumbled down the stairs.

She hid her face in her hands. 'I hate this room. I hate this house. I want another life.'

He returned. 'I've got to go. Swinging lamps in Girton. By the way, the front door was closed. You didn't leave it open.'

'I did,' she said into the empty – or apparently empty – room.

★

178

The next morning, the manager of the domestic cleaning agency phoned to say that no more help would be placed in the Manor. When Charlotte asked why, the woman hesitated at first. Apparently the city council had called to warn them about a ghost. The cleaners were afraid to return.

'How could you?' Charlotte snapped when Mervin arrived two days later. She was in an apron and had just finished dusting the dining room.

'Domestic help gets in the way of ghostbusting.'

'How can I manage this house without any help?'

'That is of no importance. Take that apron off; we've got work to do.'

Indeed, he had come with two large hot water urns, which he filled with water in her bedroom en-suite and, unrolling the electric cable, placed them at either end of the banqueting hall. Then, he investigated the small windowless space off the room and she turned her head away because she was convinced that Henry functioned from there.

'While the water is heating, tell me what activities occurred since I was here last.'

'I heard scraping noises coming from this room.'

'When? How long did they last? How loud was it?'

'Honestly, I can't say.'

'Specifics, Charlotte. You note down every single thing which is out of the ordinary and the timing. Understood?'

How domineering this dark devil was, with his black olive eyes piercing hers while he told her off. There was something inexplicably attractive about it.

When the urns boiled, he took their tops off. Vapour curled out into the air, expanding. She dared ask, 'What is that for?'

'Ghosts hate hot water. Ever heard of a ghost warming things up?'

It did always go cold around Henry, didn't it?

'And what have we got here?' He bent near Henry's chair.

She too now noticed the chair leg marks in the dust. It had been moved forward. '*Voilà*! The scraping you heard. Henry needed more leg room.' Unexpectedly, he started to applaud. 'Congratulations, Charlotte, you have a poltergeist. Rare these days. Poltergeists in England belong to the Queen, did you know that? A poltergeist is a ghost that throws objects around the room,' he explained, seeing the expression on her face.

Mother had furniture removed from this room, Charlotte thought. *She knew there was a poltergeist!*

A pale hand slid over her shoulder. She stiffened her neck and opened her mouth in a scream.

'Charlotte, dear, don't be so jumpy. It's only me. I am here to protect you.'

She managed a hint of a smile while he propelled her to one of the old inlaid panel mirrors. Charlotte saw herself outlined in the wafting steam in her narrow pleat skirt and pale blue sweater.

He came to stand right behind her, his head showing over her shoulder. 'Just keep looking into the mirror. Look into the mirror, Charlotte. Keep looking into the mirror.'

She obeyed. Her figure seemed to start floating despite the pressure of his body against hers. She drifted towards a trance – a trance so intense that she felt lifted up by it. A simple touch of his hands on her hips brought on a rush of sensual exhilaration. In the steam-misted mirror, they seemed to be one being. And then his head was not mirrored any longer, and she gave a little shriek. He pulled her body against his pelvis, which was almost grinding into her, and she gasped. In the mirror she too had become invisible. *We're gone.*

He pivoted her to face him. Devoured by the sloe-dark eyes on her, she hovered spellbound as if she had no will left of her own, whilst her body turned putty-soft. Drowning in those glinting ink pools, she longed to be touched and caressed as if she were not herself any longer. She lusted for penetration as her female parts began to convulse and spasms ran up her thighs. Just before the black dots of fainting took over, he twisted her back to face the mirror, and they both showed as before.

When she came to, she was prostrate on the sofa in the drawing room. Hottie was next to her, and Mervin sat in the chair, watching her as if she were on a psychiatrist's couch.

'You passed out.'

No, she thought, *I must have just started the menopause. That's what it had to be, those vaginal cramps.*

Mervin left after ascertaining that she was all right. It was just as well because Alexander called from Hong Kong to say that work was going well. Why wouldn't it be? The jade ring came to her mind. She got up and spent the rest of the day cleaning the house.

★

181

The next day she was relieved not to hear from Mervin as she tried to rationalise the hold he seemed to have over her. Making herself a hot chocolate, she went to bed early. Propped against several pillows, she sketched tentatively on a pad.

The bedside light went out. In the blue dimness from the gap in the curtains, the dark figure of a ghost hovered. She slipped under the cover, pulling the duvet over her head. To her dread, the ghost pulled back the bedcovers and moved into bed with her. 'What?' A warm mouth sealed hers.

'I came to find out whether you had recovered from our last experiment.'

'You... You... You can't just, just do that.'

'Charlotte, are you aware that you had two strong orgasms in front of the mirror. You are an incredibly attractive and sexy woman.'

He had such power to confuse her, Charlotte thought. It was easier to just accept what he said and what he did.

What she saw him do now was pull the black roll-neck over his head to reveal a pleasing masculine torso. Then he took the rest of his clothes off and for some reason, she did not look away chastely. Naked, he put aside her drawing pad and pencil, exposed her on the sheet and took her nightie off, before joining her faithless body, which yearned to touch his as if her sanity depended on it.

Two hours later, amid crumpled sheets, the bedside lamp on the floor and sweat beads on her forehead, she knew what an orgasm was. Never would she get enough of those.

'Love me?' he asked when he was dressed again and bent over her spent being to kiss her brow.

'Henry did not show jealousy, did he?' she called after him as he left her bedroom.

Sunday morning, nibbling at a slice of toast with thick-cut marmalade, she knew that she had fallen madly in love with the delectable black devil. Any faults or imperfection of his she could take in her stride.

When Olivia called to find out how it was going with the ghostbuster, Charlotte only admitted that he had promised to come and have a look.

'A look?'

'A feel, a whatever he does with the ghosts.'

'I see. Good luck, Mum.'

At least Charlotte had not given away that Mum was the happiest, most despicable woman in the county.

★

Charlotte hardly recognised herself in the altered life of chaos that followed. Mervin had taken over, calling it 'our life together'. 'Hello, Henry the Eighth!' he greeted the ghost loudly on arrival.

Alexander had rung again and she felt as if she were talking to a creature from another planet.

Mervin turned down her suggestion of repeating the steamed-up mirror experience, the unreal moment when her brain, her whole being had changed.

'Tricks only work with ghosts once. They wisen up.'

He decided to invite a group of his students for a nocturnal ghost hunt. Gear was set up in the banqueting hall. She had to provide piles of sandwiches for the five students who arrived with their *ghost box* on an adapted supermarket trolley. It was designed and built by Cambridge engineering students. With pride, they showed it off; it could record minute temperature drops, take infrared pictures in the pitch-dark, and register high frequency sounds beyond human hearing. She gave it due praise and Mervin seemed pleased that she was getting on with *his* youngsters.

Coming into the drawing room, he dusted his hands. 'That's it.' He locked the door.

'Aren't you staying up with them?'

'No. They're sitting up there in the corners of the room. I want them to be really scared. I can't vouch for the state of your bathroom tomorrow morning.'

'Maybe nothing will happen tonight.'

'Don't be so sure. I might have fixed a few things. At midnight you might hear yelling and begging us to let them go home. Be prepared. It's good for them.'

When she finished laughing, Mervin asked her to marry him.

She objected that she already was, and he glanced at a photograph of Alexander. 'Divorce him.'

She pointed out she hadn't even said yes to his proposal, but he said, 'You will.'

'Only if I can live in the centre of town in a small practical house.'

'Done.'

★

A wish come true. Charlotte was in an estate agent's office looking at pictures of small properties on a screen. Hottie was on her lap. She made the agent stop at one which had a sage-green door over which trailed wisteria. It had two bedrooms, two bathrooms, many original features and a charming south-facing garden. It was vacant and chain-free. 'That one, don't you think, Hottie?'

When she explained that the funds would come from selling Tudor Manor, which she owned and which he was welcome to sell for her, he excused himself. She saw him confer with two other men, one of whom tapped his temple with a finger. The agent came back to her and tried to talk her out of it, calling it madness. Charlotte was at a loss.

The next day, Mervin came with her. 'Don't you want the commission, you fool?' is all he said, to make the agents eagerly come up with papers to sign. The Manor could fetch as much as four million pounds, while the new house cost only four hundred and fifty thousand.

That evening, Alexander called and, to avoid speaking, Charlotte claimed to have a chest cold. He would be back in two weeks.

When she had finally found sleep, she was awoken by a sound like a wooden ball dropping to the floor and rolling across it. 'I don't care any more.'

Mervin introduced Charlotte to a lawyer friend who agreed to handle her divorce, quickly and efficiently. Leaving the office, she barely noticed knocking over the rubber plant; she was walking on air.

Mervin booked her into a three-star hotel in town and arranged for her personal items to be packed up and put into storage. On her last night in the Manor, on her way up to bed, the pink of human flesh glowed on Henry's staircase and a plaintive moan trailed away. The horrific appearance made her pee herself a little. Oh God, she resented this house!

Mervin was obviously well connected in town. The banns were already published despite the fact that she wasn't divorced yet. Mervin booked the Town Hall for their civil marriage in thirty days' time – a realistic guess in an uncontested divorce.

'Alexander might well contest,' she fretted.

'How can he? Abandonment, cruelty, unsuitable living conditions, psychological harm, unfaithfulness. I know the judge. Don't forget to bring me the jade ring.'

Alexander seemed now to be just a character in a book, a novel about a woman called Charlotte. Her new story would start when she closed the book.

The one thought which brought her down from the cloud was her children. How would they take it? Could they get on with Mervin? How would they judge her? Mervin was adamant that they only be told after the ceremony.

It was hard to go shopping for a wedding outfit, the right hat, hard to think of flowers. It would be a July wedding – roses, delphiniums and gerberas. How perfect would it be to do all this with Olivia?

When Charlotte dropped into the estate agent to find out how things were going, she was told that they had shown Tudor Manor to about twenty interested partners, but now had found a firm purchaser. The little house with the wisteria, however, had unfortunately been withdrawn from the market, and her search would have to begin anew.

★

The feared day of Alexander's return turned out rather different from what she had expected. He had received her divorce petition. He stated that he would sign it if he got half of the sale price of the Manor as stipulated in their marriage contract. He would reside in London and go from there. He left it to her to explain it to their children.

'Accept his condition,' suggested Mervin. 'It's his price for setting you free.'

It was becoming increasingly difficult to keep Olivia's questions at bay and find excuses not to see her. The day of the wedding eventually came, and it rained hard. They joked that the day they had met, it had rained just as much. Mervin had provided the two witnesses: one a member of the International Fund for Ghost Protection, of which Mervin was trustee, and the other his ex-wife, Philippa.

'How insensitive of you, Mervin.'

'Look me in the eyes, my darling. She is part of the past, which we both have let go. Can you feel *what has been* vanish from us? Once my ring is on your finger and we have signed the registry book, I'll take you under my wing. Together we will fly into a golden future.'

As in a dream she signed the official book, and voluptuous organ music swirled about her as she swept out of the registry office on the arm of her new husband.

On the steps outside the Town Hall, he pulled her to him and kissed her long and hard.

There was isolated clapping from bystanders. One shouted, 'Where are you going on honeymoon, Mervin?'

Mervin revealed with pride in his voice, 'I'm taking my new wife to Venice.'

Behind them, Philippa sniggered. 'He took me to Torremolinos and refused to take his black roll-neck off going swimming.'

Charlotte turned and smiled sweetly at Mervin's ex-wife.

Later that day, Charlotte packed a bag with clothes for Venice. Mervin came to pick her up in a taxi for the airport and they dropped Hottie at her kennel on the way.

★

Venice was a dream city hovering between sky and water, the way Turner had painted it. The honeymoon bed had gold cherubs painted on it. In a restaurant after the zabaglione, Mervin made her sign two official-looking documents, both to do with ensuring a legally unencumbered future for them. After that, they floated on the canal while the lights came on in the tall ornate palazzos, shimmering pools in the dark canal through which the carved bow of their gondola was being rowed. Charlotte was in heaven.

On return to Stansted the dream continued. When the brisk air hit her face outside the airport, a brand-new silver Audi soft-top was standing there, the left door held open for her by the estate agent.

Before Mervin drove off, he turned to her. 'Do you think we're going to your hotel?'

She waited, smiling to herself knowingly.

'I'll take us to our home.'

She threw her arms around his neck and whispered into his neck. 'Oh, how I love you, love you, love you.'

He drove off and her eyes were on his strong kind profile.

When he slowed down and they came off the motorway, she realised they were on the way to Tudor Manor. He drove through the gates and onto the forecourt, where he stopped with a decisive foot on the brake which made pebbles fly.

'Here we are. Just because you fell in love with me does not mean that you have to give up Tudor Manor. I have bought it, using money from the International Fund for Ghost Protection. After Alexander took his cut, you were left with two million for the house and, as your new husband, I now own half of that. The last million you have just signed over to the Fund, which is generous of you. Tudor Manor is *the* perfect setting for ghost hunts and paranormal experiments. The Fund will make it their headquarters, and I intend to run courses and attract interest from all over the world.'

She remained silent, daring to glance at the upper windows.

'I know how much you will enjoy helping me with all that.'

In a thin voice she said, 'Will I? I feel a little dizzy in my head. Have you hypnotised me, darling Mervin?'

WITH A BIT OF LUCK

Lifted from the dense foggy mass of my dreams, I wake to realise with pleasure that today has the potential to be the best day ever; one which will lead me into a more exciting life.

I reach for my iPhone – not to check it, more for its comfortable existence alongside me. The device slowly warms in my palm, which is calloused from clay pigeon shooting. I bought this small electronic gadget with my savings from serving at tables in the Alpenblick. It boasted *gorilla glass*, but a hairline crack has, from some carelessness of mine, zigzagged its way across the screen, and I would not like to test its waterproofness. At the time I got it, it seemed to offer a magic vision into everything that went on in the world: a spyhole in the door of my dark enclosed existence.

Frustratingly, there is no reception where I live. Behind us is the sheer north side of the majestic Wieselhorn, and in front the ground falls steeply down to the first dwellings of Schoendorf. About three kilometres down that winding road gets me into mobile phone catchment area. It is not good.

Nor is the fact that I still live with my parents and my young cousin, Tina, whom we call Tintin because that's how she named herself. A further encumbrance is the family chalet. This is not the type with a wide wrap-around terrace, many rooms, sauna and Jacuzzi in a cool place like Verbier or Gstaad. It is the far-from-everywhere type, where the snowplough does not get to, where cars have to be left on the parking plateau down the hill. It is stomping up through thick snow and returning the next day to find a heaped meringue under which is our van, old and rusty.

About one hundred years ago, my grandfather built the chalet, small and adequate for a rustic life. The most shameful thing about it is not the creaking and groaning of the old wood, but the ground floor being the stable for the goats the family used to have.

And if that's not the worst, then there are the three long and skinny bedrooms and the bathroom, actually a tiny shower room next to the kitchen. The walls are made of pinewood planks. If I fart in my room, the picture lifts off the wall in my parents'. All the pictures on the walls are of Swiss mountains. From my bed, I am now looking at a painting of the Wieselhorn hanging over the chest. I can see it more realistically sitting on the loo, looking out of the tiny window. An unspoken law stipulates that all of these old-fashioned horrors have to remain in place. In the chest are my clothes, crumpled because my two air rifles have to be hidden amongst them to prevent Tina from accidentally hurting herself or someone else.

Today, Tuesday the third of April, cloudy but mild, all this can change for the better, and for all of us. I stretch extravagantly in the fresh scented cotton sheets which slightly grate the skin. Mother washes on Monday, and yesterday the sun shone. The duvet is light and puffy from Swiss goose feathers.

While the sheets were flapping and pulling on the line in our meadow, Uncle Markus bowled up and drank Dad's kirsch. Mother looked surprisingly well turned out for her age; I think she even put on make-up. Geranium lips parted as she soaked in Markus's words.

The big project that has been worked towards for months will finally be decided on today during a meeting between Markus and the manager of the Astra hotel chain, which has just bought the Alpenblick and is accepting offers from would-be franchisees. This will happen at precisely ten thirty this morning. If an agreement can be reached, the thirty-nine-bedroom hotel will become part of the Astra chain, and the two brothers, Dad and Markus, will part-own and run the franchise. The chain has four other hotels in Switzerland and one in Austria. There are several would-be purchasers of the franchise as the opportunity has attracted much interest. What we have in our favour, Markus told us, is the family-run style, the solid Swiss label, the local knowledge. Markus would be the boss from his home in Lausanne, while Dad would do the day-to-day management and customer contact. Is he not able to tell tales about the area until the cows come home? Mother would oversee the housekeeping and kitchen and do the buying and budgeting. And I could move between table-serving and bar duties. Markus even threw into the plan for me to offer clay pigeon shooting to guests, and Mother wild flower pressing. Come on. We must get this. Aren't we Zellweggers of genuine alpine stock?

I should get out of bed; the zebra stripes from the shutters have started to slice my duvet. Mother and Dad have finished clomping around their room and rumbled down the creaking stairs. Tintin's feet pad past my door. The pipes start to moan, so the bathroom is not free yet.

This is an excuse to linger in bed longer in my shooting team T-shirt and pyjama bottoms. Soon I might not be wearing a checked short-sleeved shirt and cow-milking-style jeans, but a smart barman's outfit provided by Astra. Soon I might not sleep in this room which has taken on the faintly acrid odour of my masturbations, sucked up by the soft wood planks.

We will move into the Alpenblick Hotel and occupy the top floor with a carpeted corridor and, along the wall, the stuffed stagheads and horns banned from the sight of environmentally sensitive tourists. I was up there once, smoking a fag with the cook who wanted to show me his automatic rifle and bore me to death with stories about his military service: large sunny rooms, solid walls, two bathrooms for the four of us, assuming Tintin stays on – a comfortable arrangement for busy Markus. On that top floor there is also a large room with sofas, a day-room where Larissa and I will make love on the bearskin in front of the wood-burning stove.

Now I come to think of it, why should Markus be the boss? Just because he is seven years older and used to pushing people around? Dad is remarkable in his way, dependable certainly. He behaves towards me as a responsible father and towards Mother as a decent husband. Admittedly, he lacks the impulses of love and fondness, but they call him an honest man in the village and that is quite something.

Mother tries to explain Markus's selfishness as a result of his hidden unhappiness. Any old excuse. The story goes that Markus and Aunt Rose could not have children for years, or rather she couldn't for some *women-whispering-to-each-other* reason. Then Mother, much the youngest, had me. She invited Rose, to show me off probably and ask her to be godmother. Aunt Rose just fainted at the sight of me and had to be loaded onto the kitchen door and carried down into the village to go to the hospital in Grachen. It is still talked about in the village. Once Rose recovered, Markus apparently relented and they adopted. The baby girl came with the name Larissa. Larissa: that name I could say over and over. Larissa. She brought happiness to her adoptive parents because Rose got pregnant when Larissa was three. There was some *women-whispering-to-each-other* disaster at birth. Rose died. The baby lived and turned into Tintin, who came to live with us.

When one meets Tintin, one thinks she is just a fifteen-year-old girl: brown hair, green/grey whatever eyes, tall like uncle Markus, and so thin and gangly her ribs are countable under the sweaters she wears. If she does not concentrate, she walks like a crane fly which has lost one or two legs. It's when she speaks that one notices her little shakes of the head like electric shocks, and she talks rubbish. She likes to touch people, and I must remember not to sit on the sofa when she is around. She joins me and then lets herself fall sideways until her head and shoulders land on my knees. Reaching for my hand, she places it on her hair, expecting me to stroke her head.

She often waits for me, sitting on the stairs playing cat's cradle, which is for a ten-year-old. I don't dislike her. She goes straight to your heart, Mum thinks. For me, her being here means that Larissa, her adopted sister, visits from time to time, but less since Markus has moved out of the Swiss-German region to the flatlands of Lausanne. He makes money as a property investor and Larissa, who is my age almost exactly, was at a private school where they teach geometry and English. Markus has plans for her. She has been sent to London for a media course and then, no doubt, an English lord is on the cards.

There are no good schools anywhere near me and even if there were, I would not have been able to get to them regularly. Our village school stops at sixteen because the kids don't fit into the seats any longer, so for the last year I have been working in the Alpenblick. None of my schoolmates has gone on with education; they won't be anyone important either, just ski instructors in the winter and cowherds in the summer. Some may make it to tourist guide. Nowadays, parents go to work and live where there are schools with prospects for their kids.

Larissa is, of course, superior to me: big time nowadays. Everyone has forgotten that her natural mother gave her up. I remember when she forced me to go with the bus all the way to Grachen to have her ears pierced because she had bought gold-lookalike half-moon earrings with fake diamond stars in them. Markus had forbidden it, and she seemed almost happy when I did not want her to do it at first. She had lost her two mothers to rebel against.

On the way back, she moaned and whined about the pain and took one moon out to dab the blood drops, while I was made to hold the jewel which had hurt her and noticed the black gunge under my fingernails. Ashamed, I tried to scrape it from under the nail with the tip of the moon, when the bus jolted us and I dropped the earring, which slithered down into a crack in the floor. For a couple of days she walked around with grass stalks stuck in her ears, to prevent the holes growing together, and nobody said anything. I was an idiot then.

I follow her on Facebook. She is clearly changing character in England or maybe she is unhappy. Childish groups, heads together, silly hats, grimaces, stupid posts. After the marathon, all hugging, a guy pouring a bottle of Evian over Larissa's head. Pathetic. That bloke is the athletic blond type with cropped hair and gelled quiff. Probably pale blue eyes; it's hard to see on my iPhone. He appears in most of her posts, often wearing a light green pullover. He is definitely English; in profile, his top lip sticks out in a triangle. A few days ago, Larissa was in shorts, showing her good legs, lazing on grass with Quiff in a park with a photoshopped arrow pointing to Buckingham Palace in the background. She wrote about spring and hopscotching, which must mean leapfrogging. She did comment on my birthday selfie update. *Congrats, Lukas. Well done. 18!*

Now I hear irregular padding and rustles past my door, followed by dull thuds. Tintin is going down the stairs on her bum. Mother, who is so patient with her, does not like this. 'You are not an animal,' she says every time.

Just one more indulgence, dreaming up Larissa, and then I get up: Larissa's smile, her eyes before her lips rise up, the straight dark blond hair surrounding her small smooth-skinned face, the slightly rounded forehead, the chocolate eyes on me. Thinking of her is like the sun rising over the mountain, creeping red over the snow towards me and enfolding me in its warmth.

Having successfully crept unseen through the kitchen to the bathroom, I finally emerge presentable, hair washed and conditioned, in the living room where coffee, bread and cheese have been cleared away and the table-runner laid out. The radio, still Grandfather's model, babbles nonsense in Italian.

'That radio gets on my nerves.' Dad switches it off.

'No!' cries Tintin. 'I want the music.'

'It's just chatter.'

'Music will come.'

Mother paces around the living room. 'It's a quarter past ten, and I can hardly breathe from nerves. Imagine if it works and Astra accepts our offer. Imagine!'

'Yes, Mother. I have no problem with that. We'll finally move out of this place and down into the village where the others live. We'll be more than most, owning and running a hotel and meeting people from other countries.'

'Never think you're more than anyone else, Lukas. The moment you do, you're less than them.'

'I'll have to wear suits,' Dad says, as ever following his own train of thought.

198

'Now you mention it, I'll have to buy clothes, dresses, blouses. Can I do that job? Paul, tell me honestly.' Mother stops walking around and places both hands on the table before slumping sideways into a dining chair.

'You've been running the grocery store in the village for years. You can do this.'

Tintin switches the radio on again, and Dad is about to turn it off but Mother says, 'Let her. She might be nervous about a change.'

Mother is right; I know how sensitive Tintin is to tension.

'Tintin, you will be able to listen to radio music all day long down in the kitchen, helping the cook with the vegetables,' Mother says soothingly, and I learn that a plan is in place for Tintin.

Tintin hurries over to the radio and switches it off. Unheard of. Many things will change.

It is now half past ten. The meeting has begun. I check my phone despite myself. Soon this device will be connected.

'Paul, how long do you think the meeting will last? Has Markus promised to telephone us with the news?'

The strain fills the room. I go into the kitchen for some orange juice as I missed breakfast. In the fridge door, two fat-bodied champagne bottles press against the plastic shelf. Dad clearly anticipates success. He must know exactly what the outcome is going to be, surely.

When Larissa comes to visit, alone, I will be behind the bar, juggling bottles, dressed in a tuxedo and surrounded by glittering glasses and large mirrors. 'What may I serve you?' I will ask her in English, which I am practising.

If we do get to run the Alpenblick, then I will learn English in my spare time. Then it will be worth it. *Please let this happen.*

The telephone on the side-table is ringing. Mother is now standing, her wedding band hand over her mouth.

'OK,' says Dad into the receiver, irritatingly giving nothing away as he listens and then puts the receiver back into its holder.

'What did he say? Tell us, for God's sake.'

'OK. The meeting is over, and Markus is on his way up. Ah, and he is bringing along someone, a surprise.'

We run outside onto the narrow, carved balcony. I know that it is Larissa – from the tone of Dad's voice or the quick flick of the eyes he gave me when he hung up. We stare down the hill, a sight in which I know every rock and plant. Remaining snow-cushions lie in the meadows though much has melted in the mildness of this early April day.

'Look!' Mother points. 'There he is.'

We see Markus's car slowly driving up the lazy curve in the road before he is hidden again. Dad pulls Mother towards his shoulder, tucking her against him, and kisses the crown of her head.

The car is visible again on the parking plateau. The passenger door opens. Legs are visible, those of a young woman now getting out of the car. She lifts up her head and I feel the beam of her look straight at me. Larissa! It is Larissa.

Swiss radio news, midday bulletin:

At a quarter past eleven today, an avalanche swept down the north side of the Wieselhorn. It destroyed an isolated chalet and killed the family of four who lived there. Their relations, Markus Zellwegger and his daughter, Larissa, witnessed the disaster from below. It was the largest recorded mass of snow ever to come down the mountain. Some experts think it was most probably triggered by a rock fall. The mild weather could also have played a part.

HERDING GOATS

'It's paradise.' Angela lifted the chilled champagne sangria to her sun-warmed lips. In front of her was the Atlantic Ocean, shouldering wave after wave onto a dream beach that stretched from one turn of the head to the other. Further along stood magnificent cliffs in the red of an old-fashioned flowerpot, and behind her was a protected marshland with the flamingos they had come to see on their walk.

She put the glass down to pull a canvas hat out of her bag; the sun was beating down, and it was only March. 'They say the Algarve has over three hundred days of sun a year. It could be the Caribbean, the way it feels. Exotic and palm tree-y.'

One was more inclined to smile in warm climates: *a sunny smile*. Phil's faintly tanned face looked younger. His eyes had lost that strain from gazing into a computer screen at work, even only three days a week; he was now semi-retired.

'There are thirty golf courses in the Algarve, ten of which are rated in the top one hundred in Europe.'

'I bet we would make friends here. One is so much

more relaxed in a T-shirt and sandals.'

'Would we have the courage to come and live here? If we sold our house in England, used Laura's address for mail? You *are* practically retired.'

'Not permanently. It would complicate taxes and legalities.'

'Just a teeny-weensy house with a terrace for holidays then. A bit of garden.'

'And the kids?'

'A garden big enough to build a pool. Imagine the grandchildren.'

Phil had clearly imagined it at that moment, because on the way back to the hotel he parked the car in Vilamoura. Hand in hand, they eagerly sought the pictures and prices in estate agents' windows.

At the third, a young Portuguese man came out through the door, held open by a wedge, and gave them a friendly dark-eyed nod. His name was Miguel and he was eager to show them properties.

Phil flashed Angela an impish look and followed Miguel into the agency. *Why not? Nobody knew them. They did not really mean it – only dreaming.*

It had to be the 'golf without thermal underwear' that made Phil take the offered seat so eagerly.

Miguel interlaced his fingers, elbows on the glass desk. 'I imagine you are looking for a holiday home, freestanding rather than a condominium, three bedrooms with a small garden, with the potential for a pool, in the range of two hundred and seventy-five to three hundred and twenty-five thousand euros.' *That had to be the package sold to inexperienced English sun-seekers.*

'More or less. Can you show us some properties?' Angela wriggled further forward in the metal chair.

To start with, Miguel showed them some crackers on the golf courses and with marble terraces before he brought them back to his glass table. 'In your price range, it would have to be further out – a *casa do campo*.'

The visit ended with an agreement to be driven the following day to a perfect jewel of a country home, a private property with stunning views, the nearest golf course only twenty kilometres in a straight line, and the price only two hundred and ninety-five thousand euros. The owners, from Sweden, had to go home, sadly.

That evening, most uncharacteristically, the excited Heatheringtons were loud and boisterous in the hotel bar.

'We're still in good shape, aren't we?' Phil pulled up his trousers at the belt. 'All right, a bit of a belly, never remember where I put things, and a mouth full of crowns, but–'

'You can still pride yourself on a full head of hair. And neither of us has arthritis yet.' Phil designed the plunge pool in his head and she would garden, oh how she would garden, with plants which did not grow in Hoddesdon.

The next morning, Miguel drove them out of Vilamoura in the agency's sleek Mercedes V8 on gently winding roads up towards the hills. 'It always seems far the first time.'

Before they turned up a secondary, untarmacked road, Miguel pointed. 'Bus stop, only four kilometres from the property. An EVA bus brings you right into Vilamoura centre.'

Jolting up those long four kilometres, they passed a hamlet with a handful of houses. 'An English couple has bought in here. Very nice people.'

Eventually they came to the property, a stone wall with a gap in it – the entrance to the *casa*.

Rubbing stiffness from her hip, Angela appreciated the whitewashed single-floor property with deep-set windows behind wrought-iron bars. On the old Roman-tiled roof, joy oh joy, stood an ornate chimney with the lace-like topping she had seen in pictures.

'It is typical to the Algarve,' explained Miguel. 'This one is especially good, large and still has the lace holes and the hat above it. The wall around your property is made by boulders which peasants carried from the fields.'

Miguel unlocked the blue front door. They stepped into a spacious tiled living area with a substantial fireplace, wooden beams, and an arch giving into a good-sized dining room.

'Lovely,' escaped from her mouth.

Phil twisted to look up into the chimney. The built-in kitchen was not too disastrous in style; the Swedish people had done a good renovating job.

'You will want to put your own stamp on it.'

Angela nodded vigorously.

In the short corridor leading to the bedrooms was a darling alcove in which she imagined flowers in a bowl on a console table. In the three bedrooms, one larger, all had rustic painted furniture. The en-suite shower would be a first project, but the family bathroom had lovely tiles and with a new bathtub… Oh, she liked the house;

it had good vibes. How could all this cost no more than a two-bedroom house in Hoddesdon?

While Miguel showed Phil the electricity box, she stood in the neglected garden, arms spread out, taking it all in: the view over rock-scattered meadows, the trees further down and, way in the distance, the straight blue line of the sea. She had forgotten what quiet meant. There was no traffic noise, no sound of human activity; there was only undisturbed nature and the cheerful chirping of sparrows.

And then to her delight she noticed a flock of goats coming over the slant of a hill, large brown-speckled bodies with long twirled horns. The herding dog was taking it easy, and then the goatherd appeared with a biblical stick. 'Phil, come and see this!'

*

In the evening, Angela and Phil sat on the balcony of their hotel room with a bottle of red wine. The sea had a silver glittery surface, rendered magical by an almost full moon. Angela sat in silence, enchanted, her hands in her lap.

'We're going to do this, aren't we?' Phil broke the silence.

'Can we? Can we really? It will eat up most of our savings.'

'We only live once – and longer if we come here in the winter.' He raised his wine glass.

'It's complete folly but, yes, I agree.' They toasted. 'The last time I said yes to you was when we got engaged. That was folly too but look, it has worked out.'

Getting out of his chair, Phil came over and kissed her.

On their Ryanair flight back, they sat snuggled like newly-weds. A lot of happy plotting was going on behind their sun-kissed foreheads. Only when the captain announced his descent did the realisation of having to tell their son and daughter cloud their euphoria.

In Stansted it was raining and everything had the colour grey, as if the light had been switched out. Once in their cold house, they checked the e-mails and telephone messages, one of which was from Kelvin, their son. He asked to come round to borrow the hammer drill. There was also one from Laura, their married daughter: Let me know when you are back safely.

'I hope they will see this the way we do,' Angela said while unpacking her summer clothes.

*

'What a stupid idea, Mum,' Kelvin pronounced when Phil was in the garage getting the box with the drill. 'You're frankly too old to buy a doer-up in a country where you don't speak the language, a house far from anything. Imagine the legal hassle. The euro could gain in strength and then what?'

'It's done up; it just needs improving. Do you want to see the pictures?'

When Phil came in with the drill, he said, 'Lovely, isn't it?'

She hooded her eyes and shook her head.

'Dad, what are you two going to do all day sitting in that place?'

'We'll keep your mum's car there. There are English neighbours, a bus, and I will play golf while Mum gardens. Besides, we have thought about you and Laura. It's perfect for grandchildren.'

'And when would I go there?' Kelvin asked. 'I'm not retired, have little holiday and don't want to spend it on a goat farm. Laura will feel the same.'

'Don't tell her please. We will.'

'We haven't signed on the dotted line yet,' ended the conversation and Kelvin went away with the drill.

Laura was kinder to them. 'Look,' she said, 'if that is what will make you happy, why not do it? You only live once.'

'Just what we said. Thank you, Laura.'

'You will come with the children during holidays, won't you? What they need is fresh air and sunshine.'

★

Ten days later, Angela and Phil flew back to Faro to sign the promissory contract, to open a local bank account and hopefully to have another look at their casa.

Walking with Miguel to the lawyer's office, Angela and Phil felt instantly rejuvenated under the stark blue Algarvean sky.

When Jasmine Cardoso, the lawyer, came into the meeting room, Angela's jaw dropped. This young woman, who couldn't possibly be a lawyer, was a beautiful dark-eyed creature with long straight ebony hair down her back. Angela checked Phil, who was clearly transported into a world of supermodels, where this sexy feline he had hired would do things other than conveyancing.

Jasmine tossed hair over one of her shoulders and took a seat. 'I have drawn up the contract in Portuguese and English.' Thank God, she talked normally, rather dryly.

Business concluded, outside again they had to don their sunglasses. They had signed the contract, made a ten per cent down payment, and were legally committed to buying the house. It would be stamped and notarised in a couple of hours.

Back in the estate agent's, they were made to wait as the papers were not finished. A poster of a maturely aged couple gambolling hand in hand on a beach hung on the wall. It was taken just before sunset. *Algarve – O segredo mais famoso.*

'What do you think that means? The O is funny. And why do we have to wait?'

'Remember, the pace is slower here.'

They killed time by finding a name for the casa and came up with silly names like PhilAng, Angphil. Angela suggested La Cicada.

'Did we hear any cicadas?'

'Perhaps during the summer months? And anyway it might be O Cicado.' They laughed.

Finally, Jasmine appeared. Phil jumped out of his slouch in the sofa. Jasmine addressed and dealt only with him. When the necessary was done, Miguel joined them.

'Welcome to the Algarve, Mr and Mrs Heatherington.' He suggested they all go to the café.

In the road, Phil had a spring in his step, keeping up with the agile-bodied Jasmine, while Miguel told Angela that they had done the right thing by going back in time to when things were 'slow, easy, nice.'

'Simpler,' she said. 'All this electronic dependency – where will it lead?'

Sitting in the corner café, Phil, next to Jasmine, seemed in another world in which spellbinding words were offered to him from full natural lips. He even performed movements with his arm Angela had never seen before. In the tempered sunlight under the parasol, Jasmine's skin had the sheen of a fresh acorn.

What could Phil have come up with to make Jasmine laugh out loud? Leaning back in her seat, Jasmine put her arm around his shoulder collegiately – a disguise for *I've made you mine.*

★

Back in Stansted, Angela noticed with satisfaction that Phil had returned to being Phil. In the Algarve, she would not have to watch out for heat rash but for testosterone. Their Hoddesdon life resumed, but Angela bought a Mediterranean-style cookery book and laid out olives and goat cheese for nibbles. Phil spent time Google-Earthing, finding the shortest way to the golf course.

One day, an e-mail from Miguel popped up. They were ready to complete. Phil and Angela looked at each other. This was for real.

211

Unfortunately, Laura's mother-in-law had just died, and with the funeral arrangements and probate, Angela had committed herself to looking after the babies. She could not get out of it. All Phil had to cancel was his dental appointment, so they decided that he would go on his own to start with. He would drive the VW to Plymouth, take the ferry to Santander, and then drive down the length of Portugal. It would take him three days. He would finalise on the house, get it clean and do some sorting out in preparation for her arrival.

They booked Ryanair for Angela six days after his departure. Actually, she was glad not to have to do this long trip in the small car. If only the image of the gorgeous lawyer did not *push* itself into her mind – Jasmine and Phil. Alone.

'Will there be a lot more to do with the lawyers?'

He thought it most unlikely. Now it was only the bank and the estate agent.

She helped him pack up the VW. She had insisted on new sheets, and then brought an armload of her clothes on hangers. And, a little sheepish-looking, came from the house with a washing basket full of kitchen appliances.

'They have shops there,' said Phil, 'and civilisation.'

'But not what I'm used to.' She silenced him with a kiss, deciding not to bring out the second washing basket she had prepared. Phil drove off.

She called Laura to discuss the babysitting rota.

'It's a long drive for Dad,' said Laura. 'He is not the youngest any more.'

★

212

Phil phoned when he came off the ferry, and again when he was in Vilamoura, and the next day, saying, 'I'm with Miguel. Almost finished. Need to go and check the house and make an inventory. Will be given our keys tomorrow.'

'Is Jasmine helpful with all this?'

'There is no Jasmine in all this.'

If only she could believe him one hundred per cent.

Three days later, Laura drove her to the airport with the strapped-in children crying in their seats.

'Grizzly today,' Laura described them. Angela had not heard from Phil since before the inventory checking.

'Don't worry. He's lost his mobile probably, or is frantically preparing for your arrival.'

*

When Angela came through *Nada a Declarar* with her rolling case, Phil was not waiting for her. She sat on a textured metal bench and waited, one hour and then two, trying his mobile at intervals, getting into a muddle with prefixes and zeros. He did not answer. Angela called her son, who *did* answer. He promised to call Dad and, yes, let her know at once.

He did. 'Can't get Dad.'

'What am I to do now?' she asked in panic, and Kelvin told her to go to the estate agent.

'How?'

'In a taxi, Mum.'

Miguel was with a client. She chose to wait but was not offered coffee or tea. When Miguel was finally free, and she told him, he brushed the problem away. 'There is no signal in your new house.'

'Why didn't you tell us this before?'

'You and your husband wanted the simpler life.'

A little unwillingly, he agreed to drive her all the way to the property, making it clear that the agency was no longer responsible after the handing over of keys.

On the journey she noticed huge concrete pylons defaced with graffiti, gardens full of rusting metal, abandoned building sites. A horde of roaring motorcyclists overtook them, which provoked Miguel to accelerate in competition.

'Don't worry about your husband.' He had noticed her wringing her hands. 'Perhaps he had a flat tyre on his way to the airport.'

All she could think was when the brochure said *private property*, it meant *remote property*. Had Phil thanked Jasmine profusely for the work she had done?

They reached the house and Miguel parked on the grass verge.

Angela saw the VW in front and gulped. 'Please don't drive off until I know he is home.'

'Phil!' she shouted at the house. Getting closer, she saw that the blue door was closed, not just with a key but a padlock, and so was the terrace door once she had stumbled round to it. 'Phil!' she tried again, checking the windows, all of which were securely shuttered behind their iron bars. Arms hanging limply, she returned to Miguel, who had taken her rolling case from his boot. It stood forlornly on the gravel. There was something terribly wrong here. Phil clearly was not in the house.

The VW was locked, and her clothes and kitchen utensils no longer in it.

Miguel threw his cigarette stump to the ground and stepped on it. In his opinion, the padlocks must have been put there by Phil to protect the house in its remote location.

As for the presence of the car, his explanation was that Phil couldn't start it to fetch her from the airport and had set out on foot. That had to be it. And with no mobile phone reception.

Angela shouted 'Phil!' again; all she heard were sparrows. Now Miguel guessed that someone had come to pick up Phil, and she resented him for it. It made her feel completely helpless and abandoned.

Miguel had to get back. Vehemently, she begged him to call a number the minute he got there. She wrote it on the back of her boarding pass. 'My son, Kelvin. Tell him I'm in front of the house waiting for Dad, who did not pick me up at the airport.'

He promised, his hand on his trendy shirt, got into the car, changed his mind and came out again to open the trunk and take out a black rug, which he offered her. The noise of his car receded slowly. She and the case stood in the middle of the road.

Phil certainly had not touched the garden in the three days they had owned the house. After peeing behind a bush, she installed herself on the low wall. Further along, in the rough and sparsely grassed pasturage, were the long-horned goats. The dog was near the goatherd, an immobile figure wearing a cap with a long visor. She wrapped herself in the blanket.

Evening fell, and the light around her changed. Her legs felt chill and shivers ran up over her whole body. Where was Phil? She pulled the rug over her head and held it tight around her neck. Garden furniture clearly was not on the inventory.

The sun started to set, sliding down rather rapidly, so much closer to the equator.

'For God's sake, Phil.' It would not hurt either if Miguel returned to check on her.

In the dark under a canopy of stars, wearing everything of use from her case, under the rug, she sat hunched in her garden.

*

Early the next day, Angela tumbled into the estate agent's.

'Oh,' said Miguel. 'You found each other.'

Her grimly set face caused him to hesitate and make a hand gesture to ward her off.

'I sat outside the house until early morning. Here, your rug. It probably saved my life.'

'*Caramba*! I am sorry for you but you cannot blame the agency for this.'

'What did my son say?'

'I called three times. Only a recording.'

'Where is Jasmine?'

'I don't understand.'

'Where is she?'

'She is away. There was a death in the family.'

'I need to go to a hotel, simple, medium priced, near here. Can you at least help me with that?'

He now took in her dishevelled figure, the state of her shoes. 'Of course, of course. How did you get here?'

'I walked down your four kilometres, which must be at least six, and eventually got onto the first EVA bus full of workers.'

'I am sorry for you but you cannot blame the agency for all this.'

'I don't. Hotel please.'

He made some calls while talking to his colleague, who gaped at her. Then he walked her to a nearby hotel, pulling her case, and remained until she was checked in. Room 57.

The concierge promised to call Kelvin's number, and she went up to her room where she shed her clothes and took a shower with the door open to hear the phone.

Wrapped in a towel, she paced. From the tiny balcony, the view gave onto the courtyard with a palm tree and a blue pool in which two people were swimming like frogs.

The phone rang near the bed. She dropped the towel. 'Kelvin? Dad never picked me up. I lost my mobile charger. The house is padlocked. No Dad anywhere.' She started to weep. 'I'm calling from a hotel. Wait a minute. The Almandeiro.' And then she said something no mother should ever have to say to her child. 'Sorry to disturb you at work, but I need your help.' It had an effect. He promised. Pause, long pause. She heard him talking to someone, rustling noises, and then… 'The best I can do is get to Faro in two days' time. Will call again to give you timing.'

'Room number 57,' she added before saying, 'I love you'. There had been complications giving birth to him as his spine was against hers. The pain had been worth it.

Angela slept, woke, battled with demons and was sucked back into sleep. It was past midday when she looked around her, befuddled. She had two days to kill and little enthusiasm to go sightseeing.

★

When Kelvin stood in the uninspiring hotel room, she was immensely relieved at the sight of him. Everything could now be put right. He had rented a small car but had been unable to reach Dad. Despite her aversion to seeing the house again, they had to go back there. Phil had been missing since the day of the inventory when he had last called, five days by now.

'Not without the police,' Kelvin said decisively.

'Police,' she repeated with a pained expression and then, after a deep intake of breath, told her son about Jasmine, the stunning lawyer who had flirted with Dad. He had lapped it up. Now this Jasmine had gone somewhere, nobody seems to know or want to talk about. 'That's suspicious, don't you think?'

'No way, Mum. There has to be a simple explanation.'

Miguel was less than chuffed when he saw the two walk into the agency, but Kelvin insisted Miguel call the police.

'Look...' started Miguel, both hands waving in front of him.

'Yes, you told my mother already that you are not responsible any longer, but the police will need to make enquiries. A man has been missing for five days now.'

With resignation, Miguel asked them to take a seat on the sofa. Watching him telephoning on the other side of the glass had become a familiar sight to Angela.

He came back with the news that the GNR – the National Republican Police – were sending a rural inspector, a policeman who knew all about local land disputes and feuds. Angela, filled with horror, grabbed her son's upper arm and dug her nails into it.

Thirty minutes later they were winding up the roads in weighty silence behind the patrol car of Inspector Castro.

At a distance from the house she could already see the black VW.

As they drew closer, Kelvin remarked, 'This house looks deserted. The door is bricked up, windows all shuttered, and there is even a bird's nest in that chimney you are so fond of.'

The blue door indeed was not visible; it had been bricked up.

'I'll be damned,' the inspector muttered.

Rushing to the back of the house, they found that the terrace had also been bricked up.

'The mortar is still damp,' said the inspector, touching the brickwork before turning and giving his attention further afield to where the goats were grazing. In his grey suit and green wellies, he left the garden and stomped across the field in the direction of the goats.

'Phil…' Angela leaned her head against the whitewash of the house. 'Phil is bricked up in there. Someone killed him, and then…'

Kelvin, with grim determination, took his mother's arm and pulled her with him to follow the inspector.

Testing their way through the rocks and depressions in the field, they caught up but remained at a distance, Angela shooing away an inquisitive brown-specked goat.

Inspector Castro poured a torrent of Portuguese over the small sun-dried ageless goatherd in a frayed woollen long-sleeved shirt, a Fatima pendant hanging from his neck, oversized trousers held at the waist by a knotted rope. In his mouth were black-rimmed teeth, which showed as he seemed to defend himself monosyllabically but with expressive noises. More accusatory Portuguese words, and the herder yelled repeatedly, accompanied by animated gesticulations.

When Castro interrupted these passionately expressed theatricals with a sharp pronouncement, Angela revealed her suspicions about Phil and Jasmine. Perhaps the herder had seen them? The herder, who could not understand what she was saying, watched tense with alert eyes as if she were a wolf in a bush about to pounce on one of his goats.

'This case does not involve a woman. Something else has been going on here.'

'Oh God! Kelvin, what has this deranged little man done to Phil?'

More Portuguese was addressed to the goatherd.

'Please translate,' Kelvin asked, but was ignored. From the sound of the one-sided conversation, it had come to an end. The herder whistled to his dog and the goats were driven away from them. The goatherd said one more thing to the inspector, and then trudged away towards the road.

Returning to the house, the inspector explained. 'One night, about a week ago, the goats were spooked by unearthly howling from the house, and a kid was stillborn. The goatherd approached the property and realised that it had become haunted by a satanic spirit, which was raving inside and breaking furniture, growling continuously. As is the custom here, he fetched padlocks to incarcerate the ghost and protect his flock.

'The house fell silent, but a couple of days ago he saw that the spirit had managed to materialise in the garden, a black figure sitting there all night. The next morning, he bricked up the doors, and has had no trouble since.'

'The black figure was me under a blanket.'

'Exactly!' exclaimed Kelvin. 'He's making it up as he goes along. Let's open the house.'

At that moment, the goatherd returned with a crowbar and sledgehammer, the goats following him. The dog, his pink lolling tongue hanging from his panting mouth, moved ahead and, as he reached the house, he checked around it and then crapped in the front garden. The goats started to chew the flowers.

The herder started to hack down the wall covering the front door. Bricks crashed to the ground. As each inch of blue was revealed, Angela became more panic-stricken. This horrid dirty man must have tried to burgle the house, and had killed Phil. It would be revealed any minute. She turned away and paced zigzags in the overgrown garden, which was being destroyed by munching goats.

On the other side of the house, the inspector and Kelvin must have been able to open the door. She cupped her hands over her face.

'Dad is not in the house,' Kelvin announced. Her eyes slowly filled with tears. She felt so relieved that she was almost glad Phil was with Jasmine.

Stepping over the pile of bricks and penetrating into the dark inside, which slowly lightened as the goatherd took down the bricks in front of the terrace door, she saw some visible disturbance. A lamp had been knocked from a table. A chair lay on its side in front of the fireplace. On the dining table were piled up her kitchen utensils and a plate with half-eaten mush on it. Green leaves and grass were strewn on the tiled floor. It stank. How it stank!

The inspector had an explanation. 'This peasant has been using the house in bad weather, probably with the dog and some vulnerable goats, because the house was standing empty for more than a year. When he saw the car, he probably panicked and wanted to hide his crime of trespassing, first with the padlocks. And then he naively bricked it all up.'

'Great,' said Kelvin. 'But that doesn't explain where Dad is. I can't stand the stench in here any longer. Let's go to the police station, fill out the forms and get them to start a proper hunt. Mum, you'll have to come back to England with me.'

At the airport, Angela said, 'You know, Kelvin, the inspector can't be right. Phil and I were in the house only a few weeks ago and it was fine then.'

★

Angela paid the bills she received from the Portuguese authorities – and they were steep. She had to pay local rates and a tax on secondary properties in the Algarve. Phil's pension was on hold until it was proven that he was still alive. She struggled with online banking; Phil had done all that. The children explained but it did not sink in. She had lost a lot of weight. She was constantly anxious and desperately unhappy.

The GNR did not send updates on their efforts to find Phil or a complete account of what had happened in the house – because they had given up, hadn't they?

Her life, according to Laura and Kelvin, had to go on. They helped her move into a flat not too far from the grandchildren, who were her only joy.

Three years passed without news. Apparently, thousands of people disappear and are never found. Some turned up somewhere else; some simply had chosen not to tell anyone about their plans.

Jasmine had never returned to the Algarve office. Her family circumstances had changed. Jasmine's father told the police that his daughter had gone to Switzerland for work, and then changed it to America. Jasmine's mother was from Algeria and not forthcoming; it was delicate, the relationship between Algeria and southern Portugal.

Angela turned seventy but looked a lot older. She begged her children not to even mention the date. Kelvin got married and had a baby boy who looked the image of his father. *Phil is missing all this*, thought Angela, living in the silent horror of what had happened to her, for which she had no one to blame. It just happened. The past was gone; it did not exist any longer.

She started to stay in her dressing gown and slippers all day, staring at the television with glassy-eyed intensity. Her thoughts darkened and became so dense that she could hardly bear their weight. She took sleeping pills to ward off her anxiety attacks. She lost track of time, dozing through days. Only for her grandchildren did she manage to pull herself up out of the dark, knowing that children cannot be fooled easily.

Laura had long given up suggesting stimulating activities. Art classes at U3A required happier humans.

On the thirteenth of June, at a quarter past eleven in the morning, Laura and Kelvin burst into their mother's flat. 'They've found Dad!'

Angela rose from her pillows and sent her children from her bedroom so that she could get dressed. After that she poured everyone a glass of brandy.

Laura read out the report from the police in Vilamoura:

The body of Philip Heatherington was discovered on the sixth of June in his house in the Algarve. The autopsy revealed he died of blood poisoning caused by an infected abscess under a molar. The starter motor in his Volkswagen car was faulty. The pain would have been intense, thus explaining the yelling reported by a witness and the disturbed furniture. He seems to have chewed on herbs in the hope of lessening the pain.

The goatherd did indeed fix padlocks and brick up the house out of superstition, as he claimed.

The unfortunate subject, finding himself trapped, attempted to escape by climbing up the chimney, where he became stuck.

'My God!' exclaimed Kelvin. 'The bird's nest I saw was Dad's hair.'

WUOTAN

Axelrod should have tried to lose the 'rod' when he left home to go to boarding school. When his socks were named and his trunk packed, his father Rex found something more important to do that day. Jane drove her son to Eton, where his father's 'old boy' status had wangled a place for Axelrod, despite his bad exam results.

Axelrod had little sense of logic, did not understand money and was confused by politics. He got upset if someone stepped on an insect, and thought Alton Towers amusement park was the best place on earth. The headmaster at Eton who interviewed the twelve-year-old had dim prospects of keeping him.

During the first term, Axelrod revealed that he had no grasp of grammar. A clause he laughed off as a 'Santa', *past perfect* had 'gone bad', and he amused himself with 'super-laxatives' for *superlatives*. His papers were marked *D for disaster* by outraged teachers. Rex paid for extra lessons and generously donated towards a new sports hall, even though Axelrod closed his eyes when a ball flew towards him. He refused to eat meat and was mercilessly bullied by the other boys. Somehow he survived, smiling fixedly through hexagonal rimless glasses.

The straight blond hair, long on top, was worn with a side parting, cut in a bob and neatly combed over the dome of his head. His cheeks were rosy. In a dress, he could have passed for a girl.

Puberty came to his year but Axelrod was unaffected. He discovered detective stories and crime thrillers. Time and again, the headmaster battled with his conscience to send the boy away, but then there was his father and Eton tradition, and the creature seemed to have nestled itself into a role at school, a sort of mascot to the elite boys.

No university offered him a place when the time came. Because of the boy's interest in crime stories, Rex decided on a career in law for his son. The private University of Law in Leeds was willing to take him on – at a price. During those three university years, Axelrod only changed in that he became peculiar in a more mature way. He pretended to limp because he had a lecturer who was crippled by polio. This led to Axelrod walking with a black stick topped with a silver skull. Shortly afterwards, he began to enter a realm of ghouls, the remote, a mystical time of the world in chaos which seemed to be all around him. Nobody wanted to spend time with him, not even his parents or Delphina, his younger sister.

'Befriend a girl, go out with her, compliment her,' his mother urged.

Axelrod's response was that girls were yucky creatures. 'Blades are sharpened on granite,' he said. 'Fear is a dagger.'

Jane suggested therapy, but Rex would not hear of it.

The university let him graduate with a third and wished him luck in the future.

Rex got his son into the London Law School of the Chancery, a grand-sounding institution which was actually a 'crammer for the dumb ones'. The young man would have to live in London.

The help of family was called on. Back in 1895, Rex's grandfather had built a house in a most prestigious street in London near Primrose Hill, which he called Primrose House. Rex's father had bought the cottage next door, called it Lavender Cottage and joined the two with a verandah. Rex and Jane, however, had preferred to live on a country estate, and Rex's younger brother, Clark, worked for BP in remote countries, so it was Clark's wife, Claire, who whiled her lonely time away in Lavender Cottage. A brief but intense affair had ensued with Rex, whose work brought him regularly to London, and Clark was not given time enough in life to find out about it – he had died in Nigeria of a tropical disease.

The father of Rex and Clark had felt sorry for the childless widow, who had lived so long alone in the cottage next door, and he had left her both houses and a generous settlement. Rex reckoned that Axelrod could stay in the cottage while Aunt Claire occupied the house – she owed them.

At first, Jane had raised objections to the idea because Claire was depressive. It was known that she had spent time in a Quaker mental clinic, but determinedly Rex drove Axelrod, dressed in a black wing-collared shirt and black velvet trousers, to London to win Claire's agreement.

'Roddie,' she enthused on seeing him. 'How nice for me to have company, a strong young man to protect me.'

While Axelrod had a look around his future abode of Lavender Cottage, Claire and Rex were left alone in the house. He suggested they go upstairs to talk.

'Nothing has changed in my heart for you,' she said pointedly. 'Why can't you find a little time for me, the way you used to? Clark will never find out now.'

'I'd love to but I have a lot on my plate. The Inland Revenue is after me. We are packing for Zurich, which is a tax haven. Delphina is coming with us, but I'm leaving my only son with you. Doesn't that prove I still care for you? Just tell me one thing: are you clear of the mental clinic and all that?'

'I still get depressed at times, no more than any other lonely person. The Quakers have been so wonderful to me. I intend to leave them the house and my money.'

'How generous. Wouldn't you prefer to leave your possessions to someone who loves you rather than a bunch of religious quackers?'

'And who would that be?'

'Axelrod. He will love you as I did – *do*. He and I have a lot in common, did you know that? On the drive he said you'd be all he is left with once we are gone.'

Claire was pacing the room, absorbing his words.

'Stop that, my love, and come and sit next to me. I can spare one kiss. All is not over.'

When she complied, Rex pulled her towards him and kissed her on the mouth.

'Please take a photo of us like that so I can put it into the sandalwood box for secrets you gave me, and remember.'

He held his mobile phone at arm's length, then he placed his cheek against hers. 'I'll send you the picture.'

Back downstairs they found Axelrod in the lounge talking to himself.

'It is decided. Lovely Claire will take you under her wing. You have no idea what a lucky young man you are,' Rex said to his son and then declined the offer of tea and cakes.

During the drive home, to Rex's surprise, Axelrod asked why Claire lived alone in that large house. Rex had been dreading the drive back with a cognitively lacking son, so he was grateful for the intelligent question and took the trouble to explain. When the story came to Clark's death, Axelrod wanted details. Rex explained that the eggs of a Tumbu fly had burrowed into Clark's eyebrows. When the larvae hatched, they ate into his eyes and brain.

'Gruesome. I love it,' Axelrod enthused.

'Claire is sitting on ten million at least, if that means anything to you.'

*

The time had come for Axelrod to move out of his parents' house. A van man loaded up the boxes, the books, the skull collection. Jane pretended to prune the roses in the front beds. In a month they would leave for Switzerland and the house would be rented. Axelrod brought out, cradled in his arms, his beloved black metal bust of a bearded one-eyed old man with a raven on his shoulder. Axelrod called him Wuotan, his spiritual master and protector. Delphina, waiting to be picked up to go to yet another wedding of yet another old school friend, looked on.

'I'm glad to see the back of your hideous god. It gives me the shivers.'

'You wouldn't know. For Norsemen, he has magical powers. He is ferocious and prone to do things not easily explained.'

'The only buddy that gets you,' Delphina sneered as she leaned against one of the entrance pillars, touching it with her shoulder only, one arm hanging down beside her. Her flimsy party dress was decorated with prints of Chinese fans. Her thin legs were crossed one over the other, and her shoulder-length straw-blond hair was rod-straight all round her face, pushed down by a cloche hat with a wide cake ribbon.

Axelrod imagined her opening those legs like aggressive scissor blades, while her pulsating medusa sex would suck onto him.

'Stop looking that way at me,' she said. 'You give me the creeps.'

'Drop dead,' he responded.

She pushed herself off the pillar. 'Drop-dead gorgeous in my case.'

Mother slipped the pruning shears into her kangaroo apron pocket. 'You can still see each other. Delphina is planning to visit London. Axelrod can invite you to stay with Claire.'

'Me at Aunt Claire's? The one who wants to live with Axelrod. No thanks.'

Just then a car horn sounded; Delphina turned and dashed away. Walking out through the gate after her, Axelrod just saw her pull shut the door of an open-top sports car. The man at the wheel glanced at the house and the gaping Axelrod, then turned to look ahead, straining the engine with excessive revs. Delphina's hand came up to hold her hat on her straw head.

★

Axelrod moved to London and, finally, became Axel. Lavender Cottage was threatening to him. He spent weekends in the tiny living room at a computer table, watching malformed animals and morbidly obese people on YouTube. Wuotan's abode was in the upstairs bathroom. Axel ate food out of microwave containers because the Aga cooker sat, ominous, like a two-lidded Sherman tank in the kitchen. During the week, Axel went to classes. They had done *arrest and charge* and were on *sentencing*. Essays should have been written in the given time, but he did not see why.

He added a pair of black high-heeled boots and a panther-black full-length redingote to his image, and rings to his fingers, one with a ram head. He drew black around his eyes and used grey lipstick. His classmates went out for drinks. They sat in on trials in the Old Bailey and were excited about it. They challenged each other in the preparation of court case arguments. Axel saw a really nice spider earring in a jewellery shop in Soho.

Claire, in her house thrice the size, lived like a hermit. Groceries were delivered and the laundry was sent out. Tuesday and Thursday mornings the charlady came to clean, each time allowing half an hour for the cottage. Axel put his rent money from Father on the communicating verandah console where his aunt left him notes. *If you and your student chums have nothing on, do spend some time with me this weekend.* Had she not noticed that he never went out?

Eventually, they drifted together and beamed upon finding out they both liked Allsorts and Twiglets. He bought them from the corner deli next to the weird estate agent who threatened him with the police if he lingered in front of the shop window.

'You're a darling,' Claire told him. 'We give each other a *raison de vivre*.' They sat in the lounge, munching, she in a satin padded dressing gown a bit too tight over her chest – and revealing, as the top button was lost – and he in his permanent black.

To improve their employment prospects, the law students were given training in basic investigation procedures, as performed in the USA by paralegals. On one exercise, Axel had to visit a house to elicit evidence from the role-playing tenant, who suspected her landlord of rent fraud. When she opened the front door to Axel, she asked, 'Are you playing a chimney sweep?' Offended, he was unable to communicate.

In the warmth of Claire's musky-smelling lounge he confided with resignation that everything out there was turbid and incomprehensible, but that she was not. She smiled soppily and agreed. He learned that she was sixty-three and that she had married Uncle Clark at forty-two.

Once a month, mostly when it rained, she became depressed and snorted, a noisy intake of air through her nose which was partly blocked. She inhaled up to her sinuses and then swallowed the residue. 'I shall never forgive Clark...' *Sniff*. '...for having died, for not taking me abroad with him.' *Snort*. 'I feel so unwanted.' Tears produced phlegm. He held out Kleenexes but she did not think she needed them.

★

The law course continued and Wuotan reassured Axel that not understanding meant being above it. To his dismay, he was asked to participate in another exercise: a pharmacist charged with selling out-of-date medication, instead of discarding it into hazardous waste containers. 'Find out all you can. Knowledge is power in a courtroom.'

Axel was not convinced that this was a crime, and it had to be explained to him that expired medicine could be dangerous, 'fatal even for the sick and vulnerable.'

They sent him on a visit to the waste disposal plant where drugs were destroyed. He was given a white coat with a logo on the breast pocket and lilac rubber gloves. He watched employees sort through pills, ampoules, vials and suppositories, before shuffling them through holes in the worktop into bins for incineration.

Axel benefited little from the exercise and, back home, he rolled up the offensively coloured white coat and stuffed it onto the hat rack in the entrance cupboard.

Christmas approached. Rex, Jane and Delphina called to say that they would spend the holidays in a chalet in Gstaad. An opulent hamper was delivered to Claire and Axel with a Christmas card signed by Harrods. On the same day came a last will and testament which Rex had had drawn up for Claire to sign and get witnessed. *For the secret box, because I know you have Axel's happiness in mind. I do and I L Y.*

Pamphlets through the letter boxes invited the residents to participate in the traditional Christmas market in the crescent. Primrose and Lavender houses, unadorned, remained firmly closed and non-participative.

On Christmas Day a fierce wind blew from the north. Claire, in her dressing gown and wool stockings, was sitting against the cushions on the sofa next to the open hamper. Her lustreless dyed hair was unkempt and her face without make-up looked like oatmeal, the wrinkles indenting its puffy surface.

'Merry Cringles, Roddie,' she said to Axel on his pouffe. They toasted each other from crystal champagne glasses. The wind outside knocked a shutter against the house wall. In the fireplace, damp logs crackled and popped. There was something unnerving about all this for him, even though he felt a sense of belonging; his body was at ease in here. He watched the liquid in the V-shaped glass touch her lips again: *vulva* sped through his mind, *vulgar, vagina, voracious* – his sister's sex.

'Move this basket and come and sit over here with me.'

He did as he was told. Close to her on the sofa, he felt the slithery satin brush his forearm. It made him quiver with alarm. She resettled herself and now her thigh touched his. They drank and nibbled pralines, and he refilled their glasses from the second bottle in the hamper. The heat in his body was not entirely his own, as her body heat had cunningly invaded his space. It made him glow in tandem with someone else. The flames in the hearth snaked upwards sporadically, sucked by air in the flue. Putting his glass down, he placed his hand on his crotch which felt tender, and a swelling was clearly visible. It was not his doing, but Wuotan inside him was insistent.

Her upper body leaned in on him and her veined hand cupped his on his crotch, riding his movements until he gave the sigh of a man succumbing to Wuotan's basilisk bestiary and ejaculated.

'It's all right. It's going to be all right.' She straightened herself.

Is that how a man felt when a woman was involved – close to combustion? He forced his hand inside his trousers and patted his spent treacherous appendix. Next to him, she feigned calm but her chest rose and fell – *shocked or embarrassed?* he asked himself.

She turned towards him; a smile distorted her dry lips, and then fell against him in a twisted move. Her face ended up plastered against his, her body cumbersome, exuding the exciting scent of decay.

'I wish I were more drunk or drugged,' he managed to utter once she gave him air to breathe. 'Actually, I wish I were dead.'

The year was running out and he kept clear of Claire. There was lingering shame and repentance in this tactical avoidance, while at the same time he craved to feel that way again.

'Nonsense.' He calmed himself and took the bus to Oxford Street. In Hamleys he bought a kite in the shape of a dragon. He forced himself into a Costa café, absorbing looks from people. Sipping a latte, he listened intently to the ticking of his creative brain before he took the bus back, glad that he missed one so he could wait for the next one.

Forcefully, he knocked on her front door for the first time. It took a while and rumbling, but then she opened a crack while hiding behind the door, cautious about who she let into her abode.

'Tomorrow is New Year. Here, a kite. We should fly it on Primrose Hill.'

'We shall, my love.'

They didn't. The year 2010 started at midnight like any other day. His New Year's resolution to keep Claire at bay was undermined when she proposed pouring a brandy for each and going upstairs in his cottage. Her mind was obviously strong and made up.

In his bow-fronted bedroom he felt caged by her presence, watching with narrowed eyes how she took off her dressing gown to reveal flesh-coloured brassiere and U-shaped underpants. When she passed the oval cheval mirror, looking at herself, he pounced and elbowed her sideways.

'You beast! You hurt me. Don't do that again.'

'You're not allowed in the mirror. It's only for servants of the ruler, Wuotan.' After this explanation, which seemed to hover uncomfortably in his bedroom, he picked up his brandy balloon from the mantelpiece and sat on the P&O wicker trunk which had travelled with Uncle Clark to foreign places. She drained hers and, aiming poorly, her glass fell behind the bedside table.

'Take your clothes off,' she ordered him. 'You look like a black pudding.'

'I'm into black.'

'Yeah, yeah, you keep saying.' She hopped onto the bed as if imagining herself still wildly attractive and invited him to join her for *relaxation*.

He excused himself to go to the bathroom where, after consultation, Wuotan assured him that *It's all right; it's going to be all right* – Claire's words after the joint masturbation. He reached for a lipstick and painted his lips ruby red.

On return to the room, taking off his black sweater, he smacked himself in the face with the pewter alchemy pendant which he should have taken off first. He removed his trousers and stood in front of the cheval mirror. His parents and sister had abandoned him. It served them right if he was aroused and in briefs in a bedroom with his aunt Claire prostrated on his bed.

'Without you, I would go to pieces,' she said, lying sideways across the bed, arms outstretched and feet dangling to the floor, a piece of wreckage in no position to judge him. 'Think of me offering myself to you.'

Indeed, she lay like a sacrificial goat on the altar of Wuotan. Her belly vacillated with her breathing, and he

239

kissed her forehead and dry mouth, branding her with his lipstick. This was his opportunity to find out what women had between their legs. He capped her knees and prised the legs as far apart as they would go.

Scanty pubic hair sprouted on the milk-white dome, and layers of wrinkly flesh, like angry red petals, led into a deep crevice. The gunk emerging from the orifice was no doubt meant to lubricate.

'Don't look so shocked,' she said, lifting her head. 'Perhaps you prefer men.'

It was nature which had given her that mess between her legs. It was the chubby canteen matron who had put that plate of cooked red liver in front of him at Eton. *Just close your eyes and eat it.*

He climbed onto Aunt Claire and she whimpered, an infant again but in a universe where infants were born looking old. Axel rocked his pelvis over her, imagining the two-headed Muninn sailing towards him to lift him up in its talons. Before leaving contact with earth, Axel pushed his sex into the infant under him, again and again, to propagate and stock the landscape of Muninn's kingdom. *Wuotan will be proud.*

After an extended silence in the penumbra of the room, Aunt Claire heaved herself up. 'You and I are lovers now – how absolutely wonderful!'

He came to and was shocked by the transformation of the situation. Surely he had not copulated with Auntie on his bed? Horrified, with mechanical movements he helped her up, handed her the dressing gown and bent down to align her slippers.

'Next time I'll teach you to be more gentle, you little

savage,' she said in a kittenish voice and crushed him to her. When she was gone from the room, he knew that he would have to kill her.

Frighten her and hope for a heart attack? A fatal fall? It would have to be from high. There was no gas on the cooker to catch her padded coat. Claire did not eat bananas to slip on. Axel ran these options through his mind while sitting in the bath, scrubbing his body with a soapy mitten.

Slip – that was it, wasn't it? Wuotan agreed with him.

While Claire was taking her afternoon nap the next Sunday, Axel smeared a thick layer of genuine beeswax on the parquet at the entrance leading to the lounge.

When he got back from the law school on Monday, a note had been left for him in the verandah. *Disaster! Charlady fell and broke a leg. It will take months. Be a sport, my lover, and take over from her.*

The next day, Axel stayed at home to be instructed in how to clean bathrooms, kitchen floor, how to dust and hoover. All that twice a week.

It would have to be poisoning.

★

Axel spent hours at his computer printing out leaflets.

He had chosen Alver Street in Walworth at random.

Having removed his jewellery, wearing the white coat from the medicine disposal plant with the insignia on its breast pocket and carrying a danger-yellow bucket on which was painted a black skull and crossbones, he knocked on doors. The flyer described in gory detail

241

what happens to medication beyond its use-by date. After two days of collection, the bucket was full, and the variety astonishing. Wuotan helped him in the bathroom sorting it out. There was enough benzodiazepine, Xanax and Relepan to kill a dinosaur.

When it was full moon, and with Claire in a delicate swoony mood, he surprised her with a takeaway curry from the famous Taj Mahal on Gordon Street. He laid out the food containers and trimmings on her dining room table and ceremoniously poured her a glass of white wine.

She had wound a scarf around her head, probably thinking it looked Indian. 'Just because Clark never took me to Delhi, doesn't mean I'm not allowed to be exotic.' Playfully, she exhaled hot breath at the side of his neck. 'I know what is for pudding, darling Roddy.'

Wiping the poison-loaded curry residue from the side of her mouth, she gave him a beguiling smile. 'I shouldn't tell you, but I can't help it.'

He swallowed saliva and waited.

'I have made a will for you to get everything I own, seeing you already own my body.' She eagerly awaited his response.

'Wuotan and I have no idea how to react to that.'

'Just be grateful. Oh Roddie, Roddie...' and she burped, clamping both hands over her belly.

After that, she admitted to not feeling well; the dishes had not agreed with her. Some of the curry had been rather unusually flavoured, did he not think?

He suggested she lay down on the couch for a while, but she insisted on going up to his bedroom in the cottage. He supported her elbow as she reeled across the verandah and helped her up the stairs. It was midnight; Axel was satisfied with the timing.

He returned to dispose of the curry dishes and any incriminating utensils. At two o'clock, he found her thrashing on the rumpled sheets, her wet hair plastered to her head; pearls of sweat glistened on her forehead which was pale lilac. Her lips had turned blue.

He fetched the bust of Wuotan, whom he put on the P&O trunk so that he could watch Aunt Claire groan, yelp and contort herself.

By four in the morning, the moon was veiled and Aunt Claire did not move any longer. Wuotan thought she was dead. Axel needed to make sure. He unhooked the mirror from its hinges and carried it to the bed where he lay it on his aunt, almost covering her body. Crawling partly under it at the head end, he checked whether any breath clouded the looking glass. It did not.

When the sun rose, Axel, dressed in his best black, took the mirror under one arm and Wuotan under the other and left the house. He walked along the road and up to the top of Primrose Hill where he propped the mirror, *with Aunt Claire now in it*, against a tree.

★

When Rex arrived at Primrose House by taxi, he rushed in and checked the will in the sandalwood box. Then he went to the social care centre where the police had brought Axel. There he was told that people had called the police, because a man in black with a top hat was

243

talking to himself into a bedroom mirror and carrying a lugubrious bust of Satan.

Axel explained that Aunt Claire was now allowed in the mirror because her state was acceptable to Wuotan. It was decided to leave Axel in the care of the home while an autopsy was performed on Claire.

Rex hired a notorious and expensive lawyer to argue that Axel was not competent to inherit and that his father should replace him and dedicate the estate to the life-long psychiatric care of Axel.

The autopsy concluded that Claire had died from an overdose of a cocktail of medication. She had been a known depressive, the Quaker home confirmed, and had taken on the care of a disturbed nephew. Suicide was the verdict.

The family court would sit to hear Rex's case, and the judge insisted on Axel being present. Rex bade Axel appear in his best black, top hat and all. Could he bring Wuotan? Even better, he should definitely also bring the mirror.

A social worker brought Axel in a taxi. An usher opened the doors for them, and the judge from his rostrum witnessed the entrance of a young man, dressed smartly in a grey suit with a white shirt and Eton tie. His hair was neatly cut and his shoes polished. He looked intimidatingly intelligent – an Eton success product.

'My apologies. I just had to get a shoeshine at Fortnum's; they say judges assess people by their shoes.'

The judge was taken aback. 'You do not appear as I was led to believe.'

'It is never a leading question for those who are led, because they are mostly misled.'

The judge brightened and invited Axel to approach.

'Tell me about your Aunt Claire, her depressions and her will.'

'She is, was, oh so sad, a wonderful support to me during my law studies. Her cooking abilities, it is true, would have depressed anyone, but she yearned to join her beloved late husband, and no children of her own held her back. I came closest to it and she liked me, but that was obviously not enough.'

'Did you not walk around town dressed as a Goth, muttering to yourself?'

'Did not respectable Victorian lawyers wear silk top hats and black gowns? Should one not practise the art of defence closure and train one's voice and delivery? Were you not guilty of some tomfoolery when you were a law student?'

The judge nodded, his mouth clamped shut, and laughed through his nose.

'What would be your intentions for the estate?'

'I hope to open a private club for barristers, members of the inns of court. In fact, you would be the first member accepted.'

The judge addressed the courtroom, eyes on Rex. 'In my opinion, Axelrod is sound of mind and the will should be executed as was intended.'

'But…' interjected the psychiatrist, rising from a back bench, '… my assessment—'

The judge was already on his way out of the courtroom.

Axel, ignoring his furious father, hailed a taxi which brought him to the social care home where he picked up Wuotan, the mirror and his clothes, and returned him to Primrose House.

In the lounge, he propped the mirror against the wall and put Wuotan on the coffee table. 'Here we are, all three of us again,' he said and let himself fall onto the couch. 'You have no idea how excruciating it was for me to pretend to the judge that I am nuts and to say those ridiculous things I hear the others say all the time.'

LETHAL AMBITION

'If I had a million Swiss francs, I would…' Erica was sitting on a bench in the company-owned gardens, which reached into the blue of Lake Geneva, and playing her favourite game. The bench was under a covered walkway linking the Favre glass cubicle headquarters to the food safety laboratory, called the Hen House. It was a warm, scented, August Friday evening, and gnats danced in the sultry air. '… I would build myself a villa in this luscious park – after ripping out that hideous sculpture, of course.' The metal sculpture on the lawn was of two ice-cream balls in a dish, with a fan-shaped biscuit stuck into them. In 1909 the founder of the company, Maurice Favre, had invented the wafer which became the symbol of the manufacturer of top-class frozen desserts, exported across the world.

'Desecration!' She could imagine the horror of Gustav, nicknamed Old Wafer, a robust man with robotic movements, the son of Maurice and now CEO. His son and daughter and dishy nephew, Tristan, made up the board of directors.

'If I had ten million Swiss francs…' If one was imagining, one might as well do it grandly. '… I would buy the company and boss people around.' She had been hired six years before, thanks to her good diploma in biology from Lausanne tech and her two-year administrative training programme with Nestlé. 'I would fly in the corporate jet to meetings in exotic countries and would be wooed by well-travelled, mega-rich businessmen.'

Erica had not minded working late and hard, nor being told to do something again, nor even being told she had done something wrong. What she did mind, today, six years later, was that she had not advanced in the company. Indeed, no other woman had either. The female employees were restricted to the Hen House, all of them biologists. A showcase fuss was made of their analytical work on dairy food contamination, and they attended international food safety conferences in Hamburg and Barcelona. But the academics were paid small-fry expenses and blushed with grateful pleasure, while a fortune went into management travel in the corporate jets – two, because Old Wafer, with his son and daughter, did not get on with nephew Tristan. They flew separately to the Caribbean for board meetings.

Erica's first three years of employment had been a desk job in a cubicle in the Hen House, sorting out the scientists' notes, collating their biological measurements and putting them into charts, ordering lab equipment and raw bacteria, and organising conference trips. Evil microbes and rotting food were their obsession. The scientists did not talk much, let alone gossip, chat or joke. When Heidi, the senior biologist, found e-coli growth in vanilla ice cream and killed it with a virus, it was a highlight.

Every time Favre had advertised a job in the head office, Erica applied but was unsuccessful. Eventually however, her work in the Hen House had been computerised and something else had to be found for her. They shoved her under nephew Tristan, with the monotonous role of liaising between management and the scientists – a job without prospects.

Car doors slammed; the employees were leaving for their mid-August weekend. Looking back over her shoulder, Erica saw Victoria in her Bentley Continental, waiting to give her husband, Tristan, a lift home. The woman held eye-contact with her briefly, her mouth pursed, before resuming painting her lips – lips which did not know what a blow job could achieve. At thirty-four, and too selfish to go through a pregnancy, flawless Victoria, with her dyed hair and lash-extensions, did not know either what it was like to work for money in food contamination. Erica tucked her handbag close against her, a bag which would today play a vital part in her action to improve her life.

Erica's liaison job may have lacked *professional* prospects but it had the consolation of reporting straight to Tristan. Seeing him close up every day, she had to admit that he was not as arrogant as the other Favres.

'Erica, good morning to you,' he would greet her and smile sometimes. He was always impeccably dressed, and there was a youthful bounce in his step. He was good-looking with his light brown hair that was soft and straight, his dark chocolate-coloured eyes and generous mouth.

After a few months, his office had to be refurbished, a task overseen by Victoria, who obviously resented Erica's presence and began poisoning her existence with snide remarks like, 'Why do you wear skirts that short? Not everybody has good legs,' or, 'Can't you do something with your hair?'

Once, in Tristan's presence, she came out with, 'If only we could upgrade Erica to fit your new office.' Tristan, in a half-guilty, half-annoyed way, had laughed it off as a joke.

But Victoria's most hurtful comment, as they passed in the corridor, had been, 'Why they hired somebody as low-class as you, I shall never know.'

Erica had pointed her finger at the departing figure. 'Pow!'

Then and there, Erica had realised that as long as Victoria was in Tristan's life, there would be no professional future for her. She could have left Favre, but she had no family to go to. Her parents' marriage had come to an end, each having found what they called 'more suitable' partners, and she had made no effort to keep friends. Deep inside her, Tristan had taken root. Like an inspiration it came to her that her goal had to be to seduce Tristan: offer him understanding and love, in a way Victoria could not be bothered to. Erica would give him a son, a new-generation Favre, and later a beautiful daughter for him to adore, provided, of course, that by then Victoria was out of his life and that a diamond glinted on Erica's manicured finger.

Step by little step she made herself invaluable to him. He needed a file and there it was; he wanted coffee and he got cappuccino sprinkled with chocolate. At times she played helpless to bring out his manhood, and kittenish at others to make him see her as desirably young. Her hair was professionally styled and Gucci perfume enveloped her like fairy dust. She became a tower of strength when he was annoyed with Victoria's constant domestic demands. Sympathetic, Erica helped him find a new pool cleaner, and discovered the shop in Paris which sold curtain rails with the right crystal-ball ends. Victoria interrupted him at work for as little as a bee in her sauna.

In a journal, Erica recorded every smile of his and every word he said to her. This kept her company during the lonely weekends. Eventually, they became comfortable with each other, and Tristan called her into his office at the slightest excuse. He clearly preferred her to his wife of whom he was tired. He confided in her about his dislike of the green sofa with coral cushions Victoria had chosen. He gave her compliments, and they became close. It had taken a year and a half to get to that point.

One morning, Tristan had called Erica into a confidential meeting with Old Wafer and Heidi; they were going to start research on anthrax in the Hen House, a lethal bacteria that could develop in dairy substances. It required special safety measures, and Erica was to be responsible for setting them up.

That year, Tristan had still not invited her to the famous August open house party at his villa up on the hill amidst the vines. Boston lobsters and Washington Blue Pool oysters were flown in, and Tennessee whiskey was served neat in tall highball glasses. The rule was that soft drinks and water were not allowed. It was an occasion for the guests to let their hair down without consequences. The only one said never to lose control was Victoria – made of steel.

The same could not be said of Tristan. The Monday after the party a year ago, he had stumbled into the office, dark circles under small eyes in a dry putty face. He wore no jacket, and his expensive shirt was creased. He asked for coffee, trying to steady his dusty gaze on her before aiming at the sofa to crumple upon it. Erica caught him in her arms and walked him across, feeling his breath on her face and his lips against her chin, a fraction from her mouth. She was overwhelmed by this much-dreamed-of intimacy and cradled his head against her bosom, whispering comfort. He was helpless. He thanked her for being such a darling, and Erica knew that she was nearing her goal.

Comatose intimacy turned into a love affair. She had hooked him and was walking on clouds. Surely, her happiness was in sight.

But, slowly, frustration crept up on her. Their relationship did not expand; sex remained restricted to the office. On some occasions, he even talked on the phone to Victoria while caressing Erica's breasts. One day last month, while patting her naked bottom, he had said, 'Erica is heather, a plant so resilient and pliant, it even blooms under snow.'

Last week she had suggested they meet up in Geneva and, when he rejected the idea out of hand, she had finally realised, with a chill, that she had made a mistake. He was not getting rid of his wife for her. He meticulously wore condoms. He changed the subject whenever she brought up babies.

★

Erica brushed gnats from her face and checked the Swatch on her wrist. Finally, Heidi appeared at the door of the Hen House, the last to emerge. Erica got up from the bench and picked up her bag. Tomorrow was the seafood and whiskey party, and this year she was invited.

Heidi came down the steps. 'Week over,' she puffed. 'We're all done.' And then wiped her forearm over her brow. 'It's stifling out here.'

'The thunder bugs are out.'

'Crap weather is predicted. Tomorrow's party might be rained on. I hear that you are invited.'

'It's about time.'

'Honestly, Erica, don't expect too much. I only ever stay until the first of them keels over. My husband hates it. There is not even plain water, only whiskey.'

'I need to stay sober. You tell me you have spotted Victoria cheating by switching to cold tea. I might need to do that too. Any clue where she keeps the tea?'

'Nope. They are set on getting people drunk. The oysters and lobsters are superb, though. You'll be given a bib. Old Wafer wears one. That's worth seeing.'

'Isn't anyone worried about imported seafood in that heat?'

Heidi made a grimace. 'Now that you mention it.'

253

'I'm joking. Spending that much money, Favre can be trusted to serve bacteria-free food.'

Heidi drove off. Erica checked around her; the park was empty. Inside the Hen House, in the open-plan lab, she plucked rubber gloves and a white sterile face mask from dispensing boxes mounted on the wall. Then she went into her old cubicle, where she unlocked Heidi's desk drawer with the key she had kept. In her mind, she had rehearsed every move dozens of times. From a ledger, she memorised the current code numbers and then, with the weekly reports folder, she returned to the entrance where she put the paperwork down on the floor.

Back down the corridor was a door with a skull-and-crossbones sticker. She tapped in the code. Inside the room was a narrow work-table on one side and glass cabinets on the other, one of which was shrouded in a black cloth. There, she opened the combination padlock and, from the petri dishes of Anthraxis pathogenic bacteria cultures, she chose the one in which the spores, stimulated in gelatin liquid, had fully developed. Wearing the gloves, her breath on hold behind the mask, she carried the petri dish to the table. With a pipette, she carefully drew up some of the lethal substance and emptied it into a phial on a plastic stand. She snapped the hinged top shut. Starting at the wrist, she peeled the rubber glove down over the phial in her hand. It was now safely enclosed in rubber and protected from the light.

Stiff from fear of what was now in the bag next to her hip, she gathered up the paperwork from the floor, left the building and locked it behind her.

The headquarters staff had left and the metal shutters were pulled down. The lights in the corridor on the management floor were already on emergency, making blue pools on the carpet. From somewhere came the moaning of vacuum cleaning. She went through her own office to the tea-point, where she put the anthrax into the fridge before entering Tristan's office. His motionless silhouette seemed to be just one of the inanimate objects in the darkened room until he turned his head. In his sparsely lit face, the liquid of his eyes glinted. Wordlessly, following their ritual, she took off her shoes, pulled up her cloche skirt and climbed to sit astride his lap.

'Tomorrow…' he started, his forehead gently touching hers while he unbuttoned her blouse.

'It's still today,' she countered softly and took her blouse off. He unhooked the bra at her back, and she pulled it off and dropped it on the floor behind her. Bending lower, close again, he put his mouth to a nipple, glancing up to remain tuned to her, a faint glint of moisture on his lip. She nibbled the erogenous spot on his ear lobe.

When he pushed her gently from him, she climbed off, found her balance and stood in the sliced dark, taking off her skirt and pushing down her thong. He gave that involuntary gasp which she expected and which provoked her to perform a version of the Arabic enticement dance, one hand up behind her head, the other at her hip which moved in a slow circular motion.

He fetched her back to him but his warm hands felt suddenly cold on her body. The fact that he always made love to her in silent concentration seemed to show a lack of respect for who she was. Everything in that silence and the semi-dark seemed to point to shameful crudeness in their behaviour. It was hurtful never to be offered the time to babble as equals. Frustratingly he couldn't let himself go. There was Victoria, always Victoria. When he pulled away from her, she turned her head from him and felt tears run down her face.

'My relationship with you is the best thing that has ever happened to me.' His hand brushed the tears away from her cheek.

'But Victoria is still in the way, right?'

'I have a commitment. You knew that from the beginning. It does not mean that I don't love you.' He was putting his trousers back on. 'Tomorrow,' he resumed as if all was as usual, 'whatever you do, don't draw attention to yourself. Remember, I am just your boss, nothing more. Besides, don't overdo the oysters.'

She pulled herself up against the stuffed sofa arm. 'Because they might have gone off in the heat?'

'For God's sake.' He looked at her, shocked. 'And don't get drunk.'

'You don't offer soft drink or water.'

'It's the rule.'

'So how come Victoria gets away with tea? Heidi told me.'

'Ah, she hides a glass of cold tea in the flowers on the drinks table. Once she has toasted and sipped whiskey a few times, she finds her way back to the table and switches glasses.'

On the small balcony of her studio flat, Erica indulged in the soft flannel of her bathrobe and the feel of naked feet. She poured wine into her glass and gazed over the buildings below at the lake. Off to the east, clouds had gathered over Geneva. Tossing her thick hair about her head, she picked at a pork pie with her fingers. She knew exactly where Victoria kept her glass of tea, and that would make the job much easier.

A rumble came from inside the flat. Goosebumps speckled Erica's arms. It was the motor of the refrigerator and she was reminded that, inside it, anthrax cells were gathering potency in a mephitic fashion in the confines of the phial.

Beyond the balustrade, the evening dark was spreading. She was a lone figure on a small balcony, a single woman in a hopeless relationship with a rich successful man who was too decent to break it off with his wife.

It was up to her to change the situation. No one else was going to help her. Tristan did not love his wife any longer and, once she was no longer there, he would be free to start again with Erica. It was no life to just wait – in the hope that some happiness or a bit of love might come one's way.

'Nothing will change my love for you,' Mum had said, closing the door for the last time on their family home. Dad had already moved out to be with his lover. 'I will always keep your happiness my priority' – Mum's empty words. Dolly, their cat and Erica's only friend, had run away three days earlier, sensing that her happiness was nobody's priority. Mum had not found time to see her daughter for over a year now.

A first squall knocked Erica's wine glass over. The Chablis spilled across the metal tabletop. Erica turned her defiant face straight into the fierce wind. She had expected it. A second gust rattled the rolled-up blind above her head. The lake far beneath had taken on an iron look, and toward Geneva it broiled charcoal-dark. She felt at one with the uproar – resentment, loss, anger and the pain of longing all coming in upon her in blasts. On the far shore, the storm signals were pulsing at fast speed.

'It's my turn!' she shouted out, and rain smacked against her. The table sounded like a drum. 'I deserve it!' Her voice was drowned in the clamour of the storm, as petrichor scent rose from the hot earth. A sluggish grey curtain swept across the lake, erasing signs of civilisation as it went.

*

A maid ushered Erica through Victoria's living room out onto the terrace, permitting her only a glance at a large modern painting. The sun was harsh and bright after the previous night's rain. She had decided to wear a floral print dress, with a light, fringed summer shawl. Her hair was pinned up. In the handbag over her shoulder was the poison.

She had timed it right; most guests had already been to the drinks table on the gravel and moved onto the lawn, where they were being offered oysters by waiters. Some were sitting at tables, set up under red awnings. A quartet played soft blues. Further down the garden, oddly, a French harlequin was playing self-absorbedly with a large hoop. Heidi, in a plain shift and canvas shoes, stood to one side with her husband.

Victoria appeared in front of Erica. The hostess wore a snake-green dress and had drooping gold earrings.

'Oh, hello. Th-thank you for the invitation,' Erica stuttered.

'Tristan thought it necessary.'

The tall glass in Victoria's hand would still be of whiskey. This glass had to be observed and the deed done before it was switched for tea. On the drinks table, in the midst of the impressive flower spread, there it was – a three-quarter-full glass with a discreet gold rim. The guests were still too sober for Erica to make her move. She went to mingle on the lawn, yet followed Victoria's trail out of the corner of her eye.

Old Wafer slapped his large hand on the shoulders of those he was pleased to see. His daughter had gathered a noisy male group around her, while his son described something large with his hands that made his audience laugh. Tristan was over by Heidi, obviously doing his host duty. Now Victoria, surrounded by a group of women, toasted with them and then took a sip, her lips tense at the glass. The oyster trays were circulated. Buckets for the discarded shells had been stuck into the lawn. The quartet upped their tempo.

Erica looked back at the drinks table. It was still too risky.

Near the bandstand, the harlequin performed adroitly with his hoop. A gong was beaten on the terrace, heralding three chefs in white hats, high-handing platters piled with red lobsters. There was applause. The level in Victoria's glass was visibly down a notch, and a waiter with a full crystal decanter was aiming her way.

Everyone was now queuing at the food table to get at the lobster, holding out plates and tying bibs onto each other.

The moment was right. Erica stepped to the drinks table. With unfaltering determination, she pulled on a rubber glove, concealing the move in the folds of her shawl. She picked the phial out of her bag and, pretending to admire the gerbera, popped the plastic hinge with her thumbnail and tilted the twenty millilitres of bacteria into the glass of tea.

Nonchalantly, she ambled to the lobster, her glove back in her bag, her beating heart hidden. From the moment Victoria took a sip of tea, her skin would itch as the poison spread quickly through the bloodstream – a typical anthrax poisoning caused by sewage-polluted oysters. Within fifteen minutes she would be paralysed or dead, by which time Erica would have left.

Shrill laughter came from the tables where the guests were enjoying the lobster. Old Wafer's daughter was dancing the twist with the harlequin; the Tennessee whiskey was working. Erica noticed Victoria walking to the flower arrangement on the drinks table.

That was it. Looking neither left nor right, Erica walked to the arch in the tall hornbeam hedge, which led to a pebbled path down to the back gate. The formal hedge gave way to various border plants.

She stopped on hearing Tristan's voice. Peeking through the branches of the viburnum bush, she saw him in conversation with Old Wafer.

'You promise me nothing is going on?' Old Wafer's bass voice.

'No.' Tristan's voice was unsteady. 'Honestly.' He spun around and glimpsed her through the greenery.

In a move of spontaneous defiance, she lifted her skirt to reveal her leg coquettishly and placed the other arm up behind her head to perform her seductive Arabic sway. *Tristan, my love. Victoria is drinking poison right now. Once the scandal of anthrax-infested seafood and the funeral are over, you won't feel upset for long because there will be sexy me, right under your skin. Eventually you will marry me.* Erica swayed her hips.

The pain of a scalding needle shot into her armpit. She screamed. Reeling from the assault, she rubbed at the point of impact, from which it seemed fire was spreading through her body. A sense of doom invaded her, and she dropped down onto the low sweeping branches. Semi-conscious, she felt Tristan's hand on her brow and heard the distinct sound of Old Wafer's voice. 'That's your Erica, drunk as a skunk. Leave her in the bushes.'

'Push back these branches, will you? I can't see her properly. It looks as if she is swelling up.'

'The hussy is gagging too.' Through the fog of pain and confusion, Erica became aware of the musky perfume of Victoria. 'Ambulance,' she was saying.

She felt Tristan checking her body, lifting one floppy arm after the other. She wanted to make them all go away but only produced dry rasping.

'Get her water,' Tristan urged.

Erica was again dragged down into the drifting clouds. When she had enough energy to surface, someone's face was in her armpit, and then she heard Tristan spit loudly several times.

'I don't believe you've just sucked something from that woman's sweaty armpit. Disgusting.' Old Wafer's voice.

'Prop her up.' Victoria was still present.

Erica was pushed into an upright position, and Victoria poured liquid into her mouth, which ran oh-so-soothingly cool down her tight throat.

'I've just found the culprit in her shawl. It's a bee.'

'Don't touch it, Tristan.'

'Once they lose their stinger, they die.'

Victoria's large face loomed close. 'Drink. It's tea.' This time, Erica was able to see that the cooling liquid which was brought to her mouth was in a glass with a gold rim.

★

One of the paramedics jabbed a syringe into Erica's thigh. 'Adrenalin,' he explained to Old Wafer, Victoria and Tristan, standing on trampled-down viburnum branches. 'This young woman is in anaphylactic shock – it is an allergic reaction. No need to panic.'

Erica began to make loud rasping noises, those of a woman drowning within herself. A second syringe was jabbed, this time into her heart muscle. The paramedic, clearly alarmed, checked the pulse at the swollen neck out of which came the sinister noises. With agility, he climbed onto her. 'Come on.' With the heels of his joined hands, he pumped on her chest, again and again. Suddenly the rattle stopped and Erica's head fell backward.

No one made a move. Behind them were the noisy guests and the loud music. A blackbird cackled somewhere at length.

The medic stopped giving CPR and got up. With a heavy sigh, he freed his neck from the stethoscope. 'This young woman has just died, I am afraid. It seems her heart failed from a bee sting. I have never seen a reaction so fast, so ferocious and fatal.'

'Here.' Tristan held out his palm, on which was the curled furry body of a honeybee.

'Hard to believe.' The medic shook his head. 'This small insect is the cause of death.'

★

The paramedics carried Erica's body on a stretcher towards the ambulance. Tristan was by her side. The guests parted to let them through. Pale beauty was painted on the young woman's face, and the fringed white summer shawl trailed off the stretcher behind her like a bride's veil.

Victoria shrugged her shoulders. 'She would have been fired anyway.'

BLOND BABY

'Granny hair!' Evie's classmates had mocked. A sympathetic teacher had explained that the colour came from the pigmentation of the follicles, not realising that pig was all they would choose to retain.

Those little pests were not here, nearly twenty years later, to see that the frizzy white hair had turned golden blond, long, straight and weightily luxurious. The lashes that shaded Evie's light blue eyes had not darkened, though, and she had them tinted to avoid looking peaky.

She was now twenty-three, unattached, and working on reception at a Luton Airport hotel. Customers often came to the desk frustrated by the transformation works on the site. Evie dealt with them calmly, telling them the work would soon be over, as if promising that their tolerance would be rewarded. Someone once mentioned that her blondness disarmed the complainers; she did not consider it a compliment.

One Saturday she was manning the desk alone because another receptionist had quit the job to get married. Evie did not have a boyfriend, or close friend, female or male. Miroslav, working in the airport Starbucks, had been an attempt to fill the void of loneliness. He had reached out his dark hand across their awkwardness with each other, to remove the clip which retained her hair and relish in its cascading resplendence. But conversation had run out. She had gathered her hair up again.

There was no family either, apart from a sister who was eleven years older, almost a generation. Margot, with short and tight dark-blond hair, often observed Evie calculatingly, head tilted downward as if she anticipated disappointment. She no doubt thought being a receptionist in a Luton hotel was not impressive, but Evie knew that, should she challenge it, Margot would just laugh it off. And so she said nothing.

On Sunday, Evie was invited to Margot's house for lunch. It was somewhere to go. She wore a new crochet top, but Margot's compliment felt fake. New acquisitions in Margot's house were always pointed out, as if Evie needed to be educated in what mattered – simply because Margot had married Tom. 'Really? You've never seen a Georgian sugar caster? But then you lost your mother early.' Margot ignored the fact that she was Evie's sister.

For Evie, the only precious things in that home were her small nieces. They had a drowsy warm smell, and the soft plump feel of their limbs was silky against her cheek. Cuddling them was the most rewarding physical pleasure. The little one had just learned to walk, taking off like a miniature drunk. Evie overacted with them to hide her insecurity but was still rewarded with pure innocence. The four-year-old, head forwards and wide-eyed, approached her. 'Aunty Evie,' she said in a low voice, 'Mummy says you won't have babies.' Then, from behind her back, she produced a piece of crumpled paper bearing a drawing. 'For you – a blue rabbit.'

On the bus back to her rented studio flat in a new estate with immature wind-bent trees, Evie was contemplating the finger-painted gift when someone knocked against her knees. 'Sorry,' said the man with the case which had bashed against her. She looked up. He was young and tall, with lake-blue eyes and the same blond hair as hers. He exuded the air of a healthy, active, employed male. His eyes only brushed past hers to focus on her hair. There was a strange tension between them, by muted instinct one blue rabbit recognising another blue rabbit in a world of brown rabbits.

As more people got on at the Luton Road stop, her hair-mate was pushed away. She indulged in gazing at his back, his neck line, and twitched when he glanced over his shoulder, this time his look lingering on her eyes.

The next day, she found herself working with a man in his early forties, who would never become a friend. When he foisted his lost luggage customer onto her, she gritted her teeth.

Just then, she saw the man from the bus walk in: a blond head, wavy shoulder-length hair brushed behind both ears. It shone white gold in the triangle of sun through the glass. Disappointingly, he turned left to where the conference rooms were. She would not dare follow him, but marvelled at this second sighting, which seemed to indicate a fated course of events. She dealt with the customer, who moved away to reveal *him* again.

'Hi,' he said.

Obviously, once he had spotted her, he had decided to take it further. He introduced himself as Frazer Newman, an airport crowd-management planner. With authority, he told her new colleague that she had to be let off fifteen minutes early.

Together, they left the hotel through a side door. Outside in bright light he reached for a strand of her hair and twirled it between his fingers. 'Real,' he said, 'and a pretty girl into the bargain. Not peroxide and lipstick.'

She did not thank him for the compliment, being aware that this was the start of a relationship. She was neither nervous nor excited. That must mean something.

He took her to a Moroccan restaurant for afternoon tea, not far from the airport. They were the only customers. It smelled of aromatic seed pods. He described the simulation software which calculated pedestrian flow. She soaked his presence up with some pride, for he was good-looking. When it was her turn to open up, she talked animatedly about her nieces, describing their creativity until she stalled, realising that it was Margot's life and that her own was joyless. Their father had sped through life on his Suzuki Marauder and caused an accident, which killed their mother and left him brain-damaged. It had happened when she was eleven, leaving Margot to bring her up.

*

On subsequent dates to see a film and the aquarium in London, she could not help thinking how very different this was from what she had expected. Had Frazer really chosen her? Was he sexually attracted to her? He behaved faultlessly and was attentive to her, courteous, patient even. Of his private life she only learned that his mother was of Swedish origin. She and his father lived in Florida, and he had little contact with them.

He went on many business trips to other airports in Britain and abroad but called her regularly, once saying he missed her.

Margot was curious to know what he looked like, and Evie, after dithering, described him as a blond warrior, looking ahead, chin up as if to challenge life.

On a rainy day after work, lingering under the dripping hotel canopy, she noticed Frazer across the car park, despite the fact he had told her he was in Newcastle. He was sheltering a very pregnant blond woman under his umbrella. They talked animatedly. She seemed cross with him as she shoved him away from her, exposing herself to the rain. He appeared to reason successfully with her, and together they went along the row of parked cars.

Evie took out her mobile but it fell from her sweaty fingers. She picked it up and wiped it against her clothes but when she tapped in Frazer, her phone did not work.

The following day, he marched up to the reception desk. 'Your mobile's off,' he said. 'I couldn't tell you that I came back earlier. I had to deal with some issues about priorities for pregnant women.'

She listened silently.

'How about you come for supper tomorrow at my place? I'll cook. What do you say?' There was a coy blue look.

'How do I get there?' is what she said, and he gave her the address. Neither of them said anything for a moment before she thanked him for the invitation.

Margot was happy for Evie but warned her, 'Be careful.'

Leaving her high heels at work, in tennis shoes, tight black skirt and tucked-in white blouse, Evie entered his modern, expensively furnished penthouse apartment. Timidly, she sat on the sofa. *Be careful.* Margot's voice was in her head. *This is a single man's den.*

'Do you live alone?' she asked as he came in with a bottle and glasses. 'You must be well paid.'

He put the tray down. 'Is this an interview?'

'Sorry,' she mumbled and stumbled on. 'I… I'm nervous.'

'I know you are,' he said to her surprise. 'I also know you fancy me, but come on, I'm not that great. You're a gorgeous blonde. Be cool.'

Right then, she realised that she had fallen for him, and then again when he came to sit next to her, took the drink she had not yet brought to her lips, and swept her golden hair back over her shoulder. The first kiss felt like an invasion. Slowly, it eased into a melting sensation, bliss of which one could surely never tire.

She broke from him and reassembled herself. A fold appeared on his smooth forehead. Bewitched, with a drawn-out moan, she leaned forward until her lips reached his well-shaped mouth again.

He had prepared them a moussaka. She saw the table laid neatly with the candlestick. She noticed the salad bowl on the sideboard as she was led, entwined with the man of her dreams, past the kitchen and down the corridor to the bedroom. A waft of grilled cheese hovered, but she chased away the worry that he might have left the oven on.

There was a master bedroom with en-suite and two good-sized bedrooms with a shared bathroom.

Be careful. Don't rush things.

Once she noticed the condom packet on the bedside table, she relaxed. Lovemaking went well, largely because of the anaesthetic induced by kissing. Frazer was considerate, and knew women well. Even the interlude of the rubber protection did not diminish the magic. All he said before lowering himself over her gently was, 'We don't want to risk pregnancy.'

The next day she told Margot that she had found love: blond love.

★

During his frequent absences for work, she went on in a resigned manner. Time consisted of anticipating seeing him, resenting his absence and waiting.

On his returns she tempered her affection, instinctively afraid of making him feel smothered. Her touches were tentative and lingering, as if to extract some magic elixir to get her through the empty absent times to come.

The lease on her flat came to an end. Her towering worries turned to floating fluff as the decision made itself for her to move in with him.

At first, her few possessions looked self-conscious in the new place. Intimate habits had to be revealed and the

271

resulting shy embarrassment overcome. Having lived alone mostly, she passed wind often, uninhibitedly. He, she noticed, was peculiarly fussy about his hair. They had separate bathrooms. One of the three bedrooms was his *home office*, which he kept locked. There had been no mother to teach her how to cook, so Evie improvised, hiding ready meals under fresh parsley.

Margot seemed to have accepted that her little sister had found a man and invited them to Sunday lunch. At the last minute, he had to go to Lille, and Margot's doubts about him resurfaced. 'Just don't get pregnant.'

Evie reacted with vehemence. 'It's Frazer who makes sure I'm taking the pill. Once when I was getting low, he even went to the chemist's for me. He likes things done the proper way. Trust me to trust him.'

They sat down for lunch. For possibly the first time, Margot looked upon her sister as an equal, which made Evie feel vulnerable and exposed to adulthood.

Weeks passed, and spring brought green lushness. Although not a hand-in-hand man, during the light evenings, Frazer ambled with Evie through Hoo Park. They sat on the grass or reclined, looking up at endless plane traffic in the clear sky.

One day he rented a boat and taught her to row. She had brought a picnic, and they lazed. On the horizon, fluffy clouds bulged, and soon they were drifting on rocking water as the wind got up. It became dark and heavy rain prattled down on them. He lobbed his tuna sandwich into the lake and laboured through choppy waves to return the boat to land, while her wet summer dress wrapped against her like cellophane. There was a hint of hysteria in her laughter.

Back on land, he seemed angry about his precious hair being wet. She tried to humour him, but he walked into the nearest supermarket and bought a towel, which he wrapped around his head. It made him the blue-eyed Arab prince of pantomimes.

★

Soon after, Evie felt tired and listless at work. Her breasts were tender, and her morning latte made her queasy. In the ladies', she struggled to control her retching and heaving. It made no sense. Except – and the scalding heat of guilt rose in her – for that time when she had been late for work and unable to find the foil strip of pills. That once.

Two blue lines showed. How to tell him? Call a helpline for abortions? Pack her bags and go to some place where no one knew her?

Margot's initial long silence on the phone spoke for itself. 'Pray he brings up marriage within five minutes after the shock.' And then she lowered it to three.

Evie had prepared supper. Over Frazer's favourite caramel pot, she told him, starting the sentence with an apology for her carelessness. Ever so slowly he licked his tongue along the dessert spoon. She was trembling. Getting up in slow motion, he crossed the space between them to stand like a pillar close to her and caressed her hair. Was this goodbye? Even if he rejected her, she had a baby inside her – a human being which would be hers forever.

273

'I promise to do the best I can to help you through this.' She felt a final pat on her head and feared she had misheard. 'I assume you want to keep our baby?'

She felt light-headed as if she had been given a blast of helium. 'Yes, yes, of course.'

'There's going to be little sleep in six months' time. It had better be a well-behaved little girl.'

'It could be a boy.'

'Naaah.'

For the first time, she believed that he loved her.

★

'So, no proposal,' established Margot, 'but lots of "we" and anticipating shared sleepless nights. Not good enough. Work on him.'

'You'll be godmother, of course, and give me advice. Be happy for me.'

Margot accompanied her to the first scan. When Evie recognised the bean-shaped shadow as a living creature, she started to weep, and when the heartbeat was amplified, she sobbed hard. 'Mum isn't here to see this.'

At work, she made mistakes because her mind was shopping in Mothercare. Frazer was away often, but at weekends they painted the third bedroom to become the nursery. His home office, in which he worked late at night, was still out of bounds for her. He insisted on buying the most expensive cot, fussing over safety issues, turning down a cot carousel because it had a battery. Smiling, she caressed her bump. His awareness of risk

274

must come from his job, making sure people moved along in safety.

The second scan revealed the foetus was a girl. Evie returned from hospital with a picture of her. Frazer was so pleased that he pranced around the room. Margot, being kept informed about it all, saw in him a man who would spoil his little princess – irritatingly, an unmarried man.

One month before the due date, Margot finally met Frazer. Evie implored her not to ruin it by pushing him down the aisle.

He brought a box of baklava, embellished with a bow.

'Trying to sweeten me up.' Margot took the gift without hostility. He admired her decorative style, praising some knick-knacks, and she rewarded him by displaying her silver spoon collection. When the children came running into the room, he crouched down and overwhelmed them with his charm.

Out of the blue and a babe's mouth came, 'Why haven't you married Auntie Evie?' There was silence.

'I'll tell you why.' Frazer took hold of the little body and pretended to whisper close to her ear. 'I will. Don't tell anyone. Just not yet.'

Margot shot a quick look at Evie, who was silently praying that *What's wrong with now?* would remain unuttered. Tom took the children up to bed, and the two sisters filled Frazer in on their past; he showed sympathy over their mother Daphne's fatal accident, and a father who had to live in care. Frazer showed his admiration for Margot who had brought up her young sibling.

Margot was just building up to say something, when her husband came back downstairs. 'Wide awake and might appear again, but let's eat.'

Afterwards, over coffee and baklava, Margot agreed to be godmother and suggested they call the baby Daphne.

Frazer did not like this. 'If you don't mind, I don't want to hold a dead granny in my arms.'

'He is involved,' said Margot, satisfied, when Evie helped bring plates into the kitchen. 'You have to work on the *just not yet*.'

Less than four weeks later, Evie gave birth to a healthy baby girl. The twenty-hour labour was forgotten the second the white-down-covered head lay in the crook of her arm. 'Angelina.' Evie wept with joy. 'A perfect little angel.'

Frazer accepted this and insisted on holding the baby, looking down into her perfectly proportioned face, turning her round and looking at all sides as if inspecting a valuable vase for cracks or impurities.

★

Angelina was an easy baby, cheerful and trusting, slowly growing into a perfect infant with cornflower-blue eyes and a golden crown of fine hair. Evie, on maternity leave, was besotted with her. Even Frazer scooped this new wonder up into his affection, but still no budging on *just not yet.* The toddler's first birthday was approaching, and Evie felt she had to mention his parents, now grandparents. He was not forthcoming but grumbled that they were quite selfish and not interested in his life. They had just retired to Morocco as permanent expats and bought a villa. The one candle on the banana birthday cake Evie had baked was blown out.

Evie reluctantly returned to a half-day job at the hotel, while Angelina went to nursery.

On the second birthday, Angelina moved on tiptoe in a glow of blondness. Frazer was proud of her progress and called her 'my little treasure'. That night, he lingered after making love and snuggled close up to Evie. 'By your angel's third birthday she will be toilet-trained. Then we will fly to Marrakesh for my parents to see their grandchild and meet you. After that, you can plan a wedding with Angelina throwing petals along the aisle.'

'But are you…?' was silenced with an intoxicating kiss. He had finally voiced the longed-for words.

Frazer bought his toddler a potty with a hippopotamus on it. Evie suggested giving the child gold hearts in her ears, but he was horrified. 'Absolutely no holes made in the child.' Instead, she bought a small gold bracelet with a name plaque.

'As long as her name is not on it,' he said darkly. 'Strangers should not know her name.'

He was careful; he was a loving father and he was right. So she had a stylised tiny angel engraved in a corner of the plaque, the triangle skirt an A for Angelina and the wings a heart for mother's love.

★

Angelina, dainty and liking to be clean, was proud to be toilet-trained. Travel plans for Morocco were made.

Frazer had booked seats first to Faro in the Algarve, a two-and-a-half-hour flight, to give the child a rest and play before flying onto Marrakesh with Royal Air Maroc. His parents had invited them to stay at their house. Evie was dizzy with excitement.

She packed Angelina's case with new clothes, including several pretty dresses. For herself she had bought a new outfit for the introduction and a midnight-blue cocktail dress which showed off her hair, just in case.

The trio, soon to be a proper family, arrived in Faro airport which was heaving – nearly as bad as Luton. When Angelina spotted stuffed rabbits tumbling out of a tilted basket in a shop window, she wanted one. Frazer said this was not the moment but the little girl tapped against the glass. After a sly sideways look meaning sorry to Frazer, Evie went inside and emerged with Angelina crushing a powder-blue 'labbit' with long soft and bendy ears against her chest.

Elbowing their way through the crowds, they conquered a table in a restaurant for a late lunch. There was ice cream, and the Labbit had to be fed some of it. Over the din, Frazer told Evie that there was an infinity pool and a gym in his parents' villa. Also, his father had invited friends to meet them. 'Mother,' Frazer admitted, 'called it an engagement party.'

'Of course, she did.' Evie grinned at her fiancé. *How different a man behaved once he made a commitment.* Had they not been squeezed between people and luggage, she would have thrown herself around his neck.

When it was her turn to visit the toilet, the mirror confirmed that she had never looked better or happier.

278

Outside was her future husband guarding the cases, holding their adorable child. A sweet Frazer gesture had been to make Labbit wave goodbye, simply because she had to leave them for a few minutes.

Emerging, she saw their two suitcases standing there alone. He had taken his rucksack and had gone somewhere with Angelina. She waited by the cases, craning her neck, and then shouted his name into the din and chaos. A passenger on a nearby bench got up for Evie to climb onto the seat. In the mass of heads, there was nothing blond, large or small.

On the board their flight was now shown as *boarding*. Turning to the bags, she noticed that on the floor behind one of their suitcases lay Labbit with a fake angelic smile. She backed away, hand to her mouth. Her subconscious spewed poison into her mind so rapidly that she was paralysed. *He had taken her, taken her away.* Evie remained at a loss, with ice-cold fingers and legs that would not function, trying to breathe deeply to save her heart from bursting. Had she not known all along? Had she been cheating herself by ignoring the danger signs? She was less than others, and that was why she had to suffer this, wasn't it?

Her mobile was in his jacket pocket, and in his arms was her angel.

She bent down and picked up Labbit, and with it she stumbled into the crowd, blundered along the shop fronts and wove through oncoming people. She heard the final call for Marrakesh and ended up in front of the Information Desk.

Obviously someone made sense of her emotional garble because now an announcement was blasted over them in Portuguese and English, asking Frazer Newman to come to Information.

No one came. Evie had to identify the abandoned suitcases. A folding screen was set up around them for specialists to examine them, while she was led up a staircase to an office with *PSP Airport Security* written on the door. Inside was a chair for her, metal and cold. Water was in a paper cup.

She pushed Labbit against her heaving self, yearning to smell and feel Angelina. Papers were being filled in. They had taken her passport.

Her tickets were with him, and so were the child's. She did not know the name or address of his parents. In the plane he had turned the iPad off for her but retained it. *Suspicious?* No, they were one. Or so she had thought. There had been pictures of her daughter on the iPad, and of him.

She had to relive the moment of leaving them in front of the toilets, and was then asked questions, many of which she could not answer. Of Frazer she knew embarrassingly little. *Oh, how clearly she saw the baby right now, though.*

The official at the computer turned round to speak. No Frazer Newman or Angelina were booked on Air Maroc to Marrakesh or any other that morning.

The rabbit fell out of her limp palm. Black dots took over as she fainted.

Through a thick fog, voices reached her as if from far away. 'Blond babies wanted by Arabs... Harem-life... Qatar... Human trafficking.'

A nurse in a white coat helped her up from the floor where she had lain, head on a cushion. Realising that nothing had improved her situation, she shuddered. A rug was wrapped over her shoulders and shrouded her in total melancholy.

She found herself in a car and, upon getting out, she was walked along the seafront between the nurse and a policewoman. They sat on an empty bench. The sea was calm and blue. Her head was about to crack apart. She had probably suffered one of those silent heart attacks. They observed her, sitting there crestfallen, and gently tried to make her understand that she had, in all probability, been used by a man who worked as a stud. Angelina may have been sold to an Arab to be brought up in a harem.

If she screamed now dementedly, she might end up in a mental institution. It felt desirable. Instead, she sat silently, crying into Labbit on a shaded bench near the sea between two total strangers.

A mobile rang. 'Your sister, Margot, will be landing in Faro shortly.' The policewoman put her hand on Evie's arm, and Evie resented it.

★

Evie had to remain in fake-Frazer's apartment which was searched and fingerprinted. The *home office* revealed a desk and a chair, nothing else. Her contraception pill strip had been tampered with. When analysed, they turned out to be iron supplements. Fake-Frazer, she learned, had the habit of making several blond women pregnant at the same time. It was lucrative. He had contacts in airports, but did not work in any. He only ever drove hire cars. The apartment belonged to an Arab who rented it out online, and for whom Frazer most probably worked as a blond stud.

Evie had to learn to accept that Angelina would grow up in an Arab harem and be groomed. A sinister history of child disappearance existed on the Algarve.

Margot urged Evie to come and stay with them, but Evie had to live alone with the pain. It was all she had, excruciating pain, and she wanted to keep that intact at least. She rented a north-facing, impersonal room in a hostel. She returned full-time to her old job in the hotel. From Faro came police reports, showing their efforts. Interpol had not yet found Frazer.

Contact with Margot thinned out. Evie had let her sister down, as had been predicted. Her little nieces – the mere thought of touching them was agony.

She was offered promotion to head of reception but refused. On corkboards against the wall of her room, she kept track of Angelina's physical growth. She subscribed to an online Arabic language course.

One year expunged the next. Evie persisted with Arabic from books and tapes, making frustratingly slow progress. Police reports became sparse; the case seemed barely remembered. Apparently, only three per cent of abducted children were ever found again.

At free weekends, Evie sat in the airport entrance hall watching people, looking for blond hair and Arabs. Often, she took the train to Heathrow to watch there. On the cork wall, Angelina was now ten years old. The hotel management insisted she take her holidays. It was the law.

Evie booked a flight to Faro and a flight back the next day. On her return, she looked almost at peace with the world. After that, she asked to take her holiday entitlement in small rations. Regularly, she flew to the Algarve and returned the next day. When her boss asked why she did this, she answered, 'Three per cent.'

Angelina was twelve by now. The hostel owner offered Evie the two rooms on the top floor for the same rent. Evie did not need more space, but from there she could see the flight paths and so she moved upstairs.

Now Angelina was fifteen years old, a menstruating woman, if still alive. She would not be beaten because it would leave welts. Evie booked a flight to Faro and a return the next day.

Airport security recognised her with her stuffed rabbit, but pretended not to notice. They felt pity for the woman who walked to the spot in front of the toilets and stood there as if praying – the spot where she had seen her child for the last time. After that, the cameras showed her pacing around, looking into shops, scanning the sitting people. When flight boarding appeared on the screen, she went to watch the departing passengers file through passport control. On purpose she missed her flight back so that she could stay in the departure lounge. They knew the routine. The woman was broken-hearted, not mad. They let her stay all night in departures and then escorted her outside to book another flight back to Luton the next day.

★

Evie jerked up. She was once again in the departures hall at Faro Airport. An Arab, white floating thawb and black cord around the *keffiyeh* on his head, was joined by two

283

black-shrouded women, probably wives, as they came through security screening. Then Evie noticed a smaller black-cloaked Arab woman having trouble putting her shoes back on, as they got caught in the long garment. The sheik frowned with irritation. As the small woman caught up, Evie saw that she was young, perhaps a daughter. The sheik slowly turned his head to glower at her. His demeanour was slow and pompous. In silence the Arab group took the elevator to the upper floor. Evie followed.

Behind their master, the three females disappeared into the lounge. Evie idled in the corridor, checking the screen on which a Qatar Airways flight was shown leaving in fifty minutes to Doha. The lounge door opened and the sheik came out, alone. Evie pretended to read her passport. He stood for some time, rising on his toes and falling back on his heels, checking the bulbous gold watch on his hairy wrist. A young man with blond hair appeared up the escalator and then strolled across to the Arab. The two men communicated, and she thought she could guess what it was about. This was another *Frazer*, and the sheik was going through several minor airports with his family to cover his tracks.

The two men walked down the corridor, their backs turned to Evie. Now, a veiled head appeared at the lounge door, checking up and down the corridor. The plump-faced dark-browed daughter emerged fully and tiptoed to the lift, pressed the button, changed her mind and raced down the descending escalator, holding up her cloak. Something extraordinary was happening and she, Evie, was part of it.

She reached the ground floor in time to see the girl dive into a clothes shop where she frantically riffled through long summer dresses. She picked two, grabbed a handbag from a shelf, and disappeared into the changing cubicle. One sales assistant was busy with a customer; the other was at the till, and Evie blocked her view to the cubicle by standing in the way.

The curtain opened. A teenager with an absurd face emerged. Eyebrows drawn in strong kohl clashed with the long blond hair which was still forced into a rope twirl and hung like a hook down the back of a print dress which was too large. The girl made it out of the shop without being seen and, Evie still covering her back, joined the anonymous crowd, holding the handbag as a child would when playing Mummy.

Evie wanted to run to her and seize her in her arms, but the girl turned towards the toilets. Was it pure coincidence that this girl was running away exactly where Evie had last seen Angelina? Was her frustrated motherhood playing with her imagination? And yet, she knew. By instinct, she knew that this was her daughter.

Women flushed, doors opened, doors clacked shut except for one. Evie heard the tannoy announcing the last call for Doha. The toilet door stayed closed. Evie leaned against the tiled wall and yelped with surprise when she inadvertently activated the hand dryer.

The door finally opened slowly, and the teenager appeared. She had tried to wash her eyebrows, but dark smudges remained. Evie came up to her and blocked her way out, one hand on her bony shoulder. The girl pulled away. 'Don't be afraid. I will help you.'

285

Panic shot into the young blue eyes.

'Trust me.' The girl said nothing, just stared in calculating fright. *'Wasawf tusaeiduh,'* Evie said. *'Ana' aerif ma taqumun bih* – It is good what you are doing.'

'I speak English,' she said haltingly.

Evie realised how much she had forgotten the shape of her child's face, but then how much had this young person suffered?

'Will you help me?'

Evie's demonstration of affection had reached the girl.

★

While Evie was paying for the dress and bag in the shop, airport security stopped them. They were brought to the same room she had sat in twelve years before. The girl was not a thief any longer, at least that. They were made to wait in silence until the arrival of the police superintendent.

When he walked in, a stocky man, Evie knew that what would be revealed during the next hour would be her make or break.

Questioned, the girl only knew that her name was Abdia and that she was a *gem* belonging to Sheik Khalid Abu Sahib. Yes, of course she knew that she had been brought from Europe as a baby, wives and *gems* talked. 'Bought, actually,' she corrected herself. Her passport was with Sheik Khalid Abu Sahib, a diplomat with four wives and twenty-eight children.

The airport security man had his back turned to them as he searched on a computer screen. There was tapping.

Evie could not take her eyes off her possible daughter. He twisted in his seat. With frustrated contempt, he announced that Sheik Abu Sahib had left for Doha with his wives, leaving his *gem* behind. Her passport would surely be destroyed, together with any proof of her having existed.

'We can't go after him. He will claim diplomatic immunity. We've been there before,' said the superintendent.

'I have her birth certificate at home.' Evie got off her chair. 'And I believe that she is my baby, taken from me here on the twelfth of May 1998 at two thirty-five in the afternoon.' Evie searched the girl's eyes, which over the years had lost some of their cornflower-blue.

Through the frosted-glass window a light darted, running along the wall, from a sudden thundering plane. Abdia covered her eyes against it before sinking back stiffly in her chair. 'Please let her be my mother,' she almost whimpered. 'I am only fifteen.'

'You look older than that.' The superintendent looked Abdia up and down.

'It was hard work to please and always hope that things will get better.'

'Oh, Angelina, my poor darling. You had to live like an animal!' Evie cried out and went to kneel in front of the girl, who sat dejectedly in her unbecoming cotton dress, the tightly wound light-blond hair slowly unrolling. 'I found you. I have been searching for you and never gave up hope, not ever.'

'Mother?' Her voice was filled with incredulity mixed with desire. She reached out her arms and helped Evie up.

When they both stood close, face to face, the blond girl almost as tall as the blond woman, Evie murmured, 'You used to call me Mummy.'

Both were brought back to their surroundings by the arrival of a man introduced as the division commander. The small room was getting cramped. 'I am afraid we will need evidence that she is your daughter. Often, biological mother DNA profiles are inconclusive.'

'Angelina was born with a birth mark on her left thigh,' Evie said.

'They put lemon juice on it for a long time and it faded away.' Abdia pulled up her dress to show no mark. Evie noticed the coarse skin from the arid country she had had to live in.

'Here.' Evie took the rabbit out of her bag. 'You called it Labbit.'

Abdia examined the soft toy and carefully, slowly said, 'I think I remember,' and then brought the rabbit against her cheek in a loving gesture.

Evie shouted out with joy. 'I've found you! I've been searching for you, loving you every day since you were taken from me.'

'All emotional, understandably, but not substantial enough,' was the division commander's verdict.

'What about this?' Abdia clawed around in her bra cup and pulled out a tiny gold bracelet.

'Why didn't you show us that first?'

'I wanted to make sure she was my mother.'

'And now you know?'

'She is my mother. I just know!'

'There is no name engraved on the plaque–'

'Sir,' Evie interrupted. 'Please, sir, just listen to me. On one corner of the plaque is a tiny triangular angel with heart-shaped wings. The skirt is an A for Angelina.'

'That is correct,' he confirmed after inspecting the bracelet.

Some monumental putting right of an injustice had just occurred. Mother and daughter drew each other into a hug, oblivious to the bureaucratic practicalities being discussed in the stifling room.

A report had to be filled in. Photos taken. The nurse cut a bit of Angelina's fingernail for the DNA tests. Evie was instructed to go home and from there, scan and send the birth certificate, baby photos, and baby health booklets with inoculations while Angelina remained in Faro until their reunion was officially approved by the Portuguese government. The Portuguese bristled with efficiency.

Margot, whom Evie called to tell her the miracle, said, 'Don't worry. You'll get the girl. The Algarve police are eager to raise their percentage of recovered missing children.'

★

Three weeks later, the Portuguese government approved their reunion. Although the DNA result had indeed been inconclusive, the evidence of the bracelet was judged sufficient.

Angelina was escorted to Luton by an Interpol agent and stood behind Evie as she opened the door upstairs in the hostel with clumsy fingers.

289

'Is this where you live?'

Inside, Evie breathed in her child's strong alien perfume.

Angelina hesitated. 'If you have a husband and he is not a Muslim, I will not have sex with him,' she said in smooth English.

Evie refrained from hugging her daughter. Instead, she opened the door of the room which would be hers. '*Alahn wa salahn*,' she said. 'Welcome. It is south facing.' Labbit sat on the bedspread.

'What is that writing on the wall?'

'Me, thinking of you growing up and me missing it.'

'Oh.' Angelina pulled an ugly face as a response.

'You came back to me. It's a miracle. We need to get to know each other again slowly.'

'I don't like the name Angelina. My name is Abdia, *Allah ashan*. Allah be praised, my name means slave of Allah.'

To Evie's horror, the girl grabbed the rabbit, aimed, and threw it accurately into the waste bin.

In a thin voice Evie suggested, 'Let's go and sit in my room and talk. I have prepared tea and made you a banana cake.'

'And this is it? Two rooms, a kitchen corner and a shower?'

'The last time I held you in my arms, your eyes were cornflower-blue.'

'I don't think so.'

'Tell me more about yourself.'

'You want to know about favour-fights, veil dancing and giving sex? You want to see my tattoo?' She lifted her

290

skirt and pointed to the Arabic writing on her mound of Venus. She looked a lot older than fifteen.

'It means *king* or *master* in English. All women belonging to the Sheik get it.' She dropped the skirt but sat, legs apart, showing her thighs.

'Were there other blond children like you?'

'The Sheik is rich. He bought another *gem* after me and gave her the name Alqamar, which means *Moon*, but she is four years younger than me. This airplane noise is horrible. You can't force me to live here.'

'Where *did* you get that bracelet from?'

'It's not mine. It's Moon's, but I made her give it to me for safe-keeping.'

'Moon is about fifteen years old, isn't she?'

'Maybe one day she will have the courage to get lost at an airport and pretend so that she will be picked up by someone who claims her. But probably not, because she is shy and sensitive, and now the Sheik will not take his *gems* on trips any longer, not after losing me.'

GONE TO THE DOG

The lank thirteen-year-old girl with long stringy blond hair crouched at the cage, whispering to the greyhound lying on the ground. When the animal lifted its head and showed recognition, her expression softened, her eyes misting over. 'Poor sick dog,' she said. 'I wish I could make you better. Look, I brought you a piece of my sausage.' She lobbed it through the bars of the cage, and it landed near the dog's mouth. 'Come on,' she coaxed. 'Eat it, or I'll be in trouble.'

'Clara, get back to the house. Your two sisters need to be bathed,' Mum shouted down the garden.

'It's so unfair that Dad can't help.'

'Well, he can't. I'm in a mad rush to deliver the steroids to Upper Farm for Pete's sheep. Then there's supper to get. Maggie and Amy are upstairs, up to God knows what.'

In the large white-panelled bathroom Maggie, who was ten, was playing *squeeze the soap and make it scud around the floor*, while seven-year-old Amy had opened the cold water tap in the sink. They were both in singlets and knickers, and the room was chill.

The double-fronted Victorian house in Norfolk had belonged to Grandma. Dad grew up in it. He had come top of the class and became a vet, Kenny Kennington – like a stutter, according to Mum. Grandma now lived in Brighton because she would not make old bones in the draughty Fens.

Clara liked living in Wymondham surrounded by flat lands and close to Norwich, where there was a cinema. She tested the temperature of the hot water filling the metal tub. It was always quite a game to remove her sisters' underwear. Maggie made herself into a turtle on the floor, having made the soap scuttle under the bathtub irretrievably, while Amy tried to bite Clara.

Finally, they were both in the water. Resourcefully, Clara soaped the children with Mummy's shampoo and they enjoyed the bubbles. 'Grandma is coming to visit tomorrow,' she told them.

'She's boring. Always talks about the war. And she has hairs on her chin like a hog.'

It was true; she did only talk about the past and always the same thing. Sixteen years it was since the Second World War. Too many had died in the air raids on Great Yarmouth, which was a targeted port. Mercifully, Dad had not been drafted because the country needed him to doctor horses. They replaced cars and tractors to save petrol. Despite shortages everywhere, Dad was able to start his own practice. At this point, Grandma always added with a sigh that her Kenny had contented himself by marrying his secretary – Nola, Mum.

The greyhound with amber eyes lay dead the next morning, its gorgeous narrow head tipped to one side.

Clara unlocked the cage, slid her back down the crude wall to sit on the ground, legs stretched, and lifted the dog's head onto her lap. 'Did you cry before you died? If you did, no one heard you so no one knows you did.' She took her hairclips out with a tiny sigh of relief. 'No more pressure and duty and hard work. You can float and dream. You're in heaven now – much better off this way.' She gently stroked over the frontal lobe between the closed eyes of the dead animal.

★

Over the coming years, Clara redoubled her efforts at school to get As in science. There was no time to make friends. No one telephoned her. No one included her in anything. It often felt that she was a figment of her own imagination, tethered to the ground by the thinnest thread. If she let go, she would lift off and be blown away from her parents and her sisters.

Dad's practice prospered and an outbuilding was added in the garden to house an operating theatre, a recovery room and a sluice.

Mum had a soft spot for lambs who had club feet or were orphaned. They often ended up in the house. Hounds, to Clara's dismay, were not to be touched or mollycoddled as they were bred and trained to run after mechanical rabbits and had to concentrate on nothing but that.

Clara got a place at the veterinary college in Norwich. Proudly, she showed the letter of acceptance to her parents, expecting their congratulations and pride in her achievement. 'Soon you will be able to help me in the surgery and your mother can take it easier,' is all Dad said. And she felt she had no one and that it was futile to wish it were otherwise. She focused on learning to help greyhounds, which was her ultimate motivation.

When she was in her second year, a devastating thing happened. Dad had gone into the field with the cows, most of which he knew by name, to assist a birthing cow in difficulty, when out of the dark sky a lightning bolt shot like a golden arrow into a metal fence pole. The thunderclap that followed made the cows take off in panic. Unfortunately, they galloped towards him, perhaps in a plea for protection. Dad was trampled on and left on the ground in the rain for hours. He survived but ended up in a wheelchair, from which he could do little more than neuter cats and small dogs.

Grandma chose that moment to pass away, and Mum looked after Dad, and the income dwindled so much that Clara had to give up her studies. She had already written a draft of her thesis – 'The impact on the physical health of racing hounds from their exploitation for human greed' – but had to take a job with a technology company in Norwich.

Maggie, having left school at sixteen with long legs and a short memory, had since shacked up with a chain of Norfolk lads in town. She was ashamed of her crippled father and pretended she had no parents and nowhere to stay.

Amy, the apple of her mother's eye, now in her GCSE year felt cornered at home and became tyrannical, ordering her mother around and grabbing what there was for herself. Twice she received a warning for stealing in shops, but the owners felt sorry for the family and did not bring charges.

Dad became heavy from eating cake and sweets, and Clara had to come home from work at lunchtime to help her mother lift her nineteen-stone father so that he did not have to soil himself, and to help bathe him and change his clothes in the evening. Few people brought their pets to the clinic since the time Dad had cut into a cat for spaying and found no ovaries as it was a tom. Three years passed and the Kenningtons were not a happy family.

Maggie became twenty-one, celebrating with a boozy party somewhere undisclosed. Whatever happened there, she obviously met her match in a man who was stronger than her or more desperate than her, one able to keep her sexuality in suspense enough for her to drop the others. They got married and quarrelled and broke things in their tiny cottage not far from Wymondham. He worked as a truck mechanic and they *made do*. Even though Maggie's job in a petrol station shop was part-time, she still only visited home at Christmas and perhaps ran into Mum three times a year in town.

It was one less mouth to feed. Just as well, because Clara suffered from a bad back from lifting Dad. The doctor's advice, to stretch out on a thin mattress over a wooden board, did not help.

At weekends Clara attended the greyhound races, as if she could protect the hard-worked hounds from their plight. Several times she accosted dog owners and reprimanded them for straining their animals. Once she brought one home, a female called Windy Win which had collapsed and just been left there by the owner, who had no more use for her. Clara gave of herself to nurse the first greyhound she ever could cuddle, but the bitch died a few days later, and Clara cried bitter tears, holding the dog collar against her heaving chest.

Amy was no longer mother's little girl with golden ringlets. She turned twenty-one in her turn and got engaged to an Australian working for a Norwich insurance company. It was most probably Amy who talked him into returning to Sydney and taking her with him. Maggie, who made an appearance to say goodbye to her sister, was sizzling with jealousy. No love was left between the two sisters, and Amy got on an aeroplane and was gone. Shortly after that, a *do not bend* envelope arrived in which was a professionally taken wedding picture of Amy in white tulle and her Australian. No words, no matter how many times Mum turned the card over in her hand.

More years passed. Clara did not get a promotion as she could only put in so many hours. On doctor's orders she had to rest her spine to prevent further damage. Dad was now in a specially adapted wheelchair and a social worker was assigned to help out. In Australia there were now two babies; a postcard had gone to Maggie and she guessed the babies on the picture were her nieces. Maggie turned out to be unable to conceive, because she had had two abortions badly done before the age of twenty. Clara learned of this from the doctor's receptionist at the surgery in which she spent much time. She also heard from the home-help that Maggie was behind the bar of

The Hoops pub on Saturday, covered in bling and foul-mouthing the vulgar male customers.

Kenny became diabetic and something went wrong in his vast body. He was hospitalised and then put into a care home at the age of only sixty-five. Not long after that he died from the indignity around him and the despair trapped in himself, as much as of his liver failing. Never had a small woman emitted such a sigh of relief as she walked out of the churchyard, leaving gravediggers shovelling earth behind her, as did Mum. Clara sensed the exhaustion in her that was too deep for tears. With the withheld air exhaled from her body, however, she seemed to suddenly shrink as if the spark of her vigour had been blown out.

Clara now had to attend to Mum, who started just seeing things but then advanced to trying to catch them. She begged Clara not to send her away, and her daughter complied, cobbling a life for them together from her meagre salary. Eyes too large for her pale face, Clara laboured to turn cheap food into nourishing meals until Mum started a fire in the kitchen. By the time the fire brigade had doused it, there was a dark hole at the back of the house.

Clara reached a point in her life where she often sat motionless at the kitchen table with her face in her hands, taking a break from staring into hopelessness. Conditions in the care-homes she visited were appalling. Only one could she envisage for her mother but it cost money. Clara made a decision and put the Victorian house on the market.

Mum did not settle in, the staff complained and Clara had to visit at least once a day.

The house did not fetch much because of the burnt-out kitchen and the built-over garden. Nevertheless, when the money from the purchaser was in the bank, Clara transferred it to the home manager to be used up for the care of her mother.

★

The day after her forty-ninth birthday Clara, with her suitcase, was standing in front of her home. *Sold*. She had informed her sisters about Mum and the house but heard nothing. Her boss, for whom she had worked for so many years, had asked her into his office and suggested an even easier job in his company. He was a decent man, but that was not the answer.

Clara looked up into the wide sky in which dream-shaped clouds meandered and knotted into each other. Life had made her; life would leave her. How long the interim was, and how it was spent, was really not that much of a deal. She had nothing to gain and nothing to lose. 'Fate, I am yours.'

A determined tern flew high up in the sky, heading south. Clara started to roll her suitcase along the road towards the station. She got onto the next train to London. She had no bank account any longer and only £75 in her wallet, plus a handful of photographs of greyhounds, including a framed one of almond-eyed Windy Wen who had died in her arms.

There was a violent storm blowing over the Broads, and the train came to a stop in Cambridge. The line was closed for reasons they are never honest about in the loudspeaker announcements. Clara got off. She managed to walk against the wind and wild weather but, when her brolly turned inside out, she took shelter in the nearest public house. It was an old pub called The Flying Pig.

At four in the afternoon, two men were still lingering over beer. She overheard them talking about the dog races in Yarmouth. Curiously, she felt as if she fitted right in. The best dressed and groomed of them seemed to have guessed her backache, for he went to fetch a padded cushion, which he tapped against a chair-back before inviting her to join them. True, the train seat had been agony. He introduced himself as Cosmo.

Clara joined in the greyhound racing conversation and showed them pictures of dogs she had personally met, champions and money-makers. It was clear that Cosmo's mate was bitten by the betting sport; Clara knew the type only too well. Cosmo seemed different. He spotted the framed picture in her lap. Reluctantly, she showed it to him.

'Your four-legged baby is suffering from lung expansion?'

She nodded. 'Cruel,' she said.

'Don't forget. Winning thick wads at the races can change a man's life.'

She looked down to think about this.

'I used to know the old Cosmo and look at him now,' said the friend with a scar on his temple.

Clara looked at Cosmo, a man in his fifties with grey hair, wearing a blazer with a paisley cravat. 'I see,' she said, which meant that she didn't.

'Despite his money, he still comes down here to spend time with his mates. He's missing being poor, the swearing, the stench of sweaty dogs, and the release of the traps.'

'Something like that,' Cosmo finally contributed.

She gave him a shy smile and instinctively knew that this man with a slim gold watch on his wrist was a self-made man, one who has seen many aspects of life. There was something stubbornly determined in his eyes, and she guessed that he hated injustice and empathised with those who were down.

It became five o'clock, and she had to find somewhere to spend the night. She got up stiffly. Wordlessly, Cosmo helped her with her suitcase. He led her across the road as if it were the most natural thing in the world and booked her into a B&B, where he simply paid for a room and left.

Once in the room, she sat on the bed and pondered on the existence of intuitively compassionate humans like Cosmo. It was a revelation. She went to the window and looked up into the darkened sky, in which no more birds flew.

She unpacked her nightdress and washbag and went to bed on a mattress which was not too painful. Perhaps a lot of it was in her mind.

Come morning, packed again, she waited for the next stage of the interim between life and death. She heard the sound of a powerful car engine stopping outside. From her window, she saw a silver BMW in the forecourt.

A knock on her bedroom door revealed a man in his mid-thirties with floppy brown hair. Cosmo had sent him to pick her up. At the car, he helped her into the front seat and stored her case. They drove out of Cambridge into the countryside. The car engine purred at the gate of a substantial property. When the gates opened with a buzz, they drove past the house to a separate building with garage doors.

She stood on the gravel, disoriented.

'Come inside.' She was invited through an entrance to stairs leading up to the floor above the garages. 'I'm Callum. You do know that Cosmo has hired you as a housekeeper? He is often abroad.'

She waited for him to explain more, but he did not. He seemed unemotional as though everything for him was predictable. Upstairs, he opened a door and she slowly stepped into a generously sized, sun-filled room. With a gesture, he invited her to make it hers. Then he went back down, and from the window she watched him enter the large house through the double-fronted door.

From then on, Clara adopted the role of housekeeper and made it up as she went along. Callum handed her the household cash box and ledger; he had a room upstairs in the house. She clearly was now in charge of the kitchen. She also helped Maria, the elderly cleaning lady who came twice a week to the house, with easy chores.

Cosmo's sizeable drawing and dining rooms were joined by a glass sliding door. It was a pleasure to dust in these tastefully decorated and furnished premises. There was a study but Maria told her it was not to be entered. In it, Cosmo and Callum spent hours at the computer, conversing and sometimes shouting. 'Their business,' explained Maria.

Cosmo was on his mobile phone almost constantly. Only occasionally did she see him step from the patio into the green of the large garden, both hands joined behind his head, which was tilted up. His life obviously contained a lot of stress.

The first time Clara passed him in the back corridor, he smiled civilly and went on his way, as if her being there and being paid monthly was the most natural thing.

To thank him for his generosity, she applied herself to be attentive to details and to preparing more sophisticated food. She read magazines about flower-arranging and food presentation. Only once did he comment with, 'You can make bubble-and-squeak; I don't mind.'

Cosmo travelled extensively, mainly to South America. She did not ask him why. Apart from housekeeping issues, she had no conversation with either Cosmo or Callum. She guessed from the photograph on the bedside table of a striking Inca-looking woman, with two small children in colourful clothes and a baby in her arms, that this had to be Cosmo's wife in South America.

'Mistress, more like,' Maria commented. 'And his bastards.'

During Cosmo's absence, diligently and in silence, Callum and Clara cleaned the silver, which they laid out on newspaper on the dining room table. She exhaled through her open mouth against the side of the ice bucket before giving it a last vigorous buffing.

'Don't. Moisture stays and speeds up the oxidisation. It's not like gold that has to be washed.'

They left it at that.

The next day Callum was up on a stepladder pruning the ornamental topiary while she collected the cuttings in a wheelbarrow.

'Gold needs washing?' she probed tentatively, because during the night she had wondered about his remark. In the same way she had asked herself about the almost secretive bond between Cosmo and the assistant twenty-five years his junior.

Callum kept clipping with his shears. Eventually he offered her, 'Cosmo owns a gold mine in Peru.'

The next cutting she had to pull out of her hair.

When the peacock bush looked tidy again and he had put away the tools, to her surprise he took a seat on the patio bench and indicated she should join him. After hesitating because it felt wrong, she nevertheless sat down on a matching chair. Some ice had been broken between them and she guessed that he was ready to tell her more.

'My old man and Cosmo were pals up in Yarmouth.'

'I grew up there. I know it.'

'No, you don't. We were cockle-pickers: swollen legs, puffed hands, lumbago pain, the running from the tide. The only break was the dog track and the races. Cosmo had one winning streak after another. When I was a toddler, Mum died from pneumonia. Cosmo smelled a war coming. He and my old man got on a steamer to South America, shovelling coal; I was tied to the smokestack, black as your hat. Cosmo leased land with dog money. They dug. Cosmo's luck came up again. They struck gold, a lot of gold, and started mining. They were attacked by the natives. Cosmo shot two of them, but the last one shot my dad. I was twenty-five by then, and Cosmo gave me my dad's half of the mine. Later, he invested his money in Europe, and bought this house as a base for us. The mining world is rough.'

'Thank you for telling me that,' Clara said, thinking *he is a Cosmo rescue, as am I. No doubt old Maria was picked up out of some misfortune or danger too.*

In the large house, days came and went, ticking off the years of her life. They got used to each other and when Cosmo was home, the early coffee was Clara's favourite moment; it was just the two of them. In her daily-washed apron, she pushed Cosmo's coveted Popeye mug under the brew stream. When she had first brought it to him, black and strong with a delectable frothy cream topping, he had retained her by her arm, expressing in this way that he would like her to stay with him. Nowadays, she just remained standing within touching distance, as a caring mother in a fresh-linen-scented apron would to a son before he faced a day of struggle, while he sipped her coffee, elbows on the tabletop, eyes closed to savour it.

★

Each time Cosmo returned from his life in Peru, Clara noticed more white tufts in his hair. They had looked after the house and prepared for his return, more often than not Clara and Callum doing Maria's share because she was now seventy-six and no longer able to.

Cosmo was not duped. As was expected, Maria came into the kitchen one day to say goodbye. Cosmo was retiring her with enough to see her through. 'He is a generous man. I'll pray for him,' she said with moist eyes.

With Maria gone, the established harmony and hovering peace of the house and garden were disturbed, a perfect human balance out of kilter. Perhaps Cosmo was also affected by it for he returned unexpectedly two weeks after he had left, seemingly troubled. He asked for just black coffee in the morning and walked with it around the garden.

Clara busied herself near Callum in the hope that he would explain, but all he said was, 'Cosmo is not well.' She saw them leave, return and leave again with an overnight bag, and knew it was for Addenbrooke's Hospital and she started to fret. On his bedside table strips of pills appeared.

And then the moment came. She was called into Cosmo's office; a decision had been made for Callum to accompany Cosmo to Peru to pick up the business there because the responsibilities required a fit younger man. Cosmo talked in a voice which sounded strong, but in which she detected the fragility.

And how about me? she wanted to shout. *I'm sixty-five with a disastrous spine.*

'You'll remain of course, to look after my property.'

Pensively, she searched his eyes and then nodded. Her imminent future was to remain alone here, walking through empty rooms and talking to herself, with a salary which would pay for taxis, should she need to go out.

'Everything always works out in Cosmo's world,' Callum added with kindness, and the meeting was over.

This time though it seemed not to work. Clara caught a nasty virus, most probably when she had visited her GP to ask for stronger painkillers. She failed to shake it off. Her chest hurt and she could only really breathe when sitting upright. It was clear that she had a fever and her back played up more than ever. After spending two guilty nights on Cosmo's easy chair in the living room in agony and feverish confusion, she called for an ambulance while she could still tap in the right numbers.

In hospital they gave her a single room in the acute emergency section. She knew from Mum that it was *the pathway from life* – the path to the pearly gate. She asked to see the chaplain and, when he was at her bedside, she made him promise to write down and witness her last wishes, in which she left the nine thousand plus pounds she had saved 'to the hardest worked and most deserving female racing greyhound in Yarmouth'. During the next forty-eight hours, Clara heaved and rasped to get air into her lungs, while morphine slipped into her arm, gently lifting her above pain.

She had had a good life. Memories were not made up of grand events and huge expenditures. It was the quirky little things which made the mind smile: Mum saying 'one, two and hup' before lifting Dad, the feel of Windy Wen's paw on her thigh, Maggie peacocking around in a new dress worn inside out, Amy swinging upside down on a metal bar, knees bent, her tresses brushing trails into the sand and then... of course, Cosmo.

The cause of death was pneumonia paired with cerebrospinal fluid to the brain. The hospital bereavement office sent e-mails to Maggie and to Amy in Sydney. There was no reply. Clara was cremated and the ashes stored in the Cambridge crematorium for two weeks. Unclaimed, the cheap box was buried in an undesirable spot near the A14, lorries thundering by on their way north.

The state appointed a solicitor to execute the will. He sent emails to Maggie and Amy informing them of the legacy to a greyhound, but he too received no reply. He had just started to make desultory enquiries about suitable greyhounds when he was contacted by Charles Lehfeld of the posh London firm of Clacton & Lehfeld, who said he would be taking on the work. Apparently, on the same day that Clara Kennington died, her employer and benefactor in Lima had also died – actually two hours earlier once the time difference was calculated. He had left all his UK assets to Clara – several millions *in toto*.

Clacton & Lehfeld in their turn informed Maggie and Amy about the new development. Sisters who had not spoken for over thirty-six years were suddenly on the telephone for hours. Amy would fly back from Sydney, and the sisters would contest the will.

A meeting in London was arranged. In haste, Maggie hired a lawyer off the internet, one with the reassuring name of Delia, who specialised in family disputes. Delia met the sisters in the conference room of Clacton & Lehfeld, not far from Marble Arch. Amy had put on a lot of weight and gained an Australian accent, while Maggie's hair had become thin as a result of too much dyeing.

Lehfeld announced that he had already identified the most deserving greyhound in Great Yarmouth, a bitch called Allegra. Delia immediately advised the sisters to contest the will on the grounds of mental aberration in their sister and an overdose of medication at the time of writing. She prompted Maggie and Amy to contribute the thought that the will was uncharacteristic of Clara, who had always shared everything and put family first and certainly loved her sisters more than dogs.

Just then a tanned, exotic-looking man entered the conference room. Delia sucked in her breath at the sight of him. He took it all in with an unblinking gaze, conceit almost arched his back in his posture. A miniature gold ingot dangled in the V of his open shirt. 'Rodrigo,' he announced, rolling the rs. Then he winked at Delia who, in acute self-consciousness, brushed erring strands of hair behind her blushing ears.

'As Cosmo's son, I don't think I am the one who has to explain my presence here.' He pulled out a chair and sat down. 'In any case, Clara did not survive Cosmo for long enough to inherit from him under Peruvian law.'

'Shit,' said Maggie to Amy. The sisters, with their necks stretched, conferred with Delia who raised her shoulders and pursed her lips. Lehfeld and Delia asked for a moment and left the room to go and talk law.

Rodrigo bestowed on the sisters a mechanical smile, frozen in the corners of his mouth by contempt. '*Yo soy la familia de Cosmo* and you – *phui*.' His hand flicked an insect from the table.

The returning lawyers informed them that the case would take time to sort out. They would be informed about the progress of the contestation.

Amy believed that Cosmo's son was sure to get it all, but Delia commented that, according to Lehfeld, Rodrigo was an illegitimate son and that might change things.

The sisters decided it was worth persisting, despite the fact that Delia charged a hundred and twenty pounds an hour. To prove her worth, Delia assured them that there was a loophole to be found in every will if one looked closely enough. The sisters asked her to look. Amy flew back to Sydney.

★

Three months later the sisters were summoned to a second meeting. 'Fingers crossed,' said Maggie as she picked up Amy at Heathrow.

Delia began by announcing that Rodrigo's argument had failed; Cosmo's bequest to Clara was under UK not Peruvian law, and she had survived him for two hours, long enough to inherit. Now, it was up to them to overturn Clara's will. 'To leave a large house and three million to one dog is *prima facie* insanity. It can only be justified in the case of a long-standing family pet, or guide dog, or life-saving mascot of some kind.'

At least the bastard son would not get the dough.

Delia managed to raise a suit to contest Clara's will, and it would have to go before a judge. They would meet up again when a date for the hearing was set.

Rather than go direct to the airport for Australia, the sisters asked the taxi driver to make a detour via Cosmo's house. There they asked him to wait while they stood at the fence of a beautiful property in a well-tended large garden – a dream of a place.

'All that can't go to the dog,' said Maggie.

⋆

During the following months the sisters called each other regularly to make sure that neither had heard anything about the court case, or made a move behind the other's back. There was not a peep from Delia but a substantial bill.

Eventually Amy decided she had to come back to England once more, and she and Maggie presented themselves in reception in Delia's office.

'Delia is not in the office at the moment, but you have not heard anything because the case has been resolved.'

The sisters drove immediately to Cosmo's house. It glinted in the morning sun as they gazed over the hedge. A man came down the road, pulling a pug behind him on a leash.

'Excuse me,' said Amy. 'Do you know whether this house has been sold?'

'Sold? No, it wasn't sold.'

'Who lives here?'

'The late owner's son. Have a nice day.'

Maggie and Amy stormed up the road. At the gate they buzzed the intercom and buzzed again.

The double-fronted door finally opened and a uniformed maid walked slowly to the gate, where Maggie and Amy stretched their heads between the bars like greyhounds straining upon the start.

'What do you want?' asked the maid.

'To talk to fucking Rodrigo.'

'He is at the races with Allegra and her puppy, to show it how its mother got famous.' Seeing the sisters' confusion, she added, 'Look, it was a clever lawyer's trick. Rodrigo bought a dog and paid a lot of money to mate it with Allegra. Now the puppy is next of kin, and the law says Rodrigo gets to look after the dog family in the property Allegra owns.'

In the dark of the open door a woman appeared. As she advanced into the sunlight, Delia became recognisable. 'Come back here, Renata!' she ordered. 'Stop talking to those women.'

ONE MAN SHOW

Via Curiatti is situated close to the historic heart of Naples, the oldest Greco-Roman city in Europe. It was a nobleman's street, and its tall elegant houses stand in close proximity, to minimise midsummer which rules the long cloudless sky, and to retain the chill from the earth. They were built in volcanic stones and, over time, embellished with sculpted marble. Bowed wrought-iron balconies are supported by stone scrolls. On some houses, lattice shutters are fixed, and baroque lamps on brass arms, their Murano glass still intact, guide walkers at night along the tenebrous Via.

Even now, Via Curiatti is devoid of vulgar clutter. Not far from it though, cafés, gelaterias and gift-shops have nestled into the archways of houses, tables spilling out onto the road. The light air brings bursts of laughter and wafts the sounds of piped music, of a guitar being strummed, of a woman singing. The merciless July sun burns down on tourists as they dodge from one patch of shade to another, the city gasping in heat and exhaust fumes.

Those Neapolitans who reside in the Via's high-ceilinged stucco apartments indulgently suffer the graceless vendors' shouts from perennially repainted carts filled with artesania and pulled by donkeys in shabby straw hats. Already inclined to keep to themselves, the denizens note the commercialism with a blank look and protect themselves, not with hostility but taciturnity.

Some ancestral homes have been designed with more ambition, for men of greater importance. Number 17, the most prestigious, has five floors and a grand entrance; a solid stone arch reaches up to the second floor, embellished with a group of female figures in marble surrounding the family coat of arms. The stonework is discoloured and in need of restoration.

Under the shadow of the arch, the concierge in her apron tilts a watering can over enormous pots of white azaleas. In the street, cars are parked half on the narrow cobbled pavement. A brown dog trots along, sniffing in the central gutter initially laid by the Romans.

The building opposite this architectural gem wears a faded Pompeian red. Out of its Roman-tiled roof peek three dormer windows. The middle one is open, and a youth with dark curly hair looks out and down into the road. Disturbed pigeons flap in the blue air, but the young man does not move.

Marcello has to stand on an upturned crate to see over the rim of the copper gutter. His pelvis is bruised from leaning on this parapet. To pull off a great heist, sacrifices are necessary. He had not prepared his last burglary well and had lost out. There are as many thieves in the streets of Naples as there are hungry homeless dogs. This would not happen again. Through his John

Lennon spectacles, he notices the concierge watering the flowers. It fitted the pattern. Tuesday. Next the fishmonger... And there he is, driving down the road, hooting and parking right up on the pavement in front of the concierge, who gesticulates to him to go elsewhere. He ignores her, gets out and, opening the back of the vehicle, takes out plastic bags. With them, he disappears into the sombre light under the arch.

Predictably, on the third floor a glass door opens to the ornate balcony, and for a moment pellucid light springs from it. *Miss Busybody* steps onto her balcony. He has given all the residents pet names. This mature *signorina* starts to water her own modest collection of potted plants. People are often led to mimic the behaviour patterns of others and take comfort in repeat behaviour. Marcello, lingering on his crate, has studied them at length. Miss Busybody looks up and smiles at him vaguely. Her returns her smile. Shimmying in her slippers, she goes back inside, pleased with herself; it shows in her body movements.

On the top floor, without balcony, resides the Contessa, a powder-white ghost, though Marcello only ever sees the ginger fur of her cat against the sun-warmed glass. Over a span of eighty years she has been forced to sell and move up her ancestral home, floor by floor. She has a youth with a stubby ponytail deliver the Napoli news and a weekly glossy celebrity magazine exclusively to her. *Ponytail* stays in her flat for about fifteen minutes. Is he caressing her ego for a large tip? Does she tell him her memories? Marcello does not like it because the curtains are drawn at all times.

The man on the fourth floor leaves one hour later, walking down the road like any humble man but, in the Piazza Giugliano, he gets into a chauffeur-driven car. His apartment is the grandest, with the same wrought-iron balcony as Busybody but his has marble tiles with not a thing on them to spoil their inherent beauty. In the evening, when the lamps are on and the sash curtains not yet lowered, Marcello can see down into the apartment. With binoculars he believes he has identified an old master over the marble fireplace and a Cellini female bust on a plinth. Once you know such things are present, then you know that there are more, and his painstaking observations are necessary preparation for the theft of those objects.

Marcello has christened the owner *Mr Lavish*. He lives alone, never entertains, and his only guest is his elderly mother who visits occasionally. Marcello has watched the white-haired woman sitting in the armchair next to their glass balcony door, a rug over her legs. Her son does not take her anywhere but goes to work every day of her stay, returning in the evening as usual. After five days, Lavish puts her into a taxi. Not a warm-hearted son; one who has money and treasures in his apartment – maybe they even belong to his mother.

Marcello has given himself weeks to watch these three apartments so he can succeed. He finally steps down from the crate, removes the wig and glasses, and faces his abode. The horsehair mattress on a creaky metal-framed bed sags like a worn-out donkey's back, and the plywood wardrobe door, though kicked shut, always slowly gapes open again, displaying the clothes

Marcello has collected over time. In a corner of the low-ceilinged room is a pile of books about art and antiques. A sink encrusted into a corner like a mottled scallop provides the sole facility; down the corridor is a rimless toilet and primitive shower. Servants in old Via Curiatti were not spoiled with comfort.

From this small room Marcello orchestrates his life. When asked what he does for a living, he says 'Business' and spreads his arms as if offering a platter of possibilities. Women never ask about business, not of that kind. They ask whether he is available to them with their eyes, their rolling shoulders, blood-engorged lips and jutting-out breasts.

With his first cigarette, while he was still in short trousers, he decided to adopt vanity in his manners – a provocative approach – and practised it on all occasions. Thus, he lost his virginity at thirteen years of age to an older girl and became *actually* conceited before he had ever owned a suit. Now, in the wardrobe, hang several of them. In the oblong mirror stuck to the inside of the door, Marcello is worthy of admiration. His face is of classical Italian beauty, a gay man in a bar once said before Marcello punched him. His facial features are pleasingly even and the cheekbones pronounced. The sensual lips end in full stops in the right places, and the eyes looking back at him are not the brown of every Antonio or Federico, but treacle-coloured pools in which flickers mischief like petrified organisms in amber. His natural hair is glossy and dark, 'with a tinge of Russian Blue' a lady-painter once told him, not without excitement. There is something about mature Englishwomen coming here, sitting on stools, painting Italian things. The mere word *Italy* makes them tipsy. They nearly swoon when he puts a hand on their shoulder, pretending to look at the paint on the canvas. 'It's no good,' each one says; nor normally is the sex.

★

It is six o'clock in the morning on Wednesday, the twenty-sixth of July, Santa Anna's Day which is special for Marcello. He feels elated. The first pigeon croons on the ledge of his dormer, and today he will turn a major trick, the big one, the one for which he has made many preparations.

The glow of the rising sun is only just discernible. With a practised deliberate movement, he throws the now dead pigeon from his open window. After that, he leaves the building dressed in chinos, a short-sleeved Lacoste shirt, and a cashmere sweater over his shoulders, its sleeves wrapping him in a loose hug. Striding along purposefully, he crosses the piazza and walks on until he reaches an abandoned lot, where cars are parked on irregular stone slabs. He goes straight to the most expensive vehicle, a silver 3.5-litre Mercedes soft-top, and checks the tyres and bodywork. A boy in black shorts comes running, pumping his immature legs in oversized deck-shoes. With a grimacing smile, he insists, 'I did not touch the car, I swear. I did not even point at it with my finger.' Marcello reaches into his pocket and dribbles some coins into the dirty hand held out by his car-sitter.

Marcello slides onto the leather seat, starts the engine, checks the petrol gauge and activates the device to release the soft-top and fold it behind the back seat. He pops the bonnet and, outside the car, pulls out the oil dipstick, wipes its blade on tissue and pushes it back into the sump. The motor oil stands at three-quarters full. He balls up the stained tissue paper and puts it back into his trouser pocket. He checks his Rolex watch; he has left himself leeway as he always does. Two swallows sail through the bright air, emitting their high-pitched trills. This is a good omen.

He walks away and the street urchin resumes his watching position on a quarry stone, stiffly alert. 'Don't take your eyes off it until I get back and you'll earn this five-dollar note.'

On a nearby patch of greenery is a donkey, tethered to a stake and grazing the public grass in a wide ring around it. Noticing Marcello, the donkey gives an extended sobbing neigh, expressing the deep-seated pain of a lone soul seeking response, a sound familiar to Marcello. '*Poverino,*' he says to the animal.

At a wooden portal, under a niche deprived of the statue of a saint, he pushes the door and enters, letting the dry bang of the closing wood momentarily shock the brooding atmosphere. Instantly he regresses in age.

The chapel dedicated to Santa Anna seems to breathe softly at him. Familiar details dissolve in the incense-laden atmosphere into which his childish mind used to lose itself. On the side altar, she still reigns in supreme and inspired silence, clad in a midnight-blue robe of real velvet, a silver heart into which four daggers are stuck. She looks at him with her glass eyes, just at him, as she always did. Once, when no one was watching, he climbed up, one dirty knee on the white embroidered altar-cloth, to touch the translucent tear hardened on her pink cheek – he simply needed to touch – while his mother knelt in front of the eternal lamp.

Marcello grew up a hundred metres away in a ground-floor flat with a concrete yard, where his mother had washing permanently on display, underwear Marcello was ashamed of. She does not live in the flat any longer but on the outskirts of Naples. She has shrunk and feels child-sized in his arms. She tells him that she has taken pity on a widower she picked up out of kindness, one who had nothing under the sun, but Marcello knows that loneliness is the core of it. Imagining the two old lizard-skinned people grating against each other in bed panics him. *This is what I'll become when all is over*, Marcello thinks and now notices the shabbiness of Santa Anna's cloak; the rich blue has faded. Walking through the light beam from the rosette window on his way out, Marcello is wrapped in dust particles.

Outside, he checks his watch again and it is time. He crosses himself and walks back. The donkey is lying on its side now and for a moment Marcello thinks it has given up the ghost but then an ear flicks.

★

It is not just any donkey. From the beginning of June, Marcello rented it every Saturday morning and filled its leather saddlebags with a locksmith's paraphernalia. On

322

the strap across the animal's back he painted *Locksmith*. In peasant clothes, cap deep over his face, he walked the donkey down Via Curiatti. '*Fabbro ferraio*,' he shouted, 'Locksmith!' knowing that Mr Lavish would be home on Saturday mornings. His cry drew people to windows and onto balconies. Miss Busybody rushed onto hers to check what was going on. 'Locksmith!' he shouted and passed slowly with the donkey, clutching the base of its ear to control the animal which was unused to him. Thus, a Saturday morning pattern was established.

On Friday the fourteenth of July, as predicted by warning notices, restoration work began on the stonework over the arch of Number 17. Exploiting the upheaval, Marcello arrived, disguised as a priest, a personality he often adopted. The set of false teeth clipped over his own effectively altered the shape of his face. His hair was sleeked back and streaked grey. The concierge was sweeping the worn red carpet, muttering to herself about the dust she had to swallow from the sandblasting. The priest, Bible in hand, stepped over the electric cables in the hall. Seeing the man of the cloth, the concierge made to greet him, when he caught her with his finger to his lips. Pointing the same finger upward, 'Fifth floor,' he whispered. The concierge crossed herself and let him into the elevator.

On the fifth floor, as Marcello got out of the noisy wood-clacking lift, the Contessa appeared at her door, looking at him with rheumy eyes, her figure tilting on a stick. Behind her appeared the ginger cat, tail high. 'Father,' she said to Marcello, 'did you come to see me?'

'I am a little early but the angels have confided that it will not be long now before absolution.'

She emitted a shriek and turned back to save herself in her abode. She would not bother him any longer.

He crept down one floor and rang the bell of Mr Lavish's apartment. He waited for the stone-blaster to stop before ringing again. Eventually came the sound of someone approaching and a key crunched in the lock. A crack opened, revealing a third of the white-haired head of Lavish's mother, a pearl choker around her wattled neck. She stared with cold curiosity before realising that a priest was standing in the staircase – one who was about to address her when he was overcome by a coughing fit. She had time to wait patiently for it to pass.

'The dust… I was visiting the Contessa… Perhaps you could be kind enough…' and he asked for a glass of water.

'My son forbids me to open the door to anyone,' she croaked in a shaky voice. The priest's renewed coughing brought tears to his eyes. He held the Bible in front of his mouth. After all, a priest is far from anyone…

In her entrance, Marcello studied the heat sensor in the corner above him while she, wrapped in an outsized grey wool shawl, shuffled off to the right where the kitchen and utility room were. Out of sight, Marcello took the key from the lock, slipped out of the apartment and down the stairs two by two. He composed himself on the first floor to appear in the entrance lobby, dignified and serene. The concierge bickering with a workman did not even notice the priest leaving the building.

The next morning, Marcello repeated the donkey-locksmith exercise, and Lavish came out onto his balcony, hailing him to stop.

It is an old-established Italian belief that a locksmith with a donkey never abuses his craft, for if he did he would own a car.

Marcello attached the donkey to the No Parking sign and slung the saddlebags over his shoulder. On the fourth floor, Lavish asked him to replace the lock. 'My mother is completely useless,' muttered Lavish before leaving the locksmith to do his job.

Once the new lock was installed, Lavish thanked Marcello with a pursed-mouth nod and paid him pedantically. It was the growth the size of a walnut on the locksmith's cheek and several black rotten teeth which induced Lavish to add a small tip.

That afternoon, Lavish put his mother into a taxi. Watching from the dormer window, Marcello felt that all was going according to plan.

The donkey-locksmith appeared innocently in Via Curiatti the following Saturday as well, for credibility's sake.

★

Back in his garret room at eight-thirty this Wednesday morning, Santa Anna's day, having given the donkey a last pat, Marcello rechecks the items laid out in a row on his bedcover: the key to Lavish's new lock, the one Marcello installed eleven days ago; a dark holdall packed with his best suit, two ironed designer shirts, a blazer, his sport-chic outfits, leather shoes… Into the outside pocket he slips his passport, driving licence, car registration, Rolex Oyster, wallet and credit cards, and zips it closed.

Into plastic rubbish bags he stuffs his disguises: peasant clothes, priest outfit, several wigs and caps.

Marcello picks two of his books about antiques and lays them on top of his clothes in the holdall. Then he crouches and pulls an air rifle from under the wardrobe, dons the wig and Lennon glasses, climbs onto the crate, aims and shoots across the road.

The noise of the gun is no greater than a donkey's fart, but in Lavish's apartment, an upper pane of his balcony door fragments, and myriad splinters fall, tinkling onto marble.

Miss Busybody bolts out and looks around her. In some of her flowerpots are glass shards. Leaning out, she shouts upwards, 'Signor Alessi!'

Lavish is probably getting dressed for work and did not hear the glass shatter, but he hears Busybody's yelling. The postman below, about to drive off, hears. He stands at his Vespa and looks up at the balcony on which Lavish now appears and bends to pick something up. He brandishes a dead pigeon by its legs as the culprit. Busybody is scandalised and tries to take this opportunity to engage with Lavish, her cold-shouldered neighbour, but Lavish is not interested. He disappears into his drawing room with the dead bird.

'Excellent,' says Marcello. His broken-necked pigeon has done its job. He takes off the wig and stuffs it with the Lennon glasses into the rubbish bag, so confident is he that he will succeed today. He packs the rifle into his holdall and sticks a revolver from under the mattress into the back of his belt. He goes downstairs with the bags.

On the ground floor, behind the stairs, he checks the props for his next and last disguise: a trolley, on which is a wooden crate, straw peeking between its rough-hewn slats, a blue overall and protective gloves.

On his way back to the Mercedes, he gets rid of the rubbish bags in two different bins. He releases his car-watcher and hands the eager boy a note. 'As I promised.' He drives the convertible away, while the child studies the five Turkish lirasi in his hand.

Marcello parks the convertible in Via Curiatti. Back in his Pompeian red building, he slips into the blue overall onto which he has glued a label: *Express Glass.* He pushes out the trolley with the crate; *Glass – handle with care* is painted in black on the crate. He watches for Mr Lavish to leave for work and, twenty minutes later, a red-haired glazier with a limp, in a blue overall and wearing protective gloves, appears crossing the Via, pushing a new glass pane for Signor Alessi in front of him on a trolley.

'But,' protests the concierge, 'I have not had time to call a glazier yet.'

'Signor Alessi ordered the glass from us this morning. On his way to work he dropped in the key to his flat and left a note for you.'

She unfolds the note, relieved to have the information in written form, because the glazier has a speech defect which makes him quite incomprehensible.

Please allow Express Glass into my apartment. The firm does work for my company and is trustworthy. Alessi. PS I've left the alarm inactive.

Marcello produces the key to show her.

Satisfied, she lets him roll his trolley towards the elevator but changes her mind. 'I better come up with you,' she says, wiping her hands on her apron. He pushes out a loud fart, to make her step back. He forces the trolley into the elevator cage, presses number four and goes up alone.

Before opening Lavish's door, he prises the lid off the crate and takes out the glass pane. The alarm is, of course, on. Alessi did not write the note. Holding the pane in front of him with his thermal-foil glove, he defies the heat sensor in the alarm, passes beyond the alarm box, leans the glass against a wall, and deactivates the device with pliers and a spray of Superglue.

He fetches the crate and lid from the trolley on the landing and carries them into the apartment. He turns the key in the lock from the inside and leaves it there. Then he carries the glass pane through the drawing room onto the balcony, banging the balcony door several times and making sure he is heard and seen from below as a working glazier.

In the drawing room, he looks around him. The décor and the furnishings are more beautiful than he had hoped for. He gives a sigh of satisfaction.

First, he goes for the painting over the fireplace he has seen from across the Via. It is a Canaletto, there is no doubt, and in a foliate frame from the eighteenth century. He unhooks it and lays it tenderly into the straw cradle in the crate.

On a satinwood demi-lune table, he spots the Cellini bust. His fingers twitch, but first more paintings to maximise the space in the crate. He takes down three more paintings, descending in size, before grabbing the sculpture. To either side in the crate remains room for the pair of three-hundred-year-old carved candlesticks. An exquisite birdcage mantle-clock, though, does not fit. He hammers the lid back onto the crate; a glazier hammers.

Once the crate is back on the trolley on the landing, and the door is again locked from the inside, he goes for the silverware in the dining room adjacent to the drawing room and also overlooking Via Curiatti. Subdued light hovers in the high-ceilinged room, like in a museum. Marcello understands why Lavish never invites anyone; he lives an egotistical life in awe-inspiring surroundings, sheltered from human weakness.

Working systematically, Marcello empties the sideboard drawers of their silverware into a canvas bag. He hears a faint click. He holds his breath. Nothing more; old buildings make noises. In a glass display cabinet is a small Meissen donkey which he could slip into his pocket, but first he carries the full bag of silverware to the entrance door. He goes back for the donkey. Perfect, isn't it? There, another dry click. He looks around him. Perhaps it is in his mind, made up by nerves on edge.

With extended fingers he picks the donkey from its cabinet and hears another click. Slipping the figurine into his overalls pocket, he realises that the noise is coming from the other end of the apartment. He tiptoes down the corridor to the back of the building where the kitchen and utility room are, giving onto the servants' staircase. It occurs to him that, of course, it is the refrigerator in the kitchen. It clicks again just as he bends his head into the kitchen.

In the dimly lit room, he sees a shadow move. He pulls the gun from his belt. At the kitchen table sits a person. Marcello gasps. The person is alive but very old and wrapped in a grey shawl with a pearl choker under her flabby chin.

'*Avanti*,' she croaks.

'Santa Anna and all her angels!' The bloody mother of Lavish has returned, and he had missed it.

'What do you want in here?' she asks in her shaky old voice.

He stands at the kitchen door. He does not switch on the light as he prefers not to be seen clearly.

She emits a moan as if in physical pain.

He points his gun at her. 'Keep silent. I won't harm you. I am only after your son's silver and stuff. I never had any of this. It's about time I did, don't you agree?'

'You are an angry boy.'

'More than that, you old goat.'

'He calls me old goat too and, like you, only cares for money and expensive things. He hopes I die soon. He has to force himself to spend time with me. I have to shame him into looking at me and when he does, he abhors me.'

'Well, that's tough. Just stay put and don't move, and I will not hurt you.'

The old woman pulls herself up slowly.

'I said, don't move.'

As she starts to come round the corner of the table, Marcello raises the barrel of the gun to aim at her face.

'I don't want to live any longer,' she says, 'unwanted and unloved.'

'That's not my problem.'

'My memories of a baby boy in my arms are safe. I can still smell the infant, feel its warmth.'

'Good for you.'

'Shoot me.' And he sees her sway. One hand grabs the kitchen table. 'I am asking you to shoot me. Do you hear me?'

'And then what? I go to prison with a corpse in here?'

'If you cared at all, you would pull the trigger now. But do not miss my heart, my bleeding heart.'

'I am not a murderer. I am a thief.'

'Do you realise I was taking pictures of you picking up my son's treasures?' From the fold of her shawl, she reveals a small instant camera.

'Bitch! Old bat. Give me that.'

'Shoot me.'

A mechanical sound of birds tweeting comes from the other end of the apartment, disorienting Marcello. The devil has got into this burglary.

She cackles mockingly. 'You can't do it, coward, can you?'

Marcello shoots her in the heart. The knowledge that he is an excellent marksman calms him as her body slumps to the ground with a thud but without a whimper.

The camera skitters across the floor, and he stamps on it with his leather soles until it spills its guts. He gathers himself; the plan has not gone smoothly, but he is still on schedule. All he has to do is go down in the elevator with the trolley, cross the hall and be away with the loot.

Calm again, he walks back through the apartment. He has killed an octogenarian, but he will have time to think about that later.

The key is not in the door. How come? He tries it, but it is locked.

Refusing to panic, he opts for the back door to the servants' balcony. He will have to go past the body to get to it, and the taste of hysteria rises in him. He notices that his hands are trembling. Today is not an auspicious day; he should not have planned for today. Unwished for, his mind conjures up the picture of his grandmother on a woven-straw chair, reaching out her arms, her eyes lakes of love as he totters towards her to be enfolded in her love. Those arms are now crossed over her emaciated body in the box which was lowered into dug earth at his father's signal.

'Why are you doing this?' he had asked his father. 'Now she can't hear me, and I will have to dig to see her.'

'Get lost,' his father said. And he became lost, but not in prison for life.

Covering his eyes against the sight of a dead grandmother, Marcello crosses the kitchen to the utility room. The back door is locked. He searches in all the normal places – lintel, hooks, drawers, under the mat. The key is nowhere to be found.

And now there is someone ringing the doorbell. The concierge must be checking on him. His meticulous preparations have turned into a shambles.

'I know you are in there,' a male voice shouts.

Balcony, Marcello thinks. *Four floors up? Jumping eight metres down to the street?* He would have to improvise.

The door is unlocked to reveal a uniformed policeman. 'Neighbours heard a shot.'

Marcello is not a resident. Can he prove that he is a glazier? After a pat-down, the gun is taken from his belt, the porcelain figurine from his pocket, the car-key from the other. Never has Marcello been so exposed. His brain cannot find a way to slither through some gap, because of the dead body in the kitchen.

'You will stay here while I call for backup.'

The policeman closes him in. Suddenly all is silent. What happened to the key Marcello left on the inside? How come the policeman has a key? In any case, there is no way out here. The back door is made of weaker wood; perhaps it can be broken down.

Marcello runs down the corridor. In the kitchen there is no old woman lying on the ground.

Sprinting back to the front of the apartment, through the open balcony door he hears the familiar growl of a powerful car engine. He runs onto the balcony. Below, the crate nestles on the back seat of his Mercedes, the way he has designed it to fit, and a full canvas bag. A grey shawl and pearl choker are on the passenger seat. The policeman tosses his cap onto the back seat, revealing a ponytail which falls to his collar. He roars off without a look backward.

★

After hours on the autostrada, in Trieste the Mercedes crosses the border into Slovenia.

Renaldo finally pulls off the road, gets out of the car and takes off the bulletproof vest. The hours spent delivering newspapers to the old Contessa have paid off. A second time he has benefitted from watching Marcello do all the work and then stolen the loot from him. Renaldo's doting mother always said to him with admiration, 'Dear boy, you can steal anyone's heart.'

FORTUNE FAVOURS THE BRAVE

Anne died in hospital last night.

Only yesterday, I brought her in for a hysterectomy. Complications set in; a junior doctor could not explain it.

A volunteer I can barely keep up with is leading me along corridors.

In the Kandock Room, I unwind my scarf and put it on a chair. She hands me water in a white cardboard dunce's hat and tells me that the chaplain will be in shortly and that coffee is on its way. *Who or what was Kandock?*

Brochures on bereavement are piled on the round table. The water cooler, like a presence in the room with me, gulps vulgarly.

Pushing the vertical blind aside, I look along the hospital wing. Behind one of those windows is Anne, my Anne. Perhaps she has already been lowered into the basement. She carried a donor's card.

'Are you being looked after?' The volunteer looks in.

Obviously not; you killed my wife last night. She came in yesterday for a routine operation. She is – was – only sixty-eight years old.

'The chaplain has been paged, and coffee is coming.'

'To hell with the vicar, and I don't want coffee. Take me to my wife.'

The head disappears. I refill my cardboard hat.

The plastic container shows agitation, the water level drops, and I tell the contraption that my wife left me last night forever. Sip, don't cry. Forever. I am single again, the way I used to be when Bob offered me the job he feared I was not up to. In the end I worked for that carpet business for forty years. It grew from a High Street shop into twelve outlets, booming thanks to the wall-to-wall carpeting craze in the late sixties. Anne looked after things at home, raising our only son, Leo.

Before marrying Anne, I had gone out with young slips of girls of whom I was actually afraid, except for Melanie – Melanie with the corn-blond mane and the disturbing habit of walking around barefoot. For a time, I was her steady boyfriend. Her French mother had passed some foreign mannerisms on to her, admired by me at first. But she was oblivious to the discomfort her lack of inhibition caused English people, and I was cowardly. I held up a shield of conventionality and drove her away. After my Dear John letter, I imagined with remorse her utter surprise and deep hurt. To my relief she went to France, a place called Cognac, to live with her aunt, and soon afterwards I married Anne.

Did I tell the water cooler all that, or did I just think it? Only now do I notice the picture on the wall of a couple seen from behind, sitting on a bench looking out to sea.

'Bastards.' I am starting to leak from my eyes.

I draw out another cup, and the water urn glugs. Complications killed Anne. I can make a fuss about what went wrong and take the hospital to court. But she is gone forever, never to look at me again, never to poke me again saying, 'Franklin, you are muttering'. What about our trip to South America for my seventy-second birthday? We have made a down payment, started preparations.

I pick up my scarf and knot it around the pull-down tap on the water cooler. This causes the water to flow out, fill the tray and then run over the edge down to the floor. 'Weep your heart out for me, until you run dry.'

Leaving the Kandock Room, I see the vicar-woman with her dog collar and two volunteers coming towards me, arguing obviously: 'How long has he...? Nobody told me... Not qualified in bereavement...' I reach in my breast-pocket for the car park ticket.

At Silver Birch, our four-bedroom home just outside Cambridge, the beginning of the end is tough. I make it past the mat saying *Welcome* and now have to survive Anne's reading glasses looking at me from the kitchen worktop. The clock in the living room dings ten times. It is an heirloom Anne inherited from her grandmother, and we marvelled not long ago that one, not unlike it, sold at Sotheby's for seventeen thousand pounds. Most upsetting is Anne's pink cardigan draped over the back of the breakfast table chair. The buttons are imitation daisies, and the trim is flower-garlanded. It is a comfy cardigan, not for anyone else to see her in. She had it for as long as I can remember. I lift a sleeve to my face and smell Anne's cooking and Anne's eau de cologne.

I am aware that reality will draw me out of my grief. Chores and duties will reclaim me. Forms will need filling in, authorities notified, the holiday cancelled, and the word *funeral* has now something to do with me personally.

What worldly goods belonged to her are now mine. We invested our savings into four fixed-term bonds. The NatWest in town is a familiar place to me. Anne worked there for years. Colleagues trusted the easy feel-good way about her. After retirement she still *helped out*, not to lose touch she said, and I teased 'With money?' Her colleagues will be genuinely sad. They might treat me kindly therefore and be helpful.

It is Saturday midday, isn't it? Anne only died twelve hours ago. That can't be right. Surely, I have been in shock longer than that.

What is a certainty is that for three months I have not seen or spoken to Leo, my son. According to Anne, he telephoned her and showed concern about her abdominal pain. Anne proudly adored Leo, her little Lion King. I do not like what he does, or what he has become. He preys on hard-up farmers and offers to buy their land. He goes back on the agreed price after digging up flaws in land registry entries, geological faults revealed. He goes as far as causing boundary feuds, planned years ahead. Leo has a gift for sniffing out situations which he can wreck and benefit from, as he has the ability to smarm for England. He plays golf with the right people, works on his local image. Gives to charities if the media are involved. My son has conned people *for their own good* all his adult life, including his own mother.

Grandly making a major donation to the Heart Disease Crusade, Leo and his wife, Ellen, were acclaimed in the local papers. Ellen was dolled up and Anne, who mistrusts her daughter-in-law, guessed at cosmetic surgery. The charity has yet to see any of the money.

Their eleven-year-old son is at Ludgrove because it sounds good. Ellen drives a Porsche because she looks good in it. There is home-help because she deserves it. The latest fad is a white French poodle puppy with which she is already bored. I love dogs. It upsets me most about her, even more than the way she makes a fool of my grandson, Richard, who has no other option but to believe that his mother means best for him.

In the afternoon I receive an e-mail:

Dear Granddad, Mum says I will see you at the funeral. Our dog is a newsense and bit Dad. Now he has to go to someone else while we are at the funeral so nobody is upset. Got an A+ in geography. Love Richard xxx.

Nuisance is misspelled. During the night I sleep poorly. Anne's warm breathing body seems already remote, as if she were puffed away. It is Sunday morning and Leo has announced a visit. To bear sitting alone at the breakfast table I shrug on Anne's pink cardigan. Unable to eat anything, I amble around the living room and pick up the two brightly painted maracas, the samba-shakers I brought home with a CD. On an impulse I push the button. Samba rhythm enlivens the room; I start dancing, shaking the beans in the hollowed gourds. I twist and turn, bend and shake, and escape to somewhere else in my mind.

A grey face is at the French windows, that of my neighbour. He taps his curled finger against the double-glazing. I come to and stop the music, then slide open the glass door.

'I couldn't help hearing the noise,' he says. 'Are you all right?' meaning, *You're off your rocker.* 'I just heard that Anne died. We're very sorry. She was a lovely lady.'

There is nothing I can say to make this a conversation. He pads away back into his garden through our gap in the hedge. Who told him?

At eleven thirty Leo stands in the middle of my living room, in his *trust me, it is good for you to meet me* stance. For a forty-four-year-old, he looks well kept. He puts down his flash Gucci briefcase.

I have sold carpets all my life and made a good living, without ever having to show off.

Ellen has stopped in the hallway, examining the cleanliness of her teeth in the mirror. They did not bring my grandson, whom they have named Richard Cedric Price-Davies with a hyphen: Davies, the name of Ellen's family. At least Richard is comfortable at school amidst other children with hyphens.

Leo intones, 'I've just come from my lawyer who works for me round the clock. The hospital informs him that you vandalised the bereavement room and then, instead of signing papers, you ran away.'

I look down.

'You also called them late last night to say that you would drop by to bring them Mum's reading glasses – *for the one who'll get her eyes.*'

I hear Ellen snigger from the entrance.

'An hour ago, your neighbour phoned. You were dancing around, wild and demented, shaking bones in the air to some African tribal racket.'

'Samba. I bought those for your mum to warm her to Latin America.'

At the drinks trolley he lifts out the Jack Daniels bottle by its neck. Only two fingers of whisky left. This makes him accuse me of drinking.

I get up to fetch him ice from the kitchen. On passing the cabinet, I accidentally knock over the Swedish vase. On impact with the floor, it cracks and covers an area with fragments of broken glass. How clumsy I have become.

'That was the Orrefors vase I gave Mum.'

Yes, I remember. That is why it was so ostentatiously exhibited. I turn back and begin to pick up the gleaming shards from the carpet.

'Sit down,' Leo orders.

He sits close opposite me and starts to talk as if I were hard of hearing.

'You know we care for you. It is a sad blow to lose Mum, hardest for you. That is why we are here – to help. Don't interrupt.'

I had only taken a deeper breath to suppress my rising anxiety.

'However, clearly you have lost the plot and you have to admit it. Your latest behaviour… and that cardigan.

You are in your seventies and need to be somewhere small, somewhere care is available.'

Ellen taps her Botoxed forehead. I see the movement despite her now pretending to fix a stray hair.

'As it happens, I have just the right thing for you, my very exciting new project: Windsor Hall, a signature senior home, high spec throughout.' A glossy brochure is handed to me. 'As you can see, specialist care for dementia is planned for one wing. At the same time, Ellen and I feel that it has come to the point where you would benefit from my having your power of attorney. My top-notch lawyer will set this up in no time.'

I bet.

Ellen is now fingering Anne's clock and I hear her ask, 'Is this the one?'

Now I know that I am in serious trouble.

Leo pats my shoulder and changes tactics and the tone of his voice. 'We'll do all we can to give Anne a lavish send-off.'

I omit to tell him that, when calling the hospital last night to offer them the reading glasses, the arrangement was made for a simple ceremony in the hospital chapel once Anne's body has been harvested and released.

Ellen, who looks bored, announces that she needs to be driven to her hair appointment. Leo gets up but tells me that he will be back. Obviously he has not finished with me. I notice that they have come in a Vauxhall and not their Bentley or her Porsche.

'Where is the Bentley?'

'MOT. That's just a loaner.' It sounds like a lie to me.

Leo has left his briefcase behind, the one in which he brought the brochure. Idly, I flick through papers concerning the hospital and Anne's death, and then come across a legal document. Some law firm is taking Leo and his company to court pursuing a debt. There is even the possibility of prosecution for embezzlement. Despite the protestations of my son's 'top-notch lawyer', it looks to me as though Leo is unlikely to walk away unscathed. He owes honest people an awful lot of money. Prison is a real possibility unless he comes up with an initial *goodwill* payment of one and a half million pounds by the first of next month.

He and Ellen need money desperately. The first of May is in ten days' time; that's a week and three more days.

Leo returns. He lets himself in and resumes his threatening presence in the seat in front of me. I am old. I have lost my partner. All I am good for is the house and the two hundred thousand pounds I possess.

'I'll give you a whole week to think about moving to a home. OK?'

The crucial week for him to set up the power of attorney. After that, I am as good as dead, but less comfortably so than Anne. He will move me out of here and appropriate the house and my savings in order to save his ass.

'Ah, one more thing.' He turns, already at the door. 'A care assessment worker will come and assess your needs. Don't say anything; it's just a thing they do.'

Through the net curtain, I watch him climb into the cheap car because the Bentley has been impounded or sold to help pay back the debt. I bet Ellen is not at the hairdresser's either.

Left alone, I pull the cardigan across my chest and close the daisy buttons, and sit cross-armed in the chill of my house. Afternoon shadows creep in and loom. 'Anne,' I say, 'please do something to help me.' I remain like this without turning on the light.

Monday, the next day, Anne does send help which, at first, I do not recognise as such. When I answer the door, I am face to face with a woman about Anne's age – the bloody care assessment worker.

'Go away.'

'I didn't expect you to want to see me.'

'Correct.'

'Not after all this time.'

Hello, here is something which does not add up. Now that I pay attention, she does not look like a council employee on a job. She is wearing raspberry-coloured shoes with high heels and asks, her head to one side, 'You don't recognise me, do you?'

When she smiles into my eyes, I recognise her as Melanie from the time when I had smelly armpits.

She knows about Anne's death. Leo had it announced in the *Sunday Telegraph*, and online. Melanie hands me a cutting: *Dearly beloved mother and grandmother, of Leo and Ellen Price-Davies, and Richard.* I am not mentioned. My son is already acting as my empowered attorney.

'I am sorry for your loss,' says Melanie, adding, 'This is probably the wrong time for me to appear on your doorstep. Actually, very wrong. I always do that.'

I smile, remembering her ways, and invite her inside.

We connect instantly, and it feels odd to slide back in time and see her not old but how she used to look, and still looks to me.

She sits down, lots of skirt and fluff and colours, and puts a canvas shoulder bag at her feet. Bending forwards, from it she conjures a bottle of Cognac. 'Totally inappropriate again, but I brought you this in case you needed it.'

'Melanie, I am sorry I wrote you that letter. I didn't even have the guts to tell you in person.'

'It happened a long time ago, but I *have* kept the letter.'

'Dear me.'

I bring brandy balloons, aware that Anne would now insist on washing them in very hot water first. I pour the gold-coloured Cognac. Melanie and I clink glasses in toast. Then she asks me about my life with Anne, my job, my son. And I tell her as I understand it. She listens intently, a frown between her brows, how she interprets it. It feels good to talk like this.

After a natural pause, she starts to tell me about herself. She remained in France for many years but, after retiring from work in a department store in Bordeaux, returned a couple of years ago to live in a small terraced house in Royston, a house she inherited from her father. She still visits Cognac, despite the fact her aunt has passed away. There is some awkwardness when we know she will tell me about her love-life, almost as if I, who jilted her, was allowed a solid marriage, while she had to make do with whatever came along after the disaster. She never married but lived with a partner. They parted on friendly terms.

I pour us both another brandy. She gets up and paces around. She never could sit still for any length of time, I now remember.

'Why these?' She holds up the maracas and then sees the CD.

'Anne and I were going on holiday to Argentina, and…'

She switches the CD player on and sweeps along, rattling the shakers.

'You're doing it all wrong.' I take them from her to flick them alternately. She kicks her red shoes into a corner of the room, and we dance around, each flicking a shaker, her movements a swirl of skirts, her mane silver grey.

A voice shouts from the garden.

'Hide!' I push Melanie from me. She ducks behind the sofa, pulling her skirt close to her, and I slide open the French windows a polite slice.

'I've just called your son about the noise and your demented dancing.'

Pulling the glass door shut, I wonder what my son has promised my neighbour.

'What was that about?' Melanie asks. The spell between us is broken. There is so much more to our stories.

I make us coffee. At the breakfast table, she pulls Anne's chair out and sits down. I have just lost my wife and am dancing around my house with a woman I once dated, having coffee as I did with my wife three days ago.

Would Anne be upset? I think how insightful she was. As if turned guardian angel, she knows the blackness I am facing and the doom of losing our home and savings. Women are emotionally strong beyond measure.

I put both my hands flat on the kitchen table and admit to Melanie the nature of my son and the danger I am in.

In turn, she tells me that she has a forty-two-year-old daughter called Celine who is married to a Frenchman and lives in Bordeaux. With the light of pride in her eyes, she reveals that she is an engineer with Air France. 'Do you want to see a picture of her?'

Melanie's finger rolls on the iPad. She stops and holds the frame up. I look at Celine, a remarkably attractive woman with short-cut hair and intelligent face, dark blue eyes. In her arms is a toddler.

'The baby is called Tom.' Then Melanie says in a new voice, quite strangled in sound, 'Celine is yours,' and starts to cry.

Never have I felt so emotionally confused and yet alert. I reach out and crush her wrist with my right hand, wondering how to react. I am conscious of fearing her blame. I let go of her arm, and she relaxes and draws a little apart from me. Looking at me calmly, she says, 'That's what happened *then*. Now is now.'

Eventually we are worn out by each other. On the way out, Melanie promises to e-mail me the picture.

I realise that I am not able to say anything more today to anyone. I lock the door behind her and sit at my computer, waiting for an e-mail with a photograph. Melanie has given me a daughter. She has also given me a tomorrow. We have an Air France engineer in common. Thank you, Anne.

Just before I go to sleep, Melanie calls to make sure I am OK. Like teenagers, we chat for nearly an hour. I recline on the bed, head propped up by two pillows, Anne's and mine. The main topic is how to stop Leo owning me legally, locking me away to get at my home and money.

'We need to make you poor, quickly.'

'First, I will make my house over to you,' I suggest. Yesterday, I did not know she existed and now I am giving her a seven-hundred-and-fifty-thousand-pound house, and it feels the right thing to do. I trust her. 'Second, tomorrow early I will go and see the legal adviser in Anne's NatWest branch to work out how to break the four fixed-term bonds and have the two hundred thousand pounds instantly available.' These major decisions made, I find some sleep.

Tuesday, at opening time I give Jeffrey, the bank solicitor, a wad of deeds and Anne's death certificate. My instructions to him are to transfer ownership of my house and its entire contents, including the Volvo in the garage, to Miss Melanie Faulkner. He lifts his eyebrow only once, when I request a clock be mentioned specifically in the contents.

'This, and cashing in the bonds, will take five working days. And that's with the priority that bank employees get as a perk.' He adds with a softer tone, 'Anne was so helpful to us, after all.'

When I tell Melanie, she does not thank me for the gift because her mind is racing ahead. 'It will be touch and go whether it is done before Leo gets lasting legal authority over you.'

On Wednesday, I can't sit still and appear in the bank again. Jeffrey is not put out. I had no idea Anne was so highly respected. The cash from the bonds less penalty costs could be in an instant access account by late Friday. I sign on dotted lines with cold fingers.

The next question is *How to conceal this money from Leo?* 'It will be a race against time,' sighs Melanie as if suddenly my life were hers. Of course, it has become hers with our sharing a daughter and a grandson. That night, I dream about my daughter.

Thursday starts with Leo calling in his brisk *we are all happy people* voice. A lovely room in the care home has just become available. Lucky me. I can begin to pack personal items. Furniture is provided. On Sunday, Ellen and he, himself, will help me move.

A little later, the hospital calls to tell me that tonight they will have finished with Anne. I ask them to prepare her for the planned funeral service tomorrow morning.

Leo, when I tell him, does not insist on his fancy funeral idea. He has other things on his mind. He accepts that, after the ceremony in the chapel, an ambulance will drive his mother's remains to the Cambridge crematorium.

It is late Thursday afternoon and I tap my finger gently on the mouse, hesitating over the online florist's most suitable arrangements. Eventually, I settle for pink champagne roses for the coffin. This lifts my spirits.

It is short-lived, because the person in front of my door is the social worker. Black and sturdily built, she comes with a questionnaire clipped to a board. We sit at the table. She pushes her large-lensed glasses higher up on the bridge of her nose. Then she starts with the things she already knows about me, like dressing in my departed wife's clothes, tribal dancing, breaking valuables, apart from the vandalism in the hospital. She endeavours to put me at ease by smiling grotesquely. More boxes need to be ticked. How am I coping feeding and washing myself? Can I still manage stairs, and do I suffer from fainting spells? My drinking habits are already noted down.

From her, I learn that my son is expected to have power of attorney by the time I move to the home.

'Am I going to a place called Windsor Hall?'

'My word! You are going to a subsidised council nursing home. Windsor Hall has nothing to do with public care. In fact, I hear the whole project is in question.'

Another downfall for Leo.

Melanie puffs with outrage after my update. And then she comes up with a plan. It is daring, but Anne would have liked it.

Friday morning. The service in the chapel starts at eleven. Melanie and I are not there. We have driven to Leo's villa in Melanie's Volkswagen. Pushing the intercom at the closed gate, I announce us as from the Wood Green Animal Rescue Centre. The gate slowly opens.

Leo's gardener-cum-handyman bowls up and leads us to a wire dog-run at the back of the house. A white poodle sprawls on a wooden plank, eying us dully.

'How old is he?'

'Dunno.'

'Does he bite?'

'Dunno.'

'I guess you dunno his name either.'

Our mission is to fetch the dog. The bloke seems relieved; it is OK with him. He unlocks the cage door. The animal gets up.

In the car on the way to Melanie's Royston home, the animal in my arms looks up at me in wonder.

The funeral service must be over by now, and Leo is driving behind the ambulance to the crematorium. We kneel on Melanie's bathroom floor. I restrain the dog in the bathtub while she shampoos hair-dye into his pelt. The dog is not co-operating much; we're both drenched.

Once towelled, the pedigree poodle does not look the chestnut brown on the box, but a rather mottled grey, veering into lilac, especially on his back and tail.

Just before bank closing time, Jeffrey calls to tell me that the bond money is accessible and that the house deeds will be in the name of Melanie Faulkner by tomorrow, Saturday.

'You do know that you are not actually giving me this house, right?' Melanie asks.

She spends Friday evening finding out things about the care home. Care levels are according to physical or mental requirements. Melanie says that I will be better off with a physical disability.

Saturday, we go to Mobility Store looking for a walking aid. I have decided to limp towards the right-hand side. Whenever I need my right hand free, I will have to park the stick somewhere first, which increases the image of dependency.

There is a wide selection of walking frames and sticks. She suggests a Zimmer frame on wheels, but it looks incredibly jazzed up, with integral holders for a mobile phone and drink. She disentangles an elbow-support stick. It has a wide metal shaft, but I opt for an even wider aluminium-tubed one which has four bent feet with rubber stoppers to distribute the weight. I limp to the counter and pay. Outside on the pavement, my hand on the ribbed plastic handle, I trip over the walking aid's feet. Melanie, true to her nature, gives a spontaneous puff of laughter but guiltily catches it in the hollow of her hand, noticing my mortified expression.

'Hang in there,' she says.

Early on Sunday, the sky is blue and the magnolia bush at the end of the garden is in full bloom. Ellen and Leo are at the door to help me move out. My son and his wife are about to upbraid me for having missed Anne's funeral and for not answering my phone, but the ugly fall I had makes it all better.

Out of what they consider my earshot, they confer. 'So, now he is handicapped,' says Ellen. 'Does that make a difference?'

'Actually, it's bloody good news. If we go for mental health issues, they like family members to be involved in the treatment.'

We are ready. My two suitcases are brought down the stairs. Ellen does not even care about her fingernails. Melanie had suggested I pack two cases, which would be more normal for someone going away for the rest of their life.

The care home is not far from the hospital, a grey concrete purpose-built old people's home with rabbit-hutch-like living-cum-bedroom spaces. There are glass windows along the corridor for staff to check on the inmates. 'It's for your safety.' And, 'Oh look, they have their own garden.' Yes, a rectangular bit in the centre with some tough plants in pots filled with cigarette butts, a pergola in the middle, all in the permanent shadow of the surrounding buildings.

The home manager, Judy, greets us. She recognises my son from the newspapers. She blushes when Leo puts his hand on her Primark-clad shoulder, asking her to take real good care of his father. 'Don't worry, we'll help him settle in a jiffy.' My incarceration is mapped out.

Without the knowledge that Melanie is with Jeffrey picking up the deeds and keys to my house about now, I would falter and faint.

My room contains mainly the bed, a hospital affair, and a washable armchair.

'I brought you a present,' says Ellen in her playful voice and places a plastic IKEA-style clock on the only shelf available. 'The one he had at home was old. Nice, isn't it?'

Judy agrees. 'Pretty colour.'

Shit-brown?

'It is best to let him be by himself.'

'Of course.' Ellen bends towards me and plants a little kiss on my cheek, a thing she has not done since their wedding, for which I paid. Her Judas lips smell of liquorice.

'We'll put your stick right here,' says Judy loudly. 'So you'll know where it is. *Right here.* And there is the button to call in an emergency.'

I have to hold myself back from losing it. I am not allowed a mobile phone or access to a computer. There is a television in the common room, supervised. I am not allowed outside without prior permission and a relative, or without a carer bringing me to a doctor's appointment.

The window of my room on the second floor has two horizontal metal bars to prevent me falling out. It only opens a fraction and overlooks the car park area, right above the recycling bins.

A woman in the cage next to mine shouts 'Help' and 'Help' and 'Help'. Nobody responds. First, I was going to limp to her and help her, but then I realise that she has lost her mind. This will make sleeping difficult, and I need to get away from the worst day in my life. Are animals in zoos given God's grace to fall into deep sleep?

Monday. With me out of the way, Leo will be in less of a panic. He could go to NatWest, waving his power of attorney, but I guess he will appropriate the house first. Melanie, bless her, has promised to find a way to get me out of here tomorrow morning for a doctor's appointment.

In the washable armchair, I do not permit myself to dwell on who has sat here before me. Instead, I open the fat book I brought: *Stevenson's Book of Quotations.* There are two thousand two hundred and ninety-nine pages. It's the item I once said I would choose for a desert island during an idiotic dinner game. Every five minutes by the

IKEA clock, I indulge in a new quotation. Methodical discipline keeps a mind healthy. By lunchtime I am on page three. *Absence sharpens love, presence strengthens it,* Thomas Fuller. The hours are dragging and the chair smells of disinfectant. Judy enters and then pretends to knock. I am due for a wash. It is part of my needs package.

How am I going to survive this with my dignity intact? Linda, the assigned carer, has a moustache and stamps out any refusal. I choose *shower* and keep my undies on. A hand soaps in them but no eyes see the contents. It tickles but there is nothing sexual in all that. Linda is only doing her job. Someone has to.

On Tuesday, possibly the last chance to take cash out of the bank before Leo gets at it, Judy bursts in before I have finished with the entire philosophy of Rene Descartes.

'It is against our rules of prior notification, but a community nurse is here to take you to your GP for your leg.'

Melanie, in a nurse's uniform, belt and tied-back hair, with glasses on her nose, is waiting in the entrance. I bite my lower lip. She signs me out at the buzz-controlled door while I limp laboriously past Judy. Outside, the sun touches my skin.

We drive into town and Melanie parks alongside the common. The bank is not open yet.

She turns in her seat to face me. 'Yesterday, your son Leo bowled up at Silver Birch.' Her hands are sawing the air from excitement at the recall. 'Leo used his spare key. He was alone. *Gotcha!* I heard him shout from your

355

living room. Then he saw me coming out of the kitchen, me and the poodle who recognised him and growled. Leo launched onto the attack. *How the hell did you get in? Get out of this house at once, you trespassing bohemian bitch.'*

'Were you barefoot?'

'Is that important?'

'No, it's just something I like to imagine.'

'OK, so he says the property is his and he is calling the police and his lawyer.'

'The top-notch one.'

'Yes, that's the one. When I told him the house was mine, he kicked the dog. I threatened him with the police for trespassing and mistreating an animal before showing him a copy of the transfer of deeds.'

'And he went crazy with anger.'

'No, he went pale and quiet and asked me who I was and why you had given me this house. I said that we were childhood sweethearts, and he saw pigs fly. After that, calmly I asked him to leave. *Gladly*, he said, because he needed to go and contest ownership. I could stay as cleaner until then. At the door he informed me for my own good that *My father, your supposed sweetheart, is mentally ill and therefore legally incapable of making a gift.'*

Leo, with his trademark confidence, will see no problem in offering the house to his debtors as collateral. He will set out to the NatWest brandishing his power of attorney. 'We have to beat him to it.'

Melanie gives me a hooded look. 'I didn't dare ask but how will you make two hundred thousand pounds in cash disappear from sight?'

Oh welcome pure-eyed Faith, white-handed Hope, thou hovering angel, girt with golden wings! – Milton.

Leaving the car, we hurry to the main street, me limping as fast as I can. Someone is unlocking the bank's entrance. There is no sign of Leo yet. I send Melanie away to wait for me in the Moroccan coffee shop called The Beige Camel in a side street. A last look, no Leo. I hobble in. Jeffrey ushers me into his office. He is a discreet and professional man and does not mention the walking aid. I sign the receipt for the large sum realised from the investments.

The banker nods his head, his mouth pursed. 'You'll need a large purse for all that.'

At my request to be left alone in the room for about twenty minutes to *sort myself out*, he closes the door meticulously behind him.

When I emerge from the bank and cumbersomely make my way to The Beige Camel, there is still no Leo. It is ten in the morning. Melanie sits at a table in the back, folding triangular hats with paper napkins which she pulls from the metal dispenser. I have déjà-vu.

Leo will not be looking for us in here. I stand the walking aid in a corner. We can take a breather. Melanie orders more mint tea for us. She does not ask about the cash. It becomes time for my *community nurse* to take me back. Leaning heavily on my stick, progressing slowly, I return to the car. We don't speak as we both know the next step will be Leo's visit to the care home.

Back in my plastic armchair, I nibble comfort chocolates which Melanie bought me. In the afternoon, I move to the common room. A few of us are watching

357

Elmo in Grouchland, when Leo appears. My son looks unhealthily flushed and his movements are edgy. He grabs me and drags me back to my hutch. I have problems keeping my walking stick with me. Where did we fail to be father and son? When was it that we last hugged with affection? Vaguely, I remember the sticky hands of a little boy patting my forearm after he made banana-eyes, a show of milk teeth, in order to engage me in his playful mood.

'Where is the money?' Leo shouts to wake the dead before the door has a chance to close fully on my quarters. He manically rifles through my clothes in the cupboard, checks in my shoes, flings behind him the contents of the three drawers, before he comes for me to rip open my dressing gown, rage on his face. 'It's got to be in here somewhere. According to NatWest, your bonds were put into one account which is now closed. You didn't transfer the money into any other account. Despite my rights over you, which I showed them, they said you were no longer a client and they had no further information.' He started to check along the walls, concentrating on the carpet edge. 'Aha!' He went on all fours and pulled at the carpet corner, which had curled up. His fingers driven into the loop-pile, he clawed the carpet off the floor to look underneath. It crackled as it ripped off the glue. Beaten, he sat back on his haunches and looked up at me. 'You were not allowed out of here. You are not allowed visits. So where the fuck have you hidden the money? And while we're at it, this vintage hippy squatter owning my Silver Birch, a sweetheart of yours? – Come again, Dad! This woman who conned you will be evicted before the week is out.' He let go of the lifted carpet corner, which flapped down into place.

'*My* Silver Birch, surely. And not everyone cons everyone else as the norm,' I add. 'Can I go back and watch some more Elmo?'

'You senile degenerate! Don't think you're so smart. I'll find it.'

I have rendered Leo powerless and he has no option but to leave. This triumph brings me no happiness. Anne did not do him a good turn by spoiling him.

Two days later, I read in the *Cambridge News* about Leo's bankruptcy, his arrest. Ellen is shown standing in the background, looking her age. He has been unable to come up with the *goodwill* payment and has been charged with embezzlement.

That evening, Melanie appears at the door without Judy sending her away. 'I have been nosing around in lawyer-land. Apparently a man accused of serious crime is not permitted to have legal guardianship.'

*

It is now one week later, and I am on my way out of the care home for good. I left my IKEA clock with the 'Help' lady, and hugged her.

At Melanie's Silver Birch, I ring the bell.

'Come in,' I hear her shout. I give the door that swift push, because it jams a bit. Anne and I have come through this door since we had a son and I got a promotion.

Melanie, barefoot, a bouncy dog at her heels, greets me in the hall. I am led into my living room. I go over to the mantle clock, which has stopped, and wind it up with the key hidden in its back. Then I plunge into an easy chair and stand my walking stick next to the side of the sofa.

Melanie laughs like a young girl. 'You forgot. You don't need to pretend to limp any longer.'

She goes to the kitchen and returns with the oval silver tray that Anne and I bought in Italy. On it is the champagne bucket, a gold-wrapped long neck sticking from it and three Y-shaped champagne glasses plus a plate with blinis. I watch this amused. 'Since when does a poodle drink Moët?'

'Now for the big surprise.' Melanie calls out and in walks the young woman from the photograph, holding a small child in her arms – my daughter and grandson.

'It was difficult to keep Tom from making any noise,' Celine admits, and I am overwhelmed by her presence.

I am unable to say anything. I can't help it; like an old geezer who has lost it, I sob into my handkerchief and am unable to stop. 'I have gone through a lot lately. Forgive me,' I manage in an unmanly voice. What must my daughter think of me?

Tom wriggles in his mother's arms. He wants to get down and play with the dog. Celine puts the child on the carpet. The poodle loves the little person and puts up with having one ear pulled, his head yanked to one side.

She sits down closest to me on the sofa, emitting a scent of youth, apple shavings and laundered sheets. I dare glance at her profile. Her long dark eyelashes shadow the high and shaped cheekbone. I helped make a beautiful young woman. She turns her face my way, and

I smile rather shakily into the crystal-bluest eyes I was ever allowed to see.

'You've saved this house from being pulled into a money-swindling pit,' she says to me. 'And you've got Maman into the bargain. The two of you will make it without extra cash. Maman can do wonders with little.'

'Unlikely on *my* pension – and with the French dog eating haute cuisine!' I say accusingly, preparing my surprise.

Mother and daughter tense. They were not prepared for this. They do not know me all that well and are apprehensive. Celine picks Tom up from the floor onto her lap. The poodle sits upright.

I heft the walking stick over to me. First, I twist the two nuts and then I pull out the pins. Next, I lift off the heavy handle and lay it next to me on the seat.

Holding their breath, they watch.

I grab the four bent feet and, as I lift them, the stick tilts, and out of the top slide Krugerrands, one after another, slowly at first, and then in rapid succession, forming a gold pyramid on the carpet.

'Two hundred and twenty gold coins,' I say, shaking the stick, which provokes a last coin to trundle out to meet the pile with a clear *ping*.

'Ping,' says Tom.

PIXEL

The sun shone, weak and oblique. It was autumn, the season after the fickleness of summer and before the hardship of winter – the season when berries are trodden into doormats.

Clive sat on a bench in the shadow of a copper-coloured oak tree, which had grown on this crest in the parks of Wimpole Hall for more than a hundred years. He switched his gaze from the woolly black-faced sheep grazing in the foreground to the Folly beckoning deceptively on the horizon.

Out of the corner of his eye, he also noted the hesitant hovering of a human figure, which had passed and passed again below on the trodden-down track through the meadow and now came to a halt. To Clive's annoyance, the man began to walk up the hill.

The solitary man was old and thin but somehow proudly upright still. His face was garnished with a white beard, the prickly hair of which pushed out over the multiple windings of a scarf around his neck. The beard seemed to be askew as if the man had stood in a westerly wind during its growth. He must have strained into some dry hot wind judging from the deeply carved lines on his tanned forehead and flaying out over the high cheekbones.

He came to rest at the other extremity of the bench, where he clumsily disentangled his arms, one after the other, from the straps of a canvas rucksack which he then put on the bench between them. It was an unusual item, much worn and with bone buttons to fix the wide flap down over its body.

Clive was presented with the thinning crown of the man's head as he bent forward to scratch his ankle which showed, brown and fleshless, between a rolled grey sock and the frayed hem of his uncared-for trousers. He gave a deep sigh when he straightened up and his lungs were able to inhale more air.

Trying to conceal his curiosity, Clive took in the roughly woven long-sleeved shirt, over which was a vest in returned sheepskin sewn together with the coarsest of stitches. At the front, the lining emerged, wispy with brown sheep fur which seemed untreated in any way.

The scarf end rested on one shoulder, even after the windings, and the fringe suggested it was possibly an undone *keffiyeh* – wisely not on his head right now, given how people felt about Arabs with headgear.

'*This* is an odd life,' the stranger said with a hoarse voice coming from deep in his throat. The emphasis on *this* indicated that he meant the one right here they were now in, he and Clive.

It was a bit rich coming from this bizarre figure. Clive lifted his chin to look well past the man at the Canadian geese coming from the ha-ha, swaying bodies on wide-webbed feet making their way across uneven ground.

'In the great sand sea, Berber children run towards the plume of dust coming from a passing vehicle to beg. A desert wind rises, and you draw down the folds of the amamah to shelter your face. When you look again, the children have vanished, and the sand sheets lie in a different pattern. You can't trust your eyes. Therefore, you learn to see with your mind, to perceive and fathom the nature of the Sahara by intuition. When you are old, your eyes go blind from the sand. By then, the mind can still see.'

He turned towards Clive with swollen eyelids, which had reduced his eyes to slits in which, barely visible, bluish milky iris disks moved. They focussed on Clive, and he felt blitzed by this old camel-thief who must have taken refuge in England.

Clive was not a traveller; he had never gone on holiday further than Scotland. Of course, he hadn't been able to because of the dog, which was a bit of a cop-out. Clive was not curious about foreign food or adventurous about novel discomfort. His comforting *known* was his desk in the administration office of the hospital where he was an accountant. Numbers had no imagination; they just had to add up and they increasingly didn't, precisely because of types like this Arab on the bench with him. Vast amounts of money were spent on such immigrants who did not bring anything to anyone here in return. To judge from the man's eye condition, there would be repeated consultations in Ophthalmology, and he knew the price of that. More and more were let in, and more. And the British had to make room on benches for them, had to politely tolerate their ways, alter their eating pattern and stump up for translation services in hospitals.

Unearthed in his contemplative visit to Wimpole Hall, Clive took out his iPad to check the time.

'It is cowardice, fear of self, redirecting our attention into electronic toys which play visual tricks on people who have lost touch with their instincts.'

'Advanced society can't do without what you call cheap toys.' Clive was getting irate. He tapped in *temperature in the Sahar*a. 'Here we go. Today's heat in Timbuktu is 39 degrees Celsius, transmitted by satellite and being seen by me right now.'

'Nomads become aware of variations in the electromagnetic waves by sensing the compression which heats the air. You and your *seeing* – meaning only eye organs which cheat the brain with presumed information.'

'It is not my fault you neglected your eyes.'

Of course, the Saharan tramp ignored this accurate remark. *He would, wouldn't he?*

Clive sat up straight. 'We need to be informed, and an array of satellites and beacons helps us.' He slipped the tablet into his jacket pocket. 'I think we're done here.'

'Most of you depend on sensations beamed at you by visual trickery, objects doing humanly impossible leaps, transformations, physical alterations. It tricks the eye and shrinks the brain. The child, absorbed in the charade on the screen, stumbles over the root at its feet.'

'I have absolutely no idea what you are rabbiting on about. I have to go.' Clive stood up, feeling the stiffness of the bench in his back.

'You don't, but you could probably convince yourself that you do.'

'I am not enjoying your company.'

'May I ask you just one thing?'

Clive was annoyed with himself for lingering.

'Can we know *before* we have perceived? Can we perceive before we have learned how to perceive? In the Sahara—'

'Right now we are in Cambridgeshire and I came for a stroll to enjoy the view and privacy. Goodbye.'

'No, you did not. You came here, as you have done on previous Sundays, to remember your little white dog running about.'

'Great. You have been spying on me for a while. Don't you have anything better to do on Sundays – something which might benefit your host country?'

'We do not have Sundays.'

'How inconvenient. Please don't bother me anymore. We don't appreciate it.'

'You liked your dog and he went missing.'

A large bulbous cloud was slipping over the sun. It enveloped the bench, the mound, the tree behind them, in an unpleasant chill. Even the soil exuded the instant whiff of damp.

'Your dog's name was Pixel,' Clive heard behind him as he set off down the grassy slope. Merely hearing Pixel's name, *Pixel*, produced a familiar constricting lump in his chest.

'You never found him again.'

'He ran down this hill chasing a blackbird, and I never saw him again.'

'That must be hard for you.'

'I have searched everywhere. I don't know whether he now lives with someone else, whether he is treated well, looked after, cared for.' Clive lifted a limp hand in a half-hearted gesture of departure and went down to the path and along it. Tighter control had to be implemented in this country concerning foreigners. Why had he confessed his sorrow to that man who called the English cowards? The government let anyone in: *just come in and make yourself comfortable, walk around National Trust parks in beggar clothes and annoy anyone, because it was your custom back home.*

★

At the stable block, Clive went under the arch into the cobbled courtyard. The familiar scene appeased him: toddlers in pushchairs, the woman at the spinning wheel turning lamb fleece into thread, the garden centre selling bulbs for next spring. One or two dogs belonging to other people.

He bought a cup of tea with milk and took it to one of the wooden picnic tables with attached benches. After a few minutes, a woman pushed herself onto the bench on the other side of the table.

And then the infuriating thing happened again. Why had he thought he was safe in here? It was *him*, coming to the table and sliding the backpack off one arm and then the other. He put it carefully on the tabletop.

Clive ostentatiously turned his back and, askew on the bench, gazed at an expanse of brick wall. A sharp fingernail tapped on his shoulder, and he spun round in alert annoyance. 'What now?'

'I just wanted you to *see* this.'

The rucksack was gaping open. Clive got up and stooped over it. In one beat, his heart seemed to lurch. A West Highland terrier lay curled in the bag. It was Pixel, with his tartan collar and the little silver bone bearing his name. There was the endearing tuft of longer black fur in all that whiteness. The bent front paw twitched; he was obviously dreaming. The ribcage moved rhythmically in and out at a slow pace.

Overcome, Clive reached for the paper napkin which had come with the tea and dabbed it against his overflowing eyes.

When he looked up, the Arab was nowhere to be seen.

'Did you see that man leave?' he asked of the woman.

'A boy,' she corrected him. 'My son. He went to get us drinks.'

On the table, instead of the rucksack and dog, was a rolled beige anorak and, on top, a white visor cap with a silver badge clipped to it. Clive felt physically sick, beaten by an illusion he could not understand.

The son came back, carrying a round metal tray with drinks. As he made to put it down, his mother had to snatch aside the anorak and cap.

'Totally oblivious, youngsters nowadays.'

The young man took out his smartphone and his eyes darted over it, chasing shapes which moved across the screen. His middle finger rolled over the glass plate.

'But they are clever,' the mother persisted. 'It's all this electronic availability. The speed with which they can find out things. We didn't have that. *His* son will probably use robots, and I will have a grandchild who will be bored with me because I don't understand anything.' She gave a little compressed laugh, because her son had raised his head shortly to give her a punishing stare, before involving himself again in the virtual world he seemed to depend on. What could he have contributed to the conversation anyway?

INSPECTOR
MELLANBY

Glenda and Brian's downsizing ended up in a north-facing three-bedroom mid-terrace house in Norfolk.

'Take the best pieces. They will make you feel at home,' their only daughter encouraged her disoriented parents.

Glenda, who used to bring up a daughter and a dog; Glenda, who won first prize in cake-decorating; Glenda, who got at least two books a week out from the little Royston library, hated her new life. The right-hand neighbour was younger and they were not each other's cup of tea, and the woman on the left showed interest only in her own grandchildren while Glenda's daughter wasn't even in a solid relationship.

Retired, Brian, who had commuted to London for the last twenty-two years, loved it. One short conversation with the right-hand neighbour about rugby and he had an interest; another with the left one about an investment group and he had his pub and the right beer.

He declared his gardening days over and Glenda made an effort but, with so little, it was best to leave it to lawn to make it appear bigger.

He installed himself an office in the small third bedroom and came down for supper once she shouted up the stairs.

They ate in silence. She had nothing new to tell him. She washed up and he watched rugby.

The day Glenda held the Thetford Library card in her hand, she felt a little better. When she discovered the pink cream-cake shop a smile spread on her face for the first time since the move and she almost forgave Brian for retiring.

From then on, she made herself tea with cakes in the middle of the morning and afternoon in style, using her mother's Crown Derby tea service, the silver cutlery, the silver creamer and sugar bowl with cube tongue, and all that on the hand-embroidered doily which fitted exactly into the deep-set mahogany tray with curly brass handles.

Appeased with her lot, she leaned back in her easy chair and read borrowed books, leaving Norfolk for sun-toasted Italy, Spain and sometimes Florida. Her hero was Inspector Cecil Mellanby, a man with greying temples who possessed a sense of humour and an overdose of love and bags of endearments to distribute to heroines who were not young any more. He always made love to them – or almost. They put themselves in danger to help him solve his cases; and he triumphed in the end and luckily never got killed, not really.

One such heroine was short and stout, reassuringly shapely as she walked as if conferring an honour on everybody. In his customary way, Mellanby knitted his brows slightly at the sight of her and then enfolded her in his charm, which paid off because she solved his problem with the rubber glove in the piano.

Glenda called the inspector 'my dearest' in her daydreaming and felt him breathe near her.

In Norfolk it often rained and the living room was sunless, but Glenda was guided by Mellanby into the magic of a written world where they had tea, and she found clues for which he, seated on the plush couch, sucked his teeth and then rose to his feet to stare awestruck. 'You're the most desirable woman I've ever known, Glenda.'

'Where's dinner?' Brian as good as slapped her. 'Still stuffing your face with cakes. Have you noticed that I have to sleep on the edge of the bed, nearly falling out?'

He desecrated her adventure by picking up the novel, flapping it over to read the back. 'Not still Mellanby.' Then he read out from a page at random. '*Her head shot up defensively and her eyes clashed with his. For a brief moment, her foolish heart had hoped. Her rising passion began to obliterate her sanity, while the evidence of his own arousal ground against her hips.*' Brian guffawed until he coughed. 'What a load of crap. Unbelievable such drivel is not only written but published, bought and read.'

She pushed herself out of the easy chair and went to the kitchen to wash up the chinaware she did not trust in his hands, before starting on supper.

At the end of summer, Brian travelled with some buddies to France to watch the rugby and after that to Italy because England had won. Glenda discovered that eight hundred and fifty pounds had gone out of the monthly pension. Brian explained it was a loan to a friend from the investment club and none of her business.

The autumn brought persistent winds rattling the thin fence-panels surrounding the garden and she had to pull in her belt to make ends meet.

On her birthday Brian bought her a small crystal vase. A British Heart Foundation sticker for £3.75 was still stuck to the bottom. There were no flowers for the vase nor a card for the mantelpiece. That afternoon Inspector Mellanby invited her to call him Cecil, not before his mouth had plummeted down in a bruising kiss while, whimpering beneath the kiss, she fought to resist the demands of his lips. Had she not drawn his attention to the woman in the blue raincoat dropping the key into the Trevi Fountain?

At six fifteen on a dark wet October Tuesday, Glenda, who had come from the library with a new crime novel, was waiting for the bus to bring her home. It was rush-hour and through the curtains of driving rain she noticed two men having a loud argument in the car park behind her. One butted the other, who ran out of the car park, closely followed by his assailant. On the pavement they argued some more. The aggressor gripped the dun jacket of his victim until a white van drove up, when he then shoved him under the front wheels of the vehicle. The van stopped. Of the man under it, nothing showed. The driver got out, gave the killer something flat and white, and loped across the road, dodging traffic, to disappear in the dark. The van stayed where it was and nobody crawled from underneath, maimed and bleeding. The killer walked towards her and, at the rubbish bin behind the bus stop, he threw in the white evidence and strode away.

The bus arrived but Glenda let it go. She slipped on her woollen gloves and inspected the contents of the rubbish bin. An envelope seemed to be the most recently discarded item. She put it into her pocket and walked over to the place in the car park where the argument had taken place. She picked up a cigarette stub, a can ring-pull, a piece of soaked cloth, and a torn rubber washer. Under the sycamore tree where part of the scuffle had taken place and the asphalt was still dry in parts, she inspected wet footprints. With a pen, she elaborately drew the pattern of the clearest shoe sole onto the last page of the library book, telling herself that Cecil would understand. Then she returned to wait for a bus.

The TV news was over by the time she got home to a furious husband. 'I have a jolly good reason for being late. I witnessed a crime.' She took off her shoes to rub her damp toes.

'So, now I have to put up with your Mellanby messing with my life.'

She tapped three numbers into the landline phone. 'I saw what I saw,' she pronounced, her chin up while she listened to the ringing.

It was suggested she come to the police station the next day. 'But the corpse under the van?'

'No incident of that nature has been reported.'

Over sausages, bacon and powder mash, Brian cackled.

*

Perched on a metal office chair, Glenda exerted herself telling the policewoman what she had seen, while Brian stood in a corner of the room looking away. Eventually he intervened. 'Sergeant, I apologise for my wife. She imagines crimes and is taking up your time.'

The policewoman was reading the contents of the envelope Glenda had given her in a plastic Tesco bag. It was a contract from a business in Grimsby which rented vans. That seemed worth going online for, while Glenda and Brian shot each other unfriendly glances.

A policeman arrived. Together they looked at the screen, she sitting and he over her shoulder.

'They have Mafia connections, don't they? Alessandro Reinaldo Carbello, I'll bet.'

The policeman nodded and asked Glenda to describe the person who had thrown away the envelope. Proudly, for she had been aware of her surroundings despite the night and rain, she listed his attributes: about six feet tall, wearing a grey anorak with the hood up, jeans with tears under the knee, and white sports shoes which looked new and had a black tick on the heel. According to her, he had shot her a green-eyed 'criminal' sideways glance – 'grape-green,' she emphasised. Then she produced the novel, with her drawing of the shoe sole print, and Brian groaned from embarrassment.

Leaving her contact details, she was let go.

Nothing more happened; no mention of a man killed under a van. She volunteered to pay for defacing library property. However, Glenda owed it to Cecil to pursue the investigation.

The day Brian went to Twickenham for a rugby match, she took the overland bus to Grimsby and got off in the town centre. With the Google map she had printed off, she found the van rental company, where she was ignored by the lad at the desk after an appraising glance suggested her unsuitability as van rental material. She picked up a flyer showing different sizes of vans. Discreetly, she also tore a sheet of lined writing paper from a pad. 'I want to speak to the owner of this company,' she said with a straight back and aplomb.

The uncouth youth cackled. 'Nobody gets to speak to Alessandro Carbello. He has better things to do in his villa in Cleethorpes Park.'

Glenda was put out by the treatment she had received. She hailed a taxi and asked the driver how much it would cost to go to Cleethorpes Park. It was do-able and she got in. 'I am looking for Alessandro Carbello's house.'

'Are you sure, lady? All of Grimsby knows he's a shark, in that big blue house of his next to the country park.'

Glenda asked to be let out a hundred yards from it. She looked around. Behind her was a lake flanked by a golf course and on either side of the rising street stood monumental houses with large portals and rows of expensive cars in front of triple garages.

She walked slowly up the hill, stopping here and there as if to kill time. It was not a neighbourhood where people went on foot.

She stopped at a blue property governing the top position. It was enormous. Marble lions sat obediently on the entrance posts. The automatic metal gate was over six feet high. She went past it along the spiked railings and the security cameras and came to another driveway, minus the lions, with a small side-gate. Traffic in and out had brought polar-white ornamental pebbles onto the pedestrian way. She picked some up, put them into her coat pocket and loitered on the other side of the road. Eventually, a maid with a ponytail and in a uniform came out of the house carrying a plastic bag, which she put into a bin before disappearing back through the same door.

'Patience, my lover-ly,' Mellanby whispered to Glenda. Just when she needed to sit down somewhere, she noticed the ponytailed maid emerge from the servant's gate, wrapped in a wool pashmina. Glenda walked up the road and met up with the maid, a woman in her thirties who looked Italian. She accosted her. 'Excuse me. Are you employed by Alessandro Carbello?'

She nodded, her features suspicious.

'I should go through an agency but, before I move here from Wales, could you please be kind enough to tell me, from one domestic to another, is the owner hiring?'

'Not at the moment and Signor Carbello, he is fussy I tell you.'

Glenda thanked the maid and left.

★

A few days later, Glenda waved a sheet of lined paper with a smudge in one corner on which was handwritten in capitals: *YOU SAW NOTHING. YOU DO NOT TALK. ARC IS WATCHING.*

'Careful now, my lover-ly. You're getting into deep water here.' The words echoed in her ears.

At the police station this time, she was asked to step into the office of Detective Superintendent Alder. He was short and moved like a scavenging fox; his small narrow eyes did not add to his appeal. Not a patch on Inspector Mellanby who had chocolate eyes.

She told him about the pushing under the van. He asked irrelevant questions, none of which had anything to do with the crime she had witnessed. He gave her a number to call at once next time she received a threat and left the room. He certainly did not seem to fancy her.

Upon her release, Glenda went straight to the cake shop and then had civilised tea at home, during which she plotted her next step with the help of Cecil.

The following day, she bought white Nike sports shoes with a tick on the heel and, on the way home, picked up a brick from a building site. She waited until Brian had left for a pre-Christmas drinks party and then pushed the crystal vase into the middle of the sideboard. In socks, she tiptoed away from her house – it was dark and the moon's cycle was on her side. When far enough away, she slipped into the Nike shoes and returned to her front garden, where she scattered the white pebbles onto the flower bed. Then she stepped over the wall onto the pebbles and, with an energetic swing she had practised, hurled the brick with a note sellotaped to it through the front window, took the shoes off and went back into the house.

The brick had landed on the sideboard but not broken the vase. She smashed the vase on the floor.

The note Brian picked up from the shard-covered carpet at midnight read: *BITCH. YOU TALKED TO ALDER.* He called the police immediately. 'What the fuck is going on here?' he demanded, while Glenda was up in the bedroom, seemingly too frightened to move.

The next morning, DS Alder arrived accompanied by the female police sergeant, now introduced as Sandra. 'It's baffling but this new development makes us think we must be getting close to something major, perhaps even the breakthrough we've been waiting for.'

'What has my wife got to do with this?'

'We can't work that out, but there are indications that something big is about to burst, and Glenda seems to be linked to it in some way. That is why we are here. We want to put surveillance in your house right now and for the next two days at most. Because of the threats to your wife, we are moving you to a safe house.'

He handed out a list of what they could take with them.

'Pyjamas, robe, slippers, books, change of underwear,' Glenda read out. 'No mobiles, TV, no Wi-Fi or communication devices. Can I take my tea set?'

'The kitchenette is kitted out. There are mugs.'

Brian laughed out loud. 'Mugs? If you knew her at all, you'd know what a mug *you* are. She's got to have her minky little teacups and all that goes with it, prim and proper and fucking annoying. You see why we could never go camping or caravanning. Couldn't even go to a B&B.'

DS Alder scowled at Brian. Glenda fetched the tray with the tea things.

'Crown Derby,' the policeman said, picking up a cup. 'You can take it.'

Half an hour later, the blacked-out saloon car drove off, Glenda and Brian without view in the back, Alder and Sandra in the front. The drive took three and a half hours. Throughout Glenda held her tea-tray on her lap

When she was helped from the car, a fierce icy gust blew her hair askew. It was freezing cold, a rawness which had a sharp edge. Brian guessed the Yorkshire Moors. They were in front of a remote ragstone cottage in a wilderness of hoar-frosted heather.

A metal front door led into a tiny hall and to a second metal door which, in turn, gave onto the living-dining room. This space was furnished with two easy chairs, a coffee table and a bookshelf, plus a square plastic table with two plastic chairs and a fridge under a sideboard with a sink, mini-kettle and small microwave oven.

The two bedrooms, one larger than the other, had lamps set into the wall and hooks on the doors for clothing. There was a shower room; all plastic, no mirror or glass, but a shower curtain.

'Is this a hiding place for the suicidal?' Brian asked.

Unperturbed, Alder explained, 'We have all types staying here.'

Glenda turned to the window: iron bars in front of solid closed shutters.

'And the glass is bulletproof,' added Sandra.

'It's bloody freezing in here.' Brian wrapped his arms around his torso and glared around him.

Alder opened a further door, which revealed a small windowless rough-stone storage room under a strong metal roof with an earthen floor. It housed a heat-exchange device and tubes leading from it into the cottage. He clicked some tabs down and rotated a knob. A noise started up. 'I've set it for twenty-four Celsius round the clock. They expect four or five below zero during the night. Keep that door closed,' he continued, explaining that Brian and Glenda would be totally isolated from communication, 'for your own safety'.

'It's only for a short while,' Glenda said before Brian could complain again.

'There are four outside cameras monitored at the local police station,' Sandra reassured them. 'There is also a panic button to press, but only if life is at risk.'

Alder added, 'It is for Glenda's protection, may I remind you? We reckon that by Sunday evening our job will be done and dusted. We're off, then. See you on Monday morning.'

As Alder locked the first door meticulously behind him, he heard Glenda say, 'I'll put the kettle on.' He grimaced from one side of his mouth and locked the outer door. Sandra said, 'This couple will be like two bugs in a rug.'

'Squabbling.'

For Glenda and Brian inside, a short beeping indicated that the police had activated the alarm system.

'Friggin' two days hostage.' Brian opened a drawer. 'Plastic knives and forks.'

'Perhaps the police use this place for people who they need alive.'

By the time Glenda was sitting in her chair sipping her tea, Brian was still pacing like a caged tiger. He stopped abruptly. 'I can hear the wind howl outside. This place is the asshole of the world.'

Glenda closed her eyes and, within, spoke to her hero. 'Oh, Cecil, how can I earn your esteem, closed in as I am? Cecil, talk to me.'

★

On Monday morning a little after eleven, the temperature was still sub-zero when Alder and Sandra unlocked the metal door. There was a loud drumming against the second door and, from within the living room, came demented screams of 'Help! Help!'

The moment they turned the key in the lock, the door was torn open by a woman resembling the one they had closed in on Friday evening. Her hair stood on end, what looked like blood stains covered her cardigan, and rings circled her eyes in a manic stare. She was high on hysteria, virtually hopping up and down.

'Too late!' she yelled. 'You've come back too late.'

'What is going in in here?'

'Go and see in the bedroom.' Glenda sank onto a chair.

The scene Alder and Sandra were faced with in the bedroom was horrendous in its unexpected atrocity. Sandra clapped her hand over her mouth to prevent either retching or screaming.

On the bed lay a human body, its neck a soup of torn arteries severed by a blunt saw or serrated knife. The pillow and bed were soaked in fresh red blood and pulled human flesh. Through the mask of carnage which was the face, a pair of pale blue eyes stared at them lifeless in a petrified expression of horror.

The police lifted their arms as if in surrender, but in fact it was to avoid touching anything. Alder pressed the panic button and texted on his device. Glenda, beyond help, was driven to the nearest hospital, where she was sedated and kept in isolation under police protection.

Twelve hours later, the team visited her for questioning. She was groggy and *not herself* but able to answer simple questions. Brian and she had spent Friday and Saturday quietly, eating the micro-meals; he played patience and she read novels and drank tea. On Sunday night, he had two cans of beer and went to bed. Because he was snoring, she moved into the smaller bedroom about half past eleven. She heard nothing unusual.

Forensics had found no evidence of a break-in or of fingerprints other than Glenda's and Brian's. Glenda was the obvious suspect, but she had no motive, nor had any potential weapon been discovered. It was a mystery. Death was estimated at about three in the morning by decapitation with a jagged weapon applied with repeated force.

Alessandro Carbello had escaped their surveillance over the weekend and almost certainly travelled to South America on a passport borrowed from a Mafia member who was missing in Germany. The threats to Glenda had been written on notepaper from Carbello's van hire company in Grimsby. The white pebbles found in Glenda's front garden matched those from the villa.

Police investigation of the incident with the van in Thetford was also inconclusive. It seemed to relate to a drug-drop which had gone wrong, presumably because the man in the dun jacket – Glenda's 'victim' – had failed to deliver. CCTV suggested that he had, in fact, managed to roll away.

Little made sense.

Glenda recovered largely. Human beings do. Eventually, Brian's body was released and a modest family cremation took place. The daughter came to stand next to her widowed mother, telling her that she would be all right, and later left to live her life somewhere else. The library assistant from Royston sent a flower tribute.

Glenda moved back to Royston into a small two-bedroom house. She knitted bonnets for babies for the Royston hospital and had her tea on the tray with the doily and the Mellanby novels on her lap. She adopted a cat from the rescue home and called it Cecil, kissed it on its whiskers and lived peacefully in the company of the inspector, who still brought her excitement and travel to romantic places, and aroused flutters of carnal desire, even though she had read the novels several times already.

The day she learned that the inspector would *die* and that she had read his last murder mystery because the author had succumbed to cancer, she dressed in black finery. She took a taxi to Cambridge, where she had reserved a table for two in the Rotisserie of the University Arms Hotel.

Her wrap was taken from her, the seat pulled out, and the menu card offered, from which she chose rack of lamb, pink with braised fennel and gratin dauphinois. From the wine list, the sommelier proffered recommendations. She scolded the head waiter who attempted to remove the second setting of her tête-à-tête.

First, she sipped the champagne coupe and toasted to Cecil's existence and their encounter. With the lamb, she savoured the aged Morgon and her eyes challenged him over the rim of the wine glass. 'Surely you have worked it out. No? Your admiration is as delicious as this tender meat. That DS Alder was a wimp, not your class at all. All right, if you offer me Baileys with my coffee, I'll tell you. A coffee for me – unusual, I admit. There is a lot about me people don't know. Remember, it was well below freezing in the safe house. I put water in the tea tray and laid it on the floor of the storage room, then wedged a pebble under one end of the tray. The tray tilted so that the water at the top end would freeze into a sharp edge. By two a.m. it was stone-hard and Brian was still snoring. I knocked the ice out of the tray in one piece. It was like a square cutting blade. When the deed was done, and the muscles in my arms were smarting, with warm water, you know the ice…'

The coffee and Baileys were brought. After a lick, she dragged the caramel sweetness from her lips. 'I love you too,' she said. 'I've loved you since the first page.'

'Is everything all right, madam? Can we help you with anything? Should we call someone for you?'

'It's wonderful. I am free to love him as I please.'

FOUR CARATS

He bent his knee onto the sandy flagstone. She had already changed for supper and was wearing a sleek black dress, defining her waist and caressing her hips with a seductive power which singled her out. The pedicured feet, tortured by high-heeled open sandals, were part of the price of that sexual allure. She sat in a plastic wicker chair, the type which does not rot under the elements. It belonged to a table and other seats around the bar area. Hors d'oeuvres had not yet been laid out; live music not yet commenced.

Gabriela had expected him to kneel tonight, but not now when he was still not dressed. Lewis was hopeless with timing. That afternoon he had windsurfed for at least two hours without managing to stay up for any length of time, a jutting-out-bum figure hanging on for dear life. When Jojo had had to motor out and rescue him from being swept away in the current, Gabriela had picked up her towel from the sunlounger and walked away. Club Med was for sporty types, mostly laid-back young people. She had insisted they come here in the hope the buzz would make him less of a nerd and more of a stud. Had it been his decision, he would probably have taken her carp fishing in France.

Tonight's Club theme was *Elegant*, dress code: black and white. Kneeling at her feet, he was sweaty, dishevelled, with a gash on his thigh, the dried blood mingling with encrusted salt. His shorts had a Dalek print on them, a motif never seen in Barbados, and he gazed up at her expectantly through the smudged lenses in his outdated spare pair of spectacles, having lost his Porsche head-clamp ones.

'What are you doing?' she asked with an edge to her voice.

He stood up, lanky and too thin, sand caught in the sparse blond hair on his chest. 'I thought it would sort of prepare the evening for us.'

'I am prepared for the evening. Get washed and de-sand.'

'You wanted it to be natural and spontaneous.'

'Not that sort of spontaneous.'

'Are there different types?'

She watched Lewis trudge off like a defeated soldier, as if weighed down by the rolled towel across his angular shoulders. Tonight, he would propose and she would say 'yes', despite her fear that constant cohabitation would compromise her personal pursuit of happiness. Her yes would commit her to a bathroom with wet towels on the floor, to whining to get her way, to ground-down molars from listening to male snoring through the night. On the other hand, there were not as many fish in the sea as she had been given to believe, and certainly fewer than when she was twenty-five.

The first candidate for a serious relationship had come from an upper-class family, chummy with royals. Tick. However, he shouted stupidly whenever he became frustrated about something. Un-tick. The next, whom she had dated for three full years, worked in the Foreign Office in London. Super tick. She would have been ideal as a diplomat's wife – exotic postings, parties, nice clothes, help in the house – but he was fixated on her backside, demanded she wore thongs, minimal bikinis, a silk band in the crack, and the love-making was stressed, him wanting her on her stomach and she refusing. Despite the lure of the diplomatic life, she had recognised that he was a pervert.

For her thirtieth birthday, colleagues at the law firm where she worked as an assistant legal secretary had reserved a table in a nightclub, where she was hit on by her fat middle-aged married boss. The evening from hell. She knew then that she had to step up the hunt. Her first move was to change job and become receptionist to a hedge fund in Mayfair. She dressed with care, was waxed, peeled, tinted and trussed upward. By midday, the corner of her mouth trembled from the strain of constant smiling. Alpha males and focused females passed by her, twice a day at least. Most were polite, desirably successful and rich, but inevitably they all proceeded to the internal elevators or the turnstile door, leaving her as no more than part of the design of the reception desk.

Gabriela spent her thirty-first birthday in her flat getting sloshed and breaking the entrance mirror by drunkenly waving the bottle around.

In the office, she was sitting at her marble desk playing patience on the latest flat-screen computer, trying not to show her growing panic, when a rainstorm improved her life. Water was running down the high glass doors of the entrance, thunder cracked outside and everyone came in dripping, shaking mangled brollies. Just as she was picking up the phone to call the super to mop up, a latecomer rushed in, skidded on his leather soles and fell sideways, sliding to the front of her desk.

'Fuck, that hurt!' she heard and came round her desk. She recognised him right away as one of the star traders from the top-floor suites with the rosewood furniture and a bank of computer screens – a wealthy, privileged nerd with an excessive pay package and an obscene Christmas bonus. Lewis Boden, the rare one who was not yet spoken for.

He was not good-looking, more endearingly winsome in a bookish way which would make him look his thirty-four or thereabouts for ever. Such charm as he had was not enhanced by more RPMs on the treadmill, nor by staring at figures on screens. She had always had an interest in him, feeling there was more to him than showed on the surface, even though he never greeted her, walking into the building iPhoning, websiting. Surely he could be made better. She had sat in wait for her chance, and now was the moment.

Gabriela stood close to the fallen man. Asking him whether he was all right, she made sure she was close enough to offer him a look up her long legs. He did not hurry to get up. He let her take his elbow to help him back up onto his *James Bond* Derby shoes. Both knew this was a charade, and she exulted inside herself, offered him coffee, tea, medicinal brandy, a doctor, an ambulance. Eventually, she suggested he sat for a moment over there in the visitor's chair to make sure he was not suffering from concussion. She handed him his purple head-clamp spectacles, which matched his silk knit tie. Had he not hit the stone floor with his head? No, he hadn't, but he took up her suggestion and she led him to a seat.

He had to admit that the fall had quite unnerved him. And here was this attractive young woman fussing over him as if she were his mother. He could have sworn that he had never seen her before. Actually, she was the prettiest female he had seen in a long time. He started to marvel at his discovery that the receptionist one took for granted was in fact the prettiest-ever, most warm-hearted girl, willing to go out of her way to be personal with someone in distress. To his surprise, he told her all that. She, however, did not tell him how personal she planned on being with him. As concussion did not set in, they exchanged names. She already knew his, and he complimented her on Gabriela, a name worthy of her. They flirted clumsily some more.

'How can I ever thank you?'

Gabriela knew exactly how this could be done.

Eventually, he disappeared into the elevator, not without throwing her a last, slightly confused, blue-eyed look. She spent the rest of the morning planning her married life with him. Although she did not like fair-haired men all that much, his blondness was styled by Taylor Taylor. She had missed out on upper class and, sadly, on diplomatic life, but there would be two children, George and Aurelia, and the best boarding schools, expensive holidays abroad, and a smashing house in Highgate with nanny and entertaining.

Later in the day he reappeared out of the elevator and invited her for supper to thank her for saving his life. She turned down only the first evening he suggested, in fear that he might give up on the idea.

Instead of taking her where she had crossed her fingers for, the Met Bar in Mayfair where Pippa Middleton, James Corden and other celebrities hung out, he took her to a small tucked-away cabaret theatre-restaurant. She joined in laughter at jokes she did not understand, pleased her teeth had been whitened. That was the start of the compromises.

She turned thirty-two, not celebrating it alone. Her present was a week's holiday in Club Med, Barbados, and here they were, on the crucial 'elegant' evening of their holiday, and he had still not reappeared. Lewis had the ring, she knew. He thought he was subtly hiding it from her, but his whole being gave away the existence of the velvet box, wrapped so that she was unable to have a pre-peek. Who asks a jeweller to wrap an engagement ring? She could still get away with being hot and wanted at the very beginning of her thirties, and the nightmare of *later and still single* would be avoided. Of course, babies would have to be made soon.

Where was the idiot? Everyone else was here by now, dressed in black and white, the nibbles bar open, the microphone brought out and put up on the podium, tested. The stars were gleaming and glittering irritatingly in the cobalt sky.

At the next table sat a trim middle-aged man, clearly bored by a dull and silent woman. Looking around him, he took note of Gabriela. His eyes locked on hers for that significant fraction of attraction before looking innocently away again. She rose by sliding herself sideways, making sure as she bent to pick up her bag that the bored man was given a good look a fair way up her suntanned, exercised thighs. Casually, she asked him to keep her seat for her. His willingness to do so had the undertone that he would lay his honour at her feet rather than let anyone else sit there. Weaving her body suggestively past occupied chairs on the way to the bar, she felt his eyes eat into her back, and smiled, pleased.

At the bar stood JoJo, still in his hipster swimming briefs as was expected of him; he was *chef de sports*. It was all about muscles playing under his evenly bronzed skin, all about sex. Hell, he was dishy, thought Gabriela looking at him, smiling at him, while he leaned his six-pack against the bar, one foot in flip-flops on the foot rail, elbow on the glass surface, fingers twirling a Perspex swizzle-stick. She took in the straight heavy dark hair, determinedly untidy, the deep brown eyes, his square jaw and aquiline nose, and sighed.

Within this perfection, what got to her most was the mouth, more precisely the full lips, so prominent that they juiced up his classic beauty with a lascivious vulgarity in a very sexy French way. He was in such a different league to Lewis, who was slightly languid and not overtly sexy at all, ever, that she averted her eyes.

'*Salut, tu veux quoi?*' asked Pablito, the gleaming black Bajan with the naturally whitest teeth she had ever seen.

'Piña colada,' she ordered.

She sipped at the tall glass and overheard JoJo chatting with Pablito, and JoJo's repeated, annoyed '*Merde*'.

Pablito held up his arms to heaven. 'Man, coming down on that metal rod could have killed you.'

JoJo drummed on his six-pack. 'Made of steel.'

That morning, Gabriela had been in the audience when JoJo had performed on the circus trapeze with a daring double roll. Embarrassingly, the catch had failed and he landed rather un-grandly on the frame of the safety net. The onlookers booed but, taking it in his stride, he had bowed, then skipped away. JoJo had obviously taken this mishap to heart and was now lamenting over it with Pablito. Therefore, he was vain, Gabriela analysed. Lewis was not vain. Thank God for small mercies.

She offered JoJo a drink, as her package was all-inclusive and staff could not afford the bar prices. JoJo asked for a glass of milk.

'Missing your mother?'

Gabriela returned to her seat, still empty despite the disappearance of her gallant knight. Tiana had started to sing. Admittedly, she copied herself on Rihanna, the famed Barbados singer, but Tiana was up to it. Lewis thought her stunning. In black flared velvet trousers and a low-cut white frilled blouse, gold square waterfall earrings playing by her head, she brushed back her undulating hair with an elegant hand, white-varnished fingernails, to sing a Bajan slave song. Those who had already joined the queue in front of the still-cordoned-off entrance to the dining areas, stopped, listened and watched the gorgeous woman on the platform lending her soul to her art. At the end of the song, when a rare silence reigned in Club Med, she did not seek applause, but just stood there contained in herself. The enthralled silence was broken by a single loud clapping. It was Lewis returning, wearing a dark blue suit jacket over a T-shirt, trousers and deck shoes. Tiana shushed him with a piercing look and Lewis stopped attracting attention.

'My next song is a special request.'

'*Shine bright like a diamond,*' Tiana sang. '*Find light in the beautiful sea.*' Gabriela noticed the tiny wink Tiana directed towards Lewis. '*You and I, you and I, we're like diamonds in the sky.*'

'They've taken the cordon off. People are going in to dinner.' Gabriela pulled at Lewis's sleeve.

'What's the rush?'

'The others are getting the best tables and the seafood. Anyway, what took you so long?'

'Sorry. I went to the beach to think. You are right; I don't know how to be spontaneous. We are really two very different people, you and I. You throw yourself into any situation with confidence, you like people, you are life-hugging, and I am the schoolboy genius, less sporty than I hoped I was. I like science fiction and computer games.' He searched for her hand and took it into his. 'And then the sun was setting and swarms of birds were flying into the pink sky, and I thought that I needed someone who knew how to be spontaneous to get me out of myself.' He squeezed her hand. 'And I hope that you need someone who keeps it all together and calculates the risks and ventures.'

'Very sweet all that, but if you want caviar we'd better get up there and get a table.'

'Let me finish my drink and listen to Tiana. She is amazing tonight.'

'I've been sitting here so long I've grown a beard.'

'OK.' He gave up on his drink, and they proceeded towards the restaurant at the back of the queue.

Next to an artificial waterfall was the sports team in black bodysuits with black wings and white wigs, beckoning to coax the guests into devil-land. The *chef de village* dressed as Cruella De Vil greeted them and wished them bon appétit, before taking off her white top hat and walking away; they were the last ones.

'You see, thanks to you we're too late. All the candlelit tables for two are taken.' They were forced to sit inside, at a table with a German-speaking couple.

'Guten Abend,' the man greeted them with a bow of his upper body.

'Fuck my fiancé for ending me up here,' Gabriela said to no one specifically. And then checked her anger. What really mattered was George going to Harrow and Aurelia to Benenden.

'Let's just ignore the Krauts,' she whispered to Lewis, and made her way to the buffet to help herself to caviar while he pulled the napkin out of the wine glass and looked happy as the sandboy he had played all week.

When the large plates of the main course were cleared, Lewis pushed his chair back and went down on one knee again.

'Der Mann ist proposing,' said the German woman.

Lewis pulled the little package from his trouser pocket and held it up. 'Will you marry me?'

Conversation stopped at nearby tables, people came in from outside to watch, and Gabriela ripped the paper off. What really mattered was the five-bedroom house in Highgate.

She gave him back the domed velvet box.

Doggedly, he repeated his question.

'Open the frigging box,' she hissed.

He clapped the lid open and turned the box so she could see her engagement ring. It was a sizeable diamond solitaire ring, of at least three carats, probably four, table-cut. She guessed in the range of eight thousand pounds a carat, if of good quality. He had surprised her. It was good enough.

'Yes,' she said and smiled down to him. 'I will marry you.'

Everyone applauded. Tiana had appeared with her microphone and now told the whole club that they had a newly engaged couple among them.

Congratulations! Lewis was hugged by windsurfing buddies, kissed by the hostesses, and Gabriela had Pablito clutching her to his gold-chained chest. Only then was she able to slip the ring on her finger, and it fitted almost perfectly.

After dinner was cabaret in the outdoor amphitheatre, and then the newly engaged couple performed a few cheek-to-cheek dances in the nightclub built out onto the beach, Gabriela being careful not to hit anyone with the killer diamond on her finger. Walking back to their bungalow through the colourfully lit palm grove, he moved to kiss her.

'Darling,' she said, 'let me clean my face first. All those people slobbered over me tonight.'

He accepted this. They walked on, hand in hand.

Back in their bungalow, there was a silent tension between them. It was not said, but sex was not on the menu. They lay in their bed with the fan whirring softly above them and, shortly after midnight, she heard his rhythmical snoring and envied him.

Eventually, she got up and slipped on her long flowery sundress, picked up her sandals and unlatched the shutters on her way out onto their private terrace. From there she walked towards the sea, spread out in the silver sheen of a large moon. Softly lapping waves licked the sand before being pulled back by the moon. Some way off, the nightclub music spilled over the ocean, and the dark silhouettes of human shapes were dancing.

Sandals in hand, she meandered across the sand, which was still warm from the sun, towards a large rock, but it turned out to be a man. As he lifted his chin from his two knees drawn together against his chest, she recognised him as JoJo and sat down next to him. They didn't talk; she knew his English was not good. His animal sensuality was switched off, the sexual attraction gone. They were both tired. Sadly, he destroyed the peace. 'Honeymoon in English is like Hollywood. In French it is *nuit de noces*, religious.'

So that's what he had been pondering in his brain when all she wanted from him was relaxing nothingness.

'Your engagement ring is *magnifique*.'

'Four carats,' she said and stretched her hand in front of his face.

'Too big to be true. Are you sure it is not cut glass, *plutôt*?'

'Cut glass? What do you know?' She pulled off the ring. It sucked up the moonlight and threw it back into his eyes. He took the ring from her fingers and looked at it closely.

'Don't drop it.' She reached out to take it back but he pushed it between his front teeth.

'That's to check pearls. Give it back.' She jogged his shoulder.

He convulsed in coughing and then gagged. With a look of horror, he turned to her. '*Avalé*,' he said finally. 'Swallowed. Your fault.'

'Throw up. Now. Push your finger into your throat, deep.'

He tried, and she bent away from him.

He gagged and coughed and could not speak, and she panicked.

'Try again,' she shouted at him and shook him by his shoulders. He reacted by emitting a long drawn-out groan and let himself fall sideways onto the sand.

'Shit,' she said.

'*Oui, merde* is necessary,' he muttered.

Only then did she notice that they were not alone. A small boy was squatting watching, a local child no more than five years of age. In his large eyes, the white glinted.

'Is he sick?' the boy asked in English.

'He swallowed a large diamond. Now go to your mother.'

'Oh,' the child said in wonder and came closer to JoJo in the sand. 'Like a diamond in the sky. My mother sings this.'

Gabriela realised that the child was Tiana's, living wild at this hour while his slutty mother performed into all hours of the night.

'Is he dead?'

Gabriela stared at JoJo's inert curled-up figure. 'Go and get Pablito from the bar. We need the nurse, a doctor.'

Instantly, the child sprang up and ran away, a tiny dark figure moving at speed, sporadically lit by the sidewalk lights. It was not long before he returned, running beside two people carrying a stretcher. Pablito took one look and called for an ambulance. 'They'll take him to the hospital in Bridgetown,' he said.

Gabriela left the scene and walked back to the bungalow. How could she explain this to Lewis? Slipping into the bed, she woke him.

'Where have you been?' he said, drugged by sleep.

'I went for a romantic walk on the beach and something awful happened.' She buried her head in the pillow. He was fully awake now, and she told him that, while admiring the moon glint in the diamond, she had dropped the ring in the sand.

'That small ring in all that sand?' He searched for his canvas shoes under the bed.

'Where are you going? Surely you have insured it.'

'How does it look to insure a diamond for thirty thousand pounds, and then declare it lost seven days later? We need to be there when the sun gets up, to beat the local beachcombers.'

That much, she thought. How could she tell him that the ring was in the stomach of JoJo, by now hopefully defecating in hospital and solving the problem?

At the beach, as soon as purple showed on the horizon, she pretended to help Lewis search around a bending palm tree, where she *thought* she had dropped the ring. She *remembered* that further along she had come across JoJo on the beach.

'A rendezvous?'

''Course not. I can't even communicate with the guy. First, I thought he was drunk but then he collapsed. Someone in the night club must have seen it. Pablito came with the nurse, and they carried him away on a stretcher.'

'What does that have to do with losing the ring?'

'I dropped the ring as I said, but I feel guilty for having done nothing to help JoJo.'

'Gabriela, I really don't think the bloke is worth your sympathy.'

'Nevertheless…'

★

Indeed, once Club Med was awake and breakfast being served, Gabriela found the *chef de village* and talked her into taking her along to the hospital in Bridgetown. Lewis remained on the beach looking for the ring. It made no sense to him that Gabriela should be so concerned about a Club Med jock's well-being. Under these circumstances, he, Lewis, had to stop admiring impulsive behaviour and come back to his own considered ways.

Eventually he sat down, turning a shell thoughtfully between his fingers. A little boy appeared and squatted near him. '*Shine bright like a diamond. You are the woman of my heart*,' the boy sing-songed.

Man and boy started up a conversation, and Lewis learned that the boy was Tiana's child. They had been chatting for a while when the boy jumped up and shouted, 'Grangran!'

Lewis turned to see an old woman in an ample white-collared print dress walking along the beach with a rolling gait, a scarf wound around her head, a cloth belt emphasising her formidable figure.

'What you do here? I worried. Come home.'

Lewis was reassured to know that, while Tiana slept during the day, the child was being cared for by his grandmother, who pulled the boy off the ground with her dark fleshy arm, turned and started to take him down the beach.

'No,' protested the boy, and she had to stop. 'JoJo, my father, my father, he is sick.'

Grangran frowned, and her eyebrows drew together over the cushioned eyelids, her round eyes widened.

Lewis got up and explained that JoJo had been taken ill last night and was in the hospital. He had not realised that they were a family.

'Come.' Grangran invited him along, and all three walked south along the edge of the waves.

They passed the guard in his straw hut at the periphery of Club Med and the oddly assembled trio made their way past wooden boats pulled up onto the shore. Huts appeared through a banana grove. A slim

402

brown dog came running and barking, greeted the boy and sniffed Lewis's canvas shoes.

Grangran pointed to a substantial house built in the local style of bamboo over concrete base. It had the traditional wide deck with wicker chairs, and potted flowers in pierced tin-cans hanging from the rafter beams. The old woman pulled herself up the few steps, relying on the handrail.

'Is my boy OK?' came from inside and, with something of a thrill, Lewis recognised the voice of Tiana.

The boy offered him a chair and suggested lemonade, eager to please, despite the fact that his father was seriously ill in hospital. The child was dark in colour. The only concession to JoJo's French genes was the straight chestnut hair worn in a pudding-bowl haircut.

Grangran appeared at the door. 'You want benny cake?'

Lewis could not guess what that was and so declined. 'What is your name?' he asked the boy.

'He does not have a name yet.' Tiana came onto the deck in a sleeveless white cotton dress. Without make-up, and her hair around her face, she looked about fifteen years old and totally innocent and completely gorgeous.

Lewis had been exposed to many different situations in his position as fund manager, and in many different countries, but right now he was sitting in a cane chair, with a lemonade, gazing at the most desirable creature he had ever seen or even dreamed of. By asking why the child did not have a name, he hoped to hide his feelings.

403

'He is half-Bajan, half-French. When he is someone whole, a name will come his way.' She drew a circle in the air with her elegant hands when saying 'whole'. He wanted to grab her and kiss her hard.

Grangran was in the garden to the side of the house, cooking and energetically wafting away smoke from the barbecue while talking to herself.

'My mother cooks us shrimp Creole with roasted bell peppers.'

Lewis, wanting to appear domesticated, said enthusiastically how nice that was going to be and how much the art of Creole cooking was appreciated in London's best restaurants.

She laughed. 'My mother is too emotional to cook well. The peppers will be burnt, I warn you.'

How natural it all was. Lewis liked it. She sat down, curled her legs under her and talked about the sea's different colours and about her boy's clever mind. She did not once mention her fame as a singer even though inside, when he had asked to use the lavatory, he had seen a picture of her on a magazine cover framed and hung on the wall.

After some leg-crossing and uncrossing, realising that she did not smell of cosmetics but of his childhood liquorice and warm stone, Lewis dared to mention JoJo and Club Med. Her face clouded. 'Those Club guys are very healthy, and there is nothing around here, no town. It is difficult for me to work there because of them. Most move every six months. JoJo got a promotion and stayed long enough for a relationship to grow. That is all. If he recovers in the hospital, he will go home. And my life is here.' She shrugged her well-shaped shoulders and went on, 'What about you and your fiancée?'

'Gabriela insisted on going to the hospital to be with JoJo.'

'Unusual. It is not clear what is happening here.'

'I agree.'

'It will become clear,' she said affirmatively.

'When it will be whole.' He made the movement of outlining a circle with his hands, the way she had done.

She smiled straight into his blue eyes. 'You learn fast. I like that.'

Lunch was laid out on a wooden table on the uneven ground in the garden with view of the sea. It smelled good, and Lewis realised that he was hungry, for food, for everything.

An outboard engine gurgled as it was throttled down to be cut off. They watched a man jump out, grab the metal ring in the bow and pull the boat crunching onto the beach. He clapped his hands to rid himself of sand and came walking towards them.

'My brother, Benson,' Tiana explained.

Out of courtesy, Benson walked up to his mother and said something to her in Bajan Creole. She responded by clapping her hand affectionately against his cheek. Only then did Benson greet the others, lifting up the little boy and shaking him, calling him a rascal. He came up to Lewis, grabbing him familiarly by his forearm. 'You are a banker in London?'

'An investment manager. How do you know that?'

'Tiana texted me.'

Just because they were in a heavenly place did not mean that suddenly mobiles did not exist.

'I am deputy to the CEO in a bank in Bridgetown,' he went on. 'I have so much business to talk to you about.'

'First, you fill your bellies,' Grangran decided for them. 'Then you talk good.'

'You know' – Benson turned to Lewis – 'I have offered to pay for her teeth to be fixed.'

'I heard that.'

They all sat down, and as the meal progressed Lewis came to realise what spontaneity could be. He had never felt so clear in his mind, so engaged with his emotions. He knew that he would do anything to be part of this.

Over coffee and rum, Benson and he talked finance. First, Lewis thought this would just be banking small-talk but, as Benson spoke expansively of his large regionally active bank which, since the crash, had deteriorated fiscally to corporate vulnerability, Lewis understood that only financial injection and global flow could improve the situation. His hedge fund was in a position to open up the bank's horizons. Benson explained how beneficial this would be for the island as a whole, and Lewis realised that it could be a big opportunity for his hedge fund too. The two men's heads were close together as they came up with specifics.

The sun threw a sudden shadow caused by a palm tree in its course; it was late afternoon. He and Benson agreed to continue their discussions in front of a computer screen in Benson's office the next day.

Lewis walked back to Club Med and Gabriela. Only last night he had asked her to marry him, given her an enormous diamond ring, and now he felt that he would rather not see her ever again. But she was there, at the bar, drinking with Pablito and many of the staff. They were agitated and emotional. Apparently, JoJo had been suffering from massive internal bleeding and despite an emergency operation had died on the table. His crash into the metal bar of the safety net must have been more traumatic than anyone had appreciated at the time. The body would be coffined and sent back to JoJo's family in France for burial. Gabriela was hysterical and drunk.

Lewis pulled her away from the bar and took the drink out of her hand to put it out of her reach. 'Why are you doing this? What is JoJo to you?'

She stared at him with tear-bathed eyes, then began to laugh, head back. He saw the red inside of her mouth, the gallery of teeth, while hysterical laughter burst from her body.

'Can we talk?' he asked her. 'You are scaring me.'

Gabriela suddenly went limp. 'I know what you are going to say.'

'You don't.'

She gathered her drunken wits and looked at her fiancé with stoical intensity. 'Something happened with me and Jojo. I can't explain and you wouldn't understand.'

Lewis reached a decision. He half-dragged Gabriela to reception, got her booked on to the last flight home that evening, and extended his own stay by a week. Gabriela was packed and in the car to the airport more efficiently than it was normally done. Their engagement was not mentioned, nor was the ring.

He kissed her hairline with cold lips and let her go. Then he returned to the beach, which had become part of him in a short time, pulled out his mobile and called Benson to confirm their appointment in Bridgetown the next day.

★

Three days later, following hours in meetings and Skyping with London, a basic agreement was drawn up and ready for signature. It would be a big change for Barbados and many rather sleepy bank employees would have to be shaken up, but the benefits were foreseeable. Lewis would stay and work alongside Benson for at least six months to realise the project.

Benson and Lewis motorboated out of Bridgetown and through clear waters. Lewis felt his hair pulled back by the on-wind and his brow cleansed. It felt like being reborn. At the height of Grangran's house they swerved towards the beach.

'Everything is wonderful,' Lewis announced, walking across the sand to the house. 'I'll be staying here for a while. Let's celebrate.'

'You,' the grandmother said with a stab of finger at him, looking matronly pleased with herself. 'You young man not know celebration. Old women know.'

Tiana explained that today was a special day in more ways than one. The spirit of JoJo had to be laid to rest; after all, he was the boy's father. That evening they would go out onto the water and decide on a spot where flowers would be cast upon the sea and prayers made for JoJo's soul.

Once the sun had set in an array of warm colours, Benson pushed the boat far enough into the sea for it to float freely, and they climbed in and sat down. Benson jumped on and pulled the cord for the outboard motor. They swooped out to sea. The moon had waned, and the water looked oily black.

The child said, 'Here is a good place for light in the beautiful sea and, Mum, here is your diamond in the sky.' The boy dug in his shorts pocket and pulled out a ring with a perfect table-cut diamond of four carats.

'Where did you get that?'

Benson cut the motor, leaving them to drift.

'My father put it into my hand when I walked with him being carried away on that bed.' The boy held out the ring to Tiana. 'Mum, can I have a name now?'

JoJo's ash-throwing was cut short. Nobody said a word as they puttered back to shore.

In the house, Tiana gave the ring back to Lewis. 'You offered it to a woman you asked to marry only four days ago.'

'Ya ya ya,' Grangran said. 'Not important. Lewis and Benson make big business. Good money can build a house for Lewis, wife Tiana and son. Everybody happy now.'

'Grangran, it smells of burning from the barbecue.'

'Kawblema!' she muttered, gathering her ample skirts and walking away.

Further along on the beach, Lewis, the diamond ring securely in one hand, bent his knee onto the sand and caught Tiana's narrow hands with the other. 'Will you marry me?'

RELIGION

Luckily she didn't ask me to be her bridesmaid.

In St Mark and the Martyrs Catholic Church, I slip into the last pew to be furthest away from my sister, getting married in white because the mother of Tom, the groom, is Catholic. We, the Young family, never set foot inside such a church – or any other for that matter.

But Juliette had to have a theatrical production for her wedding. Hats are bobbling in the front pews. There is a lot of chattering and looking around. Tom's mother paid for the flowers, yellow and orange against dark green foliage. I am wearing a silver-dusted fascinator; the hairdresser said he could do little with such short hair. Why not just say, 'Little could be made of me'? My dress itches; I almost wish I were at work right now.

St Mark's is filling, probably with Tom's work colleagues apart from some distant relatives and acquaintances Mother has rustled up in the flurry of wedding fever. I watch the reactions of the arrivals through the door next to me; the little shoulder-jerks and tensing of face muscles show that they are ill at ease in the rococo décor, the dolls of saints and the wafting scent – and with their guilty prejudices. A hair-gelled usher shows them to seats.

A mother stoops at my shoulder. She has two children in tow. Could I please move so that the kids can see the bride? I slide across. After a while her hubby arrives and I have to slide right to the end. A wide stone pillar is in front of me now. At least I won't have to see Juliette and Tom, and nobody will see me. I am probably sitting in the leper seat.

Here Comes the Bride: the played-out tune trumpets right up to the vaulted ceiling. Necks twist. There is rustling and wood being banged as guests get up to see and photograph the 'amazing, beautiful, out-of-this-world' bride. From the corner of my eye I perceive the slow-moving snow queen who has iced me out all her life.

The inevitable is conducted at the front while I can see right into the side-chapel of the Holy Spirit. On a narrow altar stands a large wooden cross with a life-size Jesus nailed to it. He looks slightly sideways, demurely down to earth for those who stand in front of Him, but sitting I can see some gloss in His eyes, which are actually looking at me right now, a regard full of pity. From the stained-glass window His pale pinewood body is played upon like a kaleidoscope. He is endearing in His exposed nudity. I feel tears well up and the heat of emotions fills my head. The misnamed fascinator is slithering down my hair. I wrench it off and clip it into the needlework of the hassock hanging at my knees. I return my eyes to the man on the cross who clearly has singled me out to flirt with. My tensions ease; I will be able to bear the long day during which Tom marries my younger sister and not me.

The wedding was seventy-two hours ago. Today it is raining; I saw it on my lunch break. Something makes me decide on the spur of the moment to tap on the door of my supervisor. She lets me off two hours early.

Under my umbrella I walk as fast as I can all the way to St Mark and his Martyrs.

I push the door and step onto the grey flags, as thousands have before me since 1885, when the church was built. For a second time, I penetrate the sanctum, and thereby into the inner space where all that is good in me dwells. Outside, the sky is weeping. In here, eternity is beaming, shaming the ordinariness of every day.

Stepping softly, I head for the side-chapel. It is veiled in darkness but kept alive by flickering wax candles from a metal stand with spikes. No one else seems to be about.

Pulling the prayer stool up close enough for His aura to encompass me, I caress the thorn-spiked wood of His injured thigh. We're intimate; He is the only man in my life. The tips of my fingers touch the edge of His loincloth, carved in folds and tarnished where paint has flaked off. I close my eyes indulgently. The Lord is a man after all, the covering of His loin scant and His pelvis narrow and lust-inducing. My fingers spread against it, I feel the dead wood warming, and the blood coursing through my veins infuses Him with my ardour. Now His heart beats and ebbs together with mine. The candles flicker in my tears and I bring Him back to life – I, Frances, prostrated before Him. Were there not others who witnessed blood from the spear wound? And others who witnessed real tears fall from His eyes? I adore you, my Lord. Give me a sign that you can feel my sensual passion, my adoration.

My inner agitation causes the prayer stool to slide to the side from under me. I sway and hold onto His hip, a hip which is just a piece of old dry carved wood with holes made by worms. I step down and think of my own body. I have to love it in order to perform daily tasks, even though others don't. I used to be eager to please but now that incentive has worn out and I feel veiled in my unloved body. Plain and boring in my early forties, I lie in bed in cold stillness night after night. At least at work I feel the breath of others' selfishness.

The crucifix has given me hope in myself again. What I look forward to all week is Mass on Sunday. I go early to have some private time with Him. Arms spread, He welcomes me. I feel infinite love. His slender pale feet one over the other force His long elegant legs into a chaste pose. Yes, men too can open their legs vulgarly to display their much-vaunted *goodies*. But Christ with legs spread would be unacceptably vulgar.

By now I've got the hang of Mass but keep a low profile which is possible because people come in and sneak out at all times, the vestry door banging behind the shallow and unmoved.

★

Today is an extended celebration. The organ pipes thunder, the music tumbling tumultuously between stone arches and echoing vaults. The adult choir, clad in black cassocks, are singing. Two youths assist at the altar. Their cassocks have white collars as if to remind the world that they are still innocent. One has thick dark rebellious hair swept back just like Tom's when he was interested in me. I watch that boy, hands joined coyly in front of him, but his body language shows a character as indomitable as his hair, the way he wriggles and bum-bumps the boy next to him. Tom used to rock on his feet when standing and then, realising it, would pull himself together by jerking up his square chin. Tom, whom I believed to be mine for keeps.

I get up from kneeling and the priest sends us back out to our lives with the blessings of the bearded old man and his son, my secret lover. Not ready yet to walk out on pleasure, I sneak into the tenebrous apse behind the altar. The choir members have all come out of the vestry and left. One of the youths passes me in jeans and T-shirt, chewing gum and carrying a sports bag. Where is my Tom lookalike? The woman I know to be the church warden has already started to go through the rows of pews like a cleaner in an aeroplane, so the clergy must have left.

I catch sight of my Tom, still robed and lifting the metal lectern onto his shoulder to bring it down from the dais towards me. I step behind a pillar. Does he have to do chores as punishment for being naughty? He disappears in shadow. I tiptoe forward to where I can make out a narrow metal-studded wooden door outlined in light strips. It leads into a small crypt, which I know from the pamphlet explaining the church. I check around. I am alone.

415

Pushing the door, venturing down the stone steps, I come to a small wrought-iron gate, arched and also open. The one lightbulb behind me is not strong enough to illuminate the crypt, from which comes some noise.

I enter. A moving shadow reveals where Tom is closing a heavy chest, into which he must have put the lectern. When he turns and sees me, he curses crudely in fright. With the light behind me, my shadow is gigantic over him and the walls. I am blocking his way out.

'Push off!'

His predicament gets worse as I close the gate behind me and advance towards him; he retreats until his back is against the curved wall.

'Take off the cassock, Tom,' I say with a strange voice coming out of me, and then think of 'please'.

After some hesitation he obeys. Now he is in jeans and a T-shirt and obviously feels more empowered. 'Who are you and what the fuck do you want? My name isn't Tom.'

The moist, earthy smell in the confined space seems to entomb us in the same fate. I notice the thrill of terror when he looks into my eyes and reads what I have in mind. I am within touching distance of him.

'Crazy bitch. Help!' he shouts, but not loudly or convincingly enough.

I grab his arm and pull him off the wall. With one hand over his mouth and letting myself fall, I take him with me to the ground. He does not use his muscles or anger to beat me off, which he easily could. I used to hop onto Tom on the bed and he had to let himself be playfully molested.

I pin the youth down by his angular shoulders and bend down over his mouth, which quivers. 'You're mine. I want to caress your body and show you how I love you and how tender I can be.' He shivers at my touch and tries to writhe from under me, his eyes locked on mine to predict when I might go dangerously mad. 'You won't come to any harm. Just let me stroke your strong young chest, only a little.'

He freezes in panic while I roll up his T-shirt and put my hand on his slender, fat-free body. I push the garment right up to his Adam's apple, which moves rapidly up and down. Kissing the dell of his belly button, I feel his cool flesh. I force my hand into the top of his jeans, and he objects by pulling down his T-shirt.

'I lust for you. I need you. Help me take off your jeans.'

'The priest is waiting for me.'

'Everyone is long gone, trust me.'

'You're molesting me and now you want to rape me. This is a crime; I'm only fifteen.'

'That is a beautiful age to be introduced to clean carnal desire. Later in life it will be spoiled.'

'Don't touch more of me. Let me go!'

'Trousers off, you ungrateful boy.' I seem to have a lot more strength than I gave myself credit for. He spits as I kneel on his ankles, which must hurt him, and undo the button and zip. I pull the jeans towards me and move to the side. With his trouser legs around his ankles, his legs are like the Lord's on the cross. He is past worming himself away from me now. I have won.

417

His body is beautiful, soft and smells of vanilla. The curve of his pelvis is perfect and pale, just like Christ's. There is something immature, clean and honest about his sex, revealed when I pull down his underpants. Not like Tom's, who sleeps in the same bed as Juliette now. I caress his sex with my lips.

'Mum,' he calls out, but he is a man in every way and tastes of honey-drops like any adult man. Frances has ceased to be Frances; she is now a priestess dispensing love and initiation to the act of ultimate intimacy.

He lets it happen and, when it happens, he gnarls his fingers into my brown hair. I am his first woman and therefore have made him mine for ever.

★

Back in my flat, I plunge into my easy chair. My muscles hurt. Something has happened to my body to exert it without my consent or control. The front of my blouse is wet and stained and smells bland from the semen he shed for me. I stop myself from journeying into wild fantasies ending in aberrant conduct. Suddenly I notice the dark animal cowering in the entrance. I panic. What have I done here? It is not moving and now I realise that it is a black surplice – his – which I have taken with me. How did it end? Oh God, what will happen to me? No, it can't be so bad. He loved me in the end and gave me the cassock. I lift it up and, with it, collapse into genuflexion. My lovely Tom lookalike has offered me his priestly cloak as a peace token between us. I feel chosen, and therefore I am devoted to you, my Lord. It is that way, isn't it?

418

I go to bed early. Daytime is too much of a nightmare.

Monday work is as normal as it could be. In my cubicle office space, both my skinned kneecaps burn. Now I am like anyone else; carpet-burns they call it. I too had sex at the weekend.

I can, of course, never go back to St Mark and his Martyrs.

★

A week later, my imagination has made the choirboy talk to his parents, who have talked to the choirmaster, who has informed the police. In our culture, people object to under-age humans being shown what they might learn later, even though there are no kicks as precious as first-time ones experienced under the thrill of danger. It has to be a gift to a youth to experience such sensual delights.

And three weeks later, I am missing Sunday Mass. The stupendous thing which happened to me is now somewhere in the past; I almost don't believe it happened. I yearn for candlelight, the air heavy with scent and dust, and the magic and the tender flesh of Christ.

Juliette has announced that she is pregnant. Mother is showing off to friends. 'Frances, what are you waiting for to make yourself worthy of us?' is not exactly what she said but is, I know, what she meant.

I could change my appearance. The pack of dye I bought promised blond hair but did not live up to expectations. I buy a blond wig with shoulder-length curls. It is pleasing to feel hair dance on my shoulders. I shave off my eyebrows and paint on some new ones.

419

With a pair of horn-rimmed spectacles on, I don't recognise myself in the mirror.

In the black gown, off which I have taken the white collar with my nail scissors, I will join the choir next Sunday at vesper Mass, because it will be a big event. Several churches are coming together for Ascension, the day Christ rose to Heaven. Surely, the police will not be active on a late Sunday afternoon; they certainly won't expect me to be in the choir.

I sneak in from the side-door, already robed, and wait behind a pillar near the vestry. When they all file out, I join up. On the dais, they place themselves where they have rehearsed and I tuck in beside the altos. Only now, half-hidden by the back of the singer in front of me, do I dare to look around. The church is well attended. All seems as it should, except for the two men in suits – yes, they are here. One is positioned at the entrance door and another skulks in the side-nave near the front pew with his hand against his ear, which no doubt holds his radio receiver.

'Tom' and the other boy process behind the priest to the altar, where they prepare the Communion, while the organ babbles music. My eyes feast on the slender and immature neck of Tom. I indulge in a dream of touching Tom, kissing Tom, smelling Tom. The priest turns to the congregation. The nearest policeman has taken a seat. Mass is about to begin.

The choirmaster looks up and over us, and then sees me whom he does not recognise. He scratches in his hair. What now? He steps down from the dais to the sitting policeman and words are exchanged. It is too late to hide behind the sheet music of the singer next to me. The choirmaster points at me discreetly and the policeman gives me a nod. Mechanically, I nod back, lips loose and quivering. Why did I do that?

The choirmaster resumes his place in front of us, and the organ music stops for the priest's warm welcome. I notice Tom twitching and looking back over his shoulder at the choir. Did his eyes linger on me? He can't possibly recognise me, but why look back at us at all?

The Mass proceeds and the woman next to me is put out by my half-hearted sing-songing and by having to share her music sheet. The moment comes for the faithful to file forward to receive the body and blood of Christ.

This break brings the policeman next to me. 'You Special Branch? You didn't make yourself known. We have to work together.'

'I agree.' (Working together is better than being arrested for sexual assault!)

'Put your radio on Channel 8. I am Foxtrot. At the door is Golf. You're Hotel. The victim is one of the altar boys. Just watch them.'

Foxtrot ducks away and here I am, a blond female detective – and I can't laugh hysterically until I drop.

The Mass is coming to an end. The final blessing is bestowed upon us. Now it is going to get tricky for me to leave unseen. The choir files back to the vestry. Foxtrot indicates that I should join Golf.

What next? I am now with Golf at the church door watching the slow-moving crowd. Between us is Tom, ready to identify his assailant, a shameless almost smiling Judas. I can see a beckoning slice of the outside world through the door and am ready to run, but have to hold still.

The churchwarden is already at the back pews tidying the hassocks and hymn-sheets.

'Shouldn't someone go to the crypt and see whether she is waiting in there?' Tom asks.

'The door and gate are locked. We made sure of that.'

'She doesn't know that, does she?' Tom is clearly eager to catch the criminal.

'I'll go,' I say, 'to check the crypt.'

Now I am walking back into the heart of the church from which there is less chance to escape, knowing the side-doors are locked.

Foxtrot is palely lit on the far side checking the nooks and crannies. I notice that the metal-stud door to the crypt is unlocked! Strange. I tiptoe down the stairs. The light bulb is not on. Now my testing fingers reveal that the wrought-iron gate is open too. I enter the moist space and sit on the chest in the pitch dark. Has anyone ever been sucked up by total darkness?

Spontaneous combustion existed but didn't that have to do with lightning?

It is clear that Tom has unlocked door and gate so that I can be trapped down here like a rabbit in a cage and arrested thanks to his initiative. He, the hero, because he recognised me when he looked back and his eyes rested on me. Maybe he dreams of joining the police when he grows up.

Someone is coming. I sense it like an animal living underground who has the ability to detect danger without sight. Rubber soles are tapping down the stone steps. I am lost. My life is over. I cower to minimise my physical presence. The gate gives a little squeak as it is pushed to the side by the intruding policeman. And now a torch is eating me in its beam. I close my eyes and cross myself.

'Hi.' The torch travels along the wall, enough to shed light on the torch-holder. Tom grins at me, teeth white in the dark. 'Your disguise is pathetic and those glasses. Gross!'

'W-where are the police?' I stutter.

'Up there. They sent me here to get you.'

'Aren't they coming?'

'They've arrested the churchwarden and taken her away because I said it was her. She was holding a silvery bunch of feathers, and I told the Fuzz she tickled me with it before forcing me to have sex.'

'Why didn't you give me away?'

'I loved what you did to me. Let's do it again; this time I won't… you know, so quickly.'

'Surely, the choirmaster is looking for you.'

'Nah, I sent him to my parents and told him I would join them there. He's a sleazeball, always touching me up and drooling over me. If he finds out I've been with an experienced woman, he will leave me alone.'

'But…'

'No *buts*. All my mates have done it already, and I'm sixteen next week anyway, so thanks, we have hours for you to show me things. And then we can just leave because there's no churchwarden to lock up.'

RAMIRO

Ray finally joined them, pulled out the chair and then tucked himself against the wax tablecloth. Yesterday he had been absent, spending the day at a school-leavers' career path seminar.

Alice, his adoptive mother, smiled with slightly grim affection and put the plate of food in the space between the knife and fork in front of him. 'How did it go?' she asked apprehensively, and he flapped the napkin open.

'Job choices. How to write a CV. Where we saw ourselves in ten years' time. Greg saw an estate agent, and my other friend Danny will go to university. At the end, we were each seen by a counsellor.'

'A waste of time,' said his stepfather, Will. 'In three weeks you'll be eighteen, an adult. It's bleeding obvious what you're going to do.'

'Apparently because I had to change school and lose a year when my dad died, my choices are limited.' Ray heard his voice was self-consciously shrill and avoided looking into their eyes. 'I told them that I wanted to be a paramedic.'

'That's a crap job. And anyway, the one who died was your adoptive dad. The Brazilian who actually fathered you buggered off, along with your Brazilian mother. Your widowed mum here, when she married me, had to move with me to Gravesend. It's not my fault if you lost two fathers.'

'The first year I would have to get a health care qualification.'

Will put his fork down. 'You'll work for me, starting in the yard like Stuart here. He began at the bricks, moved to timber-cutting and is now creating cost sheets. I broke my back turning that builder's yard into a major merchant supplies outfit to leave to my sons.'

'Stuart, your son – not me.'

'Where does that come from, huh? Bloody do-good career advisors.'

Alice stared at her husband, appalled. 'Perhaps Ray could work in the yard for a time and see whether he likes it?'

'Laid-back Brazuca. Too lazy to lift bricks,' Will said to no one in particular but then jerked his head in the direction of Ray. 'Get a crew cut. I want my yard lads to look spruce.'

'I don't look good with a shaved head.'

'Who cares?'

'Dad, can we please stop this?' Stuart finally contributed.

'Yeah, what's for pudding?'

★

426

A week later in the builder's yard, Ray, wearing a woollen cap over his curly black hair, watched the meticulous movements of the forklift as it picked up slabs. The worst sin was damage to material. His task was to hand-pile bricks onto pallets for smaller orders. He had come prepared with gloves but took them off, faced by the mocking reaction of the yard lads. One had shimmied his hips. Ray knew only too intimately how racism worked. Alice and his now dead father had been unable to have children and had adopted him from Brazil during the eighties when unwanted babies were being sold off.

That evening, Alice knocked on Ray's door before entering the bedroom, the wall space of which was hidden under posters of Brazilian football teams. Ray was rubbing Nivea into his hands. She sat next to him on the bed and took one hand onto her lap. Blood droplets seeped through the viscous cream. She sighed.

'Don't worry, Mum. It doesn't hurt that much.'

'Something unusual has happened,' she said and let him take his hand back. 'You know Will does all my emails. Well, he has shown me one just in from the adoption agency.'

Ray frowned sideways at her; he felt the tension emanating from his mother.

'You know that the name on your birth certificate is Ramiro Ribeira. Your natural father was Carlos Ribeira.'

He waited, apprehensive.

'You were handed over by the Carmelite sisters in Sao Paulo, but your natural father was there to sign the papers and pick up the money. We promised to send photos to the agency.'

'And did you?'

'At first. You must understand that, with time, we came to feel that you were our child, and the trip to Brazil slipped into the blue yonder. We haven't heard from them for ages.'

Ray guessed that his mother was now going to say something which he had long imagined. 'Carlos is coming to see me, isn't he?'

'Not quite. He has been invited to speak at a conference in London. Afterwards, there is a reception and dinner to which he would like to invite you.' She added, 'What he actually wrote was *in that setting, my natural son will not have to be ashamed of me.* They'll tell us the exact date and time. The speech will be shown live on TV.'

They agreed to watch the conference together as a family before Ray would take the Tube into London to meet Carlos in the lobby of his hotel.

★

On the day, Will drove Stuart and Ray home early from the yard and, by four o'clock, Ray was in the armchair while Stuart and Will were installed either side of Alice on the sofa. Will had even lapsed into kindness enough to heap a plastic bowl with crisps and put a six-pack on the coffee table. The curtains over the patio doors were drawn.

Will pressed the button.

A short bald man with glasses stood at the lectern, and Ray's blood thickened in his throat but then eased when it became clear that he was merely introducing the speaker, Mr Carlos Ribeira. The camera turned to the audience, out of which rose a tall man, his black curly hair tickling the collar of the dark grey suit jacket. He made his way along the aisle to the podium.

My natural father reverberated through Ray's mind. He glanced at Will, who was rocking his upper body slightly, leaning forwards, nursing a beer can in his hands between his splayed knees. His mother stared at the screen and Stuart crunched crisps.

Carlos held the lectern tightly with elegant hands emerging from white starched cuffs. He was handsome in a rugged way, dark skin and ink-black eyes. First, he thanked the Carlton Tower Hotel for hosting the conference, and then went on to say, 'Life is an extraordinary gift.' He spoke with a cultivated voice, tinted by a slight accent. 'A gift offered by a creator, a spark-giver. What each of us makes of it is our individual choice.'

'Sounds like a bible-thumper,' Will mumbled.

'I am here to remind us about those who were deprived of that choice by the inhumane adoption practices in the eighties. Four hundred Brazilian babies a month were sold to adoptive parents abroad. The majority went to North America, some to Europe. The popularity of this traffic in helpless babies was abetted by the press. You might recall pictures of dirty toddlers standing in rusty cots in dark rooms, tears glinting in their innocent eyes.

'These babies, taken from poverty-stricken families, are now young adults and in most cases have lost all track of their origins. Adoptive parents have a tendency to crush signs of *differentness* and bend the child their way. A Brazilian child has genes which react to sun and light, to rhythm and vibrations, but these poor children were destined to live in a cold climate. The child's inner self is deprived, but does not know it. The result is a tension in life; the child does not know how to genuinely feel good. There may well be better education and job prospects, but essentially they have lost their right of individual choice.'

Alice pulled up her shoulders in a shiver. Will fizzed open another can of beer. Stuart carried on munching crisps.

'That is one side of the coin,' Carlos went on. 'The *favelas* of Sao Paulo and the city's orphanages, from which most of these babies came, were a shame to the Brazilian government who watched it happening. I am pleased to use the past tense. It is the mission of the Society Against Baby-Trafficking, the organisers of this conference, to ensure that it never happens again.

'Of the nineteen thousand babies sold or given away, one was my son. He was picked up by a couple from England forty-eight hours after his birth, and his mother and I got six hundred pounds for him. This allowed us to survive for about a year and a half – time enough to make another baby to sell. None of you here in the audience knows poverty – not the kind where you have to sell your own children. This is not an excuse. It is a tragedy. I intend to spend the gift of my life helping to improve the living conditions in Sao Paulo.

'My son Ramiro will soon be eighteen. I have invited him to join me for the reception and dinner after this conference and hope he will come. How I feel about this, it is impossible to convey – too many tissues would have to be on hand.'

Carlos stepped down. His hand was shaken, and a medal was presented to him for his relentless work in this cause. When he made to return to his seat, the camera revealed a smile spread on his face. Instinctively, Ray knew that it was for him, and indeed Carlos lifted his left hand and gave a short wave – a wave for Ray.

Will pressed the button.

'He's good-looking for an old Brazilian,' said Stuart stupidly, while Ray ran up the stairs to get ready for London, taking two at a time.

In the bedroom, he had laid out the suit and black shoes he had borrowed from Stuart, a school shirt and underwear. Alice came and wordlessly picked up the shirt.

'What are you doing?'

'Here.' From behind her back, she produced a new shirt folded under plastic. 'Tonight is special for you.'

'Rather.'

'I have still not come to terms with what Carlos said in his speech about all those babies,' she said. 'I yearned for an infant to hold and love, and my husband turned out to be infertile. There was no choice in England, and people went to Brazil, pretending to be pregnant with a cushion – a holiday during which, surprisingly, the baby was born. Your name was put on my passport; we paid the fee and home we came. We told ourselves that we had saved an unwanted baby from a dreadful fate.'

Ray unfolded the new white shirt and lobbed the crumpled wrapping to his mother. 'Why didn't you give me an English name?'

'There were complications with your birth. You were born by C-section. A priest on standby conducted an emergency baptism, but you were saved. We met Carlos in the corridor of the clinic. Your mother was lying on a trolley, and he was holding her hand. Later, we talked.'

'Did my mother say anything? You must tell me everything exactly as it was.'

'She was sedated.'

'What did she look like?'

'Like a woman after a long labour. Dark long hair in a thick braid hanging down beside her head. Pretty, I guessed.'

'Did they look deprived, like drug addicts?'

'They were undernourished and exhausted. I remember worrying that the baby had not got enough nutrition in her womb.'

'Weren't they upset about losing me?'

'In that corridor, he bent over her, his lips on her forehead, and she kissed the medallion on the chain around his neck – a Madonna, I believe.'

'Thank you, Mum, for telling me. There are things in me which I sort of know are different to who I am supposed to be.'

'Well, tonight make the best of this invitation. You have our blessing. Life is a gift to treasure, as your natural father said quite correctly.'

★

Once on the Tube in London, Ray decided to think of himself as Ramiro. There were many in the carriage who did not have the English pink skin. Two young women of Mediterranean appearance stared at a street map, obviously tourists. They chatted in Portuguese, and one caught his eyes and smiled. Ramiro knew they thought he was *one of them.*

In Knightsbridge he got off and was soon walking down Sloane Street, his new stiff cotton shirt warm under his armpits, and Stuart's shoes pinching his toes. The glassy entrance of the Carlton Tower Hotel appeared on Cadogan Street. He went inside and was dumbfounded in the blade-sharp light coming from the ceiling. Then he followed the signs to the washrooms.

The mirror clearly showed Ramiro, not Ray. He doused his comb and dragged it through his hair backward, to imitate the way Carlos had worn his in the speech that afternoon. It made him look more Brazilian. Under his arms were wet patches. He would keep the jacket on. Some unruly hair sprang up. Resigned, he combed it back the way he wore it normally. This was not the moment to experiment.

Will had told Ray that Carlos expected to meet him at six in the hotel lobby. There were ten more minutes to six. It was exciting to know that his real father was in the same building. He took a seat on one of the pale green velour-covered chairs in the lobby. The receptionist glanced alertly at him, and he quickly got up.

He paced over the beige carpet, trying not to step on the dark bits. After Will had switched off the TV, the conference must have gone on for a bit longer. Carlos

433

would have gone to his room to freshen up or rest and then change. The anticipation of meeting, any minute now, was nerve-wracking. Reaching into his pocket for a tissue, Ramiro fished out a business card for the Hopscotch Club, with a picture of a woman nude except for a glitter thong. Stuart's.

At about six, a party of animated people came out of the elevator. Carlos was not amongst them. They left in taxis, which the concierge sorted out outside.

In the calm of the entrance it became ten past six and then a quarter past. Ramiro checked the time on his mobile against the clock on the wall behind reception. He paced and read the framed dining room menu again, wondering what *roulades* were.

It was half past six. He asked the receptionist to call Carlos Ribeira in his room.

'We have no Ribeira registered.'

The concierge came inside. Ramiro almost collided with him. 'You know the Brazilian conference they held here. Where did they go afterwards?'

'I remember a group of about a dozen going to Herman's Bar in Ormond Yard, before dinner in Bishop's restaurant. They left around six.'

'They didn't. I was here all the time. How much would a cab cost to Ormond Yard?'

'About fifteen quid, but...'

Ramiro impatiently interrupted him. 'OK, OK, I'll walk then,' he said, because he had only seven pounds fifty on him. He picked up a London map from the desk. 'This hotel sucks. They don't even know who is staying here.'

'Hey,' shouted the concierge after him. 'I think you've got it wrong.'

Long-striding and resolute, Ramiro walked along busy roads, passing embassies with flags. At a street crossing he was nearly knocked over by a cyclist. By Grosvenor Place, the pain from Stuart's shoes was unbearable. He pulled out the laces to give his feet some slack.

At Hyde Park Corner he lost time getting across, waiting at many pedestrian lights. Finally, he reached Piccadilly. It was past seven. Glowing in sweat, he slapped along in his unlaced shoes. It was nearly seven thirty when he entered Herman's Bar. Through open doors, he noticed that a private room was being cleared. The party had moved on, and he had missed Carlos again.

With his balled fists, he drummed on the bar top, which made peanuts hop from a small dish. 'Damn it.'

'That bad?' The barman came over. 'She's not worth it.'

It succeeded in raising a smile in Ramiro. 'My father, my real father, was here with a group a moment ago. My bloody shoes are too small, and this suit stinks of Stuart.' He grabbed a handful of peanuts and tossed them into his mouth. 'They went on to dinner in some place called Bishop's. How the fuck am I going get there?'

'You're eighteen, right? Honestly, you could do with a drink to loosen up. I've just the thing for you.'

The rum and coke with curved orange peel, according to the tab, cost six pounds fifty, and wasn't large. He gobbled peanuts, and the barman simply replenished the dishes. 'You from Argentina?'

435

'Brazil.'

'You won five World Cups…' The barman gave him another drink. 'On the house.'

Ramiro felt the alcohol take the edge off his anxiety. The protein of the nuts helped.

'You're too young to be sitting alone at a bar,' said one of the two women to his left.

He lied to them about his age and confided that he was supposed to meet his father, who had given a speech on television earlier, but had missed him in the hotel lobby – and now in this bar as well. He had to find some restaurant called Bishop's.

To his surprise they knew of the place, thought it a lovely French restaurant, and showed him on his map where it was. They urged him not to give up but to jump into a taxi at once.

Ramiro half-hoped the women might offer him the cab money, but of course they could not guess he was still at school.

Concentrating his slightly fuzzy mind on the map, he plodded along, walking awkwardly and feeling the pangs of hunger. London was a big city. In Lincoln's Inn Fields, he slumped onto the first free garden bench. He was not that far away from Ely Place, his goal, but peeing could not wait any longer. He got up, pretending to admire the bushes planted to the side, and turned his back to the benches. The urine pattering on wood chips made a racket.

A man materialised out of nowhere and yelled at him, calling him a pervert, a criminal, a sicko, and threatened to call the police. Ramiro had not finished, but started to run away, warm pee running down one trouser leg. At the park gate, he managed to zip up but not without getting urine over his fingers.

Night had fallen. Empty office buildings glowered forbiddingly. Finally, he was standing in Ely Place, which was a private cul-de-sac onto which backed a church. In one corner, he saw a panel announcing Bishop's restaurant and pointing to a narrow passage. It led to the restaurant's main entrance. He was too much of a mess to go inside. He wended his way back to a coffee shop, where he dived into the men's room. Activating the hand dryer and making little jumps was not effective in getting the hot air to dry his trouser leg. He dragged a milk crate in from the passage and stood on it in front of the dryer. The heat blast gave the trousers back their original colour. Just as he was threading back his shoelaces, he was ordered to leave by an ill-tempered square-headed man who had stuck his head into the men's room.

Ramiro hobbled out, turned and was back in Ely Place. His father must by now have come to the conclusion his son did not want to meet him. This demoralising thought almost made him retch. It was necessary to compose himself before he moved on. He tried the door of the dark-bricked church. It was unlocked. Steps led down to a damp crypt. Gradually, his eyes adapted to the semi-dark enough to make out a carved wooden Madonna in a recess of the coarse wall. Pleading to her, he begged, 'Please, let me meet my father. I have only this one chance.'

As if in instant response, there came a hollow clanging, but then he realised that he was being closed

437

in. Shouting and hammering against the door produced an old caretaker to let him out, too lazy to have checked whether anyone was inside. Ramiro's hands, already raw from yard work, were bleeding again.

With sudden decisiveness, he took off his shoes and ran in socks back through the passage. In front of the main entrance to the restaurant, he put the shoes back on but found he had lost one lace. He wiped his bleeding hands on a panel of the shirt, which he tucked out of sight into his trousers. At the door, he was embraced by a suffused aroma of food and the resounding voices of animated diners.

A young woman, *Kate* on her lapel tag, confirmed that there was a party of twelve people inside. They had finished dessert and would have coffee and brandy.

'Is it the Society Against Baby-Trafficking?'

'That rings a bell, but I'm just a waitress.'

He beamed at her. 'Thank you.'

'They won't let you in, though. Dress code, I am afraid. And we are closing now. The last guests will have to leave through the back door into Ely Place.'

Ramiro felt good. Carlos was right behind that partition. One of the voices he heard had to be his. Nothing else mattered, not even the acrid smell on him of sweat, blood and urine. All he had to do was go back round to Ely Place and make sure Carlos did not get away again.

A bearded man in a white apron responded to his knock at the back door. 'My father is with the private party, eating in there. I can't disturb them but need to catch him on his way out. Can I wait inside?'

'Can do.'

An effort had been made to decorate the exit corridor; there was a mirror on the wall, and one of those occasional tables his mother wanted and which Will thought served no purpose. On it was a fishbowl with artificial flowers. Ramiro took a seat on the French-looking chair. Nobody could pass him unseen. What would be the first thing he said to Carlos? He had practised possibilities but still not made up his mind.

Laughter and the sound of voices announced a party of people coming his way. A few women appeared first, chattering and clutching onto each other, followed by three men, one of whom held the door open for the ladies. Two more women appeared. Ray's heart beat fast. A group with men and women appeared next, one woman holding a tall red rose. They all left through the door. Ramiro had not counted them. Perhaps Carlos had to settle the bill and would be last.

A door opened and Ramiro stood straight. Kate appeared. 'What are you still doing here?'

'My father…' He faltered.

'They're all gone. Every single one of them. It's a quarter to twelve.'

Outside, he felt like crumpling to the pavement. What could have happened to his father, and how would he ever find him now?

Kate, in a cherry-red jacket, emerged together with the *can do* man minus his apron. She frowned. 'I don't know what you are up to. Doesn't your father have a mobile? Honestly!'

Ramiro gave them a shortened version of his plight, while Kate listened, playing with the buttons on her

439

jacket. 'I am sorry I couldn't let you into the dining room, but then your father was not there. Are you sure you have the right day?'

'I saw him give his speech about Brazil live on TV this afternoon.'

'Brazilians,' said *can do* man. 'They eat here *last* Monday.' He made a gesture of two fingers pointed at his eyes and then onto the pavement. 'I see accident last Monday.'

'Albi, the kitchen assistant,' Kate explained, and then asked Albi what he had seen.

'A dark man with hair brushed back. He ate in restaurant with group. Walked into van down there.' He pointed to Holborn Circus. 'First police come, and then ambulance take Brazilian man away.'

'That was Monday a week ago? Why would the dinner be the week before the conference?' It made no sense to Ramiro.

Albi walked off to unchain his cycle from the iron railings near the church, while Kate lingered, not having given up yet. 'This really matters to you, doesn't it?' Ramiro looked at the ground, and she went on, 'The hurt man was almost certainly taken to St Thomas' Hospital.'

On the map he unfolded, he saw that it was down to the Victoria Embankment, along the Thames and over Westminster Bridge.

'You ride with me,' offered Albi and, with Ramiro sitting astride the metal carrier behind, he pedalled off. They chose side roads because it was illegal to ride like that. In one of them, the lace-less shoe fell off the foot.

440

At St Thomas', Ramiro thanked Albi and, rubbing his sore backside, clad in socks, one shoe in his hand, he entered a hospital in night mode – long empty white corridors and dimmed lights. Neither at main reception, nor in A&E, were they able to tell him who had been brought in last Monday, not at one in the morning. At the inpatient pharmacy, convincing them he was a paramedic asking after a case he had brought in last week, they pointed him to the ambulance office. On the way there, he snatched a half-eaten burger from a canteen table. He repressed the thought that it could have the saliva of an incurable patient on it.

An incapacitated ambulance woman manned the office, her wrist in a bandage. After inspecting the dark purple socks, for which no explanation was offered, and with a measure of self-importance, she showed willing to search the computer, but doubted that such a patient would still be in the hospital. She clicked and searched. Then she found the relevant spreadsheet and read out names of the injured brought in last Monday. 'Carlos Ribeira, tibia broken in two places. Tracked to Ward D.'

'Yes!' he shouted out.

She was taken aback, but he was already skating along the corridor.

The glass doors to Ward D were closed for those without an electronic tab. He pushed the bell. When a corpulent nurse eventually materialised to wave her hands in dismissal, he feigned not to understand and kept ringing the bell. Irritated, she opened the door to tell him off, but he had already pushed past her and rushed down the ward to the main desk. Nobody was in

441

attendance, and he had to wait for the nurse to make her way back to the desk and sit behind it.

He explained, harping on the words *poverty* and *adoption*, and looking often into her fugitive eyes. It was lost on Nurse Rowena McGregor.

He invented a story about his injured foreign father having always promised him they would visit beautiful Scotland and fish in the rivers, a yet unrealised dream.

She interrupted him and asked him to get his butt off the desk and not take her for a fool.

He had to earn her cooperation. Nurse Rowena swivelled her chair to turn her back to him, sorting some papers. In the silence, he pictured the breathing of all the patients in the bays.

Eventually she had to face him, a stubborn statue of a good-looking teenager. Resignedly reading from her screen, she sighed. 'Carlos Ribeira was brought in with compound leg fractures. It was so bad that his wire and plaster-cast cage was finally removed only yesterday, but he has to remain immobile in a new cast before being discharged and flying home to Sao Paulo.'

'Which bay is he in?'

'Stop shouting. You'll wake the patients.'

He jumped excitedly.

'All right then. Five minutes, but looking, no touching, and no waking the patient if asleep. I'll be watching you,' she said, pointing up to a screen above her. 'Bay 5, bed B.'

In Bay 5, there were four beds, two on either side. His heart knocked in his chest like a hammer. The man in bed B lay on his back, the plastered leg outside the cover, an injured arm bandaged. His lids were closed and his black hair swept carelessly away from his head. The strong and beautiful hands Ramiro knew from television lay flat on the bedcover, the veins showing patterns.

Ramiro approached the sleeping figure one tiptoe at a time, so close that he could hear breathing. 'Dad,' he mouthed and then, '*Papai*'. When the tears welled over and rolled down Ramiro's cheeks, he thought they made a noise.

Perhaps they did, for the patient's eyelids twitched and opened. The head turned on the pillow. Their dark brown eyes met.

★

Ray got home at four on Tuesday morning, in a cab paid for by Carlos. Even then, he did not sleep but lay awake, his mind racing. When he came down to the kitchen, Stuart had already left for work, but Alice and Will were still having coffee. He saw Will square his shoulders and thrust out his chin belligerently, but Alice leapt up with concern.

'Did you meet Carlos? How did it go?'

'It was fine, Mum,' replied Ray gently, but his eyes were on his stepfather and he caught a flicker of surprise crossing Will's face. 'I'm really tired now. I'll tell you all about it in a couple of days.'

Will looked suspicious but decided to bluster his way out of it. 'It's your eighteenth on Saturday. Why don't your brother and the yard lads take you on a pub crawl? I'll pick up the tab.'

'Well, we've got final interviews at school on Friday, and then Greg and Danny have something planned for me on Saturday, but the evening should be fine.'

'Find out what they have in mind, and we'll figure something out. See you in the yard in half an hour.'

★

'My friends have booked a paragliding jump as a birthday present.'

Will's laughter filled the kitchen unpleasantly.

Stuart put his fork down. 'They'll never get you to do that. You panic climbing up a ladder.'

'Greg and Danny sort of think it's a dare thing.'

Alice looked at Ray. 'Poor you. It must be frightening to run to the end of a cliff and jump into thin air, trusting a large umbrella.'

Will hit the table with both his spread hands, laughing as Ray had seldom heard him do. 'I can't wait to see this,' he kept spluttering. 'This has to be filmed.'

Ray looked down. 'Danny has a video camera. A film is part of the present.'

'He'll shit himself,' said Stuart. 'That's got to be on tape.'

★

The sun shone. A light wind wafted in the air over the South Downs. 'Perfect for thermals,' said the instructor as he helped a helmeted Ray get strapped into the harness.

Danny was filming these preparations, making odd comments. Then came the run-up, the end of the ridge, and Ray's ear-splitting yell as the instructor and Ray sailed through the air under their wing, high above houses, gardens, woods and fields. They turned in wide circles, and Ray's legs eventually stopped kicking. Slowly they corkscrewed down, becoming smaller and smaller on the film, while the instructor's voice could be heard on the headset radio, preparing for landing on the green field with a red cross.

★

On the evening of Ray's birthday, Danny brought round the DVD. Ray was apparently still in the pub, being revived by Greg, but he wanted them to see the recording before the pub crawl. Will chuckled and Stuart, who had been having a shower after work, came downstairs in a towel. This had to be seen at once.

Alice, Will and Stuart watched the preparations and heard Greg's jocular comments. Then came the jumping off the cliff, and the loud yell. Alice thought it looked pretty, the way they slowly turned in the air. Ray's whimpering was audible over the landing instructions. The recording finished, and they got up.

'Well,' said Stuart, 'he had great weather for it.'

After a second's silence, Will strode to the window and ripped the curtains apart. It had been grey all day. It was Friday that had been sunny. He tapped a number on his mobile, hissing, 'That bastard!'

'Who are you calling, Dad?'

'I'm calling Ray, because I'll tell you one thing – this parachute jump did not happen today. It was yesterday.'

'Why would Ray do that?'

'Because I taught him how to.'

★

'*Por favor, apertem os cintos e coloquem os assentos na posicao vertical.* Please fasten your seat belts and put your seats in the upright position. We will be landing in Sao Paulo in fifteen minutes.'

In the Varig airplane, Ramiro thought of Will watching him on the DVD, soaring away, free as a bird. He ran the Madonna medallion back and forth along its chain. 'I am going home,' he said to the businessman in the seat next to him.

FAILED

Cedric entered the Balfour home where, at the age of twenty-one, he still lived with his parents.

As ever, he felt daunted by the massive oil portrait of his dead grandfather, Edward Balfour, flanked by one no less arresting of his father, Charles, repeating the wide brow, stiff neck and strong dark hair, parted on the left and ending in a wavy sweep: two superior, almost perfect, beings, cold at heart, whom he resembled only physically.

The paintings sobered Cedric, who had drunk two beers in the sun on Market Square. *Had he not drowned his first love in Millie's haunting brown eyes at fifteen, he might have been more of a Balfour.*

Upstairs in his comfortable but messy room, Cedric looked down into the gardens at the giant cedars of Lebanon. He had now finished school and was about to enter university, two years later than expected. So far, nothing good had happened to him in his life. In the middle of the park stood the impressive original house with its clock tower which his grandfather Edward, a gynaecologist, had converted into an exclusive old people's residence, The Royale. Father, in his footsteps as an eminent gynaecologist too, was famous for helping childless women conceive. He was discreetly invited to Los Angeles, Geneva and Monte Carlo to impregnate neurotic actresses and celebrities. He had continued running The Royale, where thirty-three rich and bewildered dodderers paid through their noses. The Balfours were not short of money or of being envied.

Millie and Cedric had met at sixth form college. It was during a fire alarm practice that they ended up next to each other on the lawn. That had felt dangerously attractive, inexperienced with girls as he was.

His father had insisted he take science A levels, but the subjects were too abstract and academic for his agile and enquiring brain. He was struggling grimly in class. In contrast, Millie's dark curls corkscrewed on her shoulders as she enthused about her art and design course, making little hops on the grass. He was swept up by her plan to create a line of crazy couture hats for her label 'Millie's Millinery'. Her large brown eyes sparkling at him made him her slave. They had walked back, his hand in hers.

Three years after Cedric's birth, there had been a sister gestated all through the nine months to emerge stillborn. Few knew about this blot in Charles's copybook. Camilla, the postnatal depressive mother, had turned her back on almost everything. She got her nails gelled, her hair done and walked around in perfect groomedness. Cedric remained the only fruit of her loin and her pride, even though she could not express herself to him and he hardly dared to touch her.

Millie and he had met in a secret place behind the bins after school. He remembered her warm breath in the dark of the cold winter evenings. She told him that she lived with her mother on a council estate. They did not have a car. She had to take medication for dizzy spells. He had felt like a knight born to save his sweet princess.

Cedric had finished his two-year extra A-level crammer and had somehow been awarded a place at medical school. If he objected to his father about studying medicine, the effect would be no more than a fly on its back buzzing on the sill. He had no choice but to face drudging through five years of study and taking over the whole Balfour caboodle one day.

And then one day Millie failed to appear behind the bins. His parents had forbidden contact between them, finding her 'unsuitable', and now his coded text messages remained unanswered. Millie disappeared from MySpace. He hung around the council estate, starting to doubt her love. But then he learned that she was in hospital.

Awkward and shy, he asked his way to her ward. From behind a glass partition, he recognised her shaven-headed figure, no more than a white outline under a white sheet. Her mother was against the bed, forehead down and arms spread over Millie's body like a great felled bird. Unable to cope, he had walked away.

It was evident to Cedric that the medical college was not overjoyed to have him, but the university owed professional tribute to his forefathers.

Millie died of a brain tumour when school was out. The medical profession, for all Charles's pride in it, had been helpless. Cedric had not held her a last time or offered his love for her to take with her into death. He had walked down that horrid hospital corridor without looking back, a sad seventeen-year-old lacking courage. Never ever could he put that right.

★

Obviously, nothing good was going to happen to Cedric at university either. The course started with the structure and workings of the human body, anatomy and dissection in the morgue, where he fainted twice. He failed the examination.

There was a painful confrontation between father and son. 'Not just resit, but repeat. The whole first year!'

Trembling with nervousness, Cedric suggested to Charles that today's medical studies were harder, the material to absorb vast, the NHS overcrowded.

'Yes, yes.' Charles knew all that, and then some.

Cedric dared say, 'I am struggling because it doesn't suit me.'

Charles stared at his son with idiotic surprise. 'What nonsense! You're a Balfour.'

The son turned away from his father's fury. 'It doesn't work, anyway. I want to do something else,' he muttered darkly.

'You can't,' was the verdict. 'Pull yourself together.'

★

Cedric finally made it into year two: the operating theatre, physical contact with patients, strings of difficult words to remember and the first horrors of gynaecology. He bungled diagnoses with regularity, an obvious failure in comparison to Charles, who just happened to be enjoying widespread press coverage with pictures of himself and

Princess Augustina. *'The wonderful gynaecologist who made me pregnant.'*

With the help of a resit, Cedric made it into year three. Teamwork was a problem. He kept himself at a distance from his colleagues, none of whom felt inclined to draw him into their midst. It was only in the break-and-traction clinic, hands on in the technique of plaster-casting, that Cedric came to life. The way in which gypsum, a crystalline mineral, reacted with water seemed like nothing less than alchemy.

'Get on with it and plaster that broken leg,' he was reprimanded, as he marvelled at the transmutation of matter.

He energetically rolled plaster, *walling* as it was called, onto the patient's leg. However, the work had to be dismantled while still unset. 'We are not mummifying limbs. Cedric, your mixture is too dense, the cast padding too thick. The man's leg would shrivel to nothing, deprived of oxygen.'

Charles invited the professor to lunch in town, and Cedric was admitted to year four.

At the end of this hardship came the Bachelor of Medicine exam. The student had seven minutes to examine a patient, who was instructed not to reveal the nature of his or her ailment, and then present the case to the consultant who would ask testing questions. When the bell rang, the student had to move on to another patient.

The results would come out two weeks into the summer holiday. Cedric spent most time on his bed, listening to music.

The short letter read *Bachelor of Medicine failed*.

'How can you fail something so simple?'

Camilla uncharacteristically interfered at this moment. 'Don't kill him. You've already killed our daughter in my womb. Cedric can go be a doctor at The Royale. They won't know he failed.'

Charles looked at his wife as if he had not noticed her before. 'That's a bloody good idea,' he said. 'And after a year he can repeat year four; the option is open for up to two years. We'll make a gynaecologist of the idiot eventually.'

Had Mother suggested he should cut up cattle in a Moroccan meat market, Cedric would have preferred it.

He was marched by his father to The Royale. Over the entrance was a scrolled stone oval. Double doors led into a spacious hall from which stairs went up to the wings and down into a basement, and a corridor led to sophisticated reception rooms. Beyond them, a large floor-heated octagonal orangery had been added.

In his white coat and with the cold snake of a stethoscope around his neck, Cedric was introduced to the staff with whom he would have to work closely, led by a stout qualified nurse, Phoebe. He knew they were all well paid to spend their days in this overheated geriatric asylum, while he was there as a punishment from his father. Charles gathered the inmates into the orangery to introduce his son as 'your own personal junior doctor'. There was clapping and shouts of congratulation. Cedric squirmed at this unearned acclaim from old and demanding fools, none of whom had died young and innocent of a brain tumour.

Father left him to it only too abruptly, and Phoebe showed Cedric the premises. There were what she called 'designer' treatment rooms. The most popular was Vampire, with a décor of dark colours; it offered blood suction with plastic cup ventouses applied to the back. 'To purify the body of toxins.'

The next room was called *Exotic Massage*. 'How disgusting,' burst out Cedric. 'At their age, the skin secretes acids which oxydise to produce nonenal.'

Phoebe looked up at him slowly. 'There's a lot more to this than in the textbooks, *Doctor*.' They went into a room scented with regular puffs of pine tree aroma, and he wondered to himself whether she had guessed his failure. Phoebe called this the *Sweet Memory* room. There was soft piped music from the forties, and photographs of beautiful nature spots were projected over the walls and ceiling. At the base of comfortable seats, a water circulation system allowed foot massage.

'My father has created a world of delusion.'

'That and other lucrative successes.'

In the indoor swimming pool, Phoebe introduced a lifeguard, a muscle pack in a yellow tracksuit. Cedric noticed that the water was less than a metre deep.

'Eliza, your crawl is too slow,' the lifeguard shouted, his voice amplified in the room.

'Don't scold me,' the swimmer panted, and her feet touched the bottom. 'I know I'm improving.'

'Not enough,' shouted the hulk. 'You owe it to yourself to do better.'

Cautiously, she moved into a floating position and resumed her clumsy splashing.

Phoebe smiled like a Cheshire cat. 'Aerobics are in the adjacent room. There's nothing to see there but padded swivel chairs.'

Cedric had no idea how to react. 'Why pretend these people are not close to death?'

She ignored him. 'We use a nearby GP practice,' and then she added tentatively, 'Perhaps less now, with you here.'

Phoebe suggested introducing him to the residents individually the next day and walked off briskly because a device on her belt was beeping.

He went down the stairs to seek his new quarters. Charles had insisted he move into the old park-keeper's apartment with its own access from outside. It was a large basement room with a small bedroom at the back. The windows were level with the ground, good if you were interested in insect life. The washroom was down a corridor.

Cedric hopped onto the bed and reclined. 'Fuck,' he said up to the ceiling, which had a zigzag crack. 'Fuck my father.' Sleep did not come.

Out of the unfamiliar obscurity emerged the liquid haunting eyes of Millie, as they often did. An invisible growth in her brain had made her vanish. He had been in love with her, and she would have to come back to release him. Her short doomed life could not just have been pointless. He put his hands up to his cheeks. They were wet with tears.

★

On his first day of duty, Cedric mooched around the orangery early in the morning, and the eyes in his grandfather's bronze bust followed him in a sinister way: Edward, the founder of this haven for spoilt people

454

who thought they could cheat death. Outside it was still dark and bursts of rain drummed on the vast expanse of double-glazing. No resident was in sight yet, but a carer joined him. The glassed room darkened around them as more charcoal clouds built up and distant thunder rolled.

'It's bad weather.' The carer pointed out the obvious and then, to make conversation, asked, 'You like working with old people?'

'The purpose seems to be to help vain geriatrics delude themselves, and at a price.'

'Immortality – who wouldn't pay for that? The mind doesn't get old.'

The door to the outside was torn open by Phoebe in a glistening raincoat. 'Eliza is out there somewhere. Help me find her.'

'Again?' The carer sprinted to Phoebe at the door and Cedric followed. Once outside they were pelleted with hard rain.

'Eliza loves thunderstorms,' Phoebe shouted into the hissing wind as they ran across the grass, hands up sheltering their eyes to scan the park. 'Over there by the cedar!'

When they brought her into shelter, Eliza enthused, 'The power and majesty of nature makes me feel invincible.'

'What is your friend Stanley going to say? You could break a hip. And how did you get out?' Phoebe dabbed Eliza's face and dried her hair with a towel.

'Cook arrived at the back door with an umbrella.'

'While he folded the umbrella, you sneaked out behind him.'

The carer, picking up the wet shoes and the dripping raincoat, said to Cedric, 'That one's mind is not old. She's as sharp as a tack.'

Eliza sneezed.

'You know that Stanley thinks you'll come to harm out there one day.'

'I'll be blown away.'

*

Eating with the staff in the kitchen, Cedric learned that the cook was French-restaurant-trained and that special wishes for luxury food were catered for. Strawberries were flown in from Israel in December.

'Why not serve frozen ones?' he asked.

Apparently, the soft fruit contained too much water which crystallised and turned to mush when defrosted. The residents did not like that.

He asked about security measures and the risk of someone escaping. They thought the question funny. The inmates would never run away. Whenever a relative came to take them out for the day, they were worried they would not be brought back. Some families might deny a life of luxury to the aged to safeguard their inheritance.

Cedric, uncomfortable speaking to the residents, had much time to dwell in his room and breathe out silence while thinking about the meaning of immortality and the carer's remark about brains not ageing.

How could he spend his time constructively? Medicine had been unable to save Millie; it did not understand the brain. Here, at least, he could study first-hand the medical controversy over the relationship between physical and mental decline. The body certainly faltered, and it was now known that the brain shrank, but that did not necessarily mean reduced cognitive capability.

His attention turned to Eliza and Stanley, always sitting close, touching and whispering. Cedric approached the fleshy man with a large head and ample white hair, called the Brigadier, and asked about the lovey-dovey pair on the cane sofa.

'They haven't got anyone left except each other. That's why they're always snogging.'

'Do you think that sex is still on the cards?'

The Brigadier guffawed. 'Sex is always on the cards; sex is everywhere, always. I once had sex with a goat. It was in Austria, I think. Perhaps Bulgaria.'

In the Brigadier's case, Cedric noted that the body was less deteriorated than the brain. He went to sit next to the woman with pale hair called Lady Jean.

'You can't sit here,' she told him.

'I have to take your pulse.' Immediately she held out her mottled gold-spangled wrist. 'Give me the names of as many prime ministers as you can,' he asked of her.

'What does that have to do with my blood pressure?' She retracted her arm. 'Over there, that sage dress Eliza's wearing is mine. She stole it. It looks ridiculous on that old hag. I am Lady Jean, and her husband only had a bakery. Go and tell Eliza to give me back my dress, dry-cleaned first, of course.' Cedric took notes and moved on.

Violet appeared to have surprising stamina for a little old woman with emaciated arms and legs. Her age was difficult to guess. 'I'm ninety-one and the oldest, so there you are.' She remembered when the German army had marched into Paris, where her father was attaché at the embassy. She had worn a white-and-blue-striped dress with a red scarf in sympathy with the French and had an earphone hairdo. Her brain was still active, but her body was a mere dry shell.

Cedric wondered what happened when one of them died.

'We don't use the D word,' explained Phoebe. 'One day, one of them is simply gone. No questions are asked. Their places at the table and in the sitting room are immediately filled. Of the thirty-three, about ten die a year.'

Cedric explored the secluded part of the basement where there was a theatre equipped for small operations and clinical autopsies, with ventilation and running water. Discreetly off it were cold storage facilities with two sliding refrigeration trays. Boldly, he pulled one out to display a human figure. This pale-green cadaver had been in there for more than two months because his son was on a cruise around the world. The Royale needed the son's signed consent to get the body moved to the undertakers.

Cedric returned upstairs and walked straight into an episode. Violet had slipped on tea she had spilled. After testing along her brittle bones, Cedric confirmed a broken tibia and was slightly surprised by the authority with which he ordered them to scoop her onto a pat slide and carry her downstairs to the operating theatre while he rushed out of the clinic and across the grass to his parent's house. Camilla, at first, would not let

Cedric use the BMW but, once she relented, he drove off. When he returned to The Royale, the gardeners had to carry the equipment he had bought for plaster casting and three full bags of gypsum powder.

Violet fought on the slab like an emaciated wildcat. 'Don't fuss. It's nothing. Get off me.'

That demonstrated to Cedric that her mind did not know the state of her body, as he mixed the plaster in the bucket.

When the leg was encased and Violet wheeled out, Cedric felt good about himself. After being praised by Phoebe, he retired to his rooms to read the medical journal he had filched off the coffee table while his mother had gone to fetch the car key.

The articles were about cryonics – the freezing of organs, whole bodies even, for later resuscitation. Within minutes of cardiac arrest, the body had to be frozen to a temperature of minus 196° by immersion in liquid nitrogen. One of the still-unsolved problems was ice formation in the brain cells, causing them to dehydrate and compress. Research was hampered by the speed at which brain cells decomposed after death compared to the rest of the body. Scientists could experiment on living animal brains, but not those of humans.

Nevertheless, thousands were on the waiting list to be immortalised. The living mind might not age, but how would it emerge from cryopreservation? Would memory survive, or would the resuscitated mind be wiped clean? Or perhaps the brain could even be upgraded. All this was fascinating.

Phoebe brought him back to reality over supper when she complained about the mess he had made in the theatre with his plaster casting.

This gave Cedric an idea. 'Pottery – pottery classes! This will teach me more about them and they might be amused,' he said to Phoebe.

'Now you *do* sound like your father,' she said, and he knew she liked the idea. He ordered a kiln, four pottery wheels and stools.

Most of them wanted to do pottery right away. There was much laughter and fun, making bent vases and bashing about wet clumps of clay. He was forced to offer his living room downstairs for the activity and live with the heat of the kiln. The Brigadier managed to make a box for his cufflinks and Stanley, wrestling with arthritis, formed a tiny pink heart with his initials on it for Eliza. Both subjects gave much away about their cognitive skills.

One weekend when Phoebe was in Wales for the wedding of her niece, at night when The Royale was quiet, Cedric rolled out the cadaver. By the time the early birds were twittering in the park, the body was back in refrigeration, the craniotomy a mere circular superglued fissure around the head, partly hidden under hair. Cedric was in possession of a wealth of photographs of the dead brain as well as slices of it, plus observations on the samples' reactions to chemicals.

The pottery class advanced to making small and easily shaped animals. Eliza wore the pink glazed heart on a ribbon around her ankle. The son returned from his cruise and the body was fetched by the undertakers to be cremated.

That same day Violet passed away. Cedric assisted the pathologist with the autopsy on the still warm body. Frustratingly, Cedric could not get at the freshly dead brain until the night, when he risked being heard in the basement with his high-speed craniotomy saw. He made experiments with this brain under a microscope.

The potters, bored of forming small animals, ambitiously suggested making a bust of Charles to stand next to Edward in the orangery. Cedric provided enlarged photographs of his father's head. The Brigadier was to construct a solid head, while neck, nose, eyes, ears, lips were given to others to do. To their childish amusement, the sculpture kept falling apart and finally split in the kiln.

In *The Scientist*, there was an article about the latest findings in cryogenics with pictures of a freezer farm in America. Evidently there had not yet been a breakthrough in the freezing technique.

And then two residents died on the same day. Phoebe was not going anywhere and the days had grown longer, and useful nights shorter. Cedric was only able to cut open one skull for his research. Just as he was immersing brain bits in nitrogen, someone came down in the bed elevator. He managed to throw the body back into the drawer and the skull cap after it.

The next day he had to go for a walk and feed bits of brain to crows.

Undeterred by the bust failure, the class wanted to attempt a whole human statue. Cedric ordered more plaster. His popularity was increasing.

Summer was good at The Royale, with afternoon tea being served under the wisteria-covered pergola. The staff played croquet matches in teams supported by betting residents, while Cedric used pliers to bend wire for the base structure of the statue. Ribald shouts came from the tea party as to whether it should be male or female.

August brought thunderstorms. After three hot days, one such storm broke in the evening while they were having supper. Electric blades slashed the looming clouds. Stanley could not find Eliza and soon the staff were looking for her all over the park. This time they did not find her and Stanley was devastated. Phoebe called the police. Apparently it was a regular occurrence for them; old confused people walked away from care homes, despite the security measures taken. In ninety per cent of cases they were found within forty-eight hours, dead or alive.

The next morning, Charles took Cedric to one side to heap blame on him. After all, he was now in charge of the residents. Exhausted and drained, Cedric explained that he had searched for Eliza all night long. According to Stanley there was a stepsister in Australia, but she was out of contact. The Royale handed Eliza's papers over to her lawyer and life went on as before, except for Stanley.

Not long after, Cedric rolled the statue into the orangery. He had spent hours walling the wire cage with plaster rolls. They thought the artwork 'they' had done 'together' was great, as Cedric pushed it to stand in a corner: a crudely executed full-sized androgynous figure with primitive features and the outlines of a toga. He had made them happy children.

The front page of *The Telegraph* reported a breakthrough: a laboratory had successfully reheated cryogenically frozen sections of heart tissue. It was said to be in a better 'rested-restored' condition than before. Cedric paced around his potter's studio living room. Could a ninety-year-old cryopreserved man hope to wake up with a healthy heart and a fully restored brain?

★

Some months later, Cedric dared to go back to his medical school. After much pleading, he was admitted to see the professor, sitting at a long well-polished table.

'I have failed. I know, I know. Nevertheless, since then I have been researching cryogenics,' began Cedric.

'Really?'

He lay a fat folder on the tabletop and gave it a shove. 'Read and admire.' He turned on his heels and walked out of the room.

The next day, the professor's assistant called to invite Cedric back at any time suitable.

'You wanted to speak to me?' Cedric realised that he was using the same tone and manner as his father would have.

Both men sat. The professor, rubbing his chin, looked again at Cedric's work. He took his glasses off. 'You recorded experiments with brain tissue in different stages of deterioration. You exposed them to sodium polyacrylate at a great range of temperatures and measured the absorption of fluid. How?'

'Kiln and liquid nitrogen. Extremes often give richer results. In chemistry nothing is ever lost and nothing is ever created – all is transformation, as Isaac Newton said.'

'It was Lavoisier, actually, but I forgive you. How were you able to compile such a detailed thesis on brain cell reactions?'

'I have been in charge of The Royale for more than a year, and had the opportunity to autopsy the brains of the deceased.'

'Dead brains, their cells already dehydrated. The brilliance in your findings is in the process of live cells dying. How did you obtain these results?'

Cedric smiled. 'They speak for themselves.'

'They certainly do. You are throwing much-needed light onto an obdurate aspect of cryopreservation. I must say, I didn't think you had it in you. What triggered your interest in pure research?'

'Plaster-casting and the death of my friend, Millie.'

'That,' – the professor patted the file, no doubt thinking of the prestige for his institute – 'counts as your thesis. I will make sure you are awarded a Doctorate of Medicine.' He rose and held out his hand. 'Congratulations, Dr Balfour.'

★

Excerpts and pictures of his findings were printed in medical journals. He received an avalanche of press enquiries and invitations to give talks to universities all over the globe. Charles had to ask the gardeners to escort curious scientists off the premises. He glowered at his son, clearly unsettled by this transformation in Cedric. Mother, too, held herself at a safe distance.

I can't win, thought Cedric and accepted an offer to become a fellow of the Cryonics Institute of Missouri. The Americans were more advanced in cryopreservation anyway.

When he said goodbye to the assembled residents, there were tears. Cedric promised to write and never forget them. They insisted on a group photograph being taken, which included the statue. They shuffled around and changed the order of who was to be where and, amid the shoving, the statue fell forward, right on its face. The Brigadier just failed to catch it. In the crash, the plaster split open and Stanley, as he helped put it upright again, stared down at a gaping hole where an ankle showed, a tiny pink pottery heart on a thin ribbon tied around it.

'My God, Eliza's in there!'

Cedric fled the orangery, ran down the hall and out of The Royale to meet Charles, waiting in the BMW with his luggage.

In Heathrow's first-class lounge, Cedric was arrested for the murder of Mrs Elizabeth Mason.

Charles felt shameless relief. There was one eminent Dr Balfour, and that was him.

WEIGHT PROBLEM

'Why do we have a fat receptionist?' Lisette overheard one sleek hedge fund financier say to the others as they left through the glass revolving doors of the modern building in Geneva.

A few days later, she heard another say, 'We'll have to get her a bigger chair.' She cried at the bus stop on her way home to her bedsit in Vidollet.

Mother, with irritating cheerfulness, always brushed her weight problem aside. 'You inherited that endearing pear-shape from Grandma. Men like a bit of padding on a woman.'

No, they don't. Fifty-four young, on-the-ball men worked in the building and not one, not even the IT geeks, gave her a sideways glance, despite her expensively groomed black hair.

A delegation from Brussels visited for talks about passporting for financial services within the EU, and Lisette was asked to help out with hosting. That meant taking coats and umbrellas, and serving tea, coffee and croissants. She took the role seriously; she was from a good Swiss family with the noble name of Petit-Roland,

and her father was director of the Federation of Swiss Watches.

During a coffee break, a young Englishman accosted her. First, she thought he wanted directions to the men's room, but he asked her about herself and was interested in whether she was from Geneva, what her parents did and whether she was a skier. In turn, he told her that he was from London and had just joined the Rothschilds' bank. She wished she had actually gone to the aerobic classes she had enrolled in.

'So you hope to talk one of the Rothschilds into adopting you.'

He praised her English and asked her out for a drink to get to know her better – a quick one because dinner was planned for the delegation that evening.

She flustered about not having time to go home and change, but he told her she looked absolutely right the way she was, and she stopped hyperventilating.

★

His name was Graham Wheeler and he admired the Swiss for being rich, organised and dependable. 'Is it true that Swiss girls make the absolute best housewives?' he asked impishly over their gin and tonic with a twist.

She returned the compliment by admiring the sportiness, self-assurance and beauty of English women.

'Skinny, neurotic and unyielding more like,' he mumbled and then told her that he expected to be posted to a foreign branch of the bank. She laughed out loud – 'posted like a package' – and he ordered a second cocktail.

She started to like him a lot. He brought up the topic of different cultures, and she enthused about travelling to far-flung countries and seeing more than the Alps. He told her an English joke about the Swiss. And she told him a Swiss joke about the Swiss. They laughed a lot, and he made her feel light and desirable. Sadly, he had to go and join the others but promised they would find another moment for themselves before he flew to London. He gave her his card.

Lisette sneaked away from reception when Graham was due to leave for the airport. In front of the restrooms, he gave her a small present. She gave him a kiss on his cheek. He grabbed her by the shoulders and kissed her on her mouth, before jumping back when a colleague approached.

Back at her desk, through the glass she watched him with his leather overnight bag, her heart in turmoil. When he turned his head for a last contact, she waved a shy goodbye and he bestowed on her an intimate smile, his eyes fastened on hers, deliciously secret and exciting.

His gift was a silver bracelet.

Mother was animated by hope for her thirty-year-old daughter, and over a fondue started every sentence with an *if* – 'If this young Englishman continues to show interest…' , 'If there were to be a wedding, what would I do about my hip replacement?'

'Let's not get carried away,' Father admonished. 'The English are not given to spontaneity.'

'Behind those stiff upper lips, their emotions broil and bubble like anyone else's.'

469

★

A week later, a personal e-mail popped up on Lisette's screen just as she was munching on a Danish. Graham had to go to Milan for two days and proposed stopping in Geneva on his way to see her. Lisette threw the pastry into the waste bin.

On this second date, he invited her to the four-star Michelin restaurant in the Parc de la Grange. She had chosen black, which was said to make the bum look smaller. He watched the *maitre d'* pull out the chair for her to squeeze into.

'You look charming,' he said, and she fell in love with him. His mother had died of cancer, and his father lived in Salisbury with a second wife. Graham was in the process of buying a small house in an up-and-coming area of London but, he told her in a more serious tone, a posting abroad was imminent and he hoped to accept it on an *accompanied* basis.

She choked on the asparagus, and he stood up to pat her back and then held her hand across the table. They found out both liked tiramisu and, after the meal, they strolled through the park and looked out onto the lake which lapped gently against the Quai General Guisan.

'Surely not as impressive as the Thames and the Houses of Parliament.'

Modestly, he said, 'That's just a view. You are the one who is impressive.'

Self-conscious, she felt exposed. 'You do know that I am thirty years old and you must be only…'

'A few years younger. So what?'

There was an awkward goodbye in the lobby of his hotel. It was clear that she would not go up in the elevator with him.

The next day, they took a taxi to Cologny for an aperitif with her parents. Her father in his tweed jacket offered pink champagne; Mother had made cheese straws, left in the oven too long. After small talk about the weather in Geneva versus that of London, Graham was given an exposé of Lisette's life from baby days onward.

'Blessedly, a healthy baby. We made double-sure we loved her enough,' exclaimed Mother. Graham surprised them by replying in good French. Gleaming with *I was right with my ifs*, Mother gazed at the Englishman with adoration.

'A catch,' she enthused, before following the men out onto the terrace to admire the blue lake daubed with dashes of white sailing boats.

'This view is not to be sneered at,' Graham said admiringly.

'We had this villa built thirty-five years ago. Now it is worth more than three million francs. An Arab made me an offer for four.'

'Shush,' Mother scolded. 'English people don't talk about money; it is inelegant. Why don't you two sit in the swing lounger? It is meant for lovers.'

Graham drew Lisette towards the seat, but she resisted. 'It will only hold one of us.'

Her mother tsked. 'Always so sensitive about her weight.'

Afterwards, outside the waiting taxi, Graham put his arms around Lisette and ostentatiously pulled her to him to nuzzle his face in her dark hair while, from the upstairs window, her parents watched.

At the airport, once Graham had boarded, Lisette called her parents to say that he had asked her to go to London to find out whether she could live there.

'With him? Oh my God, it is happening,' shouted Mother. 'Has he proposed? Make sure he does. Don't stay with him; we'll pay for a hotel. They don't pop the question if she is already in their bed. We need to start planning.'

'Mother!'

Lisette quit her job at the hedge fund and gave notice to her landlord.

★

London was cold, grey, drab and dirty. In the parks, the trees were stripped of leaves. Graham had booked her into a bed and breakfast in Bayswater. The carpets had gaudy flower designs and curled up grey at the edges. The doors were of hollow plastic. He was too busy to see her often, even during lunch hour. She had to do her own sightseeing. One evening he took her to a pub close to her B&B where he introduced her to a colleague called Rob who, immediately after her 'How do you do?', ignored her. Nevertheless, she called her mother every other day to say how wonderful London was.

After a rainy weekend sitting in her dank room, she talked Graham into agreeing to a wintry Monday picnic on a park bench. With the blanket from her bed and

M&S sandwiches, she waited for him on the steps of St Paul's. Come noon, men and women emerged from the banks of the City, but he was not amongst them. At twelve thirty she lay the rug on the stone parapet and sat on it.

At one o'clock, men and women began returning to the buildings. He did not come. She became angry and was packing up when he finally appeared, striding up the road.

'Look,' he said, out of breath. 'I should never have agreed to this. I have no control over my schedule and, anyway, what would this look like to my boss?'

She complained bitterly about her abandonment since her arrival and threatened to go back home. He became agitated and explained that he liked things done in order; he would book the registry office and trust her to buy them gold wedding bands.

She was stunned. 'Is this your way of proposing?'

'Haven't I proposed? I have so much on my mind. It will be better next month, I promise.'

'And what's wrong with the proper wedding my parents expect?'

'All your people are in Switzerland, and my friends don't care enough. This way it is quicker, and you can move into my house by the new year.'

'You still haven't proposed to me.'

He helped her up, pulling both her hands, and then bent his knee.

★

Before Christmas, they were wed at Bayswater Registry Office. Her bridesmaid was the Sicilian from the corner shop and his best man was Rob, who had ignored her in the pub and now, forced to relate to her, was cold and stand-offish. She was sure he mouthed to Graham, 'It's all that melted cheese these Swiss eat.'

After the short ceremony, the wedding party of four boarded a boat for a lunch cruise with a set menu and sightseeing commentary. It motored past the Houses of Parliament to the Tower of London, turned and came back. Graham and Rob talked work. It started to rain and the boat was draughty. Nobody had yet seen the champagne-coloured Ted Baker dress she was wearing because of the black coat over it. The wind had made wearing the hat impossible. And the Italian bridesmaid suffered from queasiness on the boat.

What shall I tell my parents? Lisette fretted throughout the day. Perhaps she could claim that Graham, in his intelligence, hated fuss and thought weddings overrated. Guilt gnawed at her, for having disappointed them and herself. Surely it would be better once she had moved in with him and they could start a physical relationship.

★

His Victorian end-of-terrace house was in Clapham. She insisted on being carried over the threshold. He struggled. 'We're not exactly feather-light, are we?'

The two-and-a-half-bedroom house was sparsely furnished. He explained that it would be rented out when they were abroad. She fetched her two suitcases from the tiny front garden.

The next morning, he showered early and left in a dark suit. She remained contemplating the gold band on her finger in his bedsheets with an anchor motif: weighty cold things. No physical contact had been possible last night because, after wolfing down the meal she had cooked, he had to work at the computer until late while the US office was open. But he had kissed her on the forehead before leaving.

She called her mother that morning to say that she was now engaged and living in a wonderful Victorian house. Mother talked about the Parc de la Grange restaurant for the wedding venue and Cousin Arianne expecting to be a bridesmaid while, in Lisette's head, she screamed, *I am already married!*

The following day, their wedding night was postponed again because he had to put together a complicated business proposal. Alone in their bed, which was sized for a king, looking up at the brown crack in the ceiling she had plenty of time to contemplate the shiny gold band on her finger.

Later, she stood on the scales. 'Not fair,' she said aloud. 'Not after three days of minimal calories.' Perhaps the scales were broken. Inspecting them, she noticed a price sticker on the underside; they were newly purchased, a silent reproach to her.

Mother threatened to visit because she felt things weren't right, but Lisette excelled herself in appeasing her worries.

'Is he treating you right?' asked her father, taking over the phone. 'Ask him to fix a date.'

'Don't worry, Papa. He loves me, but he has to prove himself at work. Our exciting life has just not yet started. One thing at a time.'

'As long as you are happy, my little cabbage.'

Lisette had to find a way to provoke Graham's desire. She cleaned the whole house, put on new bedsheets, prepared a meal of boeuf bourguignon and paraded in a diaphanous nightgown. He returned late, with a briefcase. She pretended to ignore it. He said sorry; they had time to eat, but he had to work. She washed up and watched an objectionable programme about a mentally disturbed man called Fawlty running a small hotel abysmally.

Alone in bed after that, she tossed and turned, sexually frustrated, and then bounded downstairs naked. 'This marriage is not consumated. It is not legal!'

'Why are you so aggressive, Lisette? I am doing what I can, for us, for you and for a decent job abroad. There are still weighty problems to overcome.'

He meant her bottom, didn't he?

'In fact, I was going to tell you later that at the beginning of February, I will be able to take a week off and I suggest we go skiing in the Rocky Mountains. That will be our honeymoon.'

'Really?' She tried to read his body language.

'You have no faith in me, do you?' He looked up at her from his seat at the desk and a soppy smile spread. 'Silly Swiss woman. Tomorrow night, I'll bring home holiday brochures, and we will book right away.'

'OK,' she said slowly and went back upstairs.

★

They unpacked their suitcases in a fake-wood-clad room in the Redwood Lodge in Canada. It was in the middle of the afternoon. They were jet-lagged. After a meal, they crashed out on the double bed in the early evening, not hearing any of the goings-on in the bar.

In the morning, the sun shone through the shutters in stripes. Lisette turned to her husband, warm from sleep. 'How wonderful to be away somewhere, neither your country nor mine.'

He grunted and she sidled up to him and blew hot air from her mouth onto the neck next to his ear. '*Mon chéri*,' she whispered.

He reached out and patted her hair. 'Chéri comes from chérir, to protect.'

She put her finger on his moving lips. 'No talk. Honeymoon.'

'Now in Latin, *carus*…' He pushed himself up on his elbows.

She pulled him down and started to climb onto him. 'I'm on the pill but if you agree, I'll stop taking it at the end of this month. How many babies do you think we should have?'

'None.'

'Nine! We'd better start right away.'

'Lisette, the sun is shining; there is snow out there. Our rented skis are in the entrance.'

'Make love to me *now* or I'll go mad.'

'As peremptory as your mother.'

'My mother was respectful to you. And why don't you want children?'

Before disappearing into the bathroom, he said, 'My

job comes first. I need to be married so my life looks normal. Besides, I'll need some help around the house. I have never taken to children and don't want to have to account for any. I had a girlfriend before, nagging about children. She was much worse than you, but not as large.'

Outside the lodge, Lisette looked up at the mountain peaks in snow against a blue sky and, as the Swiss have for centuries, she thought arguing was petty compared to the majestic view. Graham fixed the skis on the rack of the cheap Ford Escort, the last available rental because he had forgotten to book one in good time.

'It's not suited for snow.' Lisette walked around it. 'We need a four-by-four.'

'It's a car. It'll do.'

He drove them through the centre of the ski station and onto the road which led up to the ski lifts. For a while, they flanked the train track which joined the ski station to Banff on the flat lands below. As they gained height, the railway line dropped into a deep valley, separated from the road by fifteen yards of untouched blueish snow. They were still in the shadow of the mountain, but in the distance sunlit snow glittered on the flanks of Mount Norquay.

'Arguing with you made us late. Look at the traffic. We're missing out on skiing.' And then Graham caught up with a slow-moving queue. 'This'll take forever,' he groaned.

As they snailed round a wide curve, they saw cars way up in the sunlight, leaving the road and driving on the snow-covered meadows.

'Not stupid,' he said and twisted the steering wheel to the right.

'No!' Lisette yelled. 'We're still in shadow. And the tyres are wrong. Don't! We're not heavy enough.'

'And what else, Miss Fucking-Snow-Expert?'

He had already turned onto the hard snow next to the road.

'Turn back *now!*'

'With you, we should be heavy enough.' He accelerated, which produced the curious sensation of the ground being pulled from under them, because the field was a shield of ice. He put his foot on the brake with the steering wheel locked, and they slid several yards sideways.

'Try to turn the car back to the road and accelerate as hard as you can.'

'What sort of crap idea is that?' He tried to drive in a straight line instead, but the tyres spun and slowly the rear of the car slewed towards the abyss next to them. Lisette could make out the snow-toasted tips of fir trees on the jagged granite formations. The railway was hundreds of feet down in the crevice.

'Fuck!' he spat at the steering wheel. 'Fuck.'

She unclipped her seatbelt and freed her arm.

'You bitch,' he snarled as he gunned the engine and pulled on the handbrake, before loosening it and tightening it again. It changed nothing. The sideways slide continued, bringing them closer to their doom. 'We need your weight.'

But she yanked the car door open, just before he punched the car's central locking button. He grabbed at her thigh.

'I need you now, you fat cow!' he yelled with despair, trying to hold her back.

Her heart was beating so fast that she had to shut her eyes as she kicked the car door open wide and let herself fall out of her seat sideways. Graham howled like a damned soul, and she lay on the ice in a foetal position until the back tyre touched her hair. Then she unrolled and scrambled away from the car. She heard his desperate screams but did not stop.

When she reached the road, she stood up and started running. With her forearm over her brow, she could only make out the trodden snow beneath her feet and not the horror-struck expression of those in the queue of cars who could see what was happening behind her.

Without looking left or right she reached the lodge. In the room she tossed some clothes into her bag, grabbed her passport and the plane ticket from Calgary to London, and stuffed them into her money belt. Forcing herself to walk so as not to attract attention, she proceeded to the Roam bus stop, which brought her into Banff.

Her body shook as if she were standing on a vibrating machine. She forced out of her mind the image of the Ford reaching the edge and then…

After twenty minutes, she boarded a bus for Calgary. The woman in the seat next to her must have thought she had Parkinson's. In Calgary, she had to walk quite a bit to find the airport bus. The light was fading. At the airport she changed the ticket destination from London to Geneva. The plane would leave the next morning. She spent the night sitting on a curved metal seat in the waiting area and blocked the howls of his fear and frustration from her brain. She turned her back to the television screen with the news. But the shadow of his person in that doomed car, and the crevice into which he had tumbled, gave her no peace. She had saved herself, leaving him to die, when her weight in the car might have spared him. She had murdered him.

A wave of shame washed over her. The same shame she had felt when, as a child, she had sat on the stairs and overheard her parents in the living room. There had been a little boy in the womb with her, but Louis had been stillborn – smothered, she had always thought, by her claiming all the space.

★

Above Geneva airport, the snow-capped Alps showed and she covered her eyes.

'Mother,' she whimpered, 'I am married and have made a mess of things again. You're better off not knowing.'

Instead of going home, she took a train through the St Gotthard Tunnel to Lugano in the Italian region of Switzerland.

With her savings, she rented a simple room in the attic of a four-storey house. It had a narrow window from which she could see the lake. She slept on and off for twenty-four hours. After that she bought bread, apples and air-dried sausages and looked at the lake, for days. No news could reach her. Nobody knew where she was.

Eventually, she went to the municipal offices and told them that she had lost her passport. They checked with Geneva and came up with the details of her original Swiss passport in the name of Petit-Roland. She did not tell the official that she had married but filled out a new application naming herself as Elisabeth Roland. He accepted this and made out a new passport in that name. Between her and her parents were the Alps; between her and her dead husband was the ocean.

She found a job in a hotel as accountant, because figures don't need the command of Italian. Applying herself, she slowly gained their trust. She walked along the lake and taught herself Italian, refilling the mind she had blanked with new images and thoughts.

She became thirty-one years old alone.

On a Sunday afternoon, as she sat on a bench learning the pluperfect, a rapid storm swept across the lake like a dark curtain. She was pelted by rain; lightning cracked and thunder boomed. A man ran along the promenade with elastic gait, and she noticed his heavy dark hair plastered to his handsome head.

He came to a stop and ran backwards – literally – to enquire whether she was all right, as she groped under the bench for her soggy revision sheets.

That is how Lisette met Marco. Over a cup of hot chocolate, they connected. He smiled often and mostly at her. Each time it felt as if she were emerging from the shadow into the warmth of sunshine.

The next day they met at the end of her working day. She learned that he was an architect with his own firm. She let him take her hand into his. In a carnotzet, they had raclette cheese and warm potatoes. She tucked in because she was now two stones lighter, and he said he loved to be with someone who enjoyed eating. He took her to see *The Shining* because he was frightened to go by himself. 'Lily-livered' she called him and tried to hide her own fright. It felt as if she had known him all through her new life, a parallel existence which must have run next to the botched-up one.

Spring came and camellias hung bumbling on dark-leaved bushes. It smelled of renewal and hope. Lisette and Marco went on his motor cruiser and he pointed out houses he had designed along the shore. He took her to his home, which he had also designed, with an inner court and a fountain. He kept birds and a net was strung over the courtyard, in which they flew freely. He named his house *Paradiso*, but said it was rather hell as the African Grey kept croaking 'Hello. You're a rubbish architect' – something a colleague had taught him after a jolly evening.

She learned that Marco had lost his father but his mother lived in Rome and could not be coaxed to Lugano because of old habits and old friends. He had lived with an Italian from Milan for seven years but had never quite felt comfortable enough to propose marriage. Eventually, she had admitted to loving a real Italian and not a Swiss imitation.

When it was Lisette's turn, all she revealed was, 'Similar, still unattached as well. My parents are dead. I have no siblings.' Inside her, the old guilt whispered, 'Sorry Louis, my twin, I crushed you.'

After that, they made love in his bedroom to the cackling of parrots, and his caressing fingers felt soft and smooth and her body pressed against his, safe and relaxed. Their chests rose and fell in unity.

On the day he suggested going to her place, he was shocked by the way she lived. On her thirty-second birthday she moved into his Paradise, and shortly afterwards she found out that she was pregnant.

Decent to the bone, he proposed and she explained that she was marriage-shy. He let it be. They concentrated on the pregnancy. Lisette gave birth to a little boy in the hospital he had helped design. They called the infant Luigi.

He went to fetch his mother from Rome and drove her back to see her grandson. '*Como siamo fortunate. Il mio bellissimo angelo bambino*,' her carmine-painted lips enunciated and her dry thin fingers touched the newborn's head. Then she lifted the chain with a gold cross over her white-haired head and hooked it over Lisette's, saying, 'You are the mother now. Life goes on. May you be blessed.' Marco whispered to Lisette that mother, naturally, believed them to be married.

Lisette felt a new pang of guilt. *Naturally*. But she overcame it. Nothing of her life before she became Elisabeth Roland mattered any longer.

Luigi grew into a dark-eyed child with a frown on his adorable forehead when things were not the way he understood them. She loved her son.

Marco and Lisette were happy. On her second pregnancy, he pressed again on marriage and, when she refused, he started to pry into her past, but her agitation caused him to give up. A baby girl they called Gloria was born, with a button nose and cornflower-blue eyes.

Lisette had to give up work in the hotel, and Marco suggested she became a full-time mother; he earned enough. He tentatively suggested the children might go to an English boarding school later, which produced an explosive reaction from Lisette.

'We'll see what happens,' he said placatingly and hugged her close to him.

*

When Luigi was five and Gloria three, an official letter came to the house addressed to Elisabeth Petit-Roland. It was from a lawyer in Geneva. Some system had tracked her down. With trembling fingers, she managed to tear the letter open. Her parents had died within six months of each other, her father of cancer and her mother of despair. Lisette had inherited the house in Cologny and all they owned.

She went to bed in a dark room for two days without speaking to anyone. When she emerged, she had decided to step over her trauma. She told Marco that she had lied about her parents being long dead. He, who loved his mother, was at a loss. Lisette explained that she had had a troubled childhood; her parents had subconsciously blamed her for the death in the womb of her twin brother, and their relationship had always been strained as a result.

'Lisette, my darling. None of that could have been your fault.' Marco's words were like balm to a festering wound.

'No more secrets. I love you, Marco.'

He held her tenderly while they made plans. Lugano was their home. She could sell her parents' villa and, with the millions, buy houses to let to pay for a private day school education for the children.

★

Lisette went to Geneva. First, she visited the churchyard in Cologny and, at the gravestone of her parents, she stood head bent, and tears coursed down her chin and fell onto the black quartz. 'You had such beautiful grandchildren and you did not know. I have hurt you so much because I made a horrendous mistake in my life and did not want you to know about it. Please forgive me.'

In the villa, she tiptoed around the familiar furniture, the family treasures which had meaning more than value. In her parents' bedroom she faltered, knowing she had abandoned them, but picked herself up. A new positive life would start right now, one based on the fond memory of her parents.

In front of her old bedroom, she paused with a smile and opened the door. A shadow moved in the corner where her bed was. She patted the wall and clicked the light switch.

One pale liquid eye stared at her. The other eye was missing; in fact, part of the man's head was not there. Sparse reddish hair dangled over the cavity which brain surgeons had chiselled out of the skull. The grotesque cripple lifted one stump of arm. A prosthetic arm lay on the child's desk, clad in a shirt sleeve with closed cuff.

Beside the bed were two crutches. The rest of Graham's body was mercifully covered by her daisy-print duvet.

'Help me up, will you?' said a twisted mouth under a reconstructed nose. 'Part of my brain is dead, and I have fits but there are pills. I was hospitalised for the best part of a year. Learned to cope. Your parents claimed not to know where you were. I kept watch and knew when your mother died you would come. And here you are, darling. Your parents have made us wealthy, haven't they? Millions for this house. We can give our marriage another chance. Let's have children. You can look after me, since you owe me.'